SCORPIUS

ZODIAC SERIES
BOOK 1

JOHN WEGENER

Scorpius

Written by John Wegener.
Published by Prosolin.
© Copyright, John Wegener, 2017. All rights reserved.
© Cover designed by Fiona Jayde Media.

All characters in this publication are fictitious, any resemblance to real persons, living or dead, is purely coincidental.

John Wegener asserts his moral right to be identified as the author of this book.

People fear the unknown. It is only by immersing oneself in the unknown that knowledge is obtained and, through knowledge, the removal of fear.

1

ALEX

Alex Warner had a sense of dread when he awoke. The feeling intensified as his surrounds became familiar. He had had a late night, drinking too much and trying to charm the occasional woman before deciding he didn't feel like company that night. When the alarm drilled through his brain, it seemed too early, which it always did, and he told it where to go. Only when he was fully conscious did he realize that it wasn't 6am but 2:36 and it wasn't his wake-up call but his comm going berserk trying to get his attention.

I really don't want this, he thought, but knew he had to accept the call and knew who the caller would be. He was a mess and didn't need to share the aftermath of last night's drinking session, so he pressed the audio-only button and grunted: "Alex here. I hope this is important."

"It's Commissioner Harris, and it is important."

Alex grudgingly but quickly raised his alertness level at the voice of his superior. "Sorry, boss. Didn't look to see who it was."

"I'm sorry, I know it's late, or early I suppose. I'm peeved, too. Unfortunately, this can't wait. A murder's just happened, and it's starting to escalate inter-species tensions, and that's the last thing us humans want at the moment."

"What's the go?" Alex asked, his interest piqued.

"There's just been a report of a murder of an important Cetusian government official on Caerus. That's a big enough issue, but not the actual problem. They are blaming humans and demanding revenge. Guess why I called!"

Alex's blood curdled. He also felt annoyed. *Not Cetusians again. They think we humans always persecute them, making them so bloody hard to deal with. 'You humans treat us like slaves, blah, blah, blah'.* "Why me?"

"You know why. Can you get in here in an hour to get briefed? And bring a packed case. You will have some traveling to do."

"Guess so, boss. Get there as soon as I wake up."

"Oh, sorry if I interrupted anything."

"Just asleep to get rid of a good night drinking this time."

Alex sat up in bed and it confirmed his earlier thoughts. *I really don't want to wake up today. Shouldn't have had so much to drink last night either. Still, there were a few fresh faces that may interest me.*

The office was more than an hour's flight away with his AGrav so, by the time Alex got himself ready, it was more like two hours, but he thought, *the Commissioner isn't going anywhere.* Not that he wasted any time. The flight was quick and uneventful, as you would expect in the express flight path at four in the morning.

Being a Chief Inspector, he had a dedicated parking spot in the underground garage at the agency office in Sydney, Australia. He got his promotion to Chief Inspector two years ago now. It still seemed like yesterday, he had been so busy. He was just a normal detective until then. Now his official title was Chief Inspector Detective Alex Warner, a bit of a mouthful to be honest, but his crew kept him humble. He did away with the formalities when he could.

The Galactic Intelligence Agency (GIA) originated many centuries ago, out of necessity, to appease all the different political and human species persuasions in the galactic confederation. There had to be one overarching law enforcement agency that could cross the political boundaries as the need arose. The headquarters could have been anywhere on earth, it had to be on earth, so politically, Australia was the consensus country as it was more neutral than any other location. It was also relatively free of skullduggery most of the time. They chose Sydney as the metropolis to set up office, although other cities had competed fiercely for the privilege. So that made Sydney Alex's home base when he was home, which wasn't often. He just wished the internal political bickering at the agency didn't make it so difficult to get things done. With no family and no personal attachments or commitments, Alex was the obvious choice when a foreign assignment came along, not that he complained. Sometimes it had unexpected pleasures.

He got out of his AGrav and went to the elevators. The luggage stayed in the trunk as he didn't know where he was staying. Arriving on the Commissioner's floor, he walked across to his austere but functional office, which he had visited many times before. He respected the Commissioner's practical approach; some senior members of the establishment were so pretentious, Alex didn't think he could work with them.

Commissioner Harris sat waiting behind his desk, catching up on paperwork for something to do. His desk, piled with report tabs to sign, stood angled so he could look out the window at the harbor when he needed to think. Two chairs sat in front of the desk, a coffee table and more casual seats were by the window for informal discussions or just when he felt the need. A coffee bar stood in one corner, which the chief used constantly. Probably too much. Alex also knew the Commissioner had a stash of alcohol he brought out for special occasions, but Alex had so far failed to work out where he hid it.

"Coffee?"

"Yeah, might wake me up."

"Strong, black and no sugar?"

"You've read my file."

The Commissioner prepared coffee for both of them and handed

Alex a mug. "Sit, please," the Commissioner said as he pointed to the seats by the coffee table.

"This sounds ominous," Alex replied. It was the first time the Commissioner had ever asked him to sit at the coffee table.

The Commissioner chuckled. "You've an excellent reason to feel something's up!"

They sat and sipped their coffees as the Commissioner gathered his thoughts.

"We have a bit of a situation, as I mentioned you on the comm before," the Commissioner started. "A report came in during the night of a murder on Caerus. Now, normally the local police would have handled it, but they murdered a Confederation Ambassador, the initial reports from the Caerus police show that it may have involved a human. Our esteemed political leaders are getting concerned, as it is one more thing causing ripples in our confederation with enough tensions already between Humans and Cetusians."

"You mean because of that halo thingy they've grown on their heads?"

The Commissioner looked at Alex dubiously. "Yes... the halo is one reason - it's called an Aureola, incidentally. Do I detect a bit of prejudice?"

"OK, Aureola then, I'll keep my inclinations to myself."

"Anyway, our leaders have stressed that we need to show we are taking the situation seriously. That's why they contacted us, why I appointed you to find out what happened, who the murderer is and bring him to justice."

"Yeah right! Anything else you want before lunch?"

"I know it'll be tough. There'll be pressure on all sides to solve the murder. I hope, for the sake of diplomacy, we can say there are no political motives behind it. There have been rumblings of confederation members splitting off and going independent, as some did a while back. The confederation needs to remain strong and united. Strength in numbers, so to speak."

"A bit of a pep talk for the confederation?"

The Commissioner smiled. "I don't want you to give one of your anti-establishment speeches. Anyway, at least they gave us the authority to use whatever extra resources we need for this. That'll help keep my budget under control."

Alex's professional attitude kicked in. "Do we have the report from the Caerus police?"

"It's being sent through. You must go to Caerus and inspect the crime scene in person, I think. That's why I advised you to bring a suitcase."

"What level of authority do I have?"

"You have your normal level for your position. I dare say you can stretch that significantly in this case and the authorities will back you, so long as you can justify your actions."

Alex thought for a moment, sipped at his coffee. "Is there anyone on the Caerus end who I'm supposed to liaise with?"

"Yes, there's one of our investigating agents in the system to help you in the case to help you. Let's see..." The Commissioner rose from his seat at the coffee table and walked to his desk. He reviewed some notes he had scrawled on a note chip. "It's Agent Nascha."

"Good. We'll see how good he is."

"She."

"What?"

"Nascha is female... not that it will make any difference, will it?"

"Oh, no, I suppose not," Alex replied sheepishly as he had a reputation of giving female investigators a hard time sometimes. *Just what I need, a female Cetusian to work with. The worst of both worlds.* Alex started feeling depressed. He knew the Commissioner was aware of his near breakdown over the distress of his failed previous relationship, the circumstances behind it and his social attitudes towards women since.

"I suggest you get your things packed and get on the ship for Caerus. It lifts off at 9am. I booked you a seat. Unfortunately, the only one available was first class," the Commissioner said with a tinge of fake regret.

"That is unfortunate Commissioner," Alex said with a grin, lifting him from his malaise.

Alex finished his coffee and rose from his seat. He departed the Commissioner's office and took the elevator down to his floor below. Alex was hungry but couldn't afford to waste the time getting something to eat at that moment. He decided he would get something at the spaceport.

He looked out his office window at the Sydney Harbour Bridge, thinking. *What has the Commissioner got me involved in here? I know this kind of case. It usually gets nasty before the dust settles. I hope this won't be another one like some that they've given me. Not sure that I enjoy working with a female Cetusian agent either. I suppose I need to keep an open mind on that.* Pain momentarily crossed his face as he remembered an experience from the distant past. He broke his reverie and looked at his desk. Another shiny new nameplate sat on it. He looked at the plate with annoyance. They kept appearing on his desk, and he kept putting them in the bin. He didn't like them, never had.

He went to his chair, sat down and turned on his data interface to the agency's storage hive to download the files he thought he would need for the case. He knew he could access the data anywhere, but it was always so much easier and quicker if it was already on his data plate. Opening his message bank, he noticed a file from Agent Nascha containing the murder investigation report. *She's very efficient at least,* he thought as he moved the file to his data plate. He then wrote a brief message to Agents Michael Sutton and Ruth Chavez, his two senior team members, informing them of his plans, leaving Agent Chavez in charge. *This will get to Sutton,* Alex thought. He knew Agent Sutton sometimes had issues with taking orders from females. *He'll learn one day. He knows that Chavez is the better manager.* He sent the message.

Alex closed the interface and sat back to consider his schedule. It was 6:34. He needed to leave by 7:00am to catch the ship, although he knew he could get on at the last minute, being a first-class passenger. He collected some personal gadgets, items from his desk he thought he might need and two firearms, a maser pistol and a zaser cannon that fired z-bosons, something to avoid. *That should keep me out of trouble.* He also included an oxygen enhancer in his kit as he Caerus was a low-oxygen world. He placed everything into his investigation case, which he had made to carry the tools of his trade. He required it far too often. He pondered the unfolding situation as he traveled to the spaceport. *A high-ranking Cetusian government official murdered. Intriguing. It seems they don't think it's a domestic or local criminal matter. They want GIA to investigate. What's really going on, I wonder? I suppose I'll find out when I get there. I hope this Agent Nascha is easy to work with. She probably thinks she's being persecuted like all the other Cetusians in the Confederation.*

He arrived at the spaceport at 7:53 with enough time to get some breakfast before he boarded. He checked his AGrav into the secure long-term parking facility, collected his possessions and hurried to the spaceport terminal to check in.

The area bustled with people busily hurrying to wherever they needed to be, like ants criss-crossing paths to gather food before returning to their nest. The noise, a constant hum, echoed off the hard surfaces. Alex saw the counter for the flight to Caerus and hurried over. The attendant looked surprised as he approached. "You're cutting it fine, sir," she said, activating the data screen in front of her.

"Sorry about that, I haven't had a great day so far. I hope it gets better."

"Do you have your ticket?"

Alex retrieved his comm from his pocket, looked at his message bank to find the ticket from the Commissioner. He transferred the information to the terminal on the counter.

The attendant reviewed the data and finally announced, "Everything seems in order, Mr. Warner. I see that you are flying first class. An attendant will be here shortly to escort you to the ship. Do you have luggage to check in?"

"Yes, I do. I also need to tell you I'm a GIA officer and am carrying arms with me. Here are my credentials. I need ultra secure storage."

The attendant raised her brow. *She doesn't have to deal with a request like that often*, Alex thought. "Of course." She made the required inputs to the data terminal, producing a boarding chip for him and a fast track immigration certificate so he could bypass the usual checks. The secure part of the ticket gave him the highest authentication possible. She handed Alex the boarding chip. The escort arrived to lead him to the ship.

Alex gave the escort the once over. *This'll be an enjoyable walk.* She was attractive, with a slim body and ample breasts. Her face was almost perfectly symmetrical, and she had a cute baby appearance.

"Good morning, Mr. Warner," the escort said. "Please follow me. We will have you seated and comfortable before you know it."

"Yes, thank you," Alex said. He followed her through the terminal, through immigration with no hassles and to the boarding gate.

"Here is your ship, it is ready for departure. I hope you have a pleasant flight."

"Thank you," Alex responded, approaching the boarding ramp.

He walked down the ramp, entered the hatch of the ship and produced his boarding chip to show the waiting crew member. She scanned the chip, instantly becoming more alert when she saw he was a first-class passenger. "Good morning, Mr. Warner. Welcome aboard. Your flight area is through here, in the space shown on your chip."

Alex walked towards his space for the flight. It was unbelievable, as big as a room. He knew he wasn't likely to enjoy luxury like that ever again. He placed his personal items in the locker space and seated himself with a sigh.

"Would you like a refreshment, Sir?" asked an attendant who came from nowhere.

"I'd like something to eat. I've been awake since two thirty. I'm starving. Can you arrange something?"

"Is there anything in particular that you would like?"

"Food?"

The attendant smiled knowingly. "I will see what I can find. I am sure you'll like it. And a refreshment while I prepare your breakfast?"

Alex thought momentarily. "I think I'll have Centaurian Champagne."

"You will have it in a moment," the attendant replied.

Alex relaxed in his seat, enjoying his surroundings for the voyage ahead. Once he arrived, he knew he would be far from comfortable and no-one would offer him champagne.

2

NASCHA

Nascha gazed out of her office window at the Caerus branch of the GIA, contemplating the evidence of the murder investigation so far. The sun was shining, and the trees were flowering. She was jealous of the people walking past, smelling the fragrance of the blooms. The case was so baffling. The murder of the Caerus ambassador to the Confederation Assembly took place inside his own Cetusian solarium chamber, with his aureola hacked off - a viciously brutal and barbaric torture for a Cetusian - and neck broken. Forensics said the murderer broke his neck last. Some clues gathered from the crime scene made no sense. *Maybe it's best for a more experienced GIA investigator to take over here,* she thought. *It really makes no sense to me, it's above my head.* Heaving a sigh of tiredness and frustration, she realized it had been an interminable day. She needed a good sun soak to reinvigorate her before dinner and retiring. A good bask under lights would photosynthesise some much-needed oxygen and sugars to boost her metabolism.

Nascha had been told an hour before that the political powers had heard news of the tragedy and were demanding the Confederation investigate the murder at the highest level of their law enforcement capabilities. The politicians insisted the murder was interspecies related, even though no evidence pointed to that conclusion. The severing of the aureola was rather savage, admittedly. It would have suffocated the Ambassador, eventually. He wouldn't have been able to supplement his sustenance by the photosynthesis process it provided in the low-oxygen atmosphere of Caerus. A notably slow and nasty way to die, Nascha thought. She could not imagine a Cetusian doing such a thing but she had seen them perpetrate the most sadistic of crimes in the past, so she would not have ruled it out either. The politicians had instantly jumped to the conclusion a human was the perpetrator, even though the police suppressed the details of the murder.

Her superiors informed Nascha the GIA had dispatched an investigating detective from the head office on Earth to Caerus to take charge of the investigation, arriving through the next wormhole opening scheduled for 10 in the morning, Caerus time. The detective should get to the office late afternoon. *Tomorrow'll be another exhausting day,* she mused, none too happily. *Oh, well. I can't avoid it. Hope he's good at his job and not a jerk, like some humans I've worked with in the past.*

The investigating team had been trying to locate the Ambassador's next of kin during the afternoon, but that was proving difficult. The Ambassador did not have a permanent partner. She had died some years ago. The detective that Nascha had asked to look into the family had finally located the only son from the partnership. He was working a shift out in the spaceport maintenance yards off planet. He was due back on the surface in the morning, so it delayed them informing him until he returned, Nascha's first task in the morning. She imagined it would be tragic for him; she hated that part of the job, but unfortunately, it it was her responsibility. They had withheld any details of the murder from the news feeds in the meantime until they had notified the son.

Nascha turned off the data screen at her desk, collected her comm, data plate and personal items, stood and walked out of the office for the day. *All the issues will still be there in the morning,* she thought as she went out the door.

~

NASCHA DROVE out to the spaceport, arriving at 8:10 the next morning. The transport returning the maintenance workers back to the surface was due for arrival at 8:30. She left her locked AGrav in the parking area of the company the son worked for and went to the front office.

Showing her badge to the receptionist, Nascha said, "I am here to talk to Mr. Ahiga. I believe he is about to arrive back from the maintenance yards."

The receptionist received the information with concern. "Can you please wait while I contact the day supervisor?"

"That's fine."

The receptionist pressed a series of buttons on the comm in front of her. After a few moments she connected with her supervisor and they had a brief discussion. The comm discussion ended, and she directed her attention back to Nascha. "The supervisor will be out shortly. Please take a seat. It shouldn't be long."

"Thanks."

After several minutes, a door behind the receptionist opened, and a man walked over to Nascha. "Hello, I'm Mr. Sani. I'm the Day Supervisor. I believe you're looking for Ahiga. I hope he's not in any trouble."

Nascha stood up. "No, he isn't in any trouble. I need to talk to him on a personal but somewhat tragic matter."

Sani bunched his brow together in concern. "I see. Well, his transport is due back any minute now. Would you like me to escort you to a meeting room so you can talk to him in private?"

"Yes, I would appreciate that."

"Would you like a refreshment? A coffee or tea maybe?"

"A black coffee with no sugar would be good, thank you."

Sani gestured to the receptionist to organize the coffee. "Have you signed in?"

"No, I haven't."

"OK, well could you please sign the register and I will escort you to the room?"

Nascha wrote the required details in the register while Sani waited. She then followed him to a modest meeting room where she sat facing the door. There were six chairs around the table, including hers, and a side table that had a jug of water and some glasses arranged on it. There were also two holographs on one wall. The floor was a polished anti-skid timber.

"Your coffee should arrive soon. I will get Ahiga when he disembarks and bring him to you."

"Thank you."

Sani left the room, closing the door behind him. Her coffee came moments later and Nasha took a sip while she contemplated what she would say to Ahiga when he arrived. There was never a painless way to tell someone their loved one was dead, murdered. She had learned from experience the best way was to tell them the facts, but gently. Let the information sink in at the pace the person could cope with and answer their questions if she could. It was always an ordeal. Each individual had to deal with it in his or her own way. She often hoped she would never be on the receiving end herself.

The door finally opened, and Sani escorted a man in. "Agent Nascha, this is Ahiga."

Nascha stood, "OK. Thank you, Sani, you are most kind."

"I will leave you two alone. Please press 97 on the comm when you are ready to leave." Sani left, closing the door behind him.

Ahiga looked around, worried. He was playing with his hands, trying to keep them still but not succeeding. "What's this about? Am I in trouble? What's going on?"

Nascha waved with her hands to calm down. "Please, Ahiga, you are not in trouble. Can you sit down, please? Would you like a glass of water?"

"No. I'm fine thanks," Ahiga said as he sat, becoming a little less agitated but trying to find somewhere to look other than Nascha.

Nascha tried to put on her most empathetic face. "As Mr. Sani said, I am Agent Nascha from the Cetusian branch of the GIA. There is no simple way to say this, so I will just tell you as straight as I can. Hem! It is my unfortunate duty to inform you your father is dead.

Someone murdered him yesterday. We would have informed you sooner, but we had difficulties tracking you down. I am sorry for that."

Ahiga's eyes widened in disbelief as he heard the news of his father's death. He sat motionless while the information sank in. Not even his hands moved anymore. He was speechless for a long time. He just looked at Nascha with a vacant look, trying to register what she had said. Eventually he lowered his eyes to the table in front of him. "How did it happen?" he asked.

"You need to understand that we can't tell you the details because we are still investigating the crime, but I can tell you they found him in his solarium with his neck broken." Nascha decided he did not need to know about the severed aureola, not yet anyway.

Nascha noticed that Ahiga was internalizing the news, trying to work out what he was feeling. She had seen the lack of hysterical emotion before and realized she needed to counsel him that his current feels were normal.

"I appreciate that this is a great shock to you, and it is taking some time for you to process the situation," Nascha said with sympathy and understanding at his reaction to the news. "Do you have questions you wish me to answer?"

Ahiga shook his head. "I can't believe it."

"You may wonder why you feel nothing. Some people react to such news the same way you are. There is nothing wrong with you. Different people react in different ways. Your emotions will intensify as you get further into your grief."

Ahiga looked into Nascha's eyes as if looking into her soul. He whispered, "Thank you. I think I will have that water now."

Nascha looked away, as the open honesty of the reply made it hard for her to keep her emotions in check. "You're welcome." She stood, went to the side table and poured some water.

A few moments went by before Ahiga asked, "What now?"

"Well, you will need to discuss it with your supervisor, but it might be advisable for you to take some time off. We will keep you informed when we have developments that we can share with you. We will release your father's body for burial as soon as we can."

"I'll need to plan the funeral."

"Is there anything else you would like to ask me?"

"No. I can't think of anything at the moment."

"Well, here are my contact details if you need to speak with me." Nascha handed Ahiga a data chip with her details. "We will probably need to interview you, as part of the investigation, but that can wait until later. Purely routine."

"Thank you," Ahiga replied, picking up the chip and placing it in his pocket.

"Do you want me to contact anyone for you?"

"No. That's fine. I think I will just sit here for a bit."

"OK then. I will leave. I am sorry for your loss." Nascha punched the number Sani had given her into the comm.

A voice broadcast after a few moments. "Yes, may I help you?"

"This is Agent Nascha. I'm ready to leave."

"OK. Sani will be with you shortly."

After some time, Sani opened the door and poked his face into the room, looked at Ahiga, then at Nascha. "Is everything OK?"

"I'm afraid Ahiga has had a bit of a shock. He needs time to take it in. I'll let him explain what he wants to do, but I am ready to leave."

Sani looked at Ahiga again with sympathy in his eyes. "OK. Well, if you will follow me then. I will escort you back to reception."

Nascha signed out at reception, thanked Sani for his hospitality and went to her AGrav. She looked at her chronometer. It was just after 9:30. If she hurried, she could get to the spaceport arrivals concourse and meet the GIA agent, since she was at the spaceport, anyway. It seemed like an excellent idea, although she didn't know what the detective looked like. *Well, I'll just have to do the old-fashioned thing. I'll display a plaque with his name on it on my tablet.*

～

ALEX WAS on full alert when he walked through the arrivals gate, looking around to get a feel for his surroundings, as this was the first time he had been on Caerus. He had put his oxygen concentrators in his nostrils before disembarking from the ship. He could smell the exotic aromas of the place as soon as he entered the public concourse area. He couldn't quite place the scent, similar to a cinnamon tang, he thought, but different.

He walked down the ramp and noticed his name on a data plate. A quizzical expression appeared on his face, as no one had informed him that someone would meet him on arrival. He walked over anyway. "I wasn't expecting valet service when I arrived. Given my flight, maybe I should have," he said as he neared Nascha.

He saw Nascha study him momentarily. She replied, "This isn't valet service. I was in the area and waited to pick you up instead of you having to find your own way. I'm Agent Nascha."

Alex looked surprised and slightly embarrassed for a moment and then gazed into Nascha's eyes. He found competence in her expression, a deep-seated belief in what was right as he took in her demeanor. "I appreciate that," he said, "I apologize for any misunderstanding I may have given you. It's been a long day so far."

Nascha studied Alex's body language. It showed he was uncomfortably formal, so she said, "Let's cut the crap. Welcome to Caerus."

Alex laughed. "Thanks. Formal procedure isn't one of my strong points. I'm Alex Warner of the GIA. I'm very pleased to meet a detective who's down to earth, or maybe Caerus. You're a chip off the same block as me."

Nascha looked at Alex strangely. Alex thought maybe she didn't really know what the last comment meant. He hoped she realized that he meant it as a compliment. "So. What do you want to do? Do you want me to take you to your hotel or come to the office straight away?" she asked.

"Neither actually. If it's possible, I'd like to see the crime scene."

"That's not a problem. Let's go to my AGrav and we'll be on our way." Nascha turned and started walking to the terminal exit.

Alex followed her. He cast his eyes over her form from behind.

Not bad. If it wasn't for that halo thingy, what did the boss call it, an aureola? Hold on, Alex. Why should that matter? So long as she's a good cop. He felt very confused with his emotions. His thoughts seemed to always turn to unsavory things when confronted with women who attracted him instead of treating them as beings like anyone else. He thought he was always open-minded about people, or was he? If only he could shake off his preconceived ideas about Cetusians and his disturbing attitudes towards women. *That betraying bitch has a lot to answer for!*

They arrived at Nascha's AGrav with those thoughts circulating in his head. "Here we are," Nascha gestured as she turned to face Alex again. She noticed that he seemed to be deep in thought, "You with us?"

"Huh... oh sorry, just thinking about the vagaries of the human psyche," Alex replied, as he returned to matters at hand.

"Bit of a philosopher then?"

"Ha! That'll be the day."

"Well, let's get you on the road," Nascha suggested as she opened the luggage compartment for Alex's bags. They both got into the vehicle, Nascha in the driver's seat and Alex feeling a little self-conscious, considering what he had been just mulling over.

"Your oxygen concentrators working OK?" Nascha asked to get the conversation going. "Some humans can take a while to get used to them."

"They're fine. It's not the first time I've used them," Alex replied, a little too peevishly.

Nascha seemed put out by his reply and concentrated on driving instead. She had the AGrav in manual.

"Sorry, I didn't mean to snap at you. I remember the first time I wore them and, you're right, they take a bit of getting used to," Alex offered in repentance.

Nascha opened up again. "I assume too much. Cardinal error for a detective."

Alex chuckled. "Too true. People have accused me of that more than once. So what's Caerus like? I haven't been here before."

"I can't say that I can compare too much, I haven't been away for any length of time. Let's see... I suppose it's like any other planet really, same amenities and amusements. There are differences because of our physiology, like the solariums."

"What are they?"

"They are rooms we go to once a day, if we can, to get a concentrated dose of sunlight. It re-energizes us similarly to eating."

"Oh. How long do you stay in there?"

"Probably about half an hour, depending on how much time we have."

Alex chuckled as he had a thought, "And what happens if you overindulge like if we eat too much?"

Nascha looked at Alex to see how serious he was. "We get fat."

"Really?"

"Really."

"Learn something every day." Alex pondered silently for a while, wondering what to ask next. "So, I've had a brief look at the crime report. What would happen then if they severed your... aureola, like in the murder?" Alex cringed inwardly. He had almost said, 'halo thingy.'

Nascha noticeably shivered. "I can't imagine what it would be like, but I think you would eventually suffocate, sort of like if I took your oxygen concentrators away right now."

"I see. I can appreciate the effect, I think. So... they would consider it particularly brutal and sadistic?"

"Yeah."

"You have any thoughts on why the killer might have done that?"

"Not really. I've been wondering if he was trying to send a message, but can't figure out what it would be."

"I don't like Cetusians, maybe?"

"Maybe, but I don't think so. Don't ask me why, but I think it's a callous act that the killer performed because he could."

"Oh well. I won't jump to conclusions either. How far?"

"About 10 minutes."

Alex sat in silence, wondering about the truth of his personal attitudes. *Did he really believe Cetusians were equal to humans, or were they inferior in his eyes? He had looked down on them in the past, considered them as slaves, there to do his bidding. What kind of human does that make me,* he wondered? *They were different, not inferior according to the political correctness protocol, but did he really believe that? They had done what humanity had always done, adapted to the environment in a self-imposed Darwinian evolutionary process. They had genetically engineered an organ so they could live on the planet without worrying about low oxygen levels.* He was still pondering these questions when they arrived at the crime scene. "Where are we?" he demanded.

Nascha looked perturbed at the command in his voice. "We're at the Ambassador's house."

"Oh," Alex said, regretting his tone.

They exited the vehicle and walked towards the front door. It had traditional 'Crime Scene - Keep Out' holo-tape barricading it. Two officers were guarding the entrance. They crossed the barricade and entered the house.

"Do you know how the killer gained access?"

"No. There's no sign of forced entry."

"He knew the killer, maybe?"

"Don't know," Nascha said abruptly, disguising the look of resentment on her face from him constantly suggesting the obvious to her.

Alex did not notice the change. He looked around as they walked to the solarium, taking in the scenery of the rooms they went through. Alex whistled as they entered the solarium. "Impressive."

"Typical."

Alex looked at Nascha momentarily, not sure if she was commenting on the solarium or himself. *You jackass,* he remonstrated to himself. *Why wouldn't an Ambassador have an impressive room like this? You've been behaving exactly like a typical xenophobe at his best. Let's try salvaging things, if it's not too late.* "Sorry. Does everyone have a solarium in their house?"

"No. Only those who can afford it have their own, but it is becoming more common, as they get cheaper and the standard of living improves on the planet," she said with slightly improved friendliness.

"So they would consider this a bit of a status symbol."

"Definitely, and this one is not typical. It's much more lavish than the normal solariums."

"I see. It's large. Do groups of people share the room?"

"Yes, they do. In fact, people can enter and leave as they please, sometimes having social gatherings in them for brief periods. Sort of like sharing a meal."

"Fascinating. So it would be conceivable that the victim was in here with the murderer, in a supposed amicable situation."

"Very much so, or they may have been discussing some business."

"Hmm." Alex walked around the solarium slowly, taking careful note of any smudge or iota on the walls and floor. "Is it possible to play a hologram of the victim?" he asked civilly.

"Ahh... yes. I'll just have to get the gear from my vehicle. I'll be back in a moment." Nascha left the solarium to get the equipment.

There were several couches, presumably for people to relax on as they basked. Alex looked underneath them while waiting for Nascha to return. He noticed a slip of paper under one, lodged partially under one of the couch legs. Alex got down on his knees, reached for the slip while lifting the couch slightly at the same time. The paper came out easily. Alex stood again, looking at it. There were two symbols on one side of the paper, ηℳ. He couldn't make much of what it meant, if it meant anything at all. Maybe it just came from the couch label or something.

Nascha came back carrying a bag.

"What do you make of this," Alex asked, holding out the paper slip for Nascha to see.

Nascha put down the bag and took the paper, turning it repeatedly, feeling its texture as she did. There was only writing on one side. "What is it?"

"Paper."

Nascha looked decisively annoyed. "Oh. Didn't know that. We

don't have paper on Caerus," she said sarcastically. "No idea what the writing means either," she said in a more civil voice.

"Nor do I... at the moment." Alex reddened as he realized what he had insinuated.

Nascha gave the slip back to Alex and set up the equipment for the holographic imaging. She eventually had the equipment ready. She turned it on and ran the file.

"Nasty," Alex exclaimed as the hologram appeared.

"Very," Nascha agreed.

Alex studied the image intently, walking around it to see if he could pick up anything not in the report. He couldn't and acknowledged Nascha's competence to himself. After a few minutes of study he commented, "You did a thorough report of the scene."

"Thank you," Nascha responded with a look of satisfaction.

"OK. I think I'm done here. Have you checked the victim's hive files?"

"I had people going through them, both personal and whatever he had at his offices, but someone's wiped them clean."

Alex looked at Nascha in surprise. "That's unusual."

"Sure is."

"Maybe I'll get one of my people to look at them and see if they can reconstruct them."

"They can do that?" Nascha asked incredulously.

"Sometimes. It depends on how clever the person wiped them is. I'm getting a bit warp-lagged and when I get warp-lagged, I get hungry. Can you get me to some food?"

Nascha looked at Alex testily. She relaxed. "Anything in particular?"

"No. Surprise me."

3

CHOOLI

Alex had had an exhausting day. Nascha had just dropped him off at the hotel, and he was about to check in. There was another couple ahead of him at the marble-topped reception desk. He looked around the lobby. It was a typical high-quality hotel, but not extravagant, based on other places he had stayed. Couches stood scattered in the lobby for people to sit on and various floral displays brightened up the area. He saw a business centre in an alcove to one side. It was vacant of users. The concierge directed the traffic of porters, who were busy either collecting baggage from incoming vehicles or loading them. Other porters were waiting in the lobby beside their customers, seeking instruction. Alex also had a porter waiting with him, his uniform immaculately neat.

The receptionist finally checked-in couple in front of him and they stepped aside with their room key chips and documentation. Alex stepped forward. "Hello, I'm Alex Warner. I believe you have a reservation for me."

"Let me see," the receptionist replied in hotel-politeness talk typical throughout the galaxy. The receptionist checked the reservation system, "Yes, there is a room reserved for you for one week. Is that correct?"

"Yes, that is correct."

"May I have your identity chip, Sir?"

Alex searched for his document wallet. He found it, extracted his identity chip and handed it to the receptionist. Galactic protocol dictated everyone had to provide proof of identity when booking into a hotel. That rule had provided a breakthrough for Alex on many cases in the past. When the receptionist completed the check-in, a key chip ejected from a slot in the desk. "Here is your key, Sir. You are in room 539 on the fifth floor. Here is your identity chip back. Is there anything else I can help you with?"

"Where are the restaurants?"

"We serve breakfast in the Sunrise Restaurant from six to eleven in the morning on the second floor. There is also an open-air restaurant and bar on the roof of the hotel. It is open from five in the afternoon till late."

"Thank you."

"You're welcome."

Alex replaced his chip into his wallet again and picked up his personal bag. The porter was waiting for him. "This way, Sir," he pointed to the elevator concourse area several metres away. The porter mis-stepped as they were walking to the concourse, rattling the luggage on the trolley, one bag escaping, falling to the floor. "Be more careful," Alex said grumpily. *Stupid Cetusian can't even walk properly*, his warp-lagged mind thought wearily, not thinking much about his careless comment.

The porter blushed with embarrassment, retrieved the bag and placed it more securely on the trolley. "Sorry, Sir," the porter said unhappily. They went to Alex's room, where the porter unloaded the trolley and left.

It was almost 6:30pm, local time in Arbor, the capital of Caerus. Alex stretched, exhausted and hungry. The rooftop bar and restaurant sounded like an excellent suggestion for a balmy evening. He freshened up with a quick shower, deciding to have a meal in the bar and relax afterwards.

It was after seven when he arrived and he had a drink at the bar first, while he considered what he wanted to do for a meal. Waiters were cruising the bar and restaurant floor, attending to patrons, distributing orders. It always intrigued Alex that they hadn't replaced human waiters, or in this case Cetusian, with automata centuries ago. It must have something to do with the personal interactions or something, he surmised. He ordered a local beer from the bartender and charged the cost to his room, setting up a tab at the same time. The beer arrived. Alex drank a long draught from the glass, appreciating the taste and feel of the amber fluid as it drained down his throat, the gasses continuing their release from their saturated liquid prison as they descended. He looked around the city from his vantage point. Out to the bay. The hotel was near the beach with the city lights sparkling off the surf as the evening slowly turned to night in the dusk-reducing light. Alex caught faint ocean smells as the breeze wafted past him. Mountains loomed to the side in the distance, receding into invisibility in the fading light.

The restaurant was close to the bar in a separate area and accommodated about 50 patrons. Some semi-transparent screening separated the two areas. Local music softly played in the background, and Alex noticed an area for a band. *They must have live music some nights.* He liked the music, a moderate rock sound without being too blaring, and had a foot-tapping tempo. "Nice music," he mentioned to the bartender who was standing close by watching holovision. "Is this music by local performers?"

"Yes, it is; the Cretan Novas. I don't think much of the name, but they are popular. They're coming in later tonight to play for two hours, actually."

"Really. I might hang around then after I've had something to eat. What time do they start?"

"Ten. You can have a meal in the bar," the bartender advised Alex, sizing him up with his eyes. "I'm Klah. Just sing out if you need anything."

"Alex. Thanks, I will," Alex replied, holding out his hand to shake Klah's. He took another sip of beer. *This guy might be good to know.* "What food do you serve in the bar?"

Klah went to the end of the bar and brought over a menu with an excellent selection of food, both inter-federational and local Caerus cuisine. Sipping his beer, he decided on a native bovine steak with assorted vegetables and then looked around while he waited for his meal.

ONLY A FEW OTHER people were in the restaurant at the time and they both appeared to be business types. *Nothing of interest here*, Alex thought. He watched the holographic screen in the corner instead, although it was some boring sitcom that must have been popular on Caerus at the moment. He watched it anyway.

Alex's meal arrived as he drained the last of his beer. A waitress immediately came over to attend him, "Sir, would you like another?"

"Very efficient," Alex commented as he eyed her. She was very attractive. "Yes, please." Alex looked over to Klah, who just shrugged. Alex chuckled under his breath and started eating.

The waitress returned with his beer, placing it in front of him, "Here is your beer."

"Thank you."

"What is your name?"

"Call me Alex."

"I am Doli. It is a pleasure to meet you. Please contact me if you need any further service."

"I'll remember that Doli, thanks," Alex said as he started wondering what sort of bar it was.

The bar started filling about 9:30 and Alex noticed the patrons were mainly young and female. He thought this might be a place where youthful women, struggling to survive, tried to attract a wealthy off-world man to support them. He noted there were quite a few off-world people in the bar who met that criteria. The band started setting up too. It was interesting for Alex to watch the people as they jostled for suitable seats and looked around for friends. There seemed to be quite a few regulars who were ordering drinks and trying to find the best seats. Alex continued sipping his beer.

He kept going over the case in his head. It was puzzling. *It's the type of case I enjoy. Baffling clues. No leads to speak of. Something always turns up. The culprit always slips up somewhere. There is no such thing as a perfect crime in my experience. The slip of paper intrigued him, though. What did the symbols mean? Did the murderer leave it or had it just lodged under the seat, like a frightened cat?* He was so deep in thought he didn't notice two women stealing looks while he was contemplating the unfolding puzzle. They seemed to decide their course of action and moved over to the bar next to Alex. They were beside him before he realized what was happening. *I wonder what brings you two here?* He glanced over and one was very attractive. They seemed to mind their own business, but he knew the type. They were hovering to coax him into conversation and whatever came next... *What the hell? Nothing to lose.* "Hi, ladies. Would you like a drink?"

"Never been called that before," the attractive one answered.

"What, lady?"

"Yeah."

"OK, well?"

"Well, what?"

Alex got annoyed. "Are you thirsty?"

"What if I am?"

Alex was about to give up.

"Yeah, we would like a drink, thank you," the other lady interrupted; annoyed her friend was being so difficult. She could see Alex might be profitable and gave her friend a slight dig in the ribs.

Alex hailed Klah over. "Can you get these two a drink please, put it on my tab. Just the one drink, no more." Alex had learned from experience with buying a drink for someone, only to receive a large bill at the end of the night with subsequent drinks on the tab.

Klah looked warily at the two women and then at Alex. "OK, what do you two want?"

"I'll have a martini," the attractive one replied.

"I'll have Scotch on the rocks," the other one ordered.

Klah left to prepare the drinks.

"I'm Alex. Do you two have names?" Alex said, not really in the mood for their company anymore, but he left the situation open for them to improve, since he had just bought drinks.

"I'm Mai," the other one replied.

"I'm Chooli. What ya do?"

"I'm a detective."

Chooli balked in surprise.

Alex laughed to himself. *I love it when I tell someone I'm a detective in a bar. It's so interesting to see the other person's reaction.* "Don't worry. I'm off duty. What do you have to worry about, anyway?"

"Nothin'," Chooli replied, relaxing again, but she kept looking interestingly at Alex.

"We don't see many detectives here," Mai explained. "It put us off guard for a moment. Don't mind Chooli. She's fun once you get to know her."

"I'll believe you," Alex replied, casting an eye over Chooli again. *She really is something to look at. Hope her personality improves, though.* "What do you two do?"

Klah came with the drinks and turned to Alex with a conspiratorial grin. "Watch these two. They're devils once you get them going."

"Thanks for the tip. I think I'm getting a taste of that now." Alex turned his attention back to Chooli and Mai with an expectant expression.

Both Chooli and Mai looked confused for a moment until they remembered the question Alex had just asked them.

"We're students at the local university," Chooli replied.

Alex nodded. "Did you come to watch the band?"

"Yeah. They're diablo."

Alex raised his eyebrow in confusion and looked at Mai.

"They're fantastic," Mai explained. "Chooli comes from parts with a strange vocabulary. It takes a bit of getting used to."

"I see. You want to find a lounge and watch them with me? Maybe you can explain the music. I just arrived on Caerus this morning."

"Sure. Cool," Chooli said with increased interest as she looked around. She pointed to a lounge suitable for three with a small table for their drinks. "How about there?"

Alex looked over and saw where she pointed. *That looks cozy. Almost like they reserved it for us. Play along, I suppose.* "That looks good." Alex grabbed his beer and walked over to the lounge with Chooli nuzzling up to his side. Mai followed next to her, happy to play second fiddle. The lounge was arc shaped with armrests on each end, so you didn't fall off. Alex sat, slid over to allow the two women in and was halfway across when Chooli weaved in from the other end. They wedged Alex between them. *Oh, well. I may as well enjoy. Could do worse.* Alex sat back and took in the attention. "You seem to have that down to an art."

They both giggled.

The band was tuning their instruments, almost ready to play. Chooli sat close to Alex and started explaining who the band members were, what they played and what she thought of them. Mai was happy to just sit and joined the conversation as she chose. After a little while, Chooli gave Mai a coded look, which Alex didn't understand.

"We'll be back in a nano. Just need a freshen up," Chooli explained.

Alex smiled in bemusement. He presumed Chooli needed to go to the Ladies and wanted Mai to go with her. "Fine. I'll be here when you get back, but your seats mightn't be," he said, deciding to have a bit of a joke at their expense.

Chooli looked worried.

Mai laughed. "I'm sure we can trust you to save them for us."

"Pleeze!" Chooli said, catching on to the joke and mustering her most endearing and beguiling expression.

"It'll cost you."

As they walked off, Alex realized he had almost depleted his beer and beckoned Doli. "Can I have another, please?"

"Sure. Watch those two," Doli advised, leaning her head towards the girls.

"Strange, that's what Klah said. They must be regulars."

"They are. Don't get me wrong. They're OK. They won't give you trouble, but they can be a handful."

"OK. I'll take your advice, thanks."

Chooli and Mai returned after about five minutes. Alex noticed Chooli had changed the top she was wearing to one with a plunging neckline, revealing her ample cleavage to perfection. "Get your top dirty?" Alex asked in a mocking tone.

"Nah. Just thought ya'd like," Chooli responded with sexual overtones.

"That I do," Alex responded.

As the band started playing its jazz-rock style, Alex let Chooli snuggle up to him but, several songs later, he felt a nibble on his ear and yelped in surprise. Chooli jumped too, since she didn't expect such a response. Alex gave Chooli a reproving look and wrapped his arm around her shoulders to keep her head in sight. She didn't mind and nuzzled even closer. He felt her warmth by his side and smiled contentedly.

The band took a break after about an hour, which was the cue for Alex to leave and get some sleep. The beer and the warp lag were catching up with him and he had to get up early to talk with his team on earth. "Well, it's goodnight ladies. It's been an enjoyable evening," he said as he moved to stand, disturbing Chooli's amorous play.

"Doesn't have ta end now," Chooli suggested into his ear in desperate determination, not wanting to waste her efforts for the night.

Alex looked at Chooli, sorely tempted to invite her to his room, but he was just too tired. "I'd like to, but not tonight," he said a little apologetically.

Chooli pouted in disappointment.

"I'll be here for several days. Maybe, if you're around, we can do this again. I enjoyed your company, yours too Mai, so let's see, deal?" Alex suggested, as consolation.

"Deal!" Chooli snapped immediately, a sense of pleading in her eyes. "See ya t'morrow."

Alex smiled and finally disentangled from Chooli. "Good night."

"Ciao," Chooli responded.

"Good night too," Mai replied.

Alex walked back to the bar to settle his bill while Chooli and Mai started an animated discussion. They'll probably go chase some other guys now. He gestured to Klah he was ready to settle his tab. "Quite a girl," he commented, nodding his head at the women.

"Yeah. They can be a handful, but they're basically harmless, as far as I know. Just out for an enjoyable time at no cost, looking for a man to catch if they can."

"Know the type. Some like that on every planet I've been to."

Klah handed Alex the bill.

Alex checked it over. It wasn't as expensive as he was expecting. He noted that the women were very conservative in their drinking. That was surprising, atypical in his experience. Maybe she really liked him. *We'll see if I ever see her again.* He signed off the bill and walked to the door, turning to wave at Chooli as he left.

Chooli immediately gave an energetic wave back.

4

FRICTION

Alex rose at five the next morning, having slept soundly the whole night. He still felt exhausted but was used to the feeling from the many cases he had handled. No doubt his exhaustion would increase before he solved the case. He went to the bathroom, relieved himself and rinsed off his face, not bothering to dress yet.

Removing his communication equipment from the safe in his room, he set it up to establish a link with Ruth back at the GIA headquarters on Earth, having previously arranged a time he would contact her. It would be about eight in the evening, her time. He waited at the desk in his room for a response; the link chiming occasionally as it waited to connect through the hyperspace network.

Ruth appeared on the screen after two minutes. "Hi boss," she said, adjusting her position on her seat. "Sorry to keep you waiting. Just had something urgent to finish. What can I do for you?"

"Shouldn't you be home?"

"I would be but someone loaded me up with his workload while he was away," Ruth riposted with a cheeky smile.

Alex smirked. "Touché. Anyway, did you get those hive-folder addresses that I sent?"

"Yeah. Had the cyber guru look at them but no luck, I'm afraid. They're wiped crystal clean. A real pro job, he said."

"Pity. What about the symbols on the scan of that scrap of paper?"

"That was easier. The last symbol is the astrological sign of Scorpio, and the first is presumably an ancient Greek letter. They used to designate stars making up the constellations of the zodiac signs with Greek letters, back in the past. Presumably the symbols mean the star designated eta in the Scorpio constellation. I'll send you a star map of the constellation, with the star names on it, so you can see where it is. I don't understand what it might mean, though. There are no habitable planets in that star system, as far as I know."

"Excellent work. I don't know what it means, either. Might be a clue to something the murderer wants us to figure out although, if it is, it might be a bad omen. It might mean there are more murders to follow. I've worked serial murder cases in the past, the murderer almost always wants to publicize they have struck again. I'll be interested in the map when it comes through. It might trigger something this end."

"No worries."

"I had nothing else today. How are things in the office?"

"Same so, same so. Not much happening. The whirlpool of trouble seems to revolve around you. Michael is complaining as usual. Says you're playing favorites," Ruth responded with a grin.

"Tell him to put his energy into his work, not griping about everything else," Alex replied smiling.

"He'll like that," Ruth laughed.

"Yeah. OK, I'd better go. Take care."

"You too."

Alex's screen went blank. He pondered how lucky he was to have such a talented agent as Ruth working for him. He disconnected the link and packed the equipment back into the hotel safe. Deciding it was time to have a shower, he went to the bathroom to complete his toiletries before dressing. He then went downstairs to the breakfast buffet area for food and coffee to start the day.

Nascha pre-arranged a 7:30 pickup from the hotel with him. Alex walked out of the hotel doors five minutes early and waited. The wait was not long. Her AGrav levitated towards him two minutes later, Alex got into it with a "Hi."

"Hi. Have a good sleep?" Nascha responded as she levitated the AGrav away, into one of the express flight paths.

"Yeah. Slept like a baby."

"Everything OK at the hotel?"

"Yeah. It's good. Went up to the bar last night and hung around to listen to a band called the Cretan Novas. They were good."

Nascha gave Alex a suspect look, "That bar's a pickup place."

"So I noticed. Same the galaxy over."

"You enjoy going to those sorts of places?"

Alex looked at Nascha, wondering what the comment was implying. "If you're asking if I target bars like that, the answer is no, but I don't avoid a place because certain activities occur there either."

Nascha looked embarrassed. "Sorry. Didn't mean to imply anything. I don't know you and I shouldn't have asked. Yeah, that band is excellent. I like their music. I didn't know they were playing there last night or I might go there myself, if I hear they are playing there."

Alex felt placated, his irritation subsiding. *Still, she might have a point. Maybe my hackles got up because she struck a nerve too close to the truth.* Alex cringed inside but started calming down. "I'll let you know when they're playing next."

"Thanks."

They sat in silence for a while, Nascha guiding the AGrav. She headed towards the office.

"Anyway," Alex piped up. "I know what the symbols on that scrap of paper mean."

"Yeah. What?"

"It's a star in the Scorpio constellation, apparently."

"Oh. What is the Scorpio constellation?"

"It's a grouping of stars as seen from earth, this one presumably looking like a scorpion."

"Strange. What could that mean?"

"Don't know. Could be a calling card from the killer to let us know who he is. Could mean that he's not finished."

"Hope not. Don't want to chase any more like this one."

"Yeah... Oh, and my people checked the hive folders. They were spotless, cleaner than a sanitation chamber, so no leads there except the culprit is a professional in cyberware, or someone is."

"Another dead end."

"Yeah."

They arrived at Nascha's offices and she parked the AGrav. They went to her office area. She pointed to a desk for him to park himself. "Want a coffee?" she asked.

"Yeah, thanks."

Alex sat at the desk Nascha pointed to and set up his data plate and mobile data qube. He was reviewing his messages when Nascha returned with coffee.

"Impressive set-up," she commented as she placed the coffee on his desk.

"Comes with the job, unfortunately. What I wouldn't give to just chase crims, like I did in the old days."

Nascha grinned. "Come on. You're not that old. You're still a spring chicken. I'd go out with..." She suddenly reddened slightly with embarrassment, her aureola turning a slight green. "That's not what I meant... I was... just saying that you're... not that old. That's all." She looked away from Alex. *Didn't know they did that. Must be a flushing mechanism like the face reddening. Wonder why?*

Alex suddenly started enjoying the situation Nascha had was digging for herself and played her along to see how she reacted. "Really. Sounded like more to it than that." *I wonder.*

"You're reading too much into it," Nascha snapped. "We should concentrate on the case."

"Yeah. We should," Alex agreed with a smirk on his face, which he could see annoyed Nascha even more. Her brow creased with grumpiness. "So, did you get anything more overnight?" he said, sipping his coffee, which tasted wonderful. "Not bad."

"I have a secret source," Nascha confessed. "No, nothing really. The autopsy is complete, we can review that when you're ready."

"Anything we don't already know?"

"Don't know. I haven't seen it yet."

"OK. Let's see it."

"Follow me."

Alex picked up his coffee and followed Nascha, watching her rear with appreciation. *The tribulations we must endure*, he lamented to himself. They went over to Nascha's desk; she selected the autopsy file and displayed it on the public viewing screen. They were silent for a time as they read through the report.

"Well, nothing earth shattering there," Alex commented finally. He sat on the edge of Nascha's desk for a while, working out their next avenue of enquiry. "We should go pay his office a visit. See if there are any clues there."

"You read my thoughts."

"Really?" Alex looked at Nascha, not sure whether to believe her. "Well, let's go then," he said as he finished his coffee.

They collected the items they wanted to take with them and walked out of the office together to Nascha's AGrav in the garage. Nascha seemed to be in a hurry. She had her AGrav fired up before Alex could get in properly. He almost fell out as the AGrav lifted off.

"Whoa! Slow down. You'll get me killed, or is that the plan?"

Nascha looked at Alex, a guilty look on her face, "Sorry. That's how I usually take off, yes I had thought about getting rid of you after the slip up I made before." Her face changed from guilt to a sheepish smirk. "Get rid of the evidence."

Alex chuckled. "At least I know where I stand." He mulled over what she had just said. *Might be a bit of a Freudian slip. She filled the requirements for a suitable date. Fiery and temperamental, though. She seems to have a chip on her shoulder, though. She'll open up when she's ready.* "How far is it?"

"About half an hour," Nascha replied, concentrating on the traffic.

"Why don't you put it into auto?"

"Never trusted it. Anyway, it's fun taking control. Only had a few near misses in my life."

Alex couldn't resist. "I'm confused. Are we talking about AGravs or men?" he asked, working hard to suppress a laugh threatening to explode from his mouth.

"AGravs stupid," Nascha responded with a scowl.

Alex exploded. "I couldn't resist. You fell into that so well," he said once he gained control of himself again.

"Men!" Nascha started off with a disgusted look, which slowly faded, replaced with a blossoming smile and eventually a snigger. "Not bad though. I'll have to be more careful what I say around you."

They spent the rest of the journey in silence.

When they arrived at the ambassador's office precinct, about 100 protestors with placards in hand, greeted them.

"What's all this?"

"Don't know," Nascha responded with a frown. "Looks like a protest. Don't know what it's about though."

Alex could start reading the wording on the placards as they got nearer.

<Humans Go Home>

<No More Human Interference>

<Justice For Caerus>

Alex felt a little unnerved by the messages plastered on the placards but kept his thoughts to himself. *I didn't realize there was that much resentment towards humans by the Cetusians.*

Nascha looked over at Alex. She could see the crowd disturbed him. "Are you OK?"

"Yeah. I suppose there are dissenters wherever you go. We have them on Earth, too."

"Some political radicals are stirring up things a bit. They released details about the murder to the press overnight. I suppose it has only stoked the fire. It'll die down again."

Alex thought about Nascha's comments. "Has it been an issue for long?"

"It's always been an issue ever since there have been Cetusians, but things seemed to have escalated a bit, lately," Nascha explained as a professional observation. They arrived at the office parking garage, Nascha parked the AGrav in a visitor's space, registering official police business in the parking permit system. They alighted from the AGrav, the protest forgotten for the time being.

5

TIBAH

Alex and Nascha ascended the elevator of the office complex and stood in the reception area of what had been the Ambassador's offices. Alex looked around. Apart from the reception with its desk and chairs, there appeared to be two distinct areas. To the left there was a general office area with several desks arranged in neat formation, workers busy completing the day's tasks, whatever that may have been with the Ambassador now dead. To the right was an inner sanctum, presumably the late Ambassador's office. The door was open. Alex couldn't see anything, as he was side on to the doorway.

The reception desk was unattended, and Alex and Nascha looked at each other wondering what to do. Alex shrugged his shoulders and called out: "Hello! Anybody here?"

A face darted out from the Ambassador's office, a woman's face. She looked like she had been crying with red eyes, and her cheeks were slightly damp with tears. "Oh, sorry. I didn't know anyone was there. Excuse me." The face disappeared again.

It would have been amusing to Alex, if the circumstances were not so serious.

A few moments went by the body that owned the face walked out of the door. Tears dried; she was still holding the wipe she had been using. "I'm so sorry. I just had to sit down for a while with no one seeing me. It's so tragic what has happened. Sorry. You know that the Ambassador is dead? Murdered, they say. Some horrible slaughter, they say. So horrible, so horrible..." The woman sobbed, with another fit of tears starting.

Nascha was looking impatient as the woman's hysterics escalated. "That's why we're here. I'm Agent Nascha from the Caerus GIA Office and this is Chief Inspector Detective Alex Warner from the Galactic Investigation Agency Headquarters on Earth."

The introduction seemed to jolt the woman out of her hysteria. She calmed noticeably. "The GIA! Really. At least they're getting serious about things back there, so they should. He was an important man. They must catch the culprit and..."

"That's why we're here," Alex butted in. "Could you tell me your name and your role at the Ambassador's office, please?"

The woman became flustered at the politeness, blushed slightly as she gave Alex a look over. "Um... oh... of course. I'm Tibah and I'm... was the personal secretary and receptionist for Ambassador Tse."

"I'm sorry for your loss. Could we ask you a few questions, please?"

"Well... of course. Oh, where are my manners? Please, please come into the office. Would you like tea or coffee? I'm so sorry for being so rude. Please forgive me..."

"It's OK," Alex butted in again. *What a flustered woman she is. Wonder how she ever decides about having sex and whether she apologizes for giving the lucky guy the pleasure*, Alex pondered. "Just lead the way and we'll follow. Yes, I'd appreciate a coffee. What about you, Nascha?" Alex wanted to get Tibah out of the office anyway, so he could have a quick, unobserved snoop.

"I'll have one too, please," Nascha replied, both following Tibah through the doorway.

Tibah pointed to two chairs by a conference-type table, ornate in an old-fashioned baroque style. "I'll be back in a moment. Make yourself comfortable." She disappeared through the door again.

"Flustered little biddy, isn't she," Alex commented.

"Not kidding."

"Nice table. Must have cost a bomb. I suppose he was the Ambassador." Alex dawdled around the room, looking at the layout of the furnishings. The table was to the left of the door they had entered. It had six chairs placed symmetrically around it, also baroque style. There was a window behind the table that extended the entire length of the wall, overlooked the view from the front of the building. Alex wandered over to it and looked out. He could see the demonstration still in progress below, although the local police had just turned up to disperse the crowd. Further afield was a parkland with a large river flowing through. The trees were blossoming as the renewal of Spring progressed.

Alex brought his attention back to the room and continued to dawdle around. The Ambassador's desk was directly in line with the doorway, so he could instantly see the approaching guest, or intruder, as they entered. Alex could tell the Ambassador must have been a bit of a control freak as it was quite a walk to the two chairs placed in front of the desk, a walk of courage, he imagined. The desk was also baroque in style, but the chair behind it was an immaculate black leather chair of power. The desktop was noticeably clean of data plates or anything else of a business nature. *Quite the opposite of my desk,* Alex noted, as he envisioned the clutter awaiting him when he returned to Earth. There was a holographic screen on it, but that was all. A large old-fashioned painting of the Ambassador in full regal uniform adorned the wall behind. It was at least 2 metres tall. *If you didn't get an impression of grandeur from the Ambassador sitting behind the desk, you would definitely get one from the painting,* Alex thought.

Shelving covered the wall on the right-hand side of the office with various items on display, including quite a few antique paperback books. Alex had heard they were in fashion again of late, for those who could afford them. They didn't interest Alex personally. Everything seemed natural and in order, an office befitting an Ambassador. He couldn't snoop any deeper at the moment, so he sat down.

Nascha sat watching him the whole time he was browsing the office. "See anything useful?" she asked hopefully.

"Not really."

Tibah came back into the office carrying a tray with three coffee cups, a pot of steaming coffee, a small jug of milk, a container of sugar and a small plate with some biscuits. "There you go," she said as she placed the tray on the table in front of them. "Hope you don't mind if I have a coffee too. Things were just too upsetting this morning to make one for myself before I came into work. What, with the news and all."

"Not at all," Nascha consoled.

Tibah handed Alex and Nascha their coffees after she poured them, placed the plate of biscuits in front of them and went to sit on the opposite side of the table with her coffee. She sipped it as she waited for one of them to start the conversation.

Nascha added milk and sugar to her taste. Alex had his black. Alex opened the conversation after he had a sip of coffee. "The furniture is ancient. Baroque I believe?"

"You are very good with your time periods. Yes, it is. Ambassador Tse loved that period of history. It expressed triumph, power and control, he would always say. That was his dream for Caerus within the Confederation."

"I see. Did that ever impede diplomacy that you experienced?"

"No, never. He was very strict in demonstrating the diplomatic code regardless of who he was addressing."

Nascha butted in with a question. "Did he disagree with anyone recently?"

The interference irked Alex. He was working up to the crucial line of interrogation in his own way, so he gave Nascha a look of disapproval but let the question stand.

"Not that I know of. Anyone in his position had people who disagreed with his point of view, but not to the point of killing him.

My goodness. He was such a pleasant man, when you got to know him."

Nascha had seen Alex's displeasure and backed off, allowing Alex to continue. "Who were his key contacts on Earth at the Confederation?" Alex asked.

Tibah thought for a moment. "He had frequent dealings with a person called Malo Metam from Procyon. They seemed very close. I don't know what they talked about. It was always behind closed doors."

Alex and Nascha looked at each other knowingly. *That is a clue that needs chasing up*, Alex thought.

"Do you know how they met?" Alex asked.

"I have no idea. If you ask me, they were so opposite, it amazed me they got on at all, but they always seemed very chummy with each other."

"When was the last time they met that you can recall?"

Tibah thought, concentrating as she recalled events. "It must have been about three weeks ago, I think. I can call up his diary and check."

"I thought they had wiped all his hive data."

"Yes, strange that. I don't understand how that could happen. It's meant to be impossible. Must have been some glitch, I suppose. Anyway, he kept his diary separate from the main hive folder. He said that there were some things in it he needed to keep secret for security reasons, whatever that meant. I didn't think he was in a position that required keeping those sorts of secrets. But there you go. You never know everything about anybody, do you?"

"We will need a copy of his diary as part of the investigation."

"I don't know. He was very secretive about that. Only I knew he had it and what was in it."

"We can get a warrant if you prefer."

"I suppose he's dead now. If it leads to the person who did this, it will have some further use. OK. I'll provide a copy."

"Did he have any meetings the day before yesterday?"

"He had a couple in the office but he had a light schedule that day, left early. He said he had to meet someone later, didn't say who it was."

"Did he keep any sensitive material in his desk, that you know of?"

"He always had a very tidy desk, kept very little in it. The security team emptied it yesterday anyway, so you won't see much now."

Alex and Nascha looked at each other. *What security team?*

"Did this 'security team' say where they were from?"

"Ooh! I'm not sure I can remember. They got me quite flustered. They were very pushy, you know. Not like you. They said it was standard procedure to protect the security of the planet. What standard procedure? I never heard of it in my security briefs, I have a high security clearance. I have to, you know, looking after an Ambassador and all..."

Alex cut her off. "Thank you. We will check into that. What was his relationship with his family?"

"His wife died some time ago. Very tragic, he loved her so. He has a son, but did not see him much. He's a maintenance engineer, you know, at the orbiting maintenance yards. They were both always away, it wasn't often they were on the planet at the same time. But they got along well, as far as I know. Ambassador Tse was always telling me about his son's achievements when he had news."

"Was there anything particularly sensitive that the Ambassador was working on in the office? Did your office manager have a special project?"

"Not that I know of. You can ask him if you like. He's in today. I can call him in."

"No. That won't be necessary at the moment. Well, I think that was all that I wanted to ask. Do you have anything else, Nascha?"

Nascha was not sure whether she should ask questions after the look she got a moment ago, but she persisted. "Where were you the day before yesterday?"

Tibah became flustered by the question, fussing over the position of things. "Well, I didn't know that I was a suspect. I never."

"It's OK. I have to ask. It's just routine."

"Well, OK then. I was in the office all day. You can ask anyone here."

"Thank you. And, another thing, did the Ambassador have any unusual visitors recently?"

"No. Not that I know of. That doesn't mean that he didn't see anyone privately. I wouldn't know that."

"OK. You have been very helpful. Please contact one of us if you think of anything that may be useful." Nascha gave Tibah a contact chip.

"Thank you. I'll just get that diary data that you asked for then." Tibah walked from the room.

"A few things to check out there," Alex said to Nascha.

"Yeah. That security team nonsense seems bizarre. Never heard of such rubbish. Maybe they wiped his hive folder."

"Me neither. We need to check up on this Malo character. See how he fits in. Have you heard of him before?"

"No, I haven't."

"Have you talked to his son?"

"I talked to him yesterday morning before I picked you up from the spaceport. That's why I was there. I was just informing him of the situation though. He had just arrived back from a stint in the maintenance yards. I didn't question him. He needed time to absorb the news. We can contact him again and ask some questions. I'm sure he won't mind. He seemed a decent person."

"We'll see. Chase the other stuff up first, I think."

Tibah came back into the room with a storage chip in her hand, which she handed to Alex. "Here you are. Sorry to keep you waiting with so much to do, I am sure. So many things to chase up and people to talk to. I don't know how you do it. You're so brave..."

"Thank you, Tibah. Thank you for your time and the coffee. We'll be off now."

"Yes, of course. You still have a thousand things to do yet, as do I. I don't know where to start. At least you calmed me so I can concentrate again. I was in such a state before. Don't know what came over me. Well, I'll see you off then," Tibah said as she led Alex and Nascha to the elevator.

The doors opened, Alex and Nascha said their goodbyes and entered the elevator, the doors closing behind them.

"Sure he didn't commit suicide?" Alex asked. "I think I would with a secretary like that."

Nascha grinned. "I'm sure she's very competent, it was definitely homicide."

"Just checking."

6

DINNER

The rest of the day was rather uneventful. Nascha took him to a cafe she often went to for lunch. Back in the office Alex drafted a message to Ruth at GIA in Sydney, requesting information on Malo Metam and his recent activities. He spent the rest of the afternoon looking through Ambassador Tse's diary. Nascha used the time to track down the mysterious security team that 'vacuumed' the Ambassador's office and hive folder.

"I think I'll call it a day," Alex said to Nascha at about six. He stood and stretched to get some kinks out.

"OK. Do you mind catching a taxi back to the hotel tonight? I have more to do here and I have some other things on too."

"No problem. I might do a round in the gym when I get back. I need to burn off some sedentary steam."

"I'll pick you up the same time tomorrow, if that works for you."

"That's good. See you tomorrow then."

"See you," Nascha replied with a warm smile.

Alex packed up his belongings and called a taxi before he left. The traffic was heavy on the way back to the hotel. It was almost seven before he finally entered his room. He quickly changed into gym clothes and spent an hour exercising on the various machines in the hotel gym. He would have preferred to go for a jog outside, but was wary of being overexposed on a strange planet, especially after the protest he had witnessed that morning. He showered back in his room to wash the perspiration off and regained the feeling of freshness on his skin.

What do you feel like tonight? Think I'll see what Klah and Doli are doing over a beer. Maybe see what the restaurant's like.

Alex went up to the rooftop bar and restaurant. As he walked in, he could see Klah tossing a cloth in the air as he cleaned the counter of the bar, singing to himself. Alex had a quick look around and saw a few other people there.

Klah turned as he felt someone approaching. "Hi Alex. Good to see you again. Take a seat."

"Where do you want me to take it?"

"What..."

Alex laughed. "Sorry. Standing joke with me when someone says that."

Klah finally understood the joke. "I've a few suggestions, if you keep giving me trash like that." Klah said with an enormous grin.

Alex continued to laugh.

Klah stopped cleaning, came over to Alex with the cleaning cloth still in his hand, wiping his hands dry. "What can I get you?"

"Same as last night, Klah. That's excellent beer. Must have pinched the recipe from Earth," Alex joked.

"None of your Earth muck here. One hundred percent local recipe," Klah quipped in return.

"Touché."

Klah went to get Alex's beer while Alex grabbed a stool at the bar. Klah returned with the drink as Alex pulled a mini-data plate from his pocket. "Homework tonight?"

"Sort of. Just trying to put a jigsaw puzzle together. It bugs me when I know a pattern's there somewhere, but I can't see it."

"I'll leave you to it, then." Klah grabbed his cloth and went back to cleaning.

Alex powered up the data plate, brought the Ambassador's diary onto the screen and took a draught of beer from the glass. He studied the diary for quite some time, flipping back and forth between pages, trying to find a connection between dates, events and people, but the connection continued to elude him.

"Well!" boomed a voice behind Alex, making him jump, throwing the data plate into the air, which danced a somersault, finally bouncing on the bar as it landed.

Alex turned, stunned, and saw the smiling face of Chooli. "You scared the shit out of me. Well, what!"

"Well, aren't you going to buy me a drink? I've been standing here for ages. Call y'self a detective."

Alex looked over to Klah's sniggering face. He nodded confirmation Chooli had been there for some time. Alex felt his face heat slightly in embarrassment, as he prided himself on being aware of his surroundings. She had caught him out this time. He looked back at Chooli, dumbfounded for a moment before breaking out in a grin as he realized how comical he must look. "Hi Chooli. What would you like to drink?" he said in a pretend formal voice.

They both smiled at each other with the warmth of the sun on a warm spring day.

"My usual," Chooli replied, looking at Klah who dutifully went to prepare it.

"Where's your friend?"

"Couldn't make it."

Alex looked closely at Chooli and decided that she probably hadn't asked her friend. Chooli had come alone in the hope he would be there again. He pulled a wicked grin. "Funny about that."

"Yeah, funny."

"Have a seat."

"This one taken?" Chooli asked, pointing to the seat next to Alex.

Alex looked around. "No. The woman who was sitting there must have left," Alex said, enjoying the banter. Chooli didn't take the bait.

Alex looked Chooli up and down quickly. She wore more conservative clothes tonight. The trampy clothes she had worn the previous night replaced with an elegant pleated red skirt and white top. The neckline still plunged low to reveal her cleavage but with a style of elegance. A thin gold chain hung around her neck, an emerald stone hung in the center, hemmed in on both sides with what looked like pearls. "That's a stylish necklace."

"Ta. Me Mama gave it to me for my birthday."

Chooli's drink came. She picked it up and took a sip.

"How long have you been waiting?" Alex asked, taking a punt she had been there all along when Alex arrived.

"What d'ya mean?" Chooli blushed slightly, as a green tinge colored her aureola.

"How long have you been here tonight?"

"Not long." Chooli reddened more and looked away.

Alex noticed her aureola went noticeably greener. Alex studied her a while longer. "Well, I'm glad you came."

"I wanted to see ya again," Chooli responded shyly.

"For all your boldness, you're not very experienced around men, are you?" Alex said with a kind smile.

Chooli looked back at Alex. "Not really, s'pose." Chooli smiled too when she saw Alex smiling and relaxed. Her smile almost took Alex's breath away with its freshness and symmetry radiating joy.

She looks gorgeous when she smiles. Alex felt a wonder germinate from deep within him, something he hadn't felt for a long time. There was just something special about her, but he couldn't explain what it was. Alex contemplated his next choices and decided. "You had dinner?"

"Depends."

"Depends on what?"

"Depends on why you're ask'n."

Alex threw his hands in the air in exasperation. Chooli just kept looking at him with a beguiling smile, waiting for an answer. Alex sighed and shook his head. "Would you like to go next door to the restaurant with me and have dinner?"

Chooli looked towards the restaurant and then back to Alex. "Sure they'll let me in?"

"Only if you're with me."

"OK. Don't think I'm easily bought though."

Alex threw his arms in the air again. "I wouldn't dream of it. What is it with you?"

Chooli grinned. "What were you doing, anyway?"

"When?"

"When you shit yourself."

It took a while for Alex to work out what Chooli was talking about. "... Oh. I was looking through some information on the investigation I'm working on. I was trying to work out a connection between diary appointments."

"You find it?"

"No. You probably scared any ideas I had out of me, anyway."

"Sorry."

"Anyway, shall we go to the restaurant?"

"Gotta finish my drink first."

"Bring it with."

"Can ya?"

"I'm sure we can. Klah will stop us if we can't. Isn't that right Klah?" Alex turned to Klah, who had been standing a few metres away, pretending to clean the bar counter, listening to the conversation with a bemused smile on his face. Alex noted Klah had been listening for quite some time.

Klah stopped his cleaning and looked at Alex with feigned surprise. "Sure. We're part of the same complex. The drinks come from here, anyway."

Alex picked up his mini-data plate and his beer, hopped off the stool and walked to the restaurant. "Table for two please," Alex asked the person standing behind the counter. As they waited, he looked around at the décor, formal with exquisite decorations strategically placed to give a sensation of elegant serenity. The cherubic floral arrangements on the tables complemented the rest of the furnishing impeccably, as did the golden glow of light emanating from the stalks in the center of the setting.

"Have you made a reservation, sir?"

"No. I haven't."

"I see." The Maître De said, pretending to look at the reservation list to see if a table was available. Alex grinned. The restaurant was empty. "Yes, we appear to have a table available. Please follow me."

The Maître De collected two food menus and a drinks menu and glided across the restaurant. Alex and Chooli followed. Alex glanced at Chooli, who was looking all over the restaurant with inquisitive fascination. *Maybe she hasn't been in a restaurant like this before.* They finally stopped at a table by the edge. It commanded an impressive view overlooking the city. The Maître De pulled out a chair for Chooli, who looked at him suspiciously. She looked at Alex who tried to motion discretely for her to allow the Maître De to seat her. She took the hint eventually, stood in front of the chair and slowly sat as the Maître De slid the chair forward. He did the same for Alex, gave them both a menu and placed the drinks menu in front of Alex. "One of our waiters will be over shortly to take your order."

"I'll have to teach you some etiquette, I see."

"Depends."

Alex decided not to take the bait.

Chooli looked out at the view of the city and beyond. "View's diablo."

Alex was watching her as she gazed out. He could see she had a vibrant personality and her sharp mind took in everything she observed. He liked that. "Yeah, diablo."

Chooli looked around and caught Alex looking at her. She blushed and looked down into her lap, "Ta."

"Where does 'diablo' come from, anyway?"

"Dunno. Just the 'in word' around here at the moment."

Alex looked at the menu and select his meal. Chooli, seeing what Alex was doing, followed suit. She quickly developed a confused look on her face, with a scrunched up nose and knitted brow, as she paged through the menu. Alex watched over the top of his menu with a bemused smile at her predicament. She threw the menu down in disgust. "Having trouble?" Alex asked.

"I can't understand what to order. There're things on one page titled 'Entrée' and other things on pages with 'Mains' on them."

"I take it you haven't been to a restaurant before."

"Not one as complicated as this."

"I'll talk you through it. You look at the page with 'Entrée' on it and select a dish from that. Then go to the pages with 'Mains' on them and select a dish from them."

It still confused Chooli. "Won't that be too much?"

"Believe me, it won't be too much. We'll be lucky if it's enough."

"OK, then." Chooli picked up the menu with a determined look and tried again, taking Alex's advice.

Alex finished selecting his meal. He picked up the drinks menu. He looked up at Chooli again. "Do you drink wine?"

"You kidding me. That's much too expensive for me."

"Would you like to see what it tastes like?"

Chooli had a look of expectant delight. "Sure."

Alex studied her a little. *What type of wine would she enjoy?* He decided she was the type who would enjoy a good full-bodied red wine and turned to the Reds to review the selection. The wines were all locally produced, and he was a little unsure what was good and what was average. He beckoned the Maître De over, who was hovering close by.

"Yes, can I assist you?"

"This the first time I've been on Caerus, so I'm unfamiliar with your wines. Can you recommend a good full-bodied red?"

"Yes. Fortunately for you, that is my favorite variety. I have tasted most on the list. I recommend the 53 Corbian Estate Sauvignon. It is an excellent vintage."

"OK. Thank you."

"Shall I have a waiter deliver a bottle?"

"Yes, please."

The Maître De went over to a waiter to arrange the wine.

By this stage Chooli had deciphered the menu and made her choice, turning back to the window to enjoy the city view. A slight breeze drifted through the restaurant, making the conditions particularly pleasant with the perfume of Spring in it. She looked up to the sky. Two small moons had risen, one almost full, the other waning to new, with a narrowing crescent.

"Spectacular," Alex commented, looking at the same view. "Do you just have the two?"

"Nah. There are four of them. The others are small and hard to see. They aren't visible at the moment. We call these two the twins. They seem to always be in the sky together unless they fight. They stay away for a few days, then they make up and they're back together again."

"Fight?"

"That's what the legend says."

"Oh."

The waiter came over with the wine, opened the bottle and poured a tasting sample in Alex's glass. Alex sipped. *The Maître De knows his wines. This is exquisite. I'd get a case of this if I could.* Chooli looked on, confused with the protocol. Alex nodded that the wine was fine. The waiter poured some wine in both glasses. Alex and Chooli ordered their meal at the same time.

"Would you like to order first?" Alex asked.

Chooli picked up the menu again and turned to the entrées. "Can I have the Arborian fowl salad for entrée and the Caerus Ovine shank please?"

The waiter nodded and turned to Alex.

"I'll have the spiced mollusks for entrée and the Caerusian venison steak please."

Alex picked up his glass, took another mouthful, savoring the wine in his mouth as he inhaled the aroma. He was wondering where to take the conversation as the velvety elixir slid down his throat, creating an ecstatic pleasure. "Tell me a bit about yourself."

"What ya want to know?"

Alex gave her a look of fake annoyance. "I won't have to ask 20 questions, will I?"

"S'pose not." Chooli seemed to look for inspiration as she glanced around the room. "I come from a village, Chaparral, about 300 kilometers away. Grew up there. Parents still there. Had a good childhood." Her face lit up with a smile as she recalled distant memories. "Parents aren't well off, not poor either. We got what we wanted most of the time. Anyway, I the smart one. Did well at school, got a scholarship to University here. Didn't want to leave. Papa convinced me to use me brain. So here I am."

"What are you studying?"

Chooli suddenly looked sheepish, "Criminology."

Alex laughed. "No wonder you had such a look on your face last night. Why are you trolling this place for guys?"

"Not what it looks like. We just want someone to buy us a drink. University students are poor."

"Aren't you afraid that someone might want a reward?"

"That's why there's two of us, we haven't been doing it that long."

"Why did you come tonight then?"

"Something 'bout you I had to find out."

The conversation paused. Alex noticed Chooli was relaxing in his company now, letting her guard down. He watched Chooli take a sip of wine. She almost gagged, coughing and spluttering as she tried to swallow. Alex smiled, hoping he hadn't gotten her taste wrong. "Everything all right?"

"Yeah... yeah," Chooli gasped several times as the effect abated. "First time I ever had some."

"Not to your taste?"

"No... Sure... The shock was too much. Let me have another taste." Chooli braced herself as she prepared for another sip. She smelled the aroma first this time and let the liquid settle in her mouth for a while, then swallowed, looked at Alex and smiled.

"Well?"

"I could get used to that. It's delicious."

"I thought you'd like it."

"How?"

"I'm usually an excellent judge of character."

The entrée came, which stifled the conversation while they ate. Alex could smell the exotic spices that brought out the flavors of the food.

The entrees finished, Chooli asked, "What about you then. What's your story?"

"What you want to know?"

Chooli poked out her tongue at Alex. Alex laughed.

"Let's see. I come from a typical family, really. I'm the middle of five children, so everyone usually left me alone to explore my own pursuits; too young for the older ones to tease too much and too old for the younger ones to play with. I've a passion for justice and problem solving which led me to the police force. Progressed up the ladder. The Galactic Intelligence Agency noticed me, I transferred, and here I am."

"Where's yer missus then?" Chooli probed.

"Been too busy. Never in one place long enough." Alex had a sudden feeling of deep grief, which briefly showed on his face.

Chooli saw the look. "Oh."

Alex noticed some cogs rotating in Chooli's head. He waited for her lead.

"So what's so puzzling about what you were looking at, that diary whatever it was?"

Not what I expected. "I know there's some clue in it, but I can't work out what it is."

"Can I look?"

Alex hesitated, he wasn't sure if he should. She had no authority. He didn't know her.

"Come on. Who am I gunna tell? I'm studying criminology. Good practice."

"OK." Alex took his mini-data plate from his pocket, put the diary on the display and handed it to Chooli.

Chooli took the data plate and studied it intensely. She scrolled through the screens, one by one, back and forward again, several times. "Regular meeting dates."

"What?"

"Regular meeting dates. This guy and some Malo had regular meeting dates. Looks like about a month apart."

"Let me see that." Alex grabbed the data plate and scrolled

through the diary. She was right. Why hadn't he seen it? He looked up again at her. She had a smug look on her face. "OK smarty pants. So you solved that minor mystery, doesn't mean you get a badge."

"No. Well, what if I told you that the meetings were clandestine, secret, off the books?"

"How can you know that?"

"Code. The reason for the meeting is obscure. You might have thought that's because the meeting was some secret business, but this is his personal diary. No need for secrecy in that. Must be top secret, whatever it is."

Alex's opinion of Chooli went up a notch. She was showing herself as super intelligent. He looked at her, impressed. "That was brilliant. Reminds me of myself when I was younger and more enthusiastic."

"Oh really! You wanted to solve it as much as I did. I was just a fresh pair of eyes."

"I suppose."

Their main course came. Alex packed away his data plate, and they ate in relative quiet, only exchanging chitchat as they consumed their meal. Chooli was consuming the wine with abandon, which worried Alex a bit. She wasn't used to it, from her initial reaction, although she had seemed to drink spirits like a trooper the night before. They finished their mains.

"Want dessert?"

"If I eat any more, I'll burst," Chooli said, as she sat back rubbing her stomach.

Alex laughed. She was so fresh. So honest in her behavior, yet very observant, withholding when she saw the need. He felt she was someone he could really form a genuine relationship with if he had the chance, *if I dare*. He watched her as she observed him. *What's going on in her head?* She seemed content, relaxed, assured of something, he didn't know what.

"Thanks for the meal. It was so diablo." She smiled with a radiance she hadn't displayed before. Her aureola changed to a warm golden glow that somehow gave Alex a contagious sense of contentment.

"My pleasure. Beats eating alone, as I normally do."

Chooli looked hurt. "So I'm just an eating companion."

Alex realized his slip. "No. No. No. I wouldn't have asked you to join me if I didn't want you here. I've learned that you're a special person tonight."

"Really?" Chooli responded with a sparkle in her eyes.

"Don't get too crazy. OK. I like you. You have something."

"That's OK. So long as I wasn't just company for the meal."

"You weren't. I haven't enjoyed a meal this much for ages."

The last comment seemed to placate Chooli, and Alex suddenly realized he meant what he said. They both looked out over the city as they sipped the last of their wine, Alex wondering what would happen next. Chooli seemed to come to her own conclusion and smiled. The waiter removed the plates, and Alex signed for the meal, charging it to his room. When they rose to leave Chooli crept close to Alex and placed her arm in his. Alex looked at her, wondering.

"I want to get to know you better," she said.

7

AHIGA

Ahiga left his work stunned. *My father dead! How can that be possible?* The news from the detective shocked him to the core. Now he was all alone. His mother died when he was young and he didn't have any siblings. His father should have still been alive. His father was everything to him. He had always been there for him as he grew up, even with his busy political schedule. He knew his father was always proud of him.

Ahiga sat in his small apartment moping, not sure what to do. What was he supposed to do? He suddenly remembered when his father gave him his first toy engineering kit. He would sit down with Ahiga for hours showing him how the different gadgets worked, how he could integrate them to make new machines. Tears flowed as he remembered the close times and his grief hit him, opening the door to the hollowness he was feeling, letting the pain flood out, like a burst of blindingly bright light exploding out of a room into the pitch-black night. His father was always interested in him. "Always do the best you can, that's all anyone can ask," his father would say when Ahiga thought his unimpressive school results would disappoint him.

Ahiga's tears slowly subsided, as did his debilitating grief. He was not normally a person who could sit still for long. He had to be doing things, or he'd either get bored or fidgety. His employer gave him time off to grieve for his father. "As long as it takes," Sani had said. He made himself a coffee while he thought about what he should do. *I probably don't need to work ever again,* he thought with a bittersweet smile. His father had been wealthy. He had only continued in politics for the satisfaction he got from helping people, he had said. Ahiga also knew he was the sole heir. Ahiga had ventured into engineering to make a career for himself instead of parasitically living off his father.

Maybe I should go to his house, make sure it's secure and collect any small valuables before anyone gets any ideas. Am I ready to face the house yet? Especially since that's where they killed him. Ahiga steeled himself. His father would not approve of his procrastination. "If you've got something to do, do it. Don't dither like a mother hen," he would have said. *OK. I need to go over to his house, so I may as well do it now,* Ahiga decided. He finished his coffee.

Ahiga was still in his work clothes so he got undressed, had a shower and put on some casual attire. He collected his belongings and ferreted out the spare key chip to his father's house his father had given him long ago. When asked why, his father had said, "You might need it one day". It took a while to find, as a lot of other collectables he had placed in his small secure container buried it.

Armed with what he needed, he went to his AGrav and flew to his father's house. Two police officers were standing at the front door when he arrived, and several other official-looking people were accessing of the house.

A policeman stopped him at the door. "Sorry, no entry," he said.

"But I'm his son," Ahiga protested.

The officers looked at each other. One of them radioed to someone inside the house. A few moments later a person in a suit came out. "Hello, I'm Detective Osago, the detective in charge of collecting the evidence. First, I'm sorry for your loss."

"Thanks. It really hasn't sunk in yet, I don't think."

"Yes, it must have been a shock for you. Is there anything I can do for you?"

"You can let me in. I just wanted to go through some of his valuables, make sure they are secure, take anything personal back to my place."

The detective thought through the request. "OK. Understand you can't go anywhere near the scene of the crime yet, but I think I can give you access to the rest of the property."

"OK. When do you think you will be finished?"

"Hard to say. Maybe by the end of the day, but I think we'll still be here tomorrow. We can't release the scene until Investigator Nascha gives the all clear."

"OK. She talked to me this morning. She seems a decent person."

"She's one of our best."

"Where can't I go?"

"Primarily around and in the solarium."

"Fair enough. There's nothing there I need anyway, I'm not sure I'm ready to face that yet, anyway."

"OK. Just contact one of these officers if you need anything from me," the detective said, pointing to the two door guards.

"I will. Thanks."

The detective talked to one guard and went back inside. Ahiga followed but went his own way once he was in. The house itself was unusually quiet - they had sent the staff home, not that there were many. There was a groundsman, a butler, a part-time cleaner and a cook. Ahiga headed for his father's study where he kept most of his valuables in a security safe. The key chip gave him access to the safe, but the lock also required retinal scans of both eyes, which his father had set up when he provided the chip.

The study was upstairs, so Ahiga slowly trudged up the stairway. His feet felt like lead, getting heavier as he scaled the stairs as the weight of his mission sunk in. He finally reached the top of the stairs, sighed and walked to the study, which was halfway along the hallway, on the left. A crescendo of memories came rushing in as he opened his father's office door. How often had he done so when he was younger, disturbing his father with some exciting news? His father had not hushed him or chased him out because he was too busy. He always had time to listen until Ahiga's excitement had all flowed out, like water gushing from a tipped over glass to cover the table it had been standing on, finally subsiding into a state of equilibrium again.

His father's desk stood in front of him, the polished timber bureau one of his father's treasured possessions. He walked into the room, around the desk and looked out the window, through to the solarium. A lump rose in his throat at the thought of what had happened. He sought refuge in his father's leather chair and, as he sat at the desk, trying the drawers on both sides, but they were locked. The key chip for them would be in the safe.

Ahiga rose from the chair, walked over to the holographic photograph hanging on the right wall. It was a hologram of the family when he was young, when his mother was still alive. He pushed the right-hand side of the frame and it clicked. He pulled, the frame hinged on the left to reveal the safe behind. Retrieving the key chip from his pocket, he inserted it in the slot in the lock mechanism. A scanner emerged and scanned both retinas as he stood still. Satisfied of Ahiga's identity, the safe opened to reveal an assortment of valuables, cash chips and key chips. Ahiga sorted through the key chips, found the one for his father's desk. He also saw a data chip with his name on it as he rummaged. He grabbed the data chip and the key. He put the data chip in his pocket to view later. He quickly inspected the other keys, but they didn't mean much to him. As he went to close the safe, he grabbed one of the cash chips, thinking it might come in useful. He closed the safe, retrieved the key from the lock and positioned the frame back to its original location with a click.

Ahiga walked back to the desk and sat in the chair again. He used the key to open one drawer, then the other, gliding them on their tracks to the fully open position. Rummaging through the drawers, he found nothing of interest, except a few other data chips, which he grabbed and placed on top of the desk. He was about to close the drawers again, but suddenly remembered his father telling him to feel along the space behind the facade of the desk, above the drawer cavity, if he ever needed answers. He didn't know what his father had meant then, or now, but felt the area anyway. As he passed his fingers along the left-hand side, he felt something stuck to the inside. He pulled at it. It gave way. It was another data chip. *I wonder why he put that there instead of inside the safe?* He closed the drawers, stood up and placed the data chips in his pocket.

Ahiga walked out of the study and into his father's bedroom. He looked around a room he had seen many times before. Fond memories came flooding back of running in to wake his father in the morning, for some childish reason or another, only to be tickled into submission in retaliation. He smiled lovingly at the memory. There was nothing here now, though. It was just an empty bedroom. Drapes, open since the previous day, let the sunlight stream in, motes dancing to the random push of air molecules from the Brownian motion. He turned and went downstairs again. There was nothing else for him here for now. *Let the raping violation of the murder scene subside into a mere memory first. I'll come back then and decide how best to restore happiness to the forlorn presence again.*

He left the house and informed the police guards he wouldn't be coming back soon. They nodded. He walked back to his AGrav and levitated it to join the homeward flight path.

Back inside his apartment, Ahiga emptied his pockets and placed the multiple chips on the desk with his data plate and other study items. He considered going through the chips but felt too exhausted from the stress of the day's events. Instead, he pulled a beer from his food cooler, sat in his lounge chair, turned on the holovision and watched a sitcom.

Ahiga woke with a start. He realized he must have nodded off, and it was now dark, except for the glow of the program which wasn't the sitcom he had been watching. The beer bottle lay empty on the floor where it dropped. He sat up and stretched, extending his arms to the ceiling and looked at the chronometer. It was almost midnight. He had slept for quite some time. *No wonder I've got a sore back, sitting in that slouched position for so long.* He felt hungry, so he went to the cooler and made a snack. He picked up the beer bottle and placed it in the recycle chute. Retrieving a second bottle from the cooler along with his snack, he went back to the lounge. He didn't like the program that was showing, so he surfed the channels until he found a documentary on the history of transportation from the early Stone Age to the present. It had just started. It fascinated him, especially the part where humans first developed faster-than-light space travel and the antiquated equipment used to achieve it. Technology had progressed a long way since then. It was after one in the morning when the program finished. He turned the holovision off and went to bed.

Ahiga felt refreshed when he woke the next morning. He showered and had breakfast while he watched the morning news stories. There was a story about his father. It said that the police had apprehended no one yet. They had put a detective from the Galactic Investigation Agency head office, a Chief Inspector Detective Warner, on the case. His picture displayed on the holovision, along with the detective who had talked to him the day before. *At least they are taking the murder seriously,* he thought as he munched on toast with strawberry jam, sipping coffee. He cleaned up after his breakfast and turned the holovision off.

At his desk, he fingered the many chips, placing the money chip and the key chip in his drawer. That left four data chips, the one with his name on it, the two in his father's desk and the one secreted inside the drawer. Starting with his own, the data plate revealed two files, the first one with just a sequence of letters and numbers. *I wonder what that means.* Ahiga opened the other file. A passcode screen came up. He put two and two together and went back to the first file, copying the alphanumeric sequence and pasting it into the security field. The file opened, revealing his father's account details and passcodes. *That will come in useful later, I suppose,* Ahiga thought as he closed the files and removed the data chip. The next two data chips revealed little of interest to Ahiga, just some work in progress; business his father had not yet completed.

Ahiga placed the last chip in the slot and opened the first file, a holovision file. His father appeared on the screen, seated in his leather chair in his study, wearing his ambassadorial uniform with a serious but loving expression on his face. He started talking,

"Hello Ahiga. If you are viewing this file, it probably means that I am dead because of foul play. I am sorry for that. First, remember I have always loved you and always will, and the Cetusian species. Second, do not forward this chip, or the information I will talk about in a moment to anyone, not even the police, unless you feel you must. Third, I regret to inform you I am probably not the man you thought I was."

What on Caerus is he talking about? Foul play? Not the man I thought he was?

"Through my political life, I have become a part of a clandestine movement that has questionable motives and conducts ruthless activities to achieve its objectives. Unfortunately, I had to take part in these activities, had to take part in things I regret and found distasteful. I became involved in these activities with, what I believed at the time, good intentions, but looking back, I now understand I should have found another way. Unfortunately, it became too late to back out, so I had to make the most of a very distasteful situation, salvaging my original goals and the goals of my compatriots by questionable means that are probably illegal. Please find it in your heart to forgive me. That is all I will say here, except that there is another file in the folder where you found this holovision, which contains the details of a safe deposit box in the Caerus International Bank head office in Richards Street, in the city. The information in that box will reveal all you need to know. One last thing, always remember I love you, my son."

Ahiga was weeping as the holovision concluded. His father's words confused him, as if his life had been a lie. His father had loved him, yet he said he had done despicable things that placed that love in danger. What exactly did he do? He hinted that he had involved himself in things that his father wouldn't call honorable or ethical. Ahiga had only one choice. He had to find out what was in that safe deposit box.

Ahiga wiped away his tears and thought. What was his father

really saying? The cause he involved himself in meant getting into questionable activities where things got out of hand. That seemed to be what his father was saying. His father was a principled man. Ahiga resolved to make sure remembered his father's name that way, not for any wrong he may have done.

It was almost noon, so Ahiga had a light lunch and prepared to go to the bank. He memorized data from the file; the identification details and access requirements.

Arriving at the bank, the service assistant gave him a strange look when he requested to access the safe deposit box. *Maybe I don't look the type to have a safe deposit box, he thought.* She regrouped quickly. "Sir. Come this way." She led Ahiga to a manager who was busy working on his daily activities. "Sir, this gentleman would like to access a safe deposit box," she said when he looked up.

The manager instantly made himself look official. He shut down what he was doing and stood. "Come this way, Mr.?"

"Ahiga."

"Mr. Ahiga." The manager escorted him to an elevator which descended to a room, empty except for a data input panel and retinal scanner.

"If you would Sir, can you punch in your identification code?"

Ahiga went up to the panel and keyed in the data he had memorized. The retinal scanner instantly activated. Ahiga stood in the designated area on the floor. The scanner took an image of one eye, then the other. Lights flashed green, a mechanism activated, sending an invisible trolley humming off somewhere to collect the safe deposit box. It appeared from a slot in the wall, slowly pushed forward by an invisible mechanism.

"You may conduct your business in here, Sir. Please reinsert the box into the slot, when finished, and press this button here," the manager said, pointing to a button on the wall by the door. "I will leave you to your business." The manager walked out of the door, which slid closed behind him.

Ahiga looked at the deposit box nervously. He wondered what secrets it kept. What would his father want him to have that needed locking behind steel in the depths of the bank's vault? A small table and chair stood next to the slot the box was now hanging out of. He grabbed the box with both hands and pulled it out of the slot, which remained open in readiness for its return. He sat staring at the box, indecision swirling around him. *Do I really want to know what's inside? Do I really want to know who my father truly was? Father must have had his reasons. Stop wasting time and open the damned thing.* His shaking hands finally moved to the lid, opening it slowly.

Ahiga's eyes widened in surprise as he saw the contents of the box. There were more data chips, some gemstones, which he presumed were valuable, and a maser pistol. *What would father want with a maser pistol in a safe deposit box? More to the point, why would he want Ahiga to have one?* A person needed a license to own a gun. Maybe his father had included Ahiga's name on his licence. He needed to make sure at some stage. The pistol was safe from trouble while it stayed in the box. There were some plasto-papers were inside too. He pulled them out and flipped through them slowly, realizing they might be deeds to precious metal deposits on planets all over the galaxy. *If all these mines are significant deposits and are being worked, the royalties from them would be worth a fortune!* He set the papers aside on the table and gathered the chips. There were four of them, each with a number but nothing else that identified the contents. He had brought a chip copier with him and intended to keep the originals safe. They were obviously precious for a reason he would find out in due course. He spent several minutes copying the chips, identifying the copies with the same number and placing the originals back in the box, deciding on examining them later, when he could take his time in private.

Ahiga had seen the entire contents of the box, so he returned the contents and closed the lid. He sat for a while staring at the duplicate chips, wondering what his father wanted to keep confidential until his death. What secrets would he find? What labyrinth of subterfuge might engulf him? He sighed himself out of his reverie and stood, slightly hunched over, tired and wondering if that was what he had to look forward to when he grew old. He grabbed the box and placed it back into the slot, sliding it in as far as it would go. The box hit something solid, it instantly slid the rest of the way in and the slot disappeared as if it was never there. He placed the chips in his pocket.

Ahiga was finished in the bank so he left, returning to his AGrav. A set of eyes watched from a hidden alley as he got into the AGrav and levitated away.

8

SHALLUM

A dark black mist engulfed Shallum Tsadoq as he stared into the abyss of his soul. A pinprick of white light tarnished the perfect void before him. The light grew in size and vividness as if he were approaching a blazing fiery furnace; the energy blinding him as it closed in. He recognized the shape to be human but could not make out any features yet. The specter before him confused him. It finally came close enough for him to see it was his wife.

"Cajsa!"

The apparition smiled. She now stood before him about five metres away.

"Cajsa, where have you been? I have missed you so."

Cajsa kept smiling with a wistful sorrow in her eyes.

A scorpion appeared at her feet, a brilliant magenta, scuttling around in search of a victim to devour. Cajsa looked down at the scorpion with quizzical serenity. Shallum could see her curiosity being roused. She bent for a closer look. The scorpion noticed the movement and maneuvered before her. Cajsa studied the scorpion for a multitude of seconds before she stretched out her hand as if to pet the forward carapace of the arachnid.

Shallum, sensing danger, broke out in a flood of perspiration, dread and fear encompassing his entire person. He tried shouting out to Cajsa, but his vocal chords would not work. No noise emerged from his petrified lips.

Cajsa's hand approached the scorpion, her forefinger extended to stroke it gently. The stinger on its tail slashed forward to pounce on the approaching prey. The needle sharp barb penetrated the tip of her finger with practiced ease. Cajsa jerked back her hand as the sting of the touch registered. She stood and looked at the finger. A small bead of blood oozed from the minute incision.

Shallum struggled to move with dread-filled eyes, beseeching some unknown presence to drive his feet forward to no avail.

A glowing red poison grew from the prick on Cajsa's finger. She looked at Shallum as the blemish spread up her arm. His fear for his wife blinded all other sensations he may have had. Cajsa had the look of puzzled innocence as her face started glowing like fire. She suddenly screamed in unanswerable agony as the poison took total control. Her body started fading until it vanished into the surrounding void.

Shallum finally found his voice and shouted a blood-curdling scream in desperation, but too late. The scorpion noticed the vibrations and turned to face Shallum, stared at it with hate-filled eyes. The scorpion approached. When it was close enough Shallum lifted his foot and stomped on it, squashing it. The pleasure of the execution quickly evaporated when two more scorpions appeared, blood red, running towards him. He extinguished their lives as well when they were within stomping distance. More scorpions arrived, surrounding Shallum with their menacing presence. Shallum looked closer at the scorpions, distorted faces etched into the forward visage of the creatures. They laughed in mockery at him, tormenting him, humiliating him, challenging him as they closed in.

Shallum stepped on one and then another and another. There seemed no end to them. Two more appeared for each one he exterminated. They kept laughing their spite-filled maniacal laugh, louder and louder, until Shallum could stand it no longer. He screamed hysterically, like a lunatic spluttering and dribbling as fear engulfed him. Then suddenly he felt himself shift and an evil darkness consumed him. He finally had a purpose. He kept stomping on the scorpions, removing the mocking faces from existence. He kept pounding his feet on the dreaded arachnids, faster and faster, his insane laughter increasing in volume and pitch. He saw each face fade into oblivion as he did so. His insanity finally crescendoed in an apoplexy of grief, torment, evil and despair. The scorpions finally faded away. His face froze into a look of unending hate. He would have retribution for his wife's murder. They would pay the price.

He stirred from his nightmare of imprisonment and realized he sat in his diplomatic apartment, staring at the holograph of his late wife in his hands, weeping. He had not realized the depths of his anguish. "Why did you have to leave me?" he said, to no one but himself. "What was so bad you couldn't tell me? This is worse for me, my love, than not telling me."

Six months ago, Shallum's wife had died, and he had found it impossible to overcome his grief, his confusion. 'Suicide' the official report said, but he didn't believe it. He knew there was more to it, but couldn't find any proof. The authorities had washed their hands of it, giving him no outlet for his grief. He often thought of joining her in her paradise, or prison, he did not know what, but he knew she would want him to carry on, so he did, reluctantly, doggedly.

Shallum was a foreign attaché for the Procyon Government, working for Malo Metam, the system's Confederation Ambassador. He came from the planet Racoon, the secondary planet in the Procyon star system, Procyon being the primary colonized planet. He had to travel extensively for his job and lobbied support for Ambassador Metam's Procyon policy proposals put forward to the assembly. There seemed to be a constant stream of them coming from this source. He had just returned from Caerus.

He sighed and replaced the holograph on the shelf, making sure it was in its right place. He had an obsession for neatness, a place for everything.

He looked at the holograph again. *What really happened to you?*

Why couldn't you tell me what was going on? The only conclusion Shallum could come to was that, as the personal assistant to Malo Metam, some had discovered that she had stumbled on something. Whatever it was, she was in so deep that the only solution was to get rid of her and make it look like a suicide.

Shallum could not get over his loss. They never had children. She was infertile. It had disappointed him, but now he was glad they were not sharing his grief and misery.

He looked at the time on his chronometer and saw it was time to leave for his next destination and appointment on the Chinese colonized planet Xin Shanghai in the Xi Boötis system. He had to deliver another policy proposal to yet another diplomatic bureaucracy. The lengthy trips keeping the Confederation's political system running were draining Shallum. Malo had asked whether he wanted time off after the death, but he had refused. Keeping himself active would take his mind off the tragedy. Now he wasn't sure whether he made the right decision. It was what it was.

There was a chime at the door. Shallum looked at the screen and saw it was his chauffeur to take him to the spaceport. He rose from his chair with another wearisome sigh. He stretched to his full height to get the creaks out of his bones and went to the door. "Hello. Yes, I'm ready. My baggage is over there," Shallum said, pointing to the pile of bags on the floor, near where he had been sitting. The chauffeur nodded his greeting, entered the apartment and collected the baggage.

Shallum relaxed back in the AGrav seat and poured a quality Procyon malted Scotch whisky from the small bar after he had placed a few cubes of ice in his tumbler and waited for the chauffeur to start the flight to the spaceport.

Shallum retrieved his data plate from his carry bag and brought the policy details up on the screen. He didn't know why he bothered sometimes. Each policy proposal Malo put forward was usually a variation of the same theme: preferential recognition of humans above other species in the Confederation. It was blatantly discriminatory, but he somehow got it on the Assembly agenda innumerable times, and just as often it got voted down. It was Shallum's job to whip up support for the proposals. It seemed a pointless activity, although there seemed to be an increasing momentum of support for the general principle, much to Shallum's disgust.

Malo's biggest push at the moment was to prevent inter-species breeding. He said it contaminated the sentient advantage of the human species, quoting some obscure spurious scientific research as proof. It wasn't the first time he used the results of questionable research to justify his policy proposals. Shallum had to promote these justifications, even though he knew they usually rigged the research to provide the desired result. One such finding was that interspecies breeding caused high genetic defects in offspring. It was only when one studied the details of the research, one found the sample surveyed only couples with children carrying the defects. Rather embarrassing someone pointed it out to Malo, but it showed how fanatical he was about the issue.

Shallum never understood why his wife worked for a person of Malo's political bent. He could ask the same question of himself, he supposed. Cajsa's beliefs had been diametrically opposite, always very inclusive, no matter what the species. Her boss's attitude would sometimes get to her and she would come home ranting about Malo's bigotry.

Shallum thought more about his wife, forgetting about the policy he had set out to review. He realized since her death that, in the months prior, she had become quieter, more moody than usual, as if there was something deeply troubling her. She had never opened up about it, but Shallum could tell there was something on her mind. Unfortunately, he was home so infrequently, he could not support her as much as his guilt said he should have.

He had delved into what may have caused her reticence in the months since. He got clues, but seemed to hit roadblocks whenever he thought he had a new direction. He was becoming suspicious and thought it was all a conspiracy, ludicrous as that was. His mind was playing tricks with him, and he believed his wife really did...

"We have arrived, Sir," the chauffeur interrupted Shallum's

thoughts, bringing him back to reality. Shallum packed up his data plate and alighted from the AGrav. He noticed the tumbler still sat where he had placed it, hardly touched since the first sip. The chauffeur removed the baggage from the vehicle, placed it on a trolley and walked into the spaceport terminal with Shallum. He checked the baggage in and handed the identity chip to Shallum, who took it and started walking to the waiting space ship via the diplomatic route, which meant he didn't have to wait in line - the only way to travel, as far as Shallum was concerned.

9

MALO

Malo Metam sat reviewing the latest Assembly proceedings when he received the news about the murder of the Caerus Ambassador. He placed his data plate on his desk and looked at the message on his comm again.

<Release. Caerus Ambassador murdered at home. No suspects to date. Cetusian GIA Office investigating. Assistance of Galactic GIA requested >.

Malo's blood ran cold as he read the message again. *Another one. A few more now.* The Ambassador was another member of his clandestine organization murdered in the last four months; the victims being of higher and higher rank as time passed. It was messy, but he needed to weed out the unbelievers before he started the next phase of his plan. It was fortunate he had such a willing tool to perform the unpleasant business. He counted - the Ambassador made it five deaths so far. This was the first and only Cetusian. It amazed him no one had put two and two together yet, although the murders had occurred on independent worlds so the local authorities might not have checked other star systems during the individual investigations. The story might be different with the central GIA investigators now involved. Malo hoped not, or his plans would unravel when they were entering the most critical phase of his campaign to establish the supremacy of the Human species. He hoped the Ambassador's death would spontaneously escalate civil unrest on Caerus to the degree he needed, with his agents there to help stoke the fire.

Malo stretched for a moment. He was feeling old and weary although, at 53 years of age, he was anything but old. The stress of the situation was tiring him. He thought about that and felt it was unusual for him to worry so much about things. Maybe it was because everything was finally starting to come to a head. He really couldn't put much time into the situation at the moment. An important meeting with Count Miho of Delta Pavonis was imminent, and he needed to prepare. The Count was not a very pleasant character, being pretentious and wanting the universe to revolve around him even though the star system was a minor member of the Confederation. Malo knew any support was welcome support, so he prepared to pander to the Count's pride to get his endorsement for the vote next week in the Assembly.

The Count's arrival was in 20 minutes. Malo reviewed his notes. Nouveau Franconi, the main colonized planet of Delta Pavonis, was experiencing an influx of Cetusians, as they chased menial jobs from planet to planet throughout the populated galaxy. Not an uncommon occurrence, and one Malo played to his advantage in his campaign to relegate those barbarians to the status of political inferiority they deserved. The Count's economy was straining under the influx of low-paid Cetusians, but they were the only ones prepared to do the work. Malo had to convince the Count any interbreeding between species would give him and his offspring a problem for all eternity, and Malo's proposal to the Assembly would prevent it. Malo didn't think it would be difficult once he placed the 'facts' before the Count. He finally worked out the strategy he would use to seduce the Count to agree to vote for his proposed bill. It was fortunate the Count had been visiting Procyon and could fit Malo into his 'busy' schedule.

Malo's desk comm buzzed. He pressed the answer button and his personal assistant's voice announced, "The Count of Delta Pavonis is here to see you, Sir."

"Good. Please show him in."

The Count strutted into the room in full military uniform of the Delta Pavonis armed forces, complete with an armada of medals on his left breast. Malo was half expecting a sword by his side and sighed in relief to see the Count had forsaken that item of military tradition.

"The Count of Delta Pavonis," his assistant announced formally.

Malo rose from his seat and walked around his desk, offering his hand in welcome. "It is an honor to see you Count. I am pleased that you could take time out of your busy schedule to visit me," he said.

The Count shook Malo's hand. "Well, I had a cancellation, so I could fit you in at the last moment," he said pompously.

"Please come and have a seat over here by the meeting table," Malo said, pointing to an antique leather-covered chair for the Count. "Would you like a refreshment?"

"Humph! Don't mind if I do. Coffee, strong, no milk, no sugar," the Count ordered as he marched over to the chair and sat. "I hope this will not take long. I have a rather pressing engagement."

Probably with a blonde and a bottle of champagne from what I hear. "I intend to take up as little of your time as possible. Please humor me with your presence."

The personal assistant came back in carrying a tray with the Count's coffee order on it, and coffee for Malo, a plate of biscuits, slices of cake and two individual plates for them to eat from. Placing the tray on the table, she provided both men with their coffees and plates, positioning the plate of food on the table in between them, then left the office, leaving them to their privacy.

The Count took a sip of his coffee and selected a biscuit to nibble. "I suppose this is about that silly bill you have before the Assembly."

Malo groaned inwardly and rolled his secret imaginary eyes behind his physical ones. "Let me just take you through how the bill might help you maintain your economy's prestigious position and how things might change if you allow unnatural things to happen."

The Count's ears pricked up at the mention of a potential threat to his state system's unique economy and status. "What do you mean?"

"Well, I understand that you have a significant number of Cetusians emigrating into your system."

"Yes, we do and it's rather annoying to be honest. Stretching our resources. They come in for the work."

"Why don't your people do that work?"

The Count looked affronted, offended. "You can't expect my people to do all those menial tasks. It is below our standards. We have a status to maintain."

Malo smirked internally. *You wouldn't want to get your hands dirty, would you?* "Exactly," Malo said, playing along. "It is of benefit to you that these Cetusians are there to perform these menial tasks."

"Yes."

"However, our research shows the Cetusian species is far inferior to us humans, genetically. They will never reach our potential."

"Malo, we all know this research you talk about is dodgy. Ask any scientist."

"If you believe jealousy amongst scientists. The point I want to make is, eventually you will have some Cetusians and your humans interbreeding and the more half breeds you have, the greater problem you will create."

"How so?"

"We all know that Cetusians ostracize any half breeds. They reject them entirely, so they have no cultural home with the Cetusians. Humans completely despise them too. So eventually you have a ghetto of half-breeds with nowhere to go, no cultural footing anymore. They become destitute, resulting in increased rates of drug use, prostitution, violence and mortality. You don't want that in the streets of your most prestigious areas, do you?"

The Count became gravely concerned with the scenario Malo was painting. He rubbed his chin for a bit, thinking. "I suppose you could have something there."

"Of course I do and you know it," Malo said pressing the advantage he could see opening. "The last thing you want is to have your valuable tourists shunning your system because of something that you could so easily avoid. I'm not saying get rid of the Cetusians. As you said, they serve a valuable role in the scheme of things. Just prevent them interbreeding with humans, avoid all the problems."

"What proof do you have? Where has this occurred?"

"You will see the Bill documents many instances from the research conducted on the cultural behavior of the various species and their interbreeds."

"Humph. I will have to get my people to review the documents again, brief me a summary, I suppose. How on earth will you enforce it, though? You don't intend euthanizing offenders and their families, do you?"

"Heaven forbid. We are not barbarians. We would incarcerate them for the rest of their lives. That is all. It would be openly advertised that this is the consequence of their misdemeanor."

"Maybe it would work. What about the existing ones?"

Malo sighed, "Unfortunately, there will be some casualties but for the overall common good." *I think I have him.*

The Count thought for quite some time before speaking. "OK. I think you have convinced me. If all of what you have said checks out, you can count on my vote."

"Good, good. Everything will check out, I promise, I'm pleased your exceptional intellect has prevailed in these unfortunate circumstances. Some people just don't get it. They just don't have the intelligence we have, I'm afraid."

"Just so, just so," the Count said, puffing his chest out a bit at the compliment, not realizing Malo did not mean a word. The Count sat for a while, apparently reflecting on something before he said, "Is that all you wanted to talk about then? I'm a busy man, you know."

Malo groaned inwardly again. "Yes, that is all that I wanted of your valuable time. I am pleased you could take the time to talk with me."

"Anytime, anytime." The Count rose from his chair to leave.

"I hope you have a pleasant time for the rest of your stay here."

"Thank you. It is always a pleasure to visit Procyon, always a pleasure to talk with you. Don't be afraid to stay in touch, will you?"

"No I won't," Malo replied as he held his hand out to shake the Count's. *And we all know what part of Procyon interests you most.*

The Count shook Malo's hand and allowed Malo to open the door for him. "We will see you at the Assembly then."

"Yes, I'll see you there," Malo replied.

The Count's staff rejoined him, and they left.

That went a little better than I expected. Amazing what a threat to someone's status can do to change a person's mind.

Malo pondered his next moves. He could count on the Count's support now. The numbers were stacking up. He needed more though, as it was one thing to get a motion passed into law, another for the affected to relinquish power to others. An even bigger issue was gaining acceptance from the populace, without too much bloodshed and anarchy. Yes, he would have to plan the enforcement strategies for total human rule of the Confederation. He would have to start the execution of the last phase of his master plan.

10

RESCUE

Alex was up early, in a cheerful mood for a change, and connected to Ruth Alvarez on the hyperlink.

"You look different," Ruth commented.

"I'm a day older."

"No, you look happy or something. Is everything all right?"

"Aren't I allowed to be happy sometimes?"

"Ooh! You know what I mean. Yes, you are usually happy when the bureaucracy or some clueless reporter is not harassing you. But you look... happy. Don't know how else to describe it."

"Must just be the unpolluted Caerus air," Alex quipped, not giving anything away. *Now that Ruth mentioned it, I feel happy, the happiest I've felt for a long time. Why? I had a delightful time with Chooli last night at dinner but surely it's not that, well not just that anyway.* Alex realized he hadn't had such a pleasant and enriching evening with a female for a long time. *Since her*, he thought. *Since she destroyed me.* He momentarily gritted his teeth in anger but let it pass quickly, realizing he must look like he was daydreaming to Ruth. He came back to the present. "Anyway, enough of the chit-chat. What have you got on the Malo guy?"

"I've sent you our profile. You should have it on the hive. I think he's a very creepy guy. He is xenophobic to the extreme and obsessed with putting Cetusians in their place. Otherwise, he is a typical politician, being a mover and shaker to get his proposals through. Has various staff. His personal assistant committed suicide six months ago. No suspicious circumstances, according to the local authorities' report."

"OK. You've been busy. I'll review the report today and see if there's anything else I want chased up. Anything else?"

"Yeah. Just to be thorough, I've had the guys put together a list of unsolved murders in the past six months. Check for similarities."

"Excellent idea. Any results?"

"Too early. Might have something on that tomorrow."

"OK. Well, looks like I have a day ahead of me, thanks to you," Alex jibed.

"Always a pleasure to keep the boss happy."

"Go home. You've been working too long. You're starting to get sarcastic."

They both laughed.

"Yeah. About time I got out of here. Have a pleasant day."

The connection broke. Alex sat back. Ruth's an excellent detective. She'll rise in the system. She's still young. Just needs the right opportunities and breaks. That was good thinking to check for similar murders. I'll put a comment in the case notes when I get around to writing them up. He pondered his day. His stomach was telling him he needed to have some breakfast and get some coffee. He rose, showered, dressed and went to breakfast.

At 7:30 Nascha arrived to pick him up. "Have a good night?" she asked.

Alex smiled contentedly. "You could say that."

Nascha looked at Alex, waiting for him to elaborate. Silence. "Well?"

Alex realized he was giving too much away. "I looked through the diary to see if I could find any patterns."

"Did you?"

"Yes," he lied. "The Ambassador had regular meetings with Malo Metam. Head office has put together a profile on him. They sent it overnight so we can look at it once I've downloaded it."

"How will that help?"

"Don't know yet but my people tell me he's an extreme xenophobe, so it seems weird a Cetusian would associate with him."

Nascha looked at Alex to see if he was serious. "That seems interesting. Still, I hope we can make some progress today. We don't really have anything to show for our investigation yet."

"Can you set up an interview with the Ambassador's son today? I know he wasn't on the planet, but he might provide some useful information."

"OK."

"There wasn't anything in his diary about meeting anyone after he left the office."

"Maybe it was a last-minute arrangement."

"Yeah. Maybe."

"Can you check whether he had any commitments?"

Nascha looked annoyed. She wasn't comfortable with people giving her orders in such a direct manner. "What did your last slave die of?"

The response startled Alex. "Sorry, didn't mean to upset you." *What's eating her?*

They sat in prickly silence for the rest of the trip to the office.

Alex opened his data plate once he settled into the office with a cup of coffee in hand. He saw Nascha rush off somewhere. He opened the brief Ruth had sent and started reading. *Ruth's done an expert job here. She's been very thorough. I hope she never puts together a brief on me.* Absorbed in reading the report, Alex didn't notice when Nascha returned.

"Got hold of Ahiga," she said. "We can go over this afternoon. I arranged for two o'clock."

"What? Oh. OK. Good. I was just reading the profile on this Malo guy. Fascinating brief. You may not enjoy it. He hates Cetusians. Makes his association with the Ambassador very intriguing. May have to talk to him before this is over, if we don't get a lead soon."

"Mind if I form my own opinion?"

Alex looked up and studied Nascha intensely for a moment, wondering what had got into her. "I'll send you the file."

"Got some of my people looking deeper into this supposed security team. See if we can dig up who they are and where they're from."

"OK. Good." Nascha had Alex's full attention. Something was bugging her, but he couldn't figure out what it was. He seemed to have upset her in the AGrav somehow. He couldn't understand what he had said or done.

"Still chasing up if the Ambassador saw anyone when he left the office."

"OK. Well, let's compare notes just before lunch then, shall we?"

"Will do." Nascha turned and walked away. Alex stared after her, baffled.

The morning seemed to pass slowly with no actual progress. Alex established an employee list for Malo and started chasing up any connections to Ambassador Tse but couldn't find any yet. He also started mapping the Ambassador's meetings with Malo - time, place, topic, again to find a pattern. One thing was for certain. The meetings were clandestine, as Chooli had said, whatever they were about. They were never in the same place and the agenda written in the diary was always very vague. Alex got a sense that these meetings were important to the case. He also started getting one of his uncanny vibes that all was not as it seemed. There was something else happening, something on a much larger scale. Whatever it was, Alex did not understand at that moment. His sixth sense caused him to tense as he knew that feeling and it had often led to dramatic results, sometimes disastrous. He clenched his jaw as he remembered the most notorious event for him, the betrayal that he saw in front of him but refused to accept.

"You OK?" Nascha asked as she approached. "You look angry."

"Huh! No. I mean yes, I'm OK. Just remembering an unpleasant experience."

"Want some lunch?"

"That time already?"

"Yeah. Time flies..."

"Yeah. Let's go." Alex stood up from his chair, closed the data plate and followed Nascha for lunch.

They returned to the office afterwards, collected what they needed for their meeting with Ahiga and went to Nascha's AGrav. When they rose into the designated expressway to Ahiga's apartment area, Alex looked around at the view of the city. Huge sky clawing buildings rose from the rock foundations below, glistening in the bright sunlight. These buildings gave way to less obtrusive structures as they left the city centre and moved through the inner suburbs, huge parklands opening up.

"You have massive parklands in the city. Is that how they designed it?"

"Yeah. When they first colonized the planet and started establishing a settlement, they made sure there were plenty of open spaces for the growing population to enjoy and hand down to their descendants. They enshrined it in our constitution, much to some property developers' disgust."

"It has the desired effect, I think. Even just passing over it makes you tranquil and relaxed." Alex sat back, feeling some of his stress dissipate.

They approached the Ahiga's apartment complex and Nascha slowed the AGrav to enter the underground parking area. As she was about to turn in, another AGrav sped out. Nascha braked hard to avoid a collision as she had been driving in manual, as usual.

They both peered into the other AGrav as it sped past. They saw three people in the vehicle, one looking terrified.

"That's Ahiga!" Nascha shouted. "What's going on?"

"We'll soon find out. Follow them!"

The other AGrav rose sharply, speeding up as it rose. Nascha changed direction and turned on her siren as she simultaneously contacted the local authorities. "Inspector Nascha in pursuit of a black AGrav entering the Providence Expressway traveling south with suspected detained occupant. Request backup and expressway lockdown."

Alex felt their AGrav accelerate as Nascha opened up the drive and entered the expressway, dodging traffic. "Hope you're up to date with your driver training."

Nascha gave him a wicked smile before quickly turning her concentration back to the traffic. "You haven't seen anything yet."

"I was afraid you'd say that," Alex said, grabbing his seat on either side, knuckles turning white from with clenching, as Nascha raced after the other AGrav.

"Expressway in lockdown," a voice said over the comm. "We have your position. Please detail the position of the offenders."

"Black AGrav approximately 300 metres in front of me."

"Acknowledged. Backup is five minutes away."

The AGrav in front suddenly veered off the expressway and crossed its own airspace, banking towards the city skyscrapers with increasing speed. Nascha followed, slowly narrowing the gap between them. "It's fortunate I bought the high-powered drive model," Nascha said, exposing her teeth in a grimacing grin.

Alex looked across nervously. "Enjoying yourself?"

"You bet!"

Nascha was now only 100 metres behind, entering the inner-city air space. The black AGrav started weaving through the gaps between buildings at a dangerous pace, threatening to crash as the vehicle strained to complete the turning maneuvers. Nascha followed with practiced ease. Alex closed his eyes, as buildings streaked past like seeing his life events flash before him in a near death experience. Nascha reached down to bring up her weapons console screen. She selected the particular device she wanted. With one hand on the steering and one eye on the pursuit, she activated the targeting system and waited for it to lock on the other AGrav. The screen flashed, a beeper sounded and Nascha pressed a button on the steering. The other AGrav immediately slowed and started descending to the ground.

"What did you do?"

"Drive shut-off override beam."

"Does that mean you slow down too?"

Nascha laughed as she eased back from the chase, adrenalin pumping. "Got your maser?"

"Yeah."

"Let's have them ready." Nascha retrieved hers from the compartment in the cabin.

The pursued AGrav settled to the ground, Nascha settling next to it. The doors opened, and two occupants ran out. Alex and Nascha alighted from Nascha's AGrav. Alex raised his maser and fired twice. One fugitive fell to the ground, then the other, both stunned, immobile.

"Eh," Nascha protested, looking at the two downed fugitives and pouting.

"Can't let you have all the fun," Alex shrugged.

Nascha slowly rounded the downed vehicle on one side, and Alex on the other, masers ready. They approached the doors. Ahiga was cowering on the floor, too petrified to look up. Nascha scanned the rest of the AGrav. It was clear. "It's OK now Ahiga."

Ahiga looked up, dazed. "Detective Nascha?"

Nascha put her maser away. Alex did likewise. "Yes, we were about to enter your building when this sped out. We followed."

"Thanks." Ahiga looked towards Alex inquiringly.

"Let me introduce Chief Inspector Detective Alex Warner of the GIA."

Alex looked at Nascha, annoyed. "Alex will do. I hate that title."

Two police AGravs descended on the scene and six officers alighted.

"Book those two," Nascha ordered, pointing to the two prone figures lying on the ground. "Take them in and place them in separate interrogation rooms. No collaboration beforehand."

The police noted the instructions, collected the criminals and departed.

"Are you OK Ahiga?"

"Yeah. Just scared."

"Want a ride back to your apartment?"

"Thanks."

"Hope the ride's less nerve destroying than the last one," Alex said.

Nascha laughed. She powered the AGrav up and rose into the expressway again at a leisurely pace.

"Where did you learn to drive like that, anyway?"

"Grew up in a family of rev head brothers. I had to keep up, get out of the way or die."

"Ahiga," Alex said as he turned to the rear of the cabin. "Any idea why they abducted you?"

"No," Ahiga lied, eyes averted. "They just came in and grabbed me."

Alex eyed him for a few seconds, taking in the body language. "Two people rush into your apartment, grab you and take you away and you don't know what it's about?"

"No, I don't. Maybe it has something to do with my father, I don't know." Ahiga reacted with affront.

"Why would you say that?"

"Well, he got around a bit, being an Ambassador. Maybe he made some enemies."

"Maybe, but why would they abduct you after they murdered him? Not much leverage there."

"I don't know. Maybe they thought I had something, but I don't."

They arrived at Ahiga's apartment complex and Nascha settled the AGrav in a parking bay.

"Well, we'll conduct a more in-depth interview some other time. Don't go missing in the meantime."

Ahiga got out. Nascha departed. "Rough."

"He's hiding something."

"He's had a bit of a rough experience."

"I know. He's still hiding something. I can tell. The only truthful thing he said is it's got something to do with his father. This might be the break we're looking for."

"You think? A little brazen and so soon after the murder."

"Whatever they're looking for must be important."

"Well, let's see if we can get anything out of the other two."

"Let's."

"WHY DID YOU ABDUCT AHIGA?" Nascha barked at one kidnapper. Alex was standing to the side, observing, assessing.

The man remained silent, as he had been for more than an hour, defiantly looking this way and that, avoiding eye contact.

Alex had had enough. The man exhausted his patience. He tried a different tack. "Nascha, you won't get anything out of him this way. We'll have to use the probe."

Both Nascha and the kidnapper looked at him in alarm, fear in the kidnapper's eyes.

"You won't do that. You can't do that," he said.

"Listen. Nascha is local. She has to follow the rules. I'm GIA headquarters. I can do anything I damn well like!"

Nascha looked at Alex, back at the kidnapper and then back at Alex. She stood up straight and waited for the detainee to respond.

The kidnapper gulped and thought. He looked undecided, then decided. "No. I'll talk. I've heard what those things can do."

"That's better. Now answer Nascha's question."

Nervously the kidnapper said, "They hired us to kidnap Ahiga and take him to a warehouse in the demolished district."

"Who hired you?" Nascha continued the interrogation.

"I don't know. He paid in cash, half up front, half on completion."

"But you saw him?"

"Yeah. He came to the warehouse to pay us."

"So you could identify him then. Help put an identification kit holo together with our artist?"

"I suppose."

"What did this person want with Ahiga?"

"Don't know. Didn't say. Didn't ask. He just wanted him alive and able to talk."

Nascha looked over to Alex. Alex nodded, "That's all we'll get out of him."

"You'll be charged, taken to our artist and then placed in a cell." Nascha rose from her chair. Alex and she left the room. "You weren't really going to use the probe, were you?"

"You'll never know. Got him talking, though," Alex said with a smirk. "At least we know it had something to do with Ahiga's father."

Nascha eyed him suspiciously. "It's been a tiring day. What do you want to do?"

"I don't get it though. They didn't ransack the Ambassador's place," Alex said, keeping to the case.

"Maybe he said he didn't have whatever they were looking for. Said it was in a safe place."

"Conjecture. The Ambassador knew the person. There was no struggle, no break in."

"Let's see if the holo reveals who hired these two. Maybe that can tell us something."

"Maybe."

They arrived at Nascha's AGrav, got in and left.

"Where are we going?"

"Hotel. Want a drink?"

"Let me pick up my things from the office first."

"OK. I forgot I have some things there too."

They went to the office, picked up what they wanted and Nascha drove to the hotel. She let the valet park the AGrav, and she went to the rooftop bar where Alex had become a regular.

It was past eight when they arrived in the bar, Klah packing glasses in the glass cleaner. The bar was very busy and filled with noise from conversation, laughter and clatter.

"What's going on tonight, Klah? The place is packed."

"Live band. Very popular," Klah said, moving towards Alex. "Not

the Cretan Novas. Blackhole, you might like them. The show starts at
10. People getting here for a good seat."

"You know them?" Alex asked Nascha.

"A bit. Don't like them as much as the Cretan Novas, but they're OK."

"What can I get you two?"

"I'll have the usual beer. Nascha?"

"Bloody Triton for me."

"Coming up."

Alex and Nascha sat on two stools at the bar. Alex looked around.
He spotted Chooli with Mai, this time looking crestfallen, jealous and
angry. Alex chuckled to himself, thought a bit and then waved Chooli
to come over.

Nascha looked to see whom Alex was waving to. She saw two
women walking towards them, one looking threateningly at her.
Nascha turned to Alex, raising her eyebrows questioningly.

Chooli and Mai finally arrived. "Nascha, meet Chooli and Mai.
Chooli, Mai, Nascha. Nascha is my work associate. We're investigating
the case together."

"Pleased to meet you."

"Hi."

"Yeah," Chooli said coolly, eyeing Nascha as if to assess what sort
of threat she might pose.

Nascha was similarly unimpressed. "Showing off your trophies,
Alex?"

Alex sat nonplussed for a moment, not knowing what to say, then
became angry. "No, I wasn't. These two have been very helpful to me,
especially Chooli. I wanted you to meet them. That's all. Is that a
problem?"

Nascha reddened in embarrassment. "No, it's not. Sorry." She
looked away, trying to find somewhere to hide. Their drinks arrived.

"Your Bloody Triton." Klah place the glass in front of Nascha.
"And your beer."

"Thanks," Nascha mumbled.

"What about you two?" Alex asked, looking at Chooli and Mai.

"Thought ya'd never ask," Chooli replied. "Usual," she said looking at Klah.

"Me too," Mai added eagerly.

Chooli moved to get closer to Alex and claim her man. She grabbed a stool, placed it next to him, close.

Alex looked at her and smiled. She smiled back radiantly.

Nascha brooded while sipping her drink.

"What's been with you today anyway, Nascha? You've been prickly with me all day."

"Nothing. Maybe I should go."

"Please don't. I invited you here to relax and get to know you better."

Nascha considered whether now was the right time to tell him what had been bothering her. "You are very condescending. You've been ordering me around ever since you got here."

"No, I'm not."

"You are. You should look at yourself sometime."

Chooli sat grinning. Nascha looked at her, which made Alex look too.

"What?"

"You are, you know."

"I'm not," Alex protested. "Well, I try not to be. Oh... well shit. Why didn't you tell me straight away?" Alex finally relented to Nascha, appealing to her goodwill.

Nascha smiled knowingly at Chooli. "I'm sorry I didn't, or maybe I'm not," she said as she burst into a full smile.

Chooli started laughing. Mai joined in, as did Nascha. Alex sat quietly but finally said, "You're ganging up on me now." After a few seconds of reflection, he chuckled too.

"Guess what Chooli is studying at University?" Alex asked Nascha.

"What?"

"Criminology."

"Really." Nascha looked at Chooli approvingly. "I wouldn't. It's a shit of a job. They give you people like Alex to work with." She said it half jokingly.

"Every job has its downside." The women laughed again, but Alex didn't get the joke. Chooli nudged him. "Cool up."

"Yeah, all right." Alex had a draught from his beer while the women laughed at his expense. Chooli nestled closer. Alex felt her warmth, smiled and sighed inside.

The group drank and talked for the next hour, at which stage Nascha excused herself. Alex, Chooli and Mai found a lounge, but Mai wandered off to find other interests. The band came on and Alex watched the first set.

"I think I'll go to bed now," Alex said, bending over to kiss Chooli.

"Eh! What ya do'n?"

"I was going to kiss you. What's wrong with that?"

"Not here. Not in public. Taboo. Come." Chooli stood, holding Alex's hand, leading him to a secluded spot at one end of the bar where no one could see them. "Now."

"Sure?" Alex smiled, touched her cheek, stroking it and bent over and kissed Chooli on the mouth. Chooli returned the amour passionately. Chooli's aureola instantly broke into a kaleidoscope of fluorescent color, pulsing to the beat of her heart. Alex's eyes widened in surprise, and he broke the kiss. "What was that?"

Chooli breathed deeply. Closed in on him and hugged him. "That's what happens when you arouse a Cetusian. That's why it's taboo in public."

"Oh." Alex hugged her back. "It's... delightful." Chooli hugged harder. Alex pulled away slightly and kissed her again before parting completely. "I'd better go."

"I can come with you."

Alex studied her for a moment. "Normally I'd jump at that. Drag you almost."

"So why don't ya? Aren't I good enough?" Chooli pouted, her fluorescence quenched.

"That's just it. You're better than that. You deserve better from me. I want to make it better. This is the first time for a long time that I've felt something and I don't want to spoil it by doing something stupid."

Chooli's eyes sparkled and her aureola glowed a dim gold. "That's the nicest thing anyone's said to me."

Alex stroked her cheek again. "Let's take our time, shall we?"

"OK... Wait." Chooli darted off, returning moments later. "Here," she said, shoving a scrap of plasto-film into his hand. Alex opened it and looked. He saw her comm ID scrawled on it. "Just in case you change your mind." She gave him an alluring smile.

11

REVELATIONS

Ahiga felt exhausted from the tribulations of his kidnapping but was eager to work through the files his father had left. In his apartment, he considered the detective's questions and knew he hadn't fooled him. He would be back, so Ahiga had to prepare. That meant understanding what how it involved his father. He was already acutely aware the search could threaten his personal safety.

Where do I start? Ahiga grabbed a chip and inserted it into the slot of his data plate. A list of files appeared on the screen, one named 'Scorpius'. He opened it. An image of a scorpion appeared. His brow furrowed as he tried to discern what it could mean. Pins of light dotted the scorpion's body. Underneath the scorpion was some writing:

THE SCORPIUS CONSTELLATION AS SEEN FROM EARTH

So it's a grouping of stars in the shape of a scorpion. Ahiga could see something next to each dot of light, each star, but it was too small to decipher. He zoomed in on one star. It had the symbols σ♏ next to it, then a name - Thompson. Ahiga scratched his head, wondering what the symbols meant. He inputted them into a search engine and clicked on the Galactapedia result.

Sigma Scorpius (σ) - Denebakrab, a star in the Scorpii or Scorpius constellation as seen from Earth. They traditionally gave star members of the constellations symbol designations based on the ancient Greek alphabet. ♏ is the astrological symbol for the Scorpius star sign in the ancient Zodiac system...

WELL, at least I know what the symbols mean. But what does the name mean? Ahiga looked at another star - β, Xiung Feng. Another star had - η, Tse. Ahiga stared at the screen in confusion. He didn't understand what it all meant, but it seemed like a coding system to identify various members of an organization - which his father was a part of.

Ahiga took some note film and a stylus from the drawer of his desk. He looked up the ancient Greek alphabet and examined how it compared to the one in use on Caerus. He wrote the Greek letters down one side of the page and filled in the names of the stars according to his father's coding system. He ended with the first letter of the alphabet, α and the name next to it Malo Metam. That name sounded familiar to Ahiga. He looked it up. He was the Ambassador and Confederation representative for Procyon. Ahiga understood why the name sounded familiar. He looked the others up. Some took a little longer to figure out as there was only one name, but he finally realized they were all members of the Confederation Parliament or high-ranking members of the Confederation Defense Force.

Ahiga sat back and looked at the list. Some names were familiar, but he couldn't place them. He looked them up. *That's odd. Several of these people have died recently.* The articles he found didn't mention a cause of death. He highlighted the dates of their deaths. *That's even stranger. The sequence of their death corresponds with the countdown of the Greek alphabet symbols from the omega end of the alphabet to alpha. My father is the latest, and he was ETA.* Only three symbols were left - delta, beta and alpha. Did that mean they were next on the list or was his father the last? Not all the people on the list had died. Quite a few were still alive, as if they had skipped those letters over for a reason.

Ahiga pondered the conundrum. He closed the scorpion file and went to one named 'Objectives':

SCORPIUS
Primary Objectives
- To overthrow all Cetusian Governments and subjugate them to Human rule.
- To reduce Cetusian populations to complete and utter dependency on Human masters for their survival.
- To destroy Cetusian familial, social, cultural and political identity and affiliations.

AHIGA'S MOUTH went dry as he read the objectives. He couldn't believe such an organization could exist in this day and age. That was just plain evil. What sort of people were they? How had his father become mixed up in this? He knew his father didn't and couldn't believe in those objectives. So what was his game?

Another file on the chip caught Ahiga's attention with the name 'Organization.' It showed the organizational structure of Scorpius with Malo Metam at the top of the pyramid. Ahiga's father and some other people from the other file appeared at the next level and there were two more levels below that. Some organizational positions had names in them. Some were blank or had a question mark in them.

Ahiga couldn't take much more. He wanted to stop and think about what it all meant, but another file named 'Reason' caught his eye. Ahiga opened it.

It was a hologram of his father sitting at his office desk at home. Ahiga ran the hologram. His father spoke.

"Hello my dear son, Ahiga. If you are viewing this hologram, I am dead. Regrettable. It also means that I could not complete my work, which was complex and dangerous. Let me explain.

"I first noticed the existence of Scorpius and its prime purpose about three years ago now. Understandably, it horrified me. I could not allow this to happen, but I had no proof. I decided the best way to bring the organization to justice was to infiltrate it and collect the information I needed to present my case.

"It took quite a while to convince Malo I was of a similar political persuasion, even though I was Cetusian. He eventually relented and slowly allowed my progress up the clandestine organizational ladder until I was one of the coordinating senior members, reporting directly to Malo himself. I collected much information along the way and secured the most important in the safe deposit box.

"The fact that you have this information now signifies that I did not complete my work and the Cetusian species is in danger of a great calamity and injustice at any moment.

"If you have not already reviewed them, you will see several files that detail activities I have had direct involvement in, which are objectionable, horrid. I unfortunately had to steel myself to take part in these so I achieved my objectives and not get found out prematurely. I apologize to you, both as your father and as the patriarch of the family, for the dishonor that I have placed on the family. I hope that you can forgive me and understand that my motive made these activities necessary.

"Please review the data I have collected, objectionable as it may be, and use the information to bring down this horrendous organization and prevent the catastrophe that it is orchestrating.

"I love you, my son."

Ahiga sat frozen. He felt cold as if a chill wind was blowing through his apartment. His mind was numb with information overload. He tasted bitterness in his mouth. What was he to do? Should he take it to the police? Should he destroy it? He now knew the reason for his kidnapping that day. While he was considering his options, he realized what a great personal risk his father had put himself in to collect this information. He felt proud of his father for that. He knew that whatever his father had done, it would not tarnish his father's reputation or the family name once they knew the motive.

Ahiga closed the files and removed the chip from the data plate, which he secured in a safe location. He retrieved a beer from the cooling unit and sipped as he paced his kitchen, thinking about what he should do. He needed to complete his father's work somehow and expose the organization, but he couldn't go to the police yet, not before he understood his father's plans and had all the evidence he needed to bring down Scorpius. Developing a plan, he decided he would build a dossier on all the members of Scorpius his father had listed to get an understanding of the people involved. He had to look at the other files his father had left to see where the gaps in the evidence were and how he could fill them. The task before him was mammoth and might take some time to complete, but he determined to do it, for the family honor and the protection of all Cetusians. The drama of the kidnapping and the revelations he had uncovered had tired him, so he went to bed to sleep on what he knew.

Ahiga was up early the next morning, eager to get started on his new task. He didn't want any disruptions, especially by the police at this stage, so he packed a few things, including the chips, and went to an apartment his father owned that he sometimes used if he didn't want to go all the way back to his house for the night. His father had given Ahiga the key. He set himself up and started searching the galactic hive for any information on each of the Scorpius members on his father's list, including the ones who were now dead. That took most of the day. He paid particular attention to Malo Metam, who sat at the top of the pyramid of influence. Ahiga needed to find out what he had against Cetusians.

Ahiga put his research aside and turned his attention to some other files from the safe deposit box. Another holovision file was in the folder. It showed a Cetusian tied hand and foot, beaten bloody and bruised. A Human he didn't recognize came into view.

"Where are the facilities?" the man asked menacingly, "or do you want more softening up before you talk?"

"I'm not saying a thing," the Cetusian said, a grimace of pain distorting his mouth and speech.

The man looked to someone offscreen. "Well?"

A Cetusian came into view. It was his father. Ahiga froze in disbelief. "You should tell him. It'll be easier on you," Tse said. He looked troubled.

The beaten Cetusian spat at Tse's feet, then looked up. "Traitor."

Tse's face hardened. He backhanded the captive with all the force he could muster. The prisoner slumped, stunned.

"We want him to talk first," the man said.

Tse looked at the interrogator with hatred. "I see you're getting a lot out of him."

The man turned back to the prisoner. "Look, all we want is the location of the defense station in your system."

The prisoner seemed to consider his options for a moment. "What happens if I tell you?"

"You can rest then."

"OK. It's orbiting Yaltrum."

"That wasn't hard then, was it?"

The man moved closer to the Cetusian. Before anyone had time to react, he placed his arm around his neck, grabbed his chin with the other hand and twisted it. Ahiga heard a snap as the Cetusian's neck broke.

"Rest in peace."

"You didn't have to do that," Tse protested loudly.

"What else would you suggest? We couldn't release him now, could we?"

Tse walked away without replying.

The hologram ended.

Ahiga sat looking at the blank screen for some time, wondering what sort of man his father was. He felt anger like he had never felt before. The disgust in his heart was like an icy stone. What motivated his father to get involved in such cruelty, such evil? He wanted to shout at him but couldn't. He wanted to hit him, beat him and demand an explanation. Tears trickled down his cheeks, and he wiped them away with the back of his hand. His father must have believed that the threat to the Cetusian race was so monstrous that he had to endure these actions so he could ultimately prevent them.

Ahiga had to find out more and complete his father's work before the disaster occurred and it sullied his family name for all time.

He had the resources to go anywhere now, thanks to his father's business success and the money his father left him. He would have to resign his job, which disappointed him as it was an enjoyable job and he had made many friends. Maybe he could come back to it when all this was over.

12

REVIEW

Alex arranged a review meeting with Nascha and two of her assisting officers, using one of the meeting rooms in Nascha's offices. The room was typical of an investigating organization: central conference table, chairs, comms link, data board. A window overlooking the city's parklands surprised him. The rooms normally had four walls with no windows. *To let you know there is no escape*, Alex thought. The view was picturesque at the moment. A recent shower and the sun was out again, the foliage glistening in the reflecting light. Alex sat down next to the data board opposite the window so he could look out whenever he liked. The investigation was yielding little information, not that unusual, but it annoyed Alex who was always impatient to solve a case. The team had to consolidate what they knew, which was the purpose of the meeting.

Alex sat in concentrated thought, sipping his coffee, as the others filed in. Nascha's assistants, like two bodyguards in synchronized protection detail, flanked their boss. Nascha introduced him to Atsidi and Yas.

Atsidi was a stocky middle-aged man with layers of fat under his chin. He had black rims around his eyes that made him look perpetually tired, and he yawned excessively. He had an unwashed smell to him whenever Alex got too close. Unsurprisingly, he lived alone.

Yas was the exact opposite. He was tall and spidery thin. His clothes always seemed two sizes too large, as if he was waiting to grow into them. His eyes darted around the room, as if trying to catch someone out. He had five children, which was quite an achievement on his salary, Alex thought. Although he spent a lot of time at work and put his hand up for any overtime available to provide for his family. Alex wondered where he found the time to produce all those children!

Alex placed his coffee cup back on the table and rose, looking intently at each team member, wondering what they could bring to the case.

"I called this meeting to pull together what we know about Tse's murder and work out avenues of enquiry," Alex said, getting everyone's attention. "I thought writing on the board what we already know and see where our gaps are would be a start. I'll write things up on the data board as we think of them."

Nascha started the exercise. "Well, we know that someone murdered Tse in his home and he supposedly left the office early to meet someone."

"OK. Good Nascha," Alex said as he wrote up the two points.

"He had all his data wiped by some mysterious security detail," Atsidi added.

"The murder was brutal," Yas said.

"That slip of paper with the symbols on it," Atsidi said.

"Tse had monthly clandestine meetings with Malo," Nascha said.

"Ahiga was kidnapped," Alex said as he busily wrote up all the responses.

"Yeah, and we think he's hiding something," Nascha said.

Silence followed Nascha's last observation.

"Well, I can't think of anything more that we know for sure either," Alex said finally. "So where does this leave us?"

Yas asked, "Who wiped the data and who was behind the kidnapping? Were they the same people?"

"What was Tse's connection with Malo and is he involved?" Nascha added.

"What do the symbols mean? I mean are they significant to the case or are they a red herring?" Atsidi wondered.

"Who did Tse meet?" Nascha asked.

"What is Ahiga hiding?" Alex said, connecting dot points to questions as he listed it all down.

Alex stepped back to look at the board. Everyone was quiet. He stepped forward and added a further question. "Is this an isolated incident or have there been other murders? I'm having my team on Earth look into that."

"I don't know of any on this planet," Nascha said. The assistants both nodded in agreement.

"Yeah. I figured that, or you would have said something already. That's why I have my team looking. They have better access to confederation wide databases." Alex stepped back again. "Let's assign tasks. Nascha, I think you and I should pay Ahiga another visit and we'll start digging more into Malo. I've got a feeling this involves him somehow. What about Atsidi and Yas, Nascha? You know them. Who's best at doing what?"

Nascha looked at the board and the lines of inquiry which needed following up. "I think Atsidi should chase up the mysterious security agency and Yas should look into who Tse was planning to meet." She looked at them and they both nodded.

Alex wrote the respective names beside the topics on the board. "When you find the security team, remember they could have a connection to the kidnapping," he said as he turned and looked at Atsidi.

"Will do."

"That just leaves the symbols but that can wait for now, I think."

"Yeah. I agree," Nascha said. "If they are important, they'll crop up somewhere in the other stuff we're chasing up."

She impressed Alex on that point and nodded appreciatively. "Well, let's get to it then. We'll meet at six tonight to compare notes."

"I'll see if I can arrange another meeting with Ahiga," she said.

"OK. I'll start expanding the profile on Malo while you do that."

Nascha left, leaving Alex to save the information on the data board and start a fresh page. He ran a line down the middle of the board and wrote TSE on the top left and MALO on the right. He added 'Ambassador of Caerus' underneath Tse and 'Ambassador of Procyon' under Malo. He got out his data plate and brought up the message that Ruth had sent about Malo. He read through it again. He noticed a listing of known associates. Tse was on the list and quite a few others. He wrote them up on the board under MALO and wrote Malo under TSE as Tse's diary confirmed the association. Alex wondered if there were others in common. He opened Tse's diary again and started flipping through the pages to see whom else the Ambassador regularly met.

Nascha came back into the meeting room. "I can't contact Ahiga at the moment or he isn't answering."

Alex looked up. "Would he know it was us?"

"Probably. It would have come up as the GIA."

"Might be avoiding us. Might be worth sending someone to check and bring him in if he's there."

"Hmm. He may not cooperate if we do that."

"He's not cooperating now. Anyway, they can just see if he's home or whether anything's amiss. He'd be unlucky to get kidnapped twice in two days, or very popular."

"Yeah. OK. Back in a minute." Nascha popped out again.

Alex returned to reviewing Tse's diary. He flipped through and noted meeting times and places. He spent more than an hour leafing through appointments until he felt he had gone back in history far enough. He rubbed the tiredness out of his eyes and closed them for a second to relax and regain some concentration. When he opened them again, he jumped in surprise - Nascha was standing in front of him. "What's up?"

"Nothing. I came in and it looked like you were asleep. Late night?"

Alex saw red for a second but calmed himself before he said something foolish. He saw that Nascha regretted her remark but could not unsay it. He finally said, "No, not late. I just relaxed for a moment after looking at Tse's diary for over an hour."

Nascha reddened slightly. "Any luck?"

"Don't know. I just finished going back through the diary and was about to compare the names with whom was already on the board for Malo."

"Can I help?" Nascha asked in repentance.

"Sure. Here're the names. Go for it," Alex said as he gave her the handwritten list he had produced. "I'd almost forgotten how bloody boring some of our work is sometimes."

Nascha took the list and started writing Tse's contacts under his name on the board. Where there was a match with Malo's associates, she drew a line between the two. She turned to Alex. "There are quite a few names in common."

"Yes, there are. Do you know who they are? Maybe they are just fellow Confederation parliament members."

"Some are, as I recognize the names, but some aren't. In fact, at least one name is intriguing." Nascha pointed to the board, "This guy is a very high-ranking general in the Confederation Defense Force. He's a very unusual person for Tse to associate with."

"Hmm. Interesting. All these connections can't be a coincidence, you think?"

"No. I don't think so. We need to get more background on these people and find out what their relationships are."

"I agree. Anyway, any luck with Ahiga?"

"No. He wasn't in his apartment. No evidence of foul play. Looks like he left and went somewhere. His personal items and it appears some clothing are missing."

"Hmm. What's he up to then?"

"I'll place a trace on him and see if we can track him down."

"Good."

They looked at each other for a moment. Alex was pleased to see that Nascha had that spark of excitement for the chase that every commanding officer treasured in his team. She seemed to be eager for action, just waiting for the switch to flick. He appreciated that.

The same attitude he had when he was younger and hoped he still had, although he had grown more cynical with each promotion, as if the two counter forces went hand in hand. He came back to the present. Nascha looked at him questioningly.

"We need more data on some of these names. How are you set up for this manner of research?"

"Not very well, I'm afraid. We're mainly set up for the Tau Ceti system only, not the galactic databases."

"OK. I'll send a message back to my team on Earth and get them to do some digging."

"OK. Where does that leave us?"

"What about some of these others?" Alex showed Nascha his list of names that weren't on the board.

"Some of those look Cetusian. I can get our people to see if they come from our region or some other star system."

"Do that. I have some other data to add to the board from the report Ruth sent me on Malo. I'll complete the picture on him."

"OK." Nascha left the room.

Alex went back to Ruth's message and read it again, this time noting Malo's movements and anything else about his character. Fortunately, Ruth had included a section called 'Character Profile.' There he noted that Malo was rather vocal in his prejudice against Cetusians, again something not compatible with his relationship with Tse. The report said Cetusian school children had persecuted him when he was a child. His father had been a diplomat as well and one of his postings had been on Chiron, a Cetusian colonized planet orbiting Alpha Centauri. The report also noted he was an excellent organizer and had significant influence in political circles.

It also had details of Malo's staff. Alex noted a husband and wife had worked for him but the wife who had been Malo's PA, had recently passed away. The husband was a diplomatic attaché. There were a few more staff, all office bound. Alex noted the death of Malo's PA on the board as a reminder to investigate further.

Alex turned his attention to Ambassador Tse. He didn't know much about his character profile. He would have to get Nascha to fill that in. He added the names of Tse's office staff and his personal staff to the board.

Alex stood back, perusing the information he had gathered. He didn't think he had much to show for his efforts, although the more he looked, the more convinced he was that the common associations had something to do with the puzzle. He composed a message to Ruth asking her to examine the links further. He also requested the report into the death of Malo's PA.

Towards late afternoon, Nascha returned to the meeting room and wrote some information on the board about the people she had been researching.

Alex watched as she did this, wondering if she would reach the same conclusion he had. He waited for her to speak.

Nascha turned to Alex. "Not much, is there?"

"No, there's not yet, but at least we have a basis now to delve deeper."

"I suppose."

"I can't help but think the associates in common hold the key, but I can't figure out what that might be."

"Maybe."

"Oh. Before I forget. Can you get a character profile for Tse similar to what I did for Malo?"

"Sure."

"Well, it's almost six. Might make a coffee and wait for the others."

"OK. I'll have a quick look to see if we have anything on Tse."

Alex sat with his coffee and pondered the situation. He wasn't getting any heat yet to solve the crime quickly, which was a little unusual given the political nature of the situation. *Maybe the Caerusians are happy to have the GIA's attention for now. I won't rock the boat by asking.*

Six o'clock came and Nascha, Atsidi and Yas walked in punctually. Alex waited for them to sit and get comfortable. "OK, then. What do we have so far? Atsidi. You want to go first?"

"Sure. I questioned the kidnappers again. It doesn't seem they wiped the hives. I doubt they would have the intelligence. That doesn't mean there isn't a connection between the two. I looked at the security footage of the office. Whoever they were, they were clever and knew where the cameras were. I only got a partial of one of the guy's faces. I'm trying to build a full profile and frontal image based on what I have. It's not done yet. They were wearing uniforms that seemed official enough but when I tried contacting the agency, they didn't know of the office visit and they say there was no order to wipe the hives. So that's a dead end. I hope I can get an ID from the facial when it comes through."

"Excellent work," Alex said while he wrote some notes. "Anyone got any comments?"

There was silence for a moment before Nascha said, "It still seems the two are connected, I think. The kidnappers may not have done it, but the person who hired them may have organized the hive wipe too."

"Yeah. There's a high probability there," Alex said. "Let's hope the facial gives us something. Anything else?" Silence. "OK. Yas. You next."

"It's been a hard day chasing Tse's movements. I've looked through the camera footage from when he left the office to when he got back home. Fortunately, there weren't many gaps in the coverage, but it's been a hard slog getting the footage for the entire route. He didn't go the most direct way, which was odd. Anyway, I've got him entering his estate and, as far as I can tell, he didn't have anyone else with him. The other thing that's odd is that he drove himself. He didn't use his chauffeur. When I called the office to ask Tibah if that was normal, she said 'not at all'. She was just as puzzled why he would have done that. So I'll continue looking at the footage at the estate entrance to see if anyone else entered during that time. I'll look at the security footage inside when I get it, which should be tomorrow or Monday. Monday, probably. That's it." Yas looked around for comments.

"Any questions?" Alex asked.

"None. I knew it would be hard work. That's why I put Yas on it. He has more patience that Atsidi," Nascha said.

"Thanks so much," Atsidi said in appreciation.

Yas chuckled.

Alex wrote the progress on the board. "You want to go next, Nascha?"

"OK. Well, I tried to arrange an interview with Ahiga but he has disappeared. He wasn't in his apartment and it didn't look like he had left unwillingly. He seems to have gone somewhere. I've got someone tracking him down, but with no luck at the moment. I chased some names you gave me. There are some ambassadors from other star systems. The rest don't seem to have any real relevance at present. I don't have Tse's character profile yet. That's it."

"Questions?" Alex asked.

The others shook their heads.

Alex wrote up the notes. "That leaves me then." He moved the data board to the frame he had been using during the day to show the others. "As you can see, I've been putting together a profile on Malo and Tse, with help from Nascha as she just reported. There are several names in common, as shown by the tie lines, but we don't have enough to understand why there's a connection. I've sent a message back to Earth for them to dig deeper and find out more on who all these people are. I have a feeling there's an important link here somewhere, but we won't know what it is until we get more details. Malo's PA died recently, and I've asked for the police report. I could have used Yas to do this tedious work. I'm not used to it."

The others smirked at the confession.

"Well, that's it from me. Questions?"

"Yeah," said Yas. "I can't help thinking we're missing something in all that. One intriguing thing is why would they both know the same high-ranking general? Seems too odd to be a coincidence."

"You could be right there," Nascha said.

Alex highlighted the general. He went back to the first frame and wrote a summary note next to his name. "Anything else?"

There was silence for a moment until Yas spoke, looking a little embarrassed. "I was just wondering if we're working tomorrow on our day off. Nascha knows I wouldn't normally say anything, but I've organized a sun-basking treat for the kids and they've been waiting for ages. I don't want to disappoint them again." He looked at his feet.

Alex looked at Nascha, who shrugged. He looked away for a moment, nibbling on the inside of his cheek as he considered the request. "Don't be embarrassed, Yas. It's OK to ask when there's a good reason."

Yas looked more comfortable.

"From where I sit, Tse's not going anywhere and it's not as if we're chasing a deadline or on the verge of catching anyone yet. The murderer has disappeared for now until we get something to implicate him. He probably isn't even on the planet anymore. We're all waiting on data to come in. So I can't see a reason to work you into the ground just yet. We'll take tomorrow off and come in fresh on Monday."

"You're not getting any pressure for results?" Nascha asked, a little surprised.

"Not yet, and I won't say anything until I have something concrete."

"Sounds like a plan."

Yas relaxed and smiled. "Thanks. The kids will love you."

"Have a good time," Alex said. "All of you."

Yas and Atsidi left, but Nascha held back. "What are you going to do tomorrow?"

Alex studied her, wondering where the question was leading. "I'm not sure. I'll see if I get anything from Ruth tomorrow morning. If something comes through, I'll work on that. If not, I'm sure I'll amuse myself somehow."

"Well, let me know if you want a hand or want someone to show you the sights of the city."

"OK. We'll see. Thanks for the offer." Alex was getting uncomfortable with the direction of the conversation. He didn't want to offend her, but he didn't want her to hold his hand either. He had been around enough star systems to know how to look after himself without getting into too much trouble. He was also not sure whether she had other motives. Whatever it was, he could look after himself. "I think I'll pack up and go." It was just after seven.

"Want to go somewhere for a drink?"

"Not tonight. I really want to have an early night. Thanks for asking."

"Oh," Nascha said, disappointed and suspicious. "Well, see you Monday then."

"Yeah. See you."

Alex caught a taxi back to the hotel. He didn't lie to Nascha. He felt tired and wanted an early night. He considered dinner. He thought of Chooli and wondered. He got his comm out, found her contact and dialed.

Moments went by. "Chooli. Who's talking?"

Alex smiled. *Typical.* "It's Alex."

"Oh. Hang on." There was silence and then visual came on. "Hi Alex. How's things?"

"OK. A bit tired. I was just wondering if you wanted to go somewhere with me for dinner?"

"Where?"

"Not sure yet. I'll ask someone where a suitable place is, unless you know somewhere."

"If you're looking for somewhere like the other night, then no, but if you want to slum it, student style, I can make some suggestions."

"I think I'll pass on slumming. I had enough of that in my day. Besides, I want to treat you." Alex could see Chooli blush with delight. Her aureola turned a sparkling green with a hint of yellow.

"OK. Surprise me. You sure did the other night. You're full of surprises."

"Look who's talking." They both laughed. "Let's see. It's seven thirty. Can you make it to the hotel by eight thirty and we'll go from there?"

"Diablo. You bet." Chooli was beaming with delight. Her aureola was pulsing slightly with a rainbow of colors now. She went red as she realized, but took it in her stride and smiled seductively.

"It's just dinner, remember."

"Of course." Chooli had a cheeky expression as if to say, 'how could you interpret it any other way.'

Alex laughed. "See you in the hotel lobby at eight thirty."

"See you." The comm went blank.

Alex sat back in the taxi and smiled in anticipation of the night ahead. He realized he was excited about seeing Chooli again.

13

A SPECIAL DINNER

Alex hurriedly showered and changed and was ready to go down to the lobby at 8:30. The night was balmy, so he wore a black T-shirt with jeans and navy-blue sneakers. He didn't feel like dressing up. He hoped Chooli had the same attitude.

He didn't spot Chooli when he arrived in the lobby, but soon saw her familiar profile from behind the corner of a lounge chair. *She must have gotten ready in record time.* He walked over, hoping to surprise her like she did two nights previously.

"Took your time," she said, turning to him with a cheeky grin.

"How did you know?"

"I was watching you sneak up in the reflection." She pointed to the glass windows in front of her.

"I'm not sure about fighting crime but you'll make a great spy one day."

"We'll see." Chooli stood.

Alex gasped in wonder. She was so beautiful. The effect was simple but spectacular. She wore a tight-fitting sequined mint colored T-shirt and black leather pants with black high-heeled shoes. Emerald earrings adorned her ears and a sparkling necklace, which looked like diamonds with an emerald centerpiece, hung just above her cleavage. The total effect was stunning, set off by her black hair and aureola. "You look incredible," Alex said admiringly.

Chooli blushed with delight. "That was the idea."

"Are they genuine diamonds?"

"Yeah. Me Grandma's."

"They're beautiful on you."

Chooli looked down, embarrassed but delighted. "That's why she gave them to me before she died. She said, 'I won't be needing these anymore, but you're made for them'." Sadness momentarily appeared on her face before her enthusiasm returned.

"She was spot on. They make you look... diablo."

Chooli again became embarrassed, her aureola fringing on green, but pleased with the complement. She looked up. "Well, where are we going?"

"A restaurant supposedly close to here. The Twins. Have you heard of it?"

Chooli gasped. "Really? I should have dressed up more."

"Relax. I was told it's a very casual dress code. That's why it's so popular, apparently. Anyway, I'm sure you'd get in anywhere looking like that. You want to walk?"

"Yeah. That's fine. It's only two blocks from here. Did you book?"

"Yes, we have a reservation. Let's go then." Alex held out his hand. Chooli pulled on her white jacket and grasped his hand with pleasure.

They walked out of the hotel into the warm night air and strolled to the restaurant in silence. Others were walking past, talking, laughing, musing in their own worlds as they enjoyed the sights and smells of greenery along the sidewalks. AGravs were speeding in the traffic lanes overhead.

"How was your day?" Chooli asked, breaking the reverie.

Alex turned in surprise at the very civil opening to the conversation instead of Chooli's usual brusqueness. "Filled with tedium. We delved through all the evidence and pinpointed the holes so far. Boring police work, the part I hate. I didn't realize how boring it was."

"Get anywhere?"

"Not really. There are more questions than answers at the moment."

"You'll work it out." Chooli's eyes were sparkling in the streetlight, her interest and youthful enthusiasm apparent.

"You just wait. You'll find out what I mean when you start out."

"Not me. I'll let someone else do that."

"Really. How?"

"You'd do it for me, wouldn't you?" Chooli widened her moon eyes at Alex, all innocence and vulnerability, fluttering her eyelashes for extra effect.

Alex laughed. "You'd probably get anyone to do it with that look."

"Yeah," said Chooli, satisfied.

"What about you? How was your day?" Alex asked.

"Boring, just some lectures and a tutorial. Wish they'd give us something more difficult to get our teeth into. They just keep going on and on about how important it is to keep the chain of evidence and maintain all the paperwork." Chooli rolled her eyes.

Alex laughed. "I remember all that. I get someone else to do that now."

Chooli shoved Alex slightly, playfully. "That's cheating."

"Hey! Being the boss has to have some perks."

"I suppose. Anyway, my day got significantly better when someone called and invited me to dinner."

"Who was that?"

"You, dummy!"

"Oh. Well, we had such a wonderful time last time."

"Yeah. We did, didn't we?"

They settled into silence again, turned a corner and arrived at 'The Twins' where they took an elevator to the roof-top restaurant. Chooli stood still in amazement at the spectacle before her. Alex watched the wonder traverse her face as she looked around as he, too, took in the interesting decor. A simulation of the two moons of Caerus called 'The Twins' were in the holographic display at the restaurant entrance, sparkling like the sea on a bright summer's day as the images rotated and cavorted with each other. The real moons shone that night too, reflected through the roof and onto the holographs in perfect synchronicity. The display framed the holograph on both sides of the doorway and included fresh sprays of Caerusian orchids, their flower heads larger than fists flashing iridescent modulating color that changed depending on the vantage point.

"Shall we?" Alex said, bringing Chooli out of her dream.

"Diablo."

"Yes, it is. The concierge made a good recommendation."

They walked into the restaurant and waited at the reception counter. Alex noted they had rolled the roof of the restaurant back that night, being a warm, breezeless evening, and the stars twinkled brightly despite light pollution from the city. The Maître De came over to them. "May I help you?"

"Yes, I believe there is a table for two please, booked under Alex Warner."

The Maître De looked at the reservation list. "Ah, yes. Mr. Warner. Welcome. The hotel insisted I give you the best table in the house tonight. A special occasion?" The Maître De looked to Chooli and back at Alex.

"No, nothing special. I'm a visitor from Earth and wanted to go somewhere special, that's all."

"Ah! You have made an excellent selection, if I may say so myself."

"Well, it looks promising so far."

The Maître De collected two menus and a drinks menu. "Come this way, if you please." He started weaving his way through the sea of tables to one right at the far edge. Alex and Chooli followed him. They could see the entire city from their table and the twin moons provided a spectacular backdrop.

Chooli stared for a moment, her eyes sparkling with delight. "Diablo."

The Maître De looked at Chooli quizzically for a moment before saying, "May I seat you, Madame."

Chooli looked back. "Yeah." She had learned the protocol from the previous dinner.

"Please forgive me for being rude, but where did you get that exquisite necklace? I've never seen one like it."

"Oh. That's OK. It was my Grandma's. She gave it to me when she got too old to wear it anywhere. She said it would look better on me than her."

"It does at that, Madame."

"Thank you." Chooli blushed slightly at the compliment.

The Maître De handed them menus. "The specials for tonight are a Cetusian sea shrimp chowder as an entrée and for mains there is a native bovine veal steak specially seared over a wood-fired plate topped with fresh truffles and a red wine jus. Would you like some water?"

"Yes, please," they both said.

"Very well. I shall have a waiter deliver it for you. Have a pleasant meal."

"We will," Alex replied.

The Maître De left.

"Wow," Chooli said. "This is amazing. It must cost a fortune."

"Apparently not. The concierge said the prices are reasonable, which is another big plus for those who know about it."

A waiter came and poured a glass of water for each of them.

Chooli looked at Alex for a moment, appreciation glowing on her face. "Thanks for inviting me."

"You're welcome." Alex hadn't noticed before, but their table and chairs were atop a large, slowly rotating turntable. He looked down and saw the join in the floor where the turntable met the main floor. "We're moving."

Chooli looked down, too. "Diablo." She looked up again.

"Diablo, you have one moon directly behind you," Alex said with a smile of wonder. "You look like some mysterious goddess."

Chooli looked around, saw the moon and looked back. "I want to see it behind you," she said with excitement.

"Not that you need a moon to look like a goddess."

"Stop it, you're making me blush."

"Can't I give you a compliment?"

"I'm just not used to it, that's all."

They both smiled and looked into each other's eyes. Alex was happy and content. He could sit like that all night, he thought. It felt comfortable sitting with Chooli, not caring about anything else. It had been a long time since he had that warm feeling, since his previous partner had doused his flame so completely. He was a total wreck for a long time after that betrayal. He swore he would never have a serious relationship with a woman ever again. He wasn't so sure of his commitment to that oath now with Chooli sitting in front of him. "Let's have a look at the menu," he said to break the spell.

"OK."

They both picked up their menus and looked through them. Alex decided on his selection and looked at the wine list. "Do you know what you're having yet?"

"I thought I'd have some fish," Chooli said.

Alex smiled. "So am I. I'll get a white wine to go with it." *She even thinks like me,* he thought. He looked at the wine list and selected a wine that seemed interesting but wanted to ask the waiter. "Are you ready to order?"

"Are you going to have an entrée?"

"Yeah."

"So am I."

"Good." Alex studied her more. "You're speaking different tonight."

Chooli looked down, blushed slightly and looked up again. "I'm trying hard not to be so abrupt."

"It's appreciated."

"Thank you."

Alex caught a waiter's attention. He walked over to the table and removed his order pad and stylus from his pocket, "Are you ready to order?"

"Yes, Chooli," Alex said, gesturing Chooli to go first.

"Oh. I'll have Peppered Decapus for entrée and Caerus Sea Bass for main please."

"And you Sir?"

"I'll have Crampie for entrée and the Sea Bass too."

"Very well, and would you like something to drink?"

"I was thinking of ordering this Caerus Semillon but what do you recommend?" Alex deferred.

"That is an excellent choice, Sir. The Maître De recommends it highly."

"OK. We'll have a bottle of that then."

The waiter walked away, completing the order on his pad as he went.

Alex and Chooli looked out at the picturesque view. The sky was clear, so the stars shone like diamonds. The moons were just past full but still brilliantly white, the details of the craters visible.

"The Twins. Is there a tale about what they look like?"

Chooli looked at Alex, puzzled. "What do you mean?"

"Well, on Earth, the craters form what looks like a face when the moon is full so legend has it there was an old man on the moon. I was just wondering if you have similar legends."

"Not really. Not that I know of, anyway. Caerus hasn't existed as long as Earth and technologically advanced people came here, so it probably didn't develop."

"Pity. They look so magnificent at the moment."

"Tell me about Earth."

"What do you want to know?"

"Stop it," Chooli said, annoyed.

Alex laughed. "Sorry. Couldn't help myself. Umm. Well, I live in Sydney on one of the seven continents called Australia. It's modern but not too crowded." Alex was a little stumped on how to continue. "Seriously, what do you want to know? What are you interested in knowing?"

Chooli realized the sincere nature of the question. She thought a moment. "What's nature like? The animals and plants."

"Well, I suppose it's much the same as here, really, but Australia has some fairly unique animals at least. For example, we have an animal, a marsupial called a platypus. It's got a fur body with a duck's bill and webbed feet and lays eggs. It lives near rivers and they have burrows that they can only enter by going underwater."

"You're making that up."

"It's true. Look it up if you don't believe me."

Chooli still gave Alex a doubtful look but let it stand. "What else?"

"We have an animal called a kangaroo. It can be as tall as a man and uses its hind legs to hop, which is apparently a very efficient means of travel. Its forelegs are very short and only used to grab things. The way it's built looks like a boxer. In fact, it does a form of boxing when it's fighting. Its claws are so sharp, they can rip a person's abdomen open."

"Ooh. Yuck. That's enough. Strange animals."

"They're cute. There's the koala too. It's like a small bear but only eats a certain variety of leaf from a eucalyptus tree. They are fun to hold, but they can piss on you if you're not careful."

Chooli's eyes lit up with excitement. "Wish I could see these animals one day." She gave him a stern look. "But if you're pulling my leg, watch out. I'll get you."

Alex laughed. "I'm not lying. They're real!"

They settled down again, retreating into their own thoughts when the wine arrived. The waiter opened the bottle and poured a sample into Alex's glass. Alex tasted it and nodded that it was fine. The waiter continued to pour a glass for Chooli and then topped up Alex's glass.

"Why do you do that?"

"Do what?"

"They pour a small amount that you taste."

"Oh. Well, probably tradition, but originally you were never sure if the wine was off so they poured a sample to taste. If it was off, you could reject it and they would have to get another bottle. But it is just tradition now. I've never tasted a wine was off. I've tasted some bad wines, but that's a different story."

"Interesting."

The entrées came, which quenched the conversation while they ate.

Chooli drank some water after her entrée to flush her mouth and then tasted the wine. "Wow. That's fantastic."

"It's good, isn't it?"

"I never realized wine could have such incredible taste."

"It's a way to a woman's heart," Alex said in jest.

"Really!" Chooli responded. "Not this heart buddy." She puffed her chest out in defiance, which only drew attention to her breasts. She noticed Alex admiring them and assumed a normal posture again. "Men!"

Alex laughed. While turning over his emotions, he gained the courage to tell this intriguing person what he thought. "You are an amazing woman, Chooli. I've never met anyone like you. You've healed some deep wounds that I've carried around for too long."

Chooli didn't know how to respond. Finally she said, "Thank you. You also had something I couldn't pin down when I first saw you, but you're making things difficult for me. You're experienced in these things and I'm not. I feel like I'm groping in the dark sometimes. That's why I'm trying to control my language tonight."

They looked into each other's eyes for a moment. Alex realized then that Chooli was the one. She had to be. He had thought the bitch was the one, but this was different. The feeling was so powerful. His heart raced. He looked away, breaking the moment. He looked back, seeing disappointment in Chooli's eyes. He also saw encouragement, challenge, determination and decisiveness.

The waiter came with their meals. They ate and drank their way through and bantered with each other for the rest of the meal, the intensity of the moment lost for the time being.

"Dessert?"

"You kidding? I'll explode!"

They both laughed and enjoyed the rest of the wine together. Alex paid the bill, and they returned to the balmy night air. Chooli moved close to Alex, placing her arm around his waist. He put his arm around her shoulders and was very content. He looked at Chooli and saw she was feeling the same.

"Thanks for the dinner."

"You're welcome. Thanks for making the effort to not be so infuriatingly difficult to talk to."

Chooli laughed. She looked at Alex. "You're welcome."

Alex could see Chooli's exquisite face in the subdued street lighting. It made her even more beautiful and her eyes sparkled like the stars overhead. It took his breath away. They ambled back to the hotel in silence, absorbing the romance of the moment. Alex didn't want the night to end.

Chooli looked at Alex, "You want to see what a fully aroused aureola looks like?"

Alex stood speechless at the innocence and openness of the question. "You know what I said last night."

"I know but I think it's the right time. What do you think?"

Alex pondered. He felt reluctant. He didn't want to hurt her. He wasn't sure he was ready either. He saw desire and pleading in her eyes, but it could be all for show. He somehow knew it wasn't. It was real. Was he ready to open himself up to the possibility of being hurt again? He would never know if he didn't take the risk. He decided. "Let's."

14

FAMILY LIFE

Malo opened the front door of his home after another exhausting day. He walked to the living area where his wife and two children.

"Hello dear. How was your day?" Malo's wife, Cynthia, asked.

"Hi, Sweetie. Another tiring day, I'm afraid, and I still need to do some work later. Hello Ayesha, Dagon."

"Hi dad," Ayesha and Dagon, Malo's children, said as they went to him for a fatherly kiss on the cheek.

He kissed his children, then gave Cynthia a hug and kiss too.

"Since we all seem to be in the same place at the same time for a change, I thought I would get the food preparer to make a special menu tonight for dinner," Cynthia said.

"Is there avocad?" daughter Ayesha asked with anticipation.

Ayesha was 10 but growing up too fast in Malo's opinion, or maybe he just wasn't around enough to notice the differences. A touch of sadness filled Malo as he reflected on the magnitude of his absences from family life so he could fulfill his political career and other preoccupations. "I'm sure mother has something that will please us all in mind. How was school today?"

Ayesha shrugged and sighed. "Boring. I wish they would teach us interesting things."

"I'm sure they do but you need to learn the boring things too and I think you could study more, looking at your grades."

Ayesha pouted in anguish and innocent appeal, "Awwww! Dad, you're not fair. I try hard," she wailed in protest.

Malo chuckled and gave Ayesha a hug. "I know you try, and I can only ask you to do your best. I know you do."

The acknowledgement calmed Ayesha, and a smile returned to her face.

"What about you, Dagon?"

"Yeah, OK, I guess. I'm finding mathematics hard at the moment. It's just not connecting with me," his son said in frustration. He was 15 and his studies were just starting to get harder.

"Keep at it. Let me know if you need extra tutoring to get a fresh approach, maybe."

"OK dad, I'll think about it."

"Well, if we've finished dissecting the children's school performance, maybe we can get ready for dinner," Cynthia said with mock disapproval.

Malo sighed as he feigned disappointment. "You ruin all my fun."

"Hah! That'll be the day."

Malo and the children went off to prepare for dinner. Malo changed into more relaxing clothing, a plain light gray T-shirt that he liked to wear when he wanted to unwind and some loose-fitting black pants, elasticized at the waist and around the ankles. He also put on a pair of black slippers and went to the dining room. The others were waiting.

The food supply chute in the middle of the table slid open and a tray of food rose. A spicy aroma instantly spread throughout the room to tempt the taste buds.

"That smells good," Malo said. He reached out to take one dish, which looked like was soup. The dish contained a puree of orange carro with streaks of blue cabbag, a dab of sour cream and a sprig of parsle.

"I said it would be special," Cynthia said in delight.

The others took their soups, and the gap in the table closed again.

"I saw on the news feed that someone murdered a Cetusian Ambassador a few days ago. That's terrible," Cynthia said, trying to start a conversation with Malo.

"Yes, shocking. Ghastly," Malo replied in unfeigned disgust. He realized that he felt upset by the murder despite the necessity and his involvement.

"Did you know him?"

"I did. He was a very dedicated ambassador for his star system. He debated most fervently in the parliament for his principals and what he believed was for the good of the Confederation. We often talked about various issues. I'll miss him."

"Such a pity we still have crime in our society."

"You're not in danger, are you?" Ayesha sounded alarmed.

Malo chuckled. "No Ayesha, I'm not in danger, but thanks for the concern."

"Well, I love my dad," Ayesha said with empathy, her straight-backed posture a sign of determined protectiveness.

The others laughed affectionately. They finished their soup and placed the bowls back in the center of the table. Cynthia pressed a button, and the bowls disappeared, replaced by two bowls of salad.

Ayesha's eyes lit up. "Avocad," she said with delight.

One dish was an avocad and tomat salad with thin half-moon slices of onio. The other salad had green bea and carro with walnus, also one of their favorites. Malo removed a bowl, and Cynthia removed the other, placing them on the solid tabletop. The holding table disappeared again only to reappear with their main courses. Each had their favorite dish. Dagon had a rack of Procyonian lamb on his plate, Ayesha had Spartan chicken, her favorite poultry dish on Procyon, and Malo and Cynthia both had Lobster Equador Procyon - a dish they had both experimented with and developed to their own taste over the years.

"Wow, mum!" Dagon said with delight as he grabbed his plate.

"You have outdone yourself tonight," Malo complimented his wife.

Cynthia flushed with pleasure as she also removed her plate. "Thank you."

They shared the salads and ate in relative silence, exchanging small talk now and then.

"I need to go away for a few days tomorrow," Malo finally admitted. It pained him to make such an announcement after such a beautiful meal when Cynthia had made so much effort.

The children looked disappointed. Cynthia fumed, "You could have mentioned it beforehand. The night's ruined now."

"I'm sorry, sweetie. The pressures of work have been mounting, and I need to go to Sol for a meeting. I'll make it up to you, I promise."

Cynthia stood in a huff and went over to the window, looking out over the grounds of their estate to hide the tears welling in her eyes. Malo came over and tried to touch her on the shoulders. She shrugged him aside and moved away to another window. Malo could see her reflection. The distress broke his heart. He let out a sigh of regret but did not approach her again. *It will all be over soon*, he thought in consolation. *If all goes to plan, I only need another month, and my work will over.*

The children sat like statues, not wanting to interfere in the conflict developing before their eyes. They had seen it before and it always ended in a tense standoff.

Cynthia twisted. "Why can't you find another job so you can be home more often?"

"You know why, Cynthia. This is my job. I'm good at it and many people rely on me."

"What about me and the children? We rely on you, too. You're never here when we need you. You don't love me anymore." Cynthia stormed off to the bedroom to vent her frustration in private.

"Why don't you two go do some homework or something," Malo said, embarrassed that they had witnessed the marital tiff.

The children blinked, as if the statues had suddenly received some magical power to move, stood and left the dining room.

Malo was unsure what to do. This was the worst Cynthia had ever reacted to his frequent business trips. Had he forgotten something, an anniversary or a birthday? Not that he could think of. He waited for a moment, trying to decide what to do. He went to the bedroom to see if he could placate Cynthia somehow. He knocked softly on the door and opened it.

"Go away," Cynthia said between sobs. She was sitting on the bed with her back to Malo.

He disregarded her, entered the room and closed the door behind him. He sat next to Cynthia, put his arm around her and drew her close. She struggled slightly with no genuine effort to get away and then surrendered to his embrace, her sobs increasing in magnitude. Malo gently encouraged her to turn so she could place her cheek on his shoulder while he stroked her hair slowly and softly. "I'm sorry sweetie," he whispered into her ear. "But never forget I love you more than anything."

Cynthia pressed closer. "You have a funny way of showing it," she said between sobs, not ready to capitulate totally to him yet.

"Shh, sweetie, Shh my love." Malo continued to stroke her hair until the wave of emotion passed.

Cynthia's sobs slowly subsided into slow breathing. She finally raised her head to look at him. Her face was still flushed, her cheeks streaked with tears and her eyes were red. Her sadness sent needles of pain through Malo's emotional armor. "I know. It's just I feel it's not fair sometimes, and I tried to make such an effort tonight."

"I know you did, and it was delicious and really appreciated. It was maybe insensitive of me to bring it up when I did. I'm sorry."

Cynthia raised her hand to stroke Malo's face so she could feel the man she had married. She gave a wan smile and gently punched him with the fist of the other hand. "It wasn't very good timing. It's a wonder how you can be such a superb politician sometimes."

Malo went to the bedside table for a tissue and wiped away his wife's tears. He pulled her to him and kissed her tenderly. She recip-rocated with mounting desire.

Cynthia looked into Malo's eyes as an animal would regard its prey. "You're impossible." She rose, pushed Malo back on his back and mounted him. He didn't resist.

MALO EMERGED from the bedroom an hour later, a renewed spring in his step. He went to his study and closed the door. He had to go to Sol for two Confederation committee meetings, one being budget forward estimates, the other involved reviewing the mounting civil unrest on the Cetusian populated worlds and deciding on policy recommendations to put forward to the parliament to deal with the escalating threat. He had volunteered to chair that committee. It complemented his other plans and manipulations perfectly.

He had to use the time to bring the senior members of his organi-zation together to discuss and instigate the next stages of his plan. It was this part of his itinerary he had to arrange personally and in secret.

The name 'Scorpius' had been his idea. He liked its implications. A scorpion's nippers are menacing and bewitching, tricking its prey into defending against the approaching danger while the lethal part of the scorpion stands ready. The actual weapon is in the tail that strikes with deadly speed, rendering its prey incapacitated for languid consumption. His plans for the Cetusians mirrored that strat-egy. While everyone was watching the danger in front of them and making defensive plans, the actual attack from the rear would sweep them aside. Malo contemplated his plan.

From his study, he invited select members of his covert organiza-tion to a meeting on Mars, at one of their secret locations. It was convenient, and a perfect cover for his purposes. The facility was the headquarters of a mineral processing conglomerate he and the senior members of Scorpius had controlling shares in, allowing them to become board members and converge on Mars for the requisite board meetings. This would look like just like any other board meeting.

He quickly reviewed his agenda to check he had arranged everything. It was all in order, so he packed what he needed for the morning. His hyper ship was leaving at 10am. He had completed what he needed to do. He stood up and stretched before opening the door, turning the lights off and going off to bed for some sleep at last.

15

FIRST CLASS TO XI BOÖTIS

Ahiga's sleep had been disturbing. He kept having nightmares of his father performing violent, disgusting acts on Cetusians. In his most distressing dream, he was being chased by a huge scorpion. The creature scurried after him with a sting in its massive tail. He had woken in a cold sweat. Ahiga rubbed sleep from his eyes as he lay in bed, reliving his nightmares. He finally found the energy to get up and prepare for the day.

The apartment was very spacious. *Typical of Father*, Ahiga thought. The personal bathroom connected with the bedroom and had a large Jacuzzi in one corner and a shower cubicle in another. A separate room to one side contained the toilet. A basin and large mirror was immediately in front of him as he walked through the doorway. Gold-coated fittings gleamed. The rest of the apartment was equally opulent.

Ahiga wondered if his father was always alone when he used the Jacuzzi. He momentarily felt disgusted but then realized his father was an adult with no marital commitments, so if he occasionally found companionship, who was Ahiga to judge him? Ahiga thought for a bit and realized he would probably do the same under similar circumstances. He had a shower.

Going to the kitchen afterwards, he chose his breakfast from the food preparer selection and dialed up his favorite coffee, which filled the apartment with the aroma of freshly ground beans.

As he sipped his coffee, Ahiga thought about what he should do. He looked out one of the apartment windows for inspiration. He could confront Malo, but he didn't think that was the safest thing to do without more background work and a firmer basis for an accusation. He went over the key points so far. There was a clandestine organization founded by Malo to subjugate Cetusians under Human control. A strategy was being developed to carry out this plot and Malo was the lead designer. His father, at least, had infiltrated the organization to stop the impending coup. Ahiga wondered if others in the group had the same purpose. Maybe those who could no longer speak for themselves were also spies? He had no evidence, apart from his father's hologram, but that wasn't proof. Were delta and beta also traitors? He didn't know. He couldn't go to Malo.

Acting on a hunch, Ahiga got out his data plate and brought up the list of the deceased members of his father's secret organization. There was Nguyen of Aquarii, Koanang of Lalande and Renshaw of Draconis. Nothing in the profiles showed any connection between the men or their planets. He looked at the foreign policies of each star system. Slowly a pattern emerged.

Aquarii had foreign policies friendly to Cetusian star systems, as did Lalande and Draconis. Following that line of thought, he looked at the foreign policy of Eta Cassiopei (delta). That star system had a rather neutral foreign policy. With a tinge of disappointment, Ahiga thought he might be mistaken. But when he moved on to Xi Boötis (beta), it confirmed his theory. Xi Boötis had a very strong foreign policy friendly to Cetusian systems. It had recently signed free trade agreements with many of them.

He then looked at some other members of Scorpius and the foreign policies of their star systems. Sure enough, they were all either neutral or hostile toward Cetusians. He searched further for information on the military personnel in the organization. That took some digging, but he eventually found all he was looking for. They too were hostile towards Cetusians to varying degrees. He now felt confident his working theory was valid and the other deaths were also murders, like his father's and not some other accident, although he had no proof. So, Eta Cassiopei was neutral, and Xi Boötis was friendly. It seemed logical to arrange a meeting with Xiang Feng to get some answers rather than Samir Kumar of Eta Cassiopei. Ahiga consulted time zone charts for Xi Boötis and saw that the time was favorable for a hyperlink call to Feng, so he established the connection and waited.

The black screen gave way to an Asian-looking male face of middle age. The hair was graying. The eyes were dark brown and radiated intelligence and wisdom. Ahiga could see the top of a white business shirt, blue striped tie and charcoal gray suit jacket.

"Hello. Ambassador Xiang speaking. How you get number?"

"Hello to you, too. I am sorry to disturb you. My name is Ahiga. I am the son of Ambassador Tse. Your number was in his contact list."

Feng softened with compassion. "I sorry your loss, Ahiga. Tragic. Very tragic."

"Thank you."

"How I help you?"

"I was wondering if I could come and see you to talk about my father?"

"Hmm. I busy but not go anywhere soon. When you think?"

Ahiga considered. It was a lengthy trip to Xi Boötis. "How about three days' time, in the afternoon?"

Feng consulted his calendar, which was off screen. "Yes, I free then. Make three in afternoon?"

"That will be great. Thank you so much for taking the time to see me."

"No problem for son of friend Tse. Will see then."

"Yes, I will see you then and again thanks."

The screen went blank. That was all organized. Ahiga got into the travel-booking clip and looked up flights to Xi Boötis. One was leaving later that evening, at 9pm. He booked a first-class seat. He looked at the visa requirements and saw there was an agreement between the two systems and he could get a visa on arrival for his type of visit. With his travel arrangements sorted, he looked up accommodation on Xi Boötis and booked a room in one of the luxury hotels. *May as well use the money my father gave me to show some status now, I suppose,* Ahiga thought. *It will be a little strange though. I need to make sure it doesn't go to my head.*

Ahiga's future seemed predestined now. He placed a called through to Sani.

"Hello. Sani here," Sani said in a distracted voice.

"Hi, it's Ahiga."

"Oh. Ahiga, how are you getting along?"

"OK. Still not over the shock and my life has changed given the circumstances."

"Good to hear. What do you mean changed?"

"Well, as you probably know, my father was quite a wealthy man, and I took a job to show him and prove to myself I understood the true meaning of working for a living."

"Yeah. I wondered why you were with us. You're a dedicated worker, though. When do you think you will return?"

"Well, that's just it. For a start, I don't really need to work now. Also, I have all of father's business interests to look after so I don't think I'll be coming back."

"That's a pity. I understand. Hey, call us if you get bored with all that high life and want a working vacation for a change."

Ahiga laughed. "I might just do that. So, I suppose I'm tendering my resignation."

"Yeah. I suppose you are. OK. I'll process the paperwork here and forward anything you need to sign and any last payments."

"I'd appreciated that. I'm going away for a few days so it might be hard to get hold of me, but leave a message."

"I will. I suppose this is it then. I expect great things from you. Your father would have been proud of you."

"Thanks. See you later." Ahiga cut the call.

He just had to pack now and get to the spaceport in reasonable time.

Ahiga had taken little when he left his apartment but didn't want to go back to get anything. His father's apartment was close to the retail district, so Ahiga did some shopping in the exclusive retail area. He bought a multitude of clothes, both casual and business, and shoes. By the time he finished, shop assistants were falling over each other to get a cut of the sales commission. He also bought a suitcase, a carry-on bag and top of the range chronometer, comm unit and data plate and some other gadgets. He felt exhausted by the time he got back to the apartment.

He packed his bags, including the items he already had that he wanted to take with. The carry bag had a secret compartment where he stored the data chips and more money chips just in case. By then it was almost time to go to the spaceport. He made a small snack and ordered a taxi.

At the check-in counter, the operator's eyes widened in surprise. "What are you doing in this line, sir? You should have gone over to the first class check-in."

"Oh, I didn't take notice. Well, I'm here now."

The operator smiled and continued processing his check-in while trying to get the attention of the first-class staff at the same time.

Eventually someone from that service area noticed and came over. "Is there a problem?"

"Mr. Ahiga has chosen this check-in instead of the first-class one. I thought you needed to know."

The revelation instantly aroused the person's attention. "Mr. Ahiga, please allow me to assist you through to the spacecraft after you have checked in."

The check-in operator completed the procedure and handed Ahiga his boarding chip and emigration documents. "There you go, Mr. Ahiga. I hope you have an enjoyable flight."

"Thank you."

The fuss amused the people waiting behind him, which made Ahiga slightly embarrassed. He followed the assistant to the emigration area and then into the first-class lounge awaiting the call to board the spaceship.

Ahiga felt self conscious with all the fuss and just wanted to hide. He then thought about his situation. Yes, it was good he supposed to have help with all the tedious tasks and, if he didn't want something, he should be assertive and tell them what he wanted. So when the call to board came, and the assistant arrived to escort him, he said, "I can look after myself, thank you," and walked away towards the gate to board the spaceship. He left the assistant open mouthed, not knowing what to say. Ahiga had a slight smile on his face.

He boarded and settled into his spacious seat as two very attractive young Cetusian women walked past. They looked him over with interest as they walked ahead. *I could get used to this*, he thought.

After the ship took off, Ahiga flipped through the channels on his entertainment system and started watching a holovision program. Before long, one woman approached his seat, champagne glass in hand. "Hi. I haven't seen you aboard before," she said with a cultivated voice.

The intrusion surprised Ahiga, and he fumbled a reply, "I haven't flown first class before," he said. "It was beyond my means."

"Really?" the woman said, piqued by the revelation. She sat down next to Ahiga, invading his personal space and making him slightly uncomfortable. "May I ask what exactly changed your means?"

"My father died."

"Really. My condolences. And who was your father?"

"Ambassador Tse."

"Really?" The woman was now very interested.

Her companion soon joined them, also carrying a glass of bubbly. "Oh, there you are," she said to her friend. "I've been looking all over for you. Thought you were throwing up in the toilet already."

The first woman looked annoyed, eyes piercing straight through her traveling partner. "We aren't all like you, darling. I was just getting acquainted."

"Really, and what has interested you, pray tell?"

"This here is the son of the late Ambassador Tse."

"Really." The second woman's eyes sparkled with interest as she walked to the other side of the lounge and sat, trapping Ahiga between them.

Ahiga was becoming very uncomfortable with his predicament.

"Why don't you order a champagne and drink with us? Who knows, we might join the hyperspace club later," the first woman said. Both women forced a laugh.

"I'm fine, thank you," Ahiga stammered.

"Why? Wouldn't you like to enjoy some of this?" the second woman asked, placing her glass on the table and pulling the front of her top open and thrusting her chest into his face, fully exposing her breasts to him.

"You're so crass sometimes," the first woman said, but laughing with the other anyway.

Ahiga reddened with embarrassment, his aureola turning a bright green. "I would like you to leave me alone, please," he asserted.

Both women stopped laughing, affronted by his rejection. Ahiga realized they were used to getting what they wanted. The crass one pulled up her top and picked up her glass. "Your loss." They both walked out, talking and giggling to each other in fading voices.

I hope that's not a sample of what I have to get used to now, Ahiga thought as he returned to his holovision program.

16

SAMIR

Shallum landed on the primary planet of Eta Cassiopei, Shambhala. Shambhala was a planet of contrasts. It had hot, dry deserts and steamy tropical forests. The planet was warmer than most and the only cool regions were the polar areas and an enormous mountain range traversing half the planet. It had a large Indian population. Shallum arrived in Skardu, the capital, mid morning. He felt tired from the hyper-drive flight. He seemed to be sensitive to the hyperspace environment and found it difficult to sleep. He met the embassy driver at the spaceport and directed him to his hotel.

"How was your flight, sir?"

"Usual. Nothing exciting happened."

"Have you heard about the death of Ambassador Tse of Caerus, sir?"

"Yes, terrible business. It was a bit of a shock."

"And what brings you to Shambhala this time, if I may ask, sir?"

"Just some diplomatic discussions with Samir." Samir Kumar was the Confederation representative for Eta Cassiopei.

"I see. I hope they will be successful."

"So do I."

They flew the rest of the way in silence and eventually arrived at the hotel where Shallum asked the driver to wait for him to change before heading to Samir's office, in the diplomatic part of the city.

As they neared the office, Shallum soaked up the view of impeccably manicured, lush greenery lining the streets. Tall, precisely pruned pencil pine trees colonnaded the access way into the distance on either side. Among the greenery were government buildings of every persuasion. They were homing in on the Confederation Representative's building ahead. The layout of *Eta Cassiopei is very compartmentalized,* Shallum thought. *There is a building for every function and a function for every building.* They even regionally based the restaurants. No restaurants that he could think of served anything other than food from the particular region they represented.

They finally arrived in front of the Representative's building where Shallum alighted from the AGrav. He instantly felt hot and sticky from the humid monsoonal atmosphere, his suit clinging to his body. *I don't know how they live like this.* The sky was a brilliant blue without a cloud, and yet the humidity was unbearable. He wanted to get into the air-conditioned interior of the building immediately.

"Please wait for me," Shallum said to the driver.

"Sir."

As soon as he crossed the threshold, Shallum's body welcomed the coolness. Although he had been in the Representative's building many times before, the adornments beckoning the visitor to the entrance foyer always amazed him. There were many statues of Hindu religious significance on display, their skin shining gold from the lighting's reflection, positioned to create the most stunning visual effect.

Shiva sat in front of him, majestic in her glory in the center of the foyer, radiating her golden brilliance. Vishnu sat on one side by the wall and Brahma on the other. Various other deities which Shallum did not know by name dotted the walls. The flooring was polished marble. A fountain bubbled in front of Shiva, the flowing water a pleasant coolness to the heat of the day.

Shallum took stock of his appearance and adjusted his suit to make sure his appearance was impeccable when he met Samir. He walked to the security check-in and presented himself.

"Hello. I am Shallum Tsadoq. I am here to see Samir Kumar. I have an appointment," he advised the security guard.

The guard called through to check. "If you would be so kind to place your case on the table and walk through the security portal."

"Oh. Security has tightened since the last time I visited. Has there been a heightened alert?"

"You'll have to ask someone else that question. I just do my job."

"OK."

As Shallum walked through the portal, he had the usual nervousness that he might set off the scanner, but nothing pinged. The security guard passed his case through a scanner which displayed a three-dimensional hologram of the contents. The person looked at it before giving it a pass and handing it back. Shallum grabbed his case and continued to the elevators to ascend to Samir's office area.

Exiting the elevator, Shallum walked into the reception area of Samir's office, where the receptionist sat behind a large wooden desk. Flowers of yellow, orange and blazing red stood in a vase on an elevated shelf at the front of the desk, a comfortable height for visitors as they approached it.

The receptionist looked up. She had deep black pupils matching her jet-black hair and dark skin. "Hello. How may I help you?"

"Hello. I'm Shallum Tsadoq. I have an appointment with Samir. I believe he is expecting me."

"Let me check, sir." The receptionist buzzed the comm, having a quick conversation with her boss. "Yes, Representative Kumar is expecting you. Let me show you to his office."

Samir rose from behind his enormous desk and had to squeeze his vast frame around the edge. Jowls of fat hung from his chin. His suit hung loosely on his body. "Welcome again, Shallum. How are you?" They shook hands. "Please have a seat."

"Hello to you, too. It's good to see you again. Malo sends his greetings and regrets that he cannot be here personally. You know how it is," Shallum said as he sat.

"Yes, yes, never enough hours in a day. Would you like a drink before we start? A Scotch, perhaps?"

"A Scotch on the rocks would be fine."

Samir went to his drinks cabinet and prepared a Scotch for them both. "To successful parliamentary proceedings," he toasted.

"Yes, to successful proceedings." Shallum raised his glass and tapped Samir's lightly as he watched the Confederation Representative intently. He tried to get a sense of Samir's frame of mind, distrusting him to the extreme. He could never tell what was going on behind the professional facade.

Samir was equally suspicious. "And to what do I owe the pleasure of your presence?"

"Malo just wanted to shore up support for the Bills he is presenting."

"Malo knows he has my support."

"Of course, of course. You have been one of his most loyal supporters. He was hoping for a more direct involvement in ensuring the outcome of the vote."

"Well, I thought I was contributing as much as he wanted me to. I don't quite understand his sudden need for more involvement. The Bills seem to have the required support to pass. What has changed?"

"It would seem some backers are having second thoughts."

"Why would they change their positions now?"

"There's some very aggressive lobbying against the Bills at present. An influential group is presenting a damning case, saying it is against the Confederation constitution and anti-species. Only the usual politically correct non-speak that surrounds this kind of situation, but it seems to be gaining traction in some quarters."

"I see, I see. Well, that's news to me. I was only just discussing the situation with some other members and they seemed to be still strongly behind the Bills."

"Yes, well. It's only been in the past week that the momentum has gained some leverage. Those damned Cetusians from Chiron are crying foul. They're saying they won't have it, whichever way the vote goes. They will tie up the Bill in the constitutional court forever, if they have their way."

"Yes, they like to stir things up from time to time, but surely it's just a distraction, isn't it? I mean, the main Bill is just trying to put some rational migration policies in place so we don't get to the situation where there are too many slum communities on the affected planets. Goodness knows, we have enough of them already."

"Yes, we do. Anyway, Malo would like you to have a talk with some non-committals to make sure they vote the way they said they would the last time we discussed the Bills."

Samir looked away for a moment, face as blank as a brown paper bag. Shallum couldn't read his intentions. Sometimes he wondered about his commitment to the policy considerations, but Malo was adamant he was a staunch supporter.

Samir returned from his thoughts. "I can have a talk with some of them. They usually trust what I say, I think."

"Good. Malo knew he could count on you."

"He knows he has my full support."

"Yes, he does." Shallum took another sip of his drink. "This is damn good Scotch."

"Yes, it is. It's a 50-year-old vintage from Sirius."

"They make an excellent spirit."

"So, what are your movements? Would you like to dine together tonight?"

"No. I have other commitments, but thanks."

"OK. Well, I'll probably see you in the parliament soon."

"Yeah. Probably."

Shallum drank the last of the Scotch and rose from his chair. Samir rose, too. Shallum held out his hand. "Till next time."

SHALLUM ENTERED AN EERIE CONCLAVE. There was a fire in the center. It let off no heat, only an evil red glow. The walls of the conclave washed with waves of devilish red light as it flickered and flashed out of a cauldron.

He moved to the center of the room and looked around. The enclosure was bare except for the fiery cauldron and a circle of ghoulish entities dressed in the same blood red detritus boiling in the pot. The faces of the monstrosities changed. They all looked like his wife, Cajsa. They seemed to accuse him of something, but he couldn't make out the words. It filled Shallum with dread and terror. Again the faces changed and Shallum saw the people who murdered his wife, living and dead, as the shapes transformed into scorpions. They started chanting, but Shallum couldn't make out what they were saying. It seemed to be in a foreign tongue.

One scorpion stepped forward, its face blurred, pixelated as if to obscure the identity. It spoke with the deep resonance of a lion's roar. "Welcome to the forecourt of Hades, Shallum. We have heard your anguish. We gather to celebrate your descent."

The chanting grew louder, but Shallum could still not decipher what the blur-face scorpion was saying.

He started swaying as if entering a trance.

"You are with friends. We must answer a death with a death. The death of love must have the retribution of many deaths." The scorpion started laughing a hysterical and evil laugh, one that initially filled Shallum with horror but gradually soothed him and moved him to take part in the ritual underway.

"What is your wish?" Shallum asked, completely captivated by the unholy sacrament being performed.

"Come," the blur-faced scorpion said as he ushered Shallum towards the cauldron. Shallum shuffled forward in rhythm with the chanting. He was before the cauldron. Blur-face reached into the pot and pulled out a beating heart. "Eat," it said.

Shallum took the heart and placed it in his mouth. He bit. Red fluid squirted out and into his mouth. It tasted sweet as honey to him. He bit off a portion of the heart and chewed. One of the surrounding scorpions screamed and writhed in agony as he consumed the organ. He took another bite, with more screams from the scorpion. It was fading. As it collapsed, he saw the face of one person he had murdered. He kept eating until he consumed the heart and the scorpion was no more. Red liquid trickled down his chin.

Blur-face raised another heart from the cauldron. "Eat."

Shallum took the next heart and did the same. Another scorpion vanished, as did all the scorpions of the dead.

Blur-face took another heart from the cauldron. "You cannot eat this one yet," it said, raising the beating organ in the air. The owner of the heart pleaded for mercy. Shallum begged to devour it. "You cannot take the living in this place."

Shallum laughed in hysterical delight, as he now knew in his insane mind what he must do to gain possession of the heart for his psychopathic epicurean pleasure.

17

ANOTHER MURDER

Alex woke to sun streaming through the screens of his hotel room. Chooli still slept beside him, her warmth providing a sensuality that made Alex content. He recalled the night before with pleasure as he lay there and wondered what he should do for the day. Would Chooli want to spend it with him? Why did she give him such happiness? He thought back to his other relationship with bitterness. Was he changing inside? His relationship with Chooli seemed to purge the humiliation that culminated in a near hatred of females. He used to enjoy one-night stands with whoever came along, usually after drinking too much, getting satisfaction from dominating the woman, sometimes to her displeasure. He just couldn't see himself doing that with Chooli. She was so fresh, so naturally naïve, not simplistically but in opening herself to him without reservation. He wanted to know her intimately. She was so infuriating sometimes, but that was almost comical. Alex smiled as he remembered their first encounter.

He emerged from his reverie and decided he wanted to do more with the day than lay in bed. He slowly tried to extract himself without disturbing Chooli.

"About time you woke up."

Alex jumped, "I thought you were still sleeping."

"I've been awake for ages." She slowly turned to face him. An enormous smile spread across her face, radiating pleasure and total tranquility.

Alex smiled too before kissing her leisurely.

Chooli sat up, drew her knees to her chin and wrapped her arms around her legs. She looked at Alex. "Well?"

"Well, what?" Alex replied, trying hard not to laugh at Chooli's typical exclamation. He sat up in bed.

Chooli continued teasing. "Well, what are we going to do now?" she asked, being deliberately vague.

Alex parried. "Well, what do you want to do?"

"Depends."

"Depends on what?"

"Depends on whether you want me to beat the shit out of you in a minute if you don't answer me properly."

"Me not answer you properly? That's cheek." Alex lunged for her sides and started tickling.

Chooli jumped, but didn't laugh as Alex expected. She frowned. "What are you doing?"

Alex stopped, chastised by the change of tone. "I was trying to tickle you."

"I don't tickle."

"I noticed. You're no fun."

"That's not what you said last night."

"That's different."

They were at an impasse which Chooli finally broke. "What are we going to do now?"

"I suppose we'll have a shower and go have some breakfast."

"Then what?"

"Dunno."

Alex's comm buzzed. He looked at it with a puzzled expression. It was Nascha. "I wonder what she wants."

"Who?"

"Nascha." Alex picked up his comm, pressing the audio button. "Hi, Nascha. Alex here. What's up?"

"Hi. Where are you?"

"In the hotel. Why?"

"Good. Stay there."

"Why?"

"A massive protest is brewing in the city and Humans may not be safe if they're seen wandering around. The talk is that it will get violent."

"What, can't I even get an AGrav to somewhere outside?"

"That might be OK. Be careful where you go. Don't go anywhere in the central city. The country should be safe if you want to go there."

"OK. Thanks for the tip."

"No problem. Can't have our wonderful GIA agent die on me now, can I?"

"No. I suppose not," Alex said, wondering what the last statement was all about. "See you then."

"What was that about?" Chooli asked.

"There's supposed to be some big protest in the city today. Nascha just called to tell me to watch where I go."

Chooli knitted her brow together in disgust. "Someone's trying to cause trouble with Humans. It doesn't even make sense but there seems to be plenty who agree."

"Why? What's the issue?"

"It doesn't make sense. They say that Cetusians are letting Humans run all over us. That we don't have any say and we're being repressed. It's utter rubbish to me, but it's gained some traction in the general community. That's why there's such an uproar over the murder of Ambassador Tse. They say it's a Human conspiracy."

"Thanks. So if I can't solve the murder, they'll accuse me of covering it up to protect a Human."

"Probably, but you will solve it."

"Thanks for the show of confidence."

"You're welcome. Good of her to warn you."

"Yeah."

Chooli sidled out of the bed and walked with practiced poise to the bathroom. She turned as she approached the doorway. "Well... coming?" she said with a cheeky grin.

Alex watched her slender body disappear into the bathroom. He jumped up and rushed after her.

They toweled themselves off after the shower and Alex dressed. Chooli looked at her clothes with annoyance.

"What's wrong?"

"I can't go to breakfast in those," she said, pointing to the clothes she had worn the night before.

"Why not?" Alex said naively.

"Duh! Wonder where she comes from and why she's all dressed up like some tramp who stayed the night."

"Oh. What do you want to do?"

Chooli sat forlornly on the bed, looking at the ground. "I don't know."

Alex felt sorry for her but understood her predicament. He had an idea. "What's your size?"

"Seven," Chooli said, looking puzzled.

"And your foot size?"

"Six. Why?"

"Wait here. I'll be back." Alex had noticed a clothes shop in the hotel complex.

"OK." Chooli rose, intrigued, wondering what Alex was up to. She went to the wardrobe and grabbed a bathrobe, put it on and sat on the bed again.

Alex grabbed the room key and his credit chip and left, going downstairs to the women's clothes shop. He started flicking through the clothing on a rack near the door.

A shop assistant came over. "Can I help you?"

"Um. Yes. Maybe. I'm looking for some casual clothes in size seven."

"What exactly were you thinking? Dress or top and slacks?"

Alex thought about what Chooli might prefer and decided. "Top and slacks, I think."

"OK. Let's see. We have some outfits over here that have just come in." The assistant walked over to a different rack and leafed through dress shirt and slacks combinations.

Alex didn't think they were Chooli's taste. "They're a little upmarket for what I was looking for. I was thinking more low key."

"OK," the assistant said and thought a moment. She walked over to another set of racks. Alex followed. "What about something like this?"

The assistant pulled out a plain white short-sleeved dress shirt. It had unobtrusive white frills around the sleeve ends and no collar. "What about this one?"

Alex looked at it. He liked it. He imagined it on Chooli and thought it would suit her. He took the shirt from the assistant and held it up at various angles to get a better picture, "Yes, I think that would be good."

"OK." The assistant turned to an adjacent rack, which had various pants on it. She paused and asked. "How old is the woman you're buying for?"

Alex reddened slightly. "In her twenties."

The assistant nodded. She didn't seem to notice Alex's embarrassment. "OK." She fingered through the pants and eventually pulled out three pairs for Alex to select. One was plain black satin, which would fit loosely on the person. Alex didn't like them as he thought they looked too old for Chooli. The next was a dark brown leather pair. Alex liked them but they were body hugging around the legs so it would have been easy to get it wrong and they might be too tight. The third pair was a sky blue denim fabric with black studs at the pocket corners and a red and green flower strip decorating the pocket outline. Alex looked at the pants and then the shirt. He imagined them on Chooli and liked what he saw. He took the denim pants and placed them together. It looked very casual but elegant to him. "I'll take these."

"OK. Good. May I suggest another shirt I think looks fabulous with these pants?" She walked over to another rack and pulled out a bright ruby red button-up shirt and held it out, deliberately placing it next to the pants that Alex was holding.

Alex fell in love with the combination instantly. "That is very elegant. Yes, I'll take that too. I need some shoes. Do you have shoes?"

"Yes, we have a small selection, if you will follow me." The assistant walked over to another area of the shop. "Just to walk around town?"

"Yes."

"What size?"

"Six."

The assistant looked through the shoes in a display area. She finally selected a pair of slip-on black walking shoes with a slight heel and a bow where the lace would normally have been. "How about these?" She pulled them out of the display.

Alex looked. He thought they went well with the clothes he had chosen. "Yes, they will be good."

"Anything else?"

"No. That should do it."

"Let me take those from you and I'll see if we have a size six in the shoes. You can wait at the counter if you like."

"OK." Alex had been concentrating on the clothing selection. When he looked up, he saw two women, also in the shop, looking at him with bemused smiles. They quickly looked away when they realized he had noticed. Alex's mind started wandering as he waited for the assistant to return. He smiled to himself as he considered what he was doing. It really wasn't in his character at all, but it somehow felt right. He hoped that Chooli would like what he had bought.

When Alex returned, Chooli was lying on her front, face cradled in her hands, watching the news on the holovision. She looked his way, saw the bags and burst into a radiant smile. She squealed with glee as she ran to Alex. "What have you got?"

"Clothes. I hope you like them."

"Let's see. Let's see," she said excitedly.

Chooli took the bags and pulled out the clothes. Her eyes bulged. She looked back at Alex, sparkling. "Thank you so much."

"Don't thank me. Put them on. I'm starving."

Chooli giggled. She looked at the two shirts Alex had bought and selected the red one, after inspecting herself in the mirror. She threw off the bathrobe and put the shirt on together with the pants. Alex could see her pleasure by how she moved and the aqua-blue shading of her aureola. She retrieved the shoes and slipped them on. She then inspected herself again, turning one way, then the other, a look of contented satisfaction. "Well?"

"They look fantastic on you," Alex replied with a satisfied smile. "Now let's get some breakfast before I gnaw on your arm."

"You wouldn't," Chooli said with a challenging look.

"I definitely would," Alex riposted as he tried to grab one of her arms.

Chooli avoided his advancing, probing hands with delight as they moved toward the door. They stopped. Chooli looked into Alex's eyes. "Thank you. That is the most diablo thing anyone has done for me." She arched on her toes and kissed him, wrapping her arms around his neck.

"You're welcome," Alex said. "I was serious about gnawing your arms."

"Ugh," Chooli said with fake disgust as she punched him on the shoulder.

It was late morning when they arrived for breakfast. The restaurant had a deck area, and the morning was pleasantly warm. As they relaxed, sipping coffee and enjoying the sunshine, Alex's comm sounded. He frowned when he saw it was from his boss, Commissioner Harris. "This can't be good." He opened the message and read.

<Call me immediately>

"Hmm. I need to go back to my room. I have a hyperlink call to make."

"I'll come with. I'm finished my coffee."

"Maybe not. It might be sensitive and my boss might not like it if he sees me with company."

"Whatever. I'll stay here. Message me when you're finished."

"OK." Alex rose and went back to his room.

Alex connected to the hyperlink and placed the call to the Commissioner. He came on the screen after a few moments.

"Hello Alex. How are things?"

"Slow at the moment. Nothing is making much sense yet and clues aren't jumping out of the woodwork."

"Well, keep at it. This is important."

"Yeah. What's so urgent that you want to talk?"

"There's been another murder. There might be a connection between the two."

"What? Where?"

"On Shambhala, Eta Cassiopei. The Confederation Representative..." the commissioner looked at his notes "... Samir Kumar. It happened last night. The report says they found him sitting in his AGrav. You need to get there and have a look. See if it's connected and how."

Alex scowled. "Seems like being a representative is a dangerous business."

Harris sniggered despite the gravity of the situation. "You could say that."

"I'll take Nascha with me. We seem to work OK as a team in between something I can't understand."

"Your choice but you need to get moving now."

Alex sighed. "And I was having such an enjoyable day."

He worried Chooli would be disappointed but knew she would understand. Maybe even a little excited about the twist in the case. Or maybe he shouldn't be sharing that information just yet. Thinking about her made him realize his feelings were growing. He sent her a message to say he had finished the call and then called Nascha.

"Pack your bags. We're going to Eta Cassiopei. There's been a murder there we need to look at. I'll brief you on the way. Can you arrange seats on the next flight and let me know..." Alex thought "... Business class."

Nascha stared into her comm open-mouthed for a moment,

trying to take in all Alex had said. Her eyebrows rose at the request for business class seating. "Um... Yeah... OK."

Alex heard a knock on the door. It was Chooli, looking relaxed.

When she saw Alex's concerned expression, she asked "You all right?"

Not knowing how to break the news, he blurted, "I have to go to Eta Cassiopei ASAP."

"What! You can't." Chooli collapsed on the bed as the news sunk in. She started crying. "I'll never see you again, will I?"

"Of course you will."

Chooli looked at Alex suspiciously. "You're just saying that." She started getting angry. "You probably want to get out of here as fast as you can."

Alex stood by the door, nonplussed at the sudden change in Chooli's mood. Why did she think he wouldn't see her again? He sat next to her on the bed, but she moved away. Then she lashed out and started punching him with both fists as hard as she could. "You're no different to all the others. I should have taken Mai's advice." She stopped punching and broke down in tears.

Alex stared at her. "What do you mean I'm no different from the others?"

"Mai warned me all you wanted was to get me into bed with you and that'd be the last I'd see of you. That always happens."

Alex felt miserable. "I deliberately waited even when you wanted to, didn't I?"

Chooli thought for a moment. She wiped away some of her tears with the back of her hand. "I suppose. But you're still leaving."

"I have to. It's work. I'll be back."

Chooli sniffed. "Promise."

"Promise. I have to wrap up the case, if for no other reason, and I'm looking at another reason," Alex said, looking directly at her.

Chooli still looked hurt but hoping what Alex said was true. She was uncertain yet full of desire for this man.

Alex got her some tissues, and Chooli wiped her eyes. "Thanks."

He wasn't sure why he had said what he said, but he knew deep down that he meant it. He had been around long enough to know what he wanted in a relationship and he could see what he wanted with Chooli. He didn't want to leave that go, and it confused him. He hadn't had that feeling for a long time. "I knew the moment I set eyes on you Chooli there was something special about you and I'm right. I don't want to lose you. That's why I'll be back."

Chooli sniffed away the last of her sadness. "OK."

Alex's comm sounded with a message from Nascha.

<Hyper ship leaves in three hours at 2:30. See you at the spaceport. Meet you at check-in>.

"I have to pack and go. My ship leaves in three hours."

"OK." Chooli looked at Alex lustfully. "I suppose I should go then."

"I suppose," Alex agreed reluctantly.

Chooli collected her clothes from the night before and started for the door.

"Chooli."

"Yes?"

Alex went to her, wrapped his arms around her and kissed her passionately. She did not resist. "I'll see you soon."

"Better," Chooli replied teasingly.

18

MANEUVERS

Malo arrived on Earth two days after he left Procyon. He felt relaxed and rested after the voyage. He had worked out early on how to get enough sleep so he could bounce right into work when he arrived. His government limousine took him to the Confederation Building where he prepared for his first meeting, a forward estimates committee to review the Confederation budget.

He was one of the examining reviewers who sat at the front of the auditorium. Yas, a Cetusian from Barnard's Star, was the chairperson of the committee. Most of the meeting was mere formality. The last item on the agenda was about military spending. General Langdon, the Chief of the Confederation Defense Force (CDF) Strategic Operations, was before the panel.

"Your expenditure over the past months seems to be far outstripping the current budget, General Langdon. Do you have any explanation for the excess expenditure?" Yas asked.

"We usually have military training maneuvers this time of year," General Langdon replied.

"This seems in excess even of those. We adjust the cash flow in the budget for the increased expenditure."

The General gave Malo a brief glance before turning to Chairperson Yas again. "We are conducting specially coordinated maneuvers this year which require a larger budget. We were not anticipating the extra budgetary requirement when we presented our figures previously."

"What sort of maneuvers?"

"That's classified, sir."

"Humph! Why should maneuvers be classified? Are we going to fight ourselves?"

"Sir, we all know there are systems not aligned with the Confederation and even those within are showing signs of increasing unrest at the moment."

This comment struck a chord with the chairperson, as his system at Barnard's Star was one of them. He shifted uncomfortably in his seat. Malo spotted an opening. "It would seem that, given the increased unrest in the Confederation, there is justification for the additional expenditure over and beyond budgetary requirements given that the defense forces maintain law and order in the Confederation. It would seem to me that such a coordinated defensive maneuver requires practice and planning. Is that what you have been trying to tell the learned Chairperson, General?"

"Well, that is one way of putting it. Yes."

The Chairperson glared at Malo. *It would seem that the learned Chairperson does not like the truth*, Malo thought.

"Well, we will be closely monitoring the expenditure, General," Yas said as he resumed his position. "We hoped you can report that your budgetary situation is better controlled at our next review."

"Yes Chairperson."

Yas looked around. "Does any other member of the panel have a question for the General?" He caught Malo's deliberately. "Very well. Thank you for your attendance, General. We will have another review in two months."

"Very well, Chairperson. I look forward to briefing the committee again."

As everyone rose to leave, Yas spoke: "Member Malo, can I have a quick word with you?"

"Yes Chairperson."

Yas waited for the others to leave. "I would appreciate your not condoning such unprecedented expenditure of our military budget. We're criticized enough for the mere size of the budget as it is."

"I only said it as I saw it, Chairperson. If we want a peaceful Confederation, we must ensure we prepare our defense forces to react at a moment's notice with well-rehearsed deterrent capability."

"Yes, and we all know where you would prefer that deterrence to lead."

"You know very well my views of certain policy situations."

"That's what frightens me sometimes. Very well, then."

It should frighten you, Malo thought.

General Langdon was standing in the corridor talking to his aides as Malo went past, but none of them would have noticed the discreet nod directed at their boss as the military and the government were ignorant of their actual relationship.

An hour later Malo walked into the Policy Review Committee meeting to consider the mounting civil unrest on the Cetusian-populated worlds. He was Chairperson of the six-member committee and took his chair at the head of the conference table. Other members were Tahona, a Cetusian from Chiron in Alpha Centauri; Miles Thompson, a human from Sirius; Pierre Snieders, a human from Epsilon Eridani; Santo Alvarez, a human from 61 Cygni and Atsa, a Cetusian from Lalande - shortened from Lalande 21185 for ease of naming the system. Alvarez and Thompson were also members of Scorpius, so Malo could count on their votes. They all filed in at the appointed time and sat. One characteristic attribute of the Confederation system was timeliness, much to Malo's satisfaction. He hated people being late.

Malo cleared his throat, poured himself a glass of water and took a sip. "Shall we begin?"

"OK, Pierre. Do you have the latest assessment of the civil security status of the Cetusian systems?"

"Yes, I do. I will run through the list if I may."

"Please inform the committee then."

"Chiron is experiencing increasing violence in the streets. The local authorities are becoming increasingly frustrated about what to do in response without inciting further violence."

"That's a lie," Tahona said with considerable force, his aureola turning a greenish-black. He glared across the table at Pierre.

"I'm just reporting what others have forwarded to me. You may protest if you consider the authorities' reporting biased."

"I just came from there. There's been no violence reported in a week. The violence that has been occurring has been sporadic and inconsequential."

Pierre waited with practiced patience, like letting an impetuous child exhaust their tantrum. "Shall I continue?"

"Representative Tahona, could you please wait to express your thoughts till the discussion part of the meeting," Malo said, chastising the Representative from Chiron.

Tahona sat back in his chair, sulking as he fumed about the false-hoods in the report.

"Please continue, Pierre."

"The situation at Tau Ceti has become increasingly inflamed with the news of the Ambassador's murder being released. There is outright rioting and humans on the planet and the authorities have issued advice to be cautious in their day-to-day activities. In fact, they have advised people to evacuate the system if their business is not essential."

Malo could see Tahona biting his tongue, resisting another outburst. *This is all going very well*, Malo thought.

"Lalande seems to have the situation under control for now. Various riots have They have quelled various riots in the system, and some ringleaders arrested. The situation there is being closely monitored.

"Barnard's Star is also suffering increasing tension. The security forces are only just contain the situation.

"That's the report summary from the intelligence collected by the agency."

"Thank you, Pierre. Well, it would seem that the situation is becoming increasingly grim. The Cetusian authorities seem to be slowly losing their grip on law and order..."

"That is just not right," Tahona spluttered as his face purple and his aureola darkened further with rage. "Those reports are completely false. I don't know what your game is, but we will discover it, eventually."

"My game, Representative of Chiron, is to ensure the Confederation has the right policies to deal with law and order within it," Malo explained slowly, staring Tahona down as he did so. "I like the situation as little as you do but we must ensure the security of the Confederation."

"But it's all untrue," Tahona carried on defiantly.

"If we cannot trust the integrity of our agencies, who can we trust, Representative Tahona?"

"I'm not saying the agencies are falsifying the reports."

"Then what are you saying?"

"Someone is changing the reports the agency posts."

Several of the members around the table sniggered in derision.

"Sounds like you believe there's a conspiracy or something," Malo said patronizingly. *You don't realize how close you are to the truth of the matter*, he thought.

"Don't be silly," Tahona replied. "I'm not that paranoid."

You should be. "Well, what do you think the situation is then?"

"As I said before, when I left, the unrest was under complete control."

"That hasn't made it to the report. Anyway, the crux of the matter is there appears to be increasing violence and disruption to the smooth running of things in all the Cetusian systems. The Confederation needs to formulate a policy response ahead of any situation escalating to the stage where the local forces can no longer cope."

"I do not believe we need the interference of the human systems in our affairs," Atsa said, calmly observing the atmosphere. He was an experienced campaigner in the Confederation's politics.

"Well, it would seem increasingly obvious that you are straining to manage the situation yourselves," Alvarez said, showing his political colors.

"When human politicians fan the flames by making outlandish comments about the evolutionary capabilities of the Cetusian species, one must expect the general populace to raise a few objections," Atsa continued in his logical tone.

Malo knew Atse meant the comment for his ears, but he let it go over his head, hoping to take some heat out of the meeting.

"I'm sure that your security forces can cope with most situations that could occur," Pierre said. "The question is, what support should the Confederation provide if requested by an individual system, or if the local forces are overwhelmed."

"That is exactly the policy recommendation we need to make," Malo agreed, delighted that one of his cohorts was maneuvering the discussion in the direction he wanted without obvious coercion.

"Well, I think we need to have the Confederation Defense Force readied for immediate deployment if it becomes obvious the local forces cannot manage," Alvarez said.

"This is outrageous," Tahona shouted, beside himself with frustration. "You're talking about the defense forces taking control of the system. That just will not do. That is just too Draconian to even suggest." Tahona stood up. "I will have no further part in this committee if that is its decision." He stormed out of the room.

Malo looked down to hide his smirk. The meeting was going much better than he planned. With Tahona out of the way, the committee might actually settle on a policy. As he lifted his gaze and resumed his professional mask, he asked, "What do the others think?"

"I agree with Santo. We need to be ready to offer our support," Pierre said.

"I believe that is a prudent course of action also," Miles Thompson said.

Atsa sat blinking in silence as he listened to the others. He looked bewildered. Malo knew that the unanimous approval for preparation of the CDF would have been distasteful at one level for Atsa but also appreciated at another, if they needed temporary intervention to restore order.

"What is your opinion, Atsa?" Malo asked.

Atsa moved uncomfortably in his seat. He cleared his throat. "As much as I would like to protest such drastic action, I too can see the prudence in initiating such contingency arrangements. The report is correct in that we have the situation well contained at present, but even I cannot say that has been the case at all times in the past. I will endorse such a policy. However, the area of my concern is that the unrest seems coordinated throughout the Confederation."

Miles said contemptuously, "We aren't getting paranoid again with conspiracy theories, are we?"

"Not at all," said Atsa, miffed. "I'm just pointing out that it is a little unusual that only Cetusian worlds seem to have these problems, and the issue has flared up in synchronicity, so to speak. I mean, there are plenty of Cetusians on other worlds too, but they do not appear to be having the same unrest."

"Maybe the other worlds better manage their populace."

Atsa stared with indignation at Miles.

"Let's keep to the topic at hand, shall we," Malo interjected, as he could see a shouting match developing and he wanted the motion passed. "So it would appear there is a unanimous agreement for recommending that the CDF make preparations for contingent support of the individual system forces in the Cetusian states so they are ready, should there be a need or request for their utilization. Does that sum up our discussion?"

The others around the table nodded agreement, Atsa a little reluctantly.

"Very well. I shall make the recommendation to the parliament at the earliest opportunity. Is there anything else to discuss?"

The others sat in silence, some shaking their heads.

"I will call the meeting adjourned till the next scheduled date."

After everyone had left, Malo thought *all went very well. It surprised him Atsa didn't fight harder. The subversion on Lalande must worse than we realize.* He smiled to himself. Things were coming together nicely. He was now ready for his next meeting on Mars. He had to catch the overnight shuttle so he shouldn't loiter. Santo and Miles would be on the same flight.

19

FINAL PLANS

The shuttle landed on Mars with a thump. *Must be a junior pilot*, Malo thought. He left the ship and encountered the usual diplomatic immigration protocols before the company chauffeur met him and drove him to the headquarters of his minerals processing company. Other members of Scorpius had smaller shareholdings. He had a few hours before his meeting so he went to the cafe on the ground floor to have some breakfast and gather his thoughts, deciding on traditional bacon and eggs. He ordered freshly squeezed orange juice, fresh from Earth, and a cup of steaming hot coffee. His comm buzzed. It was General Langdon.

"Mind if I interrupt?"

"Not at all," Malo said as he surveyed the café for eavesdroppers. "What's on your mind?"

"The forward estimates went well."

"I wasn't expecting anything too exciting."

"The expenditure will increase, I hope you realize."

"It will all be over by the next meeting."

"Really?"

"Yes, I need to see you after this meeting to make detailed plans."

"I have to return to headquarters now. You're welcome to come over and we can talk then."

"That sounds like an excellent idea. Let's see." Malo looked at the transportation schedules to get to CDF Headquarters from Mars. "I should get there day after tomorrow. Let's meet in the late afternoon."

"OK. I'll schedule it for after four, say two hours. We can have dinner together afterwards."

"That sounds good."

Santo Alvarez walked into the cafe and over to Malo's table. "May I?"

"Doesn't look like I have much choice." Malo sighed, watching his breakfast get cold.

"Please, continue eating."

"Thanks. How can I help?" Malo cut off a slice of egg and some bacon.

"I wasn't comfortable with Atsa's veiled accusations at the meeting. It seems the Cetusians have seen through our interference."

Malo swallowed. "Don't be. It will all be over by the time they figure it out."

"So... we'll move soon?"

"Let's leave this for the meeting, shall we? There are too many ears around." Malo's eyes shot about, concerned they may have already overheard them. Santo should know better.

"OK. Have you heard? Samir's dead, murdered!"

Malo jerked his head up, trying to read Santo's reaction to the news. "No, I hadn't."

"It's a bit of a worry, don't you think? First Tse and now Samir?"

"Don't forget the others. That is unfortunate."

"You don't sound too concerned. Isn't it going to affect what's happening?"

"I am concerned. As far as affecting what's happening, I have contingencies and succession plans for these circumstances." *I even have a succession plan for you. I have to remove the rot from my organization before it takes hold.*

"Well, I hope that's the last."

"What's wrong? You worried you might be next?" Malo smiled sinisterly.

Santo reddened with indignation. "Of course not." He stood and left.

That was quick work with Samir, Malo thought. *I wonder if that GIA guy will connect the two? He would have to investigate at least. Anyway. Nothing lost with Samir. He was becoming a problem with his fretting.* Malo finally finished his breakfast.

When he entered the meeting room, he sat at the head of the conference table watching each member file in and sit down. He sat back, elbow resting on the armrest, his head cradled by his thumb and middle finger. His forefinger played with his bottom lip as he pondered the group assembling before him. There were absences, some permanent, some deliberate. He had only his most trusted here. There were many vacant seats.

Malo started the meeting once everyone settled, the door closed and the security cloaking system switched on to prevent eavesdropping. "Welcome everyone. I know you all have busy schedules and I appreciate it you could attend at such short notice."

"Is this it? Where are the others?" Jason Zander, the Confederation Ambassador to Chiron, asked as he looked around the room.

"Yes, this is it today. As you know, some are no longer with us and I refrained from inviting certain others."

"I just heard that Samir Kumar's dead," Santo piped in.

A buzz of consternation circulated the table as the news enveloped the attendees.

Malo continued, "We must press on. We are now at a point in our plans where we have the end in sight at last."

"What do you mean?" Miles Thompson asked.

"What I mean is that the violence and protests on the Cetusian worlds are about to reach unprecedented levels with the help of all in this room."

The attendees looked at each other, perplexed.

"Yes, we are at the stage where we can start the endgame."

"What is our end game?" Safrini asked, a puzzled look on her face. Safrini was the Confederation Ambassador to Barnard's Star as opposed to Yas, who was only a Cetusian Representative.

"What I am about to tell you should not surprise or alarm you. I recruited you for this express purpose, and your political affiliations are in alignment with the goals of our organization. You all know our goals."

A chatter of assent went around the room.

"Well, we are about to realize those goals. The Cetusian worlds will soon know the true meaning of being ruled by a superior species, one that can use and control the resources at its disposal much more efficiently than they could ever dream of. They will know what it feels like to have an iron fist rule them. They will know who are the masters, and who are the servants. Humans will no longer tolerate the humiliation of their smugness and embarrassing innuendoes of human frailty just because they can breathe a reduced oxygen atmosphere without enhancers. This is it. This will be our victory."

"Here, here," rose from the participants around the table and applause. Some stood.

"Now, here is the plan," Malo returned to his formal manner. "I will see General Langdon at the CDF Headquarters after this meeting to detail the military strategy for winning control of the Cetusian systems in the Confederation. Once I finalize the strategy, and the fleet has positioned itself into the planned locations, I will send out the order to our operatives in the systems to step up the rhetoric and unrest, increasing the levels of disruption until it is obvious they require intervention by the CDF as recommended by the Policy Review Committee covering the Cetusian Issue. I will have previously had the recommendations ratified by the Confederation Assembly.

"The CDF will then move in, remove the existing governing powers and take control of the systems as administrators. The unrest will stop immediately, vindicating the action and proving the effectiveness of the intervention. Are there questions?"

A symphony of silence filled the room. All eyes were on Malo as the delegates took in the implications of his plan.

"Brilliant," Safrini uttered in awe.

"Amazing," Miles agreed.

The silence turned to a chorus of excitement that crescendoed and finally abated into a soft hum of anticipation.

"I take it I have your approval then," Malo concluded.

The representatives answered with a round of applause.

"Now, I have talked to you before about your role in all this when the time comes. The timeliness of your actions is of the utmost importance to the success of our plans. I do not intend to reiterate each item here. All I wish to ask is whether any of you have questions about your part."

No one in the room raised any issues about what they were to do.

"OK then. I'll send you a timeline once I've finished my discussions with General Langdon. Is that clear?"

Everyone nodded.

"That is all I wanted to discuss today."

The others packed up and left the room in dribs and drabs. Malo hung back, watching them as they left. He wondered if he could count on them to perform the tasks he had assigned them. He concluded that he wouldn't have had them in his organization if he didn't trust them, although others had disappointed him. This was the endgame. Everything depended on his leadership, timing and others doing their tasks as planned. He yawned and stretched. It was becoming a long couple of days and it wasn't over yet. At least he had a lengthy trip to CDF Headquarters to get some rest. In the meantime, he needed to see how the current operations of the company were performing.

20

AHIGA MEETS FENG

Ahiga arrived on Xi Boötis early. He had slept well on the hyper-ship, fortunately. His appointment with Feng was at 3:00 in the afternoon. He went to the hotel, freshen up and prepare for his meeting. The arranged limousine was waiting to pick him up. Many people looked towards him to see who the important person was. Ahiga chuckled. *Maybe I should have arranged for some girls to accompany me,* he thought.

They arrived at the Imperial Citadel Hotel and he received the same VIP treatment as he entered the lobby. He had booked the penthouse suite, and they gave him personalized service, including an exotically beautiful female butler who escorted him to his suite. She inducted him in the operation of all the devices in the room. "Is there anything else I can assist you with, sir?" she said when she finished.

"You'll probably have to show me half of what you just went through again, but that will do for now and please call me Ahiga."

"Would you like a refreshment, s... Ahiga?"

Ahiga thought. "Yes please, I'll have a beer."

As the butler prepared the drink, Ahiga looked at the Xi Boötis scenery out of the window.

"Would you prefer room service for lunch or one of our restaurants perhaps?" the butler asked.

"I'll have lunch in one of your restaurants. You choose."

"OK. What time would suit you?"

Ahiga thought. "Make it 12:30."

Ahiga's attention returned to the view. He could see out over the expanse of the city and suburbia as it disappeared in the distance. Two vast mountains dominated the background, peaked white with snow. The sky was clear with the most vibrant azure blue. It gave him a sense of peace. He appreciated the design of the room and the furniture placement, which made the most of the outlook. He closed his eyes briefly until he heard a noise.

The butler had reentered the suite. "I have made a reservation in our Ming Dynasty restaurant on the rooftop of our hotel. I can escort you if you desire, Ahiga."

"That sounds good. Thank you. Yes, you can escort me. It's not every day one enjoys the services of a butler so beautiful."

She blushed slightly. "Thank you, Ahiga. Will that be all?"

"Yes, thank you."

Ahiga finished his beer and had a shower. When he went to his suitcase for clothes, it was empty. They hung neatly in the wardrobe and stored in the drawers. *I wonder when she did that.* He retrieved his data plate and started reviewing what he wanted to ask Feng. He wrote notes for himself. Twelve thirty came, and the butler returned. "Shall we go, Ahiga?"

"Yeah." They went to the restaurant.

"Excuse me for asking, but you don't seem to be the type who normally takes the penthouse suite."

Ahiga laughed. "Very observant. No, I'm not, but I have the opportunity now, because of some misfortune, so I thought I should see what it's like living like a king." Ahiga thought for a moment. "Have you eaten?"

"No, Ahiga."

"Would you join me for lunch?"

"That is not possible, sir. It is against hotel policy to fraternize with the guests." The butler returned to her formal mode.

"It's not fraternizing. You are keeping me company and explaining the workings of the hotel."

The butler wavered momentarily, undecided about what to do.

"I will upset me if hotel policy causes unhappiness and distress for me," Ahiga said, using the same policy argument to put more pressure on her.

"Well, if you put it like that, I have no option Ahiga." She smiled.

The butler and Ahiga sat at the reserved table together. The Maître De looked disapprovingly at her. She just shrugged. "Customer's orders." The Maître De snapped his fingers, issuing orders to a waiter to set another place at the table. Ahiga and the butler talked jovially while Ahiga ate his lunch. She didn't eat to show some sense of adherence to hotel policy.

Settling into his new status, Ahiga arrived at Feng's office just before 3:00 in the afternoon. The limousine parked and stood waiting for his return. He alighted, walked to the entrance of the building and went in. It was poorly lit, so it felt like one was at the entrance to a cave. The elevators to the offices on the floors above stood at the other end of the passage. Tolerating the discomfort of the dimly lit corridor, he used the elevator and ascended at Feng's office A reception area lay before him as he walked out.

A large hologram of a person in traditional Chinese attire was hanging on the wall directly in front of him. Ahiga thought it might be Feng, but there was no caption and the face looked different. The image dissolved into a doorway, and an impeccably dressed man walked through, solving the mystery of the hologram. He was wearing a charcoal gray business suit, white shirt and a tie with black ying & yang symbols running down the center on a jade green background. He wore shining jet-black leather shoes. He was about 150cm, shorter than Ahiga, and looked slim and fit. His hair was black with streaks of ageing gray. He looked serious.

"Hello, Ahiga. I'm Feng. Good to see you. Hope you had pleasant trip."

"Hello Feng. Yes, the trip was pleasant. Good of you seeing me at such short notice."

"Not at all. Being Tse's son, you welcome any time. But please, come through to my office where we can talk in private."

Ahiga followed Feng through the opening in the wall, which rematerialized after they walked through. He stood in an office, partitioned into several areas. They occupied the lounge where various chairs encircled a coffee table.

"Please, sit," Feng invited.

Ahiga chose a seat with a view of the city while Feng went into another room to talk to someone and returned.

"Did you like effect of opaque wall in reception area?"

"I haven't seen that design of door before. Yes, it was interesting, but the hologram wasn't you. He looks like you. A relative?"

"Yes, my father. He held this position in Confederation before me. Our people honored him in elect me to continue with representation when he retired. They installed the device in his time and I had no desire to change it when I took over."

"I see. How long has your family represented Xi Boötis?"

"Over 30 years now."

"That is a long time. My father was into his eleventh year and he said that was too long to take out of his life." Ahiga grew somber when he brought up his father and looked at his hands in his lap.

"Something Tse would say, too. The business with your father's unfortunate demise is tragic. It is untenable, really. I truly hope they apprehend the culprit."

"Yes, so do I."

A woman came in at that moment carrying a tray with tea and biscuits, which Feng offered to Ahiga. "So Ahiga, how can I help you?"

Ahiga took a sip of his tea. "Well, my father left me some data chips which I found when I was looking through his personal effects. He also rented a safe deposit box for my use. It is now apparent to me he did that because he thought what he was doing had some risk associated with it and he wanted me to know certain things in the event of this situation occurring."

Feng was attentive as Ahiga spoke, his demeanor wary at the mention of the safe deposit box and risky activities. "I see, but how does this relate to me?"

"Some information stored on the chips showed an organization that he was a part of called Scorpius." Ahiga watched Feng's reaction as he dropped the name. He was not disappointed. Feng's eyes radiated alarm, which he quickly covered up.

"That is interesting but, again, how does that relate to me?"

"Your name was on the list of members."

"That cannot be possible. This is the first I have heard of this matter."

"You're not Beta Scorpius?"

Feng reddened when Ahiga mentioned his code name. He looked around in alarm, hoping no one had entered the room unnoticed.

"Please do not say that."

Feng quickly rose from his chair and went over to each door, looking through to see if anyone was within earshot. He returned, pulled a device from his pocket and pressed a button on top. He placed the device on the table. A shimmer appeared around them.

"We may speak freely now. I have a screen around us preventing anyone from hearing us. I was not aware Tse had left such information for you to find. It was unwise, I believe. It could place you and others in the organization at significant risk."

"Nevertheless, he did. I think I understand why he did. I have a reasonable understanding of what Scorpius is and what its intentions are, but why are you part of it?"

"What makes you think I wouldn't share the values of the organization?"

"I have looked at each member's profile and a disturbing trend is emerging."

"What is that?"

"They have a tendency of dying recently."

"Yes, well. These things happen."

"If I'm not mistaken, you're on that list."

Feng jumped from his chair and paced nervously back and forth. He faced Ahiga again. "Why do you think I am on that list?"

"The political systems of all those who have died recently have friendly policies toward Cetusians. My father was Cetusian, but I think they murdered him for another reason, or maybe not. Your system also has friendly policies towards Cetusians."

"There must be some that were not on the list."

"Not that I can see. Another interesting thing is that the deaths seem to occur in reverse alphabetical order. My father was Eta. Before him was Lambda, before that Mu and the first Pi. Coincidence? I think not."

Feng broke out in a sweat. "But Delta is before me."

"Yes, that is puzzling. His system seems to be neutral towards Cetusians. He jumped over the name of people with hostile policies."

Feng pulled a handkerchief out of his pocket and dabbed the perspiration away from his brow. He replaced it and fidgeted with his hands. He looked at Ahiga with concern. "There was a certain faction within the organization that was becoming nervous about the direction it was taking. I have expressed my concern from time to time. They seemed to receive it with proper democratic reception. I have had discussions about the issue with the others you mentioned, including your father."

"Uh-huh, and what was the direction of that conversation?"

"It is too dangerous for me to say."

"It may be more dangerous for you not to say. Let me guess, Scorpius would organize a forced takeover of Cetusian systems by human overlords."

Feng looked at Ahiga, blinking in surprise. "Hah! You are your father's son, that's for sure."

"Am I close?"

"There had been some talk about it when we met. I haven't heard mention of it of late, but I also get the feeling I haven't been to all of our meetings, either. I might be on the outside."

"Who would be behind such a repugnant idea?"

"Malo, of course. I presume you know Malo Metam is Alpha."

"Yes, I do."

"Malo hates Cetusians with a passion. That's how the organization first started. He initially put a faction within the Confederation together to discuss and develop policies more favorable towards Humans than Cetusians, but it seemed to become more sinister in its secrecy and intentions as time passed. That's when I started becoming nervous of our direction."

"My father said he joined the organization for his own intentions. Do you know what they were?"

"It was strange that they admitted your father. From what I could tell, he convinced Malo that Cetusians could learn from humans, although I suspect Malo had his own motives. He used him in some unusual situations."

"Like torture?"

Feng glanced at Ahiga uncomfortably. "I heard rumors of torture to extract information. How do you know that?"

"My father left me a recording. It ended unpleasantly after they got the information they needed. Maybe he left it so I could use it as evidence at some stage."

"Your father and I had some extensive discussions. He wasn't comfortable with what was happening and I believe he was trying to gather enough evidence to expose the ultimate aims of the organization."

"He left me quite a selection of evidence."

"I'd be careful who I told that to, if I were you."

"Someone has already tried to kidnap me, so I think they already suspect my father may have left something. So what do you think will happen next?"

"Kidnapped? What happened?"

"Some thugs dragged me out of my father's apartment when I was there looking through his things. Maybe they didn't expect to find me there, I don't know. Anyway, the GIA agents rescued me."

"Thank goodness. You must be careful, Ahiga. It seems like something is about to happen. Activity is intensifying. Unrest on Cetusian systems is increasing, which is the first stage of the strategy to take control, as far as I have been able to fathom. I feel the final phase of the plot may be starting."

"Which is?"

"I'm not sure. I haven't been privy to that information but, from inference, I would think they require military action to enforce any takeover of government."

"But how could the Confederation ever condone such a thing?"

Feng thought for a moment. He took his handkerchief out and wiped his brow again. "Malo is an excellent strategist. He will have worked out his intentions to the minutest detail. If you followed the proceedings of the parliament over the last couple of years, you will have seen a pattern in the bills he has put forward for adoption. The parliament is quite tired of the bombardment. There is often a general groan around when he presents another one. Anyway, the bills are very strategic but affronting to the Cetusian delegates. Now, with the unrest and rioting starting to escalate, I'm sure Malo will say 'I told you so'. If he takes over to restore peace - peace that he disturbed in the first place - they will see him as a forward-thinking leader by most of the Confederation. That and gaining the result, he can beg forgiveness later, once the damage is done and there can be no return to what was."

"Clever."

"Yes, you don't share your father's aptitude for diplomacy?"

"I wouldn't know. I'm an engineer. You need little diplomacy for that."

"I see. What will you do now?" Feng asked.

"I'm not sure. I would like to confront Malo but I don't know if I have enough information yet."

Fear covered Feng's face. "You must be very careful."

"Yes, I know. I think you need to have your wits about you, too. If Malo is behind the murders, who would he get to carry them out?"

"I don't know, how would I know? That is something you have to ask Malo."

"Yeah right. 'OK Malo, who's your hit man?'"

They both laughed despite the gravity of the situation.

Feng hesitated, unsure if he should take Tse's son into his confidence. Finally he said, "I have two more clues for you. One is Malo's PA mysteriously died about six months ago. They put it down to suicide but I know her husband was very distraught and I don't think he believed that."

"Uh-huh, what's the husband's name?"

"Shallum Tsadoq, Malo's political attaché."

"And the second piece of information?"

Feng turned off the shielding devices and went into another room, returning with a data chip. He gave it to Ahiga. "This might help you work out the next moves in the game. It depends what your father left you."

"Game?"

"Diplomacy and politics is like playing a game of chess in many ways. Have you heard of the game?"

"My father taught me. Yes, I suppose you are right there. Thank you very much for this." Ahiga wagged the chip in front of Feng and put it into his pocket.

21

ETA CASSIOPEI

Alex rushed into the spaceport. It was bustling with people. He went to the Eta Cassiopei check-in area and looked around for Nascha. He saw her standing by a building column looking at her data plate. He hurried over to her, being careful not to bump into anyone.

Nascha looked up when she noticed him. She smiled. "You made it. I was getting worried."

Alex pointed outside. "The protests were in full swing. The taxi driver was very concerned. He told me to get onto the floor a few times so the crowd wouldn't see me."

"Yeah. I was wondering if they would hold you up because of that. Well, you're here now. Let's check-in."

"You get business class?"

"Yeah."

When they handed over their credentials, the check-in operator looked up at Alex. "Mr. Warner. I see you came here first class. Let's see if we can upgrade you."

Alex looked at Nascha, a little embarrassed. "No, it's fine. It was the only available seat at the time and I don't want to sit separately to Ms. Nascha."

"You won't have to. We have two first class units still available."

Alex made to protest, but Nascha kicked him and said, "That is most kind of you."

Alex winced at the pain, looked at Nascha grumpily and said, "Yes, most kind."

The operator completed their check-in and handed them their boarding chips. Attendants arrived from somewhere to assist them with their first class boarding procedures.

Nascha whispered, "Why were you going to object?" as they walked off, Alex limping a little.

"I didn't want to get into trouble. That kick hurt," Alex whispered back.

"Sorry. Why would you get into trouble? They suggested it, and it won't cost more."

"I wasn't thinking."

"Yeah, you weren't."

They went to the gate, Nascha looking pleased with herself, Alex grumpy from the kick and also from missing Chooli, which surprised him. Maybe it was Nascha that encouraged the distinction between the two. Chooli always seemed to absorb almost any situation she found herself in, and Nascha seemed to have a chip on her shoulder all the time.

They boarded the flight and went to their seating area.

"See you for a drink later," Nascha said with a wicked smile.

"Yeah. Let's have a drink or two," Alex replied sullenly.

His morbid response puzzled Nascha.

As if reading his thoughts, a flight assistant asked for his order.

"A Scotch on the rocks, make it a double," Alex said, planning to drown his sorrows.

He flipped through the holovision channels for a distraction.

An hour into the flight, Nascha visited Alex's pod. She seemed to have been drinking a little, as she was unsteady on her feet. She had a glass of champagne in her hand.

"Want a drink?"

"Not really. Looks like you've had enough, anyway."

Nascha couldn't hide her annoyance. "What is wrong with you?"

"Nothing's wrong with me. I just don't want a drink at the moment."

"No. Not just that. You're odd around women. You look at them funny, as if we don't matter or something."

Alex wasn't sure what to say, what he should say, what the right thing to say was. Had she unraveled a part of him he didn't understand? *Did* he treat women differently? He finally admitted, "I had a painful experience in a relationship that went bad. I've found it hard to trust women since."

The confession stunned Nascha. It sobered her a little. "I'm sorry."

"Not your fault and if I have been obnoxious from time to time, I'm sorry for that."

"Yeah... OK. Listen, sorry about before, but would you have a drink with me now?"

Alex saw sincerity in Nascha's eyes, a maturity and desire for companionship. "Yeah. OK. Let's go to the bar." He rose and led Nascha to the bar where they talked for a long time.

They finally arrived at Eta Cassiopei in the afternoon. Mahendra Pradesh, a representative of the local enforcement agency, met them at the customs hall. He had been investigating the Representative's murder and told them, "They found Samir in his AGrav by someone approaching their vehicle. He was sitting in his seat, unmoving, and didn't respond when the person knocked, so they contacted us."

"I see. Has the medical examiner had a look yet?"

"Yes, he has. There is a puncture mark in the nape of his neck. It would appear someone inserted a hypodermic device up into the brain and an explosive charge liquefied the cranial matter. Death instantaneous."

Alex and Nascha winced. "Well, our killer is inventive at least, especially if it's the same person," Alex commented. "Anything else?"

Mahendra thought for a moment. "There was a scrap of paper on the instrument panel."

Alex and Nascha looked at each other. "Did this paper have anything written on it?"

"Just some scribble from what we could tell. We have taken it into evidence."

"I want to look at it when I get the chance."

"Of course."

They arrived at the AGrav, loaded their luggage and Mahendra took them to the murder location.

"Do you have a holo of the scene?" Alex asked.

"Yes." Mahendra directed an officer to run the holovision. An image of Samir Kumar appeared.

Alex and Nascha walked around the vehicle and looked from every direction. "How much have you disturbed it," Alex asked.

"Only what has been necessary."

"What about around the AGrav door where he was sitting?"

"We had to remove him once the medical examiner had conducted his initial examination."

"I see." Alex squatted by the door and inspected the garage floor. He took a flashlight from his pocket and shone the beam at an oblique angle. He couldn't see anything out of place. He looked at the doorframe and spotted a scuff mark on the bottom foot protector. He stood up again. "What do you think Nascha?"

Nascha held her chin, pondering. "I think he knew his attacker. He was about to get into his vehicle, and the person caught him off guard. The door was open so when he slumped forward, dead, the attacker sat him down and arranged the body to look like he was sitting there naturally."

Alex looked at Nascha with respect. "Very good hypothesis. How can we prove it?"

"I take it there is no security footage," Nascha asked Mahendra.

"Unfortunately not. The cameras mysteriously crashed during the time of interest."

"Same perpetrator?" she asked Alex.

"Probably," Alex said cryptically. "I've seen enough here. Can you take me to the evidence locker?"

As they flew to the station house considering the possibilities, Alex asked Mahendra: "Who was the last to see the Representative alive?"

"His PA. He said goodbye to her as he left the office the night before."

"What was his schedule for the day?"

"He had an appointment with Shallum Tsadoq in the afternoon just before he left. Nothing other than that."

"Shallum Tsadoq? Where have I heard that name before?"

"He's Malo's attaché," Nascha reminded him.

"Yes, I suppose it would be normal for him to meet with Samir."

"They had regular appointments. I checked," Mahendra said.

"Hmm. Still. We need to check if Shallum met Tse recently."

"I'll get Atsidi to ask."

They arrived at the evidence lockup and Mahendra retrieved the bag with the curious slip of paper. It perplexed Alex more than surprised. He showed it to Nascha.

"Coincidence?" Nascha asked sceptically as she examined the symbols: δℳ..

"I don't think so. It seems the murderer is leaving clues for us."

22

FENG MEETS DEATH

Feng was feeling relaxed after his discussion with Ahiga. Maybe they could avert the disastrous direction Scorpius had taken. Maybe there was hope. He went back into his office and sat in his chair in thought. Feng could see much of Ahiga's father in Ahiga. Tse's characteristic directness was a trait that Feng admired. He wondered how he might support Ahiga in the political arena when the opportune time came, if it came. If he used the intel wisely.

His comm interrupted Feng's thoughts. It was his PA. He wondered what she wanted. He had no appointments as far as he knew. He pressed the accept button, "Yes?"

"Shallum Tsadoq is here to see you, Mr. Xiang," the PA announced.

Feng's brow creased as he wondered what Shallum could want with him, unannounced without an appointment. "OK. I'll be there in a moment." Feng cast an eye around his office to determine if there was anything he didn't want Shallum to see. Shallum was Malo's attaché, so Feng was careful that Shallum couldn't relay some incriminating evidence back to him.

Satisfied that his office was clean of embarrassing material, Feng opened the interconnecting door. A blinding flash met him.

SHALLUM LOOKED at the mess in front of him. Feng lay on the floor, a wisp of smoke from the burned flesh surrounding the hole in his head rose in the air. Blood slowly oozed from the cauterized wound. Some blood had splattered Shallum's suit. He looked over to the PA's desk. She lay slumped back in her chair with a matching hole.

Shallum had to move fast. First, he needed to clean the blood from his suit. He went to the private bathroom that adjoined Feng's office. He had used it often. Grabbing some toweling, he dampened it and rubbed his suit briskly, then rinsed the blood under the tap. He looked at himself in the mirror, adjusted his jacket and tie, and returned to Feng's office.

He removed a piece of paper from his pocket with his gloved hand, walked over to Feng's desk and placed it in front of his chair. He sighed. His work was almost done. The retribution is almost complete. It was such a waste of life but an eye must pay for an eye, a life for a life and many lives for lost love. This way, the culprits would not get away with the murder of his wife using some legal technicality, as this type always did, to protect them from the punishment that they deserved. They knew what they were doing.

It was regrettable about the PA though, Shallum thought. She had to go as she could have identified him. Did that make Shallum no better than the people he had exacted his revenge upon? He wondered if she had a husband who would grieve like Shallum had, who would want retribution himself for the love he had lost. He would rest content when he had completed his task.

SHALLUM THRASHED ABOUT FOR AIR. He was in a sea of blood, covered with floating bones. His misery was beyond forbearance. What drove him to such malice and barbarism? He could no longer say. He could no longer distinguish between fact and fantasy in his mind, in his soul, if he had a soul any longer. He wondered if he had given it to the devil through some warped barter for the retribution of Cajsa's death.

Human excrement and offal covered the bone. Intestines threatened to entangle him as a criminal in chains. The stench was unbearable. He was not sure if the stench emanated from the offal or from him. He screamed for escape.

Corpses assembled from the bones, lamenting their demise, drops of blood dripping from their eye sockets like tears. They raised their arms in unison, demanding release from their prison, beseeching a deity that was not there. Where was the justice the entropy of creation promised? Where was the mercy that the universal deity assured? They had done no wrong. They had committed no evil deserving of this purgatory. Babies rose from the sea, screaming for their mothers who could no longer love or cherish them.

Shallum was sinking in sorrow. Where was the release he was expecting with the removal of the culprits behind his wife's death? Where was the satisfaction of justice? His misery and despair was just increasing with each step he took. He was slowly drowning, drowning in a sea of hate. There was no land of love and peace on the horizon, only more bones, more human excrement of misery and more blood of guilt.

A red scorpion approached as he thrashed in his torment. It looked at him quizzically and then quickly turned and scampered off. Shallum knew then how to escape Devil's Island.

23

XI BOÖTIS

lex was sleeping soundly when his buzzing comm woke him. He opened his bleary eyes at 1:40 in the morning on Eta Cassiopei and looked to see who was calling him. It was the Commissioner. Alex tensed and his stomach became queasy. He was sure whatever the Commissioner had to say would not be good for him. He placed the comm on audio. "Hello Commissioner. You're making an awful habit of calling me in the middle of the night."

"Not my choice, I'm afraid."

Alex rubbed his eyes clear of sleep and yawned. "What's up?"

"There's been another murder, unfortunately. This time it's on Xi Boötis. A Confederation Representative again."

"That's a very hazardous occupation at the moment."

"It would seem. This time there was someone else too. His PA. You need to get there immediately. I suggest you charter a private space yacht, something with some speed."

"Where am I going to get something like that at this time of night?"

"Just ask around at the local spaceport. There's always someone eager to make a quick buck. The local office might know of someone."

"OK. Anything else?"

"Just solve this. It's making me lose more hairs and I can't afford to lose too many more."

Alex chuckled. "No, I suppose not. So you suspect it's the same perpetrator too?"

"Bloody big coincidence if it's not."

"Yeah. It would be."

"Well, just solve it."

This will impress Nascha. She had a few drinks last night. I wonder how hard it'll be to wake her up. Alex found Nascha's contact number on his comm. It took some time for her to answer, as Alex expected.

"Hello..." Nascha croaked.

"It's Alex."

"Ohh... What do you want?"

"You need to get up."

"Nooo..."

"Yes, we need to get a ship to Xi Boötis. There's been another murder."

"Nooo... you go. Leave me here."

"Can't do that," Alex said with obvious enjoyment.

"Ohh... please."

"See you in half an hour."

"Bastard..." Nascha disconnected.

Alex sniggered. *I'm not looking forward to seeing what she looks like.* He needed to find out about chartering a yacht and called the station.

"Precinct 1432C. How may I help you?" the contact operator answered.

"Hello. This is Chief Inspector Detective Alex Warner of the GIA. I need to charter a yacht to take me to Xi Boötis. Can you suggest how I could get hold of one at this time of night?"

The operator was silent for a moment. "A bit out of my league, sir. I'll put you through to someone who might help. He's on tonight and he seems to be able to get hold of anything else when he needs to."

"OK. Thanks."

The operator transferred the call.

"Devi."

"Hello. Chief Inspector Detective Alex Warner from the GIA."

"Ah, yes. Mahendra told me about you. Shouldn't you be sleeping?"

"I wish. I need to charter a yacht to Xi Boötis. Apparently the operator thinks you might help."

"Hmm. That's a tough one at this hour. Not impossible, though. I know some people down at the port. I'll see what I can arrange. Is it just to Xi Boötis or do you think you'll need it longer?"

"The way this case is going, who knows? Let's say a week with the option to extend the charter longer."

"That's actually better. More likely someone will be interested. Cost limit?"

"No. I have an open credit chip on this one. It needs to be fast."

"OK. Give me 15 minutes and I'll call you back, hopefully with a chartered yacht."

Right on time, he called back. "Hello again. Devi here. You have good luck. I have secured a yacht for you. It usually ferries clients to Delta Pavonis, but he's quiet at the moment and is looking for some work. He'll be ready to leave the spaceport when you arrive. His yacht is in bay C21D and the captain's name is Jacques."

"Good."

"He's not cheap, but he's one of the best in the business."

Alex headed for Nascha's room on the floor below. He chimed on her door comm and waited. He chimed again.

Eventually the door opened to a hideous sight. Nascha looked like she hadn't slept for days. She looked miserable. Her face looked drawn and white, and she only just had her eyes open. Her aureola had a grayish hue. Alex struggled to contain his smile. "Ready?"

"No, and shut up before you say anything or I'll kill you when I get the energy. Come in."

Alex walked past Nascha as she held the door open, but was then almost knocked over by her as she rushed to the bathroom, just making it to the toilet bowl where he heard her retch. He looked her way with understanding pity and decided not to say anything as he placed his bag on her bed and sat down to wait. The vomiting eventually stopped, and he heard the toilet flush.

Nascha appeared in the bathroom doorway, leaning against the doorpost. "Sorry."

"It's OK. I've been there. I know how you're feeling at the moment. You'll be able to sleep it off in the yacht I've chartered."

"Yacht?"

"Yeah, the boss wants us to get there fast. We'd have to wait till mid morning to get the first commercial flight and it would take at least two or three days I think."

"Oh. Do I have time to shower?"

"If you do it now."

Alex heard the water from the shower. He looked around the room. *She isn't very tidy,* he thought, as he saw her clothing scattered all over the place. *It's quite a mess for one night.* He yawned, feeling the early rise catching up with him.

The shower turned off and Nascha appeared with a towel wrapped around her. "Sorry, forgot my clothes." She gripped the towel as she passed Alex and retreated to the bathroom, emerging 10 minutes later looking slightly better. She had put on makeup and tidied her hair. Her eyes were still bloodshot as a red-veined leaf.

"Feeling better?"

"No." Nascha said annoyed as she quickly picked up her clothes and stashed them into her bag along with her toiletry and makeup bags. She had to stop twice to regain her breath. Alex presumed she had to wait for a wave of nausea to subside. She eventually had everything packed. "Ready."

The spaceport was unsurprisingly quiet. Alex didn't need to dodge bodies to get to his boarding gate this time. Nascha struggled behind as best she could. Alex spotted a man leaning up against the wall wearing what looked like a captain's jacket. The rest of his clothes didn't match the uniform. Alex walked up to him. "Hi. I'm Alex Warner. Are you Jacques?"

"Yeah. Been waiting for you." Jacques looked towards Nascha, "What's wrong with her?"

"She had a late night."

"Oh. She makes a mess and it'll be extra."

"Yeah, OK. You got some paperwork?"

Jacques pulled out his data plate with the chartering contract and handed it to Alex. His eyebrows shot up when he saw the price. He looked up at Jacques. "Quite the price."

"You want to get there fast or not?"

Alex went back to reading the contract. The Commissioner will have a fit, Alex thought amusedly. Everything else was in order, so Alex signed the contract and transferred the money.

Jacques checked the money transfer. "Come this way," he said as he walked away deeper into the spaceport and to his yacht, giving Nascha a look of indifference.

"Remember what Jacques said about making a mess. You do and it comes out of your pay," Alex said.

Nascha poked her tongue out at Alex.

"Friendly girl," Jacques commented.

"She'll be OK once she's slept it off."

Nascha staggered to the nearest sleeping compartment and closed the door.

Jacques left and went to the flight command cabin and took off for Xi Boötis.

After settling in and finding a snack, Alex placed a hyperlink call to headquarters.

"Hi Ruth. How are things on Earth?"

"Just routine. Nothing special happening. Can't wait till you get back though. Getting sick of doing your work for you."

"Wash your mouth out."

Ruth smirked. "I have something for you, though."

"Really?"

"Yeah, looks like your scraps of paper with their mysterious markings are turning up elsewhere."

"Really? Where?"

"Three other Confederation Representatives have died in the last few months. The locals put it down to misadventure at the time, but we dug deeper and found some interesting similarities, along with another body."

"Enlighten me."

"Nguyen from Proxima Aquarii. He died three months ago in a boating accident. But... when the police investigated, they found a piece of paper on his boat. It read Pi Scorpius. A month later, Owen Renshaw from Draconis died from alcohol poisoning. Again, they found a scrap of paper, this time the marking read Mu Scorpius. Five weeks later, Koanang from Lalande fell off a cliff. They found his symbol where he fell: Lambda Scorpius. Then we have Tse and then Samir. They were Eta and Delta. There is a pattern here. It's a count-down of the ancient Greek alphabet."

Alex's heart raced. They finally had a proper working theory and a link between the murders. "That would show a firm connection between all the deaths. Why else would we find the notes at the death scenes?"

"Yes, that's what I thought. I would have told you earlier, but I needed confirmation."

"Why has this only come to light now?"

"The local authorities all thought the incidents were isolated, so the investigation never went any further."

"Excellent detective work, Ruth. We don't want to be chasing down black holes when the actual evidence is in a different direction all together. What's the bet we'll find another piece of paper with symbols when we inspect the murder scene on Xi Boötis?"

"Well, the killer is running out of letters. The next one will have to be Beta or Alpha, unless the perp breaks the pattern."

"Hmm. OK. Thanks for letting me know the options."

"Well, that's all I have for you at the moment."

"I thought you said there was another suspicious death."

"Oh. Yes, thanks for reminding me. About six months ago the PA to Malo Metam died. They put the cause of death down to suicide."

"So. What makes that suspicious?"

"For a start, they didn't conduct an autopsy, even when her husband requested it."

"What was the cause of death?"

"She allegedly overdosed on sleeping medication. She also left a note apologizing to her husband."

"And...?"

"Why didn't anyone confirm the medication that they found with her was what killed her? They wrapped up the case quickly, apparently at the request of Malo himself. I was told the husband has been in denial ever since."

"Hmm... that is suspicious. Malo keeps getting more interesting the more we find out about this case. What does her husband do?"

"He's Malo's attaché, a Shallum Tsadoq."

"Well! More interesting."

The door to Nascha's cabin opened, and she walked out, still groggy but looking a lot healthier.

"Well, have to go. I have my next problem to deal with," Alex said to Ruth. Nascha's ears pricked, and she turned to see what Alex was doing.

"Who was that?"

"Ruth. Some of us have to work. We all can't sleep off our over-indulgences."

Nascha poke her tongue out again at the gibe Alex made. "I feel much better than before," she said in repentance.

"You look better."

"I'll just go clean up." Nascha went to the bathroom area. She opened the door and her eyes bulged, "Have you seen this?"

Alex rose and walked over to Nascha. He looked into the bathroom and let out a whistle. "Impressive. It ought to be for the preposterous fee the guy's charging me." The fittings in the bathroom were of the obviously highest quality on the market and the sheer space was enormous for a spaceship. It even had a Jacuzzi if one desired the luxury. "Anyway, get cleaned up and we'll talk." Alex said and returned to his seat.

Alex jolted back to wakefulness from nodding off when the bathroom door opened.

"Where can I find some food?" Nascha asked.

"Over there," Alex said as he pointed the general direction of the galley. He stretched and yawned and stood up to stretch his legs before sitting down again. He looked over as Nascha walked toward him with a plate piled full of food and a drink. She sat down on the seat opposite him, placing her food and drink on the table. "Got enough?" he said.

"I'm starved."

"It will replace the stuff that you removed last night."

"When?"

"Don't you remember?"

"Remember what?"

"You were vomiting your guts out in the hotel," Alex said with a playful grin.

"You're lying," Nascha said with puzzled shock.

"I wish I was. You honestly don't remember? You must have had a time of it."

"No, I don't," Nascha replied.

"Oh well. You'll learn eventually."

"I usually don't drink so much."

"First time ex-system on an assignment?"

"Yes."

"That's what got into you. Most people get over enthusiastic on the first trip. I've seen it many times."

"What about you?"

"What about me?"

"What happened on you first assignment?"

Alex tapped his nose, "That's for me to know and you to find out."

Nascha looked annoyed. "Anyway, what did you want to talk about?"

"We have a development in the case. Ruth has uncovered three other murders where a slip of paper left at the scene of the crime had Scorpius symbols scribbled on it."

Nascha's eyebrows rose in surprise as she munched on some food. "Really?"

"Yes, they were all diplomats, all the symbols are letters of the Greek alphabet and the deaths seem to happen in order. The first was Pi..." Alex consulted his notes, "then there was Mu, then Lambda, Tse was Eta and Samir was Delta. What's your bet that this one on Xi Boötis is Beta or Alpha?"

"Very high I think."

"Another thing, Malo Metam's PA allegedly committed suicide six months ago, but they never verified the cause of death, even though the husband demanded an autopsy. The husband is none other than Malo's attaché, Shallum Tsadoq."

"Those two names keep coming up."

"A bit too often for my liking. We need to pay them both a visit when we're finished on Xi Boötis."

"Definitely. Especially if we get to use this again. How long till we get there?"

"Let's see." Alex pulled up the flight information screen. "About two hours. Fastest flight I ever had." Alex looked at Nascha eating. "You're making me hungry." He got up and went to get some food.

ALEX AND NASCHA arrived on Xi Boötis just after three in the afternoon. They quickly collected their belongings and exited the spaceport on the capital planet and hailed a taxi to the local law enforcement headquarters.

Alex and Nascha introduced themselves to the constable on duty when they arrived, who led them to a waiting area and informed his superiors they were there. Half an hour went by before someone came to see them.

A middle-aged man arrived wearing the traditional Xi Boötis law enforcement uniform, deep red trousers and tunic with a navy blue shirt. He had black hair cropped short, presumably to regulation length as far as Alex knew. Alex and Nascha rose as he entered.

"Welcome, I am Chief Inspector Bingwen Chiang. I am sorry to have kept you waiting. It took some time for someone to inform me of your presence and someone of comparable authority needs to greet you. Regulations here. Call me Chiang."

"Hello, I'm Alex Warner from the GIA," Alex said shaking Chiang's hand.

"I'm Nascha from Tau Ceti, an agent for the GIA." Nascha also shook Chiang's hand.

"I understand you are interested in the murder of Xiang Feng two days ago."

"Yes we are," Alex said. "We are investigating some other cases and wish to check if there are any similarities."

"I see."

"Can you give us a rundown on the case or can you direct us to the right person for this?"

"You are in luck. I am investigating the crime. It is the murder of a very prominent public figure."

"As are the incidents we are investigating."

Chiang looked questioningly at the agents.

"It would seem that being a Confederation Representative is a dangerous career choice at the moment. Both Representatives for Tau Ceti and Eta Cassiopei have also been murdered."

Chiang frowned. "Hmm. That is interesting. We always cooperate with the GIA, so how can I help you?"

"As I said, can you give us a rundown on the incident and then maybe we could review the crime scene and any evidence that you have collected so far?"

"That seems reasonable. I can accompany you to the crime scene. We can discuss on the way."

"I would like to see a holographic image of the crime scene if you can arrange that?"

"Indeed." Chiang took out his comm, contacted someone and talked to the person before breaking the contact. "Follow me."

Alex and Nascha followed Chiang to an elevator and into a garage area where they got in an AGrav and headed to the murder scene.

"Now, let's see," Ching said once they were on their way. "Evidence so far shows that one of Feng's staff returned to the building late in the afternoon and found Feng's PA with a maser blast through her head. The staff member went in to Feng's private office and saw him lying face up with a hole in his head. Death would have been instantaneous for both. It would appear the perpetrator surprised them, as there was no sign of a struggle or disturbance. They left the scene clean."

"Have they have found the murder weapon?"

"No."

"You say Feng's staff member found them. Do you know who was the last person to see them alive?"

Nascha sat dutifully silent, understanding Alex's modus operandi of interviewing from Tse's murder.

"There's a note in the PA's diary saying Shallum Tsadoq was meeting Feng around the time of the murder."

"What?" Alex and Nascha looked at each other in surprise. "That name crops up again and again."

"Do you know him?" Chiang asked.

"Only that his name keeps coming up in our investigations. Have you been able to interview him?"

"No. Unfortunately he left the system before we could locate him. He has returned to Procyon, where he comes from, I believe."

"Hmm. We definitely need to speak to him," Alex said. "Looks like we'll be going there after this. Anybody else see Feng?"

"Only someone called Ahiga earlier in the afternoon. He's left too, this time for Tau Ceti."

"This Ahiga wouldn't be Ambassador Tse's son, would he?"

"Yes, he is. How did you know?"

"Lucky guess." Alex looked at Nascha while directing his question to Chiang: "Was anything unusual found at the crime scene?"

"There was a scrap of paper on Feng's desk. It certainly didn't go with the rest of the items there."

"Was anything written on it?"

"Not really. Just some scribble. We bagged it. It's back at the station."

"You don't have an image of the scribble you can show us now?"

"Hmm. Possibly. Give me a minute." Chiang removed his mini data plate from his pocket and spent some time retrieving information from the police hive. "There it is." Chiang gave the data plate to Alex.

"Beta Scorpius," Alex said, as he showed Nascha the image.

"Means something to you then," Chiang said.

"Sure does. Scraps of paper with Greek symbols were left at the other crime scenes we're investigating. This adds to the perpetrator's list of kills."

"Here we are then," Chiang said as they arrived at Feng's office.

Alex and Nascha examined the crime scene, aided by a holographic image taken before they removed the bodies. The PA sat in her seat, slumped back, with her two natural eyes open and one artificial eye that showed the view through the back of her head.

"Clean shot," Alex said to no one. "She would have died instantly."

They walked through to Fengs office and examined his body. Alex saw an identical head wound. He too died instantly. He squatted dow to inspect the carpeted floor surrounding the body but found nothing of interest. He stood again. "You seen enough?" Alex asked Nascha.

"Yes, nothing we didn't already know. The murderer has been very inventive with his different techniques," Nascha replied.

Alex declined Chiang's offer to return to headquarters and physically examine the evidence as they needed to get to Procyon urgently to track down Shallum and Malo. "Can you drop us off at the spaceport?" he asked.

"Certainly. Anything that will help me in my investigation?"

"Nothing for certain. I'll be able to give you a better answer once I talk to Shallum Tsadoq and Malo Metam."

Alex contacted Jacques and told him to prepare the yacht for a voyage to Procyon.

24

CDF HEADQUARTERS

Malo flew to Earth after his meeting with the Scorpius group on Mars and took the day off for a change to recuperate before traveling to the CDF Headquarters to see General Langdon.

CDF Headquarters stood on Europa, a moon of Jupiter. Member states of the Confederation keenly contested its location when it was being established. Earth representatives insisted its location be close to the mother system of the Confederation to protect it permanently, if Earth came under a surprise attack. The other members of the Confederation objected. As usual with political decisions, they found a compromise, and selected Europa. Europa also had plenty of water needed for human consumption and other purposes after purification. They erected an extensive complex on the surface with docking, maintenance and other facilities orbiting the moon. Jupiter was on the opposite side of the sun to Mars, which made a stopover on Earth logical for Malo.

He rose early to board the private yacht he had chartered for the voyage to Europa. He had spent his lay-by day in New York, home of the Confederation Parliament. Supposedly, it replaced an organization called the United Nations, but that was hearsay.

Malo arrived at the military spaceport orbiting Europa mid afternoon and boarded a shuttle that took him down to the moon and the CDF Headquarters. He was alone in the shuttle for the 30-minute trip and could see the moon through the window, growing larger and moving as they approached on a spiral path. It was too close to see the whole moon from the orbit of the spaceport. He saw the moon's smooth sheen reflecting the sunlight when they traversed the side facing the sun, together with the familiar crisscross lines from the cracks that had split the surface over millions of years. The CDF base appeared and enlarged as they approached one of the landing bays. The shuttle finally landed with a slight jolt as it touched the surface. Several minutes later the hatch opened and a CDF assistant entered to escort Malo to General Langdon.

Just after the agreed 4:00 start time, General Langdon arrived. "Good afternoon Malo. I trust you had a pleasant voyage," he said.

"Good afternoon General. Yes, I did, thank you."

"Good. We have a secure room so you can say anything you want in here. There are refreshments and snacks over on the side table, if you're hungry."

Malo patted his stomach. "I had enough on the way here, I think."

The General chuckled. "Well, let's get our plans finalized, shall we?"

"Yes." Malo said as he considered the most urgent issue. "So, what are your plans to immobilize the security stations in the Cetusian-loving systems?"

"The crews consider it a military exercise and not the actual thing. Only the senior officer in each location knows otherwise. We will locate the fleets just outside the system surveillance limits, waiting for the message to proceed with the operation. When we give the signal, the destroyers will move in, jamming any signals as they go. Shuttles of spacer squadrons will secure the stations and lock them down."

"How long will that take?"

"It will be different for each system. The distances are different. However, it won't affect the integrity of the operation as, once the attack starts, no-one outside that system will know. We will have all their communications blocked. The longest part of the operation should take about three hours. Sometimes two."

"Are you expecting resistance?"

"Not in the first phase. It will take them that long to work out what's happening. Maybe later on, depending on how effectively and quickly we put the military juntas in place."

"So, what's next?"

"While the destroyers are disabling the security stations, the attack carriers will move in on the populated planets in stealth mode. They will block planet-based defense system, thanks to the codes you acquired."

"Let's hope they work. They cost us a lot."

"Yes, let's hope. Things could get messy otherwise. The attack craft will lock down the spaceports, media outlets and planetary military headquarters. Senior operatives will fly to the government buildings, place the government in confinement and take over the reins of power, declaring military rule!"

"Once they make that declaration, our agents on the ground who have been stirring up the riots will end the violence, giving the impression that the coup has saved the day," Malo smirked.

"How will our forces know when this has occurred, Malo?"

"Your senior personnel will receive a coded message. If there is any further violence or disruption, your personnel will be obliged to deal with it accordingly."

"Good."

"What contingencies do you have in place?"

"There will be some roaming squadrons on alert."

"What about the Cetusians in the fleets?"

"There aren't many of them. I filtered out as many as I could without arousing suspicion and there aren't any in senior positions. The ones left have to take their orders or suffer the consequences at their court marshal hearing."

"Good."

General Langdon moved uncomfortably in his chair, wary of

what he was about to say. "This is a big operation, Malo. I think I have it covered militarily, but how will this go down politically? I mean, you're ruffling a lot of feathers here, some powerful and important people, particularly in trading circles."

Malo studied the General, wondering if he was getting cold feet, but saw conviction on his face. "That's why this operation has taken so long. That's why I've been putting forward bill after bill in the parliament for the last two years and creating political divide over the issue. You know the saying, 'Say something often enough and people will start believing it.' Well, that's what I've been doing. The approval by the Policy Review Committee for CDF forces to move in if the violence gets out of hand is really the trigger for us to proceed to this next step. Without that we would have been on very shaky ground. The policy will go through the parliament in the next few days without too much fuss. I intend to go back to Earth and make sure they pass the recommendation in the senate. I'll start the operation once I get back to Procyon."

"Yes, but we all know your accomplices primarily make up the committee. Tahona stormed out from what I hear. That won't help either."

"It won't make any difference. It's still a parliamentary committee. Everybody knows how temperamental Tahona is."

General Langdon looked warily at Malo, studying him. He sighed. "I guess you're right. Nerves before an operation, I always get them even with my experience."

"It's OK to be questioning things. That's how you stumble on overlooked issues and potentially jeopardize the entire operation sometimes. I've questioned myself many times." Malo chuckled, "I'm getting nervous too. I put it down to excitement and seeing the plan come to fruition."

General Langdon smiled in recognition, "Yeah. I suppose you're right."

"So, on that note, can you see any shortcomings from your end? I'm not sure you know how much I've relied on you to question the strategy."

General Langdon studied his notes for a few seconds. He looked up at Malo, studying his face, then gave another sigh. "No, what we have developed is an excellent strategy from my perspective. It's been a long chess game. Let the end game begin and move our pieces in for the checkmate."

Malo regarded the general with appreciation, "Yes, let's."

General Langdon looked at his chronometer. It was 5:30. "I've got a few things to complete before I leave today. You OK for dinner at seven?"

"Sure. I have plenty to amuse me with my parliamentary activities to fill in the time."

"You can stay here or I can get a corporal to show you to a more comfortable residential accommodation with open hive access and other business facilities."

"I would appreciate that."

25

THE RECOMMENDATION BEFORE PARLIAMENT

M alo left CDF Headquarters the following day and returned to Earth. Finding out that the recommendation for CDF support of Cetusian systems was being presented to the parliament the next day, he contacted the Representatives he knew he could count on one last time, to make sure he had the numbers.

He arrived at the parliament concourse between sittings. His recommendation was next. The parliament was a vast amphitheater for the various Representatives and their retinue of secretaries and attaches. The President of the parliament sat in the middle on an elevated platform with his many staff. Malo went to the designated area for Procyon and waited for the vote.

Others started filing in after the recess, and the chamber was almost full. The recommendation *must interest all of them*, Malo thought. He wondered how heated the debate would get before they called a vote. Representatives were milling around, having last-minute discussions before the President's arrival.

A loud rap sounded and the Page of the chamber announced, "The Parliament of the Confederation of Galactic States is now in session."

The President sat, as did the Representatives. The President reviewed his notes on his data plate. He said, "The Policy Review Committee on Civil Unrest has proposed a policy for the Confederation to consider. The proposal reads thus, 'That the Confederation approve the utilization of the Confederation Defense Force with excessive civil unrest on Cetusian worlds, at the request of the governments of these worlds, to restore law and order.'"

Sections of the parliament erupted into uproar.

"Order, order," the President shouted, as he tried to restore civility to the chamber.

The shouting eventually subsided.

The President turned to Malo. "I ask the Chairperson of the committee, the member for Procyon, to provide the reasoning behind the recommendation and any other details relevant to the parliament."

Malo stood. "Certainly, Mr. President. Mr. President, as this assembly is aware the review committee has deliberated the unsettling situations that appear to be spontaneously erupting on the Cetusian member systems of the Confederation..."

"Liar," someone shouted.

"... The situation would appear to be escalating to the stage where the local security forces are... struggling... to maintain civil control of the populace. The latest report to the committee, only a few days ago, provided disturbing revelations of even further disturbances..."

"That is an outright lie."

"Order, order... proceed Member for Procyon."

"... Mr. President. After reviewing the options available to the Confederation, the committee concluded that extra support from the CDF when requested by the member system governments is warranted. Using such a powerful force should be as a last resort and not requested lightly. However Mr. President, the disturbing news brought before the committee has led to the bill being placed before the assembly today so there is no political impediment to the instigation of such action should the need arise. Thus the motion before the parliament." Malo sat.

Tahona rose to his feet and shouted, "That is an outright lie, Mr. President. The supposed unrest is a figment of Malo's and the committee's imagination…"

"Order, order, Member for Chiron or you shall force me to remove you from the chamber."

Tahona opted for a more official protest and pressed the red button on his desk, formalizing his request to speak.

As no one else had pressed theirs, the President said, "Member for Chiron, you may have the floor."

Tahona stood up and spoke calmly, "Mr. President, as the members of this parliament are aware, I am also a member of the CDF committee, chaired by the Member for Procyon. I am fully aware of the reports that the member for Procyon is quoting and can assure the parliament that intelligence have fabricated or altered them to mislead…"

Chaos broke out in the chamber as accusations and counter-accusations flew from member to member.

"Order, order," the President shouted, pounding his gavel. The clamor reverberated throughout the chamber until the assembly calmed again. "Order, please. We must have order." The chamber quieted again. "Please continue, Member for Chiron."

"Thank you, Mr. President. Mr. President, as I was saying, they intentionally fabricated or altered the information so that the committee could recommend only one course of action, that being the proposed bill before us today. My concern is that it gives too much power to the CDF to instigate action as it sees fit, at its own discretion, without due diligence and discussion between the CDF and the local system government. I therefore must forcefully oppose the recommendation before this parliament and suggest its withdrawal for further development, Mr. President."

Malo had pressed his 'Request To Speak' button halfway through Tahona's speech and waited for the President to address him.

"Member for Procyon, you may have the floor."

Malo rose. "Mr. President, as to the allegations and accusations that the Member for Chiron has brought before this parliament, let me advise the parliament, Mr. President, that they are false and unhelpful for resolving this recommendation. First, may I point out, Mr. President, that the Member for Chiron walked out of the committee meeting while the issues leading up to the recommendation were being discussed. Mr. President, how can the Member for Chiron credibly suggest that the recommendation is unwarranted when he wasn't there?"

"Hear, hear," came from a sizeable group of the assembly.

"Second, Mr. President, I cannot understand how the Member for Chiron can have better information on the state of civil unrest in all the affected systems than the personnel whose job it is to formulate such reports for the committee, Mr. President. He must be a very busy man, whisking from one system to the next to gauge such matters."

Laughter circulated through the chamber, angering Tahona.

"May I suggest, Mr. President, that the crux of the matter is that the state of affairs in the affected systems, of which the planet Chiron is one, is worse than the Member of Chiron wishes to admit. Therefore, we cannot take his objection seriously, Mr. President. Let the Member for Chiron bury his head in the sand, but the members of this Confederation owe it to our citizens to pass this recommendation and make the Confederation a safer place. Let us vote in the affirmative for this recommendation."

Malo received widespread applause.

Claims and counter-claims swept across the chamber for over three hours before the President decided it was time to bring the matter to a vote.

"Members of the Parliament of the Confederation, on the matter of the recommendation that the Confederation approve the utilization of the Confederation Defense Force with excessive civil unrest on Cetusian worlds, at the request of the governments of these worlds, to restore law and order., the result of the vote is 27 affirmative and 19 negative. The recommendation is passed."

People came over to congratulate Malo for his outstanding performance, which Malo accepted graciously. He sighed in relief and slightly surprised at the magnitude of the win. The debate must have swayed some members. He could now get down to the actual work. He organized a flight back to Procyon, awaiting the call from General Langdon.

26

ESCAPE

Ahiga rushed back to his father's apartment on Caerus. He was eager to see what was on the chip Feng had given him but knew the spacecraft wasn't the right forum. He had seen how nervous Feng was when he gave it to him. It was eleven in the morning when he arrived.

Three files were on the data chip: Malo's Plan, Tse's Plan, and finally Tsadoq. Ahiga's heart leaped into his throat. Maybe this was the evidence he was looking for so he could finally confront Malo for answers. He had his suspicions about the Tsadoq file but looked at Malo's first.

The security alarm sounded and Ahiga jumped up. Several heavily armed men were creeping towards the apartment. Ahiga panicked, but took a few deep breaths and remembered that the doors were dead-code lockable. He hoped that would delay them.

Ahiga quickly went back to the study desk and collected the data plate and chip. He also retrieved the other chips he had hidden previously. He then rushed to a secure safe room built by his father especially for situations like this. His father had shown him the concealed entrance and how to get in. It opened just as the intruders started destroying the entrance of the apartment. He quickly entered the room and closed the door behind him. Ahiga's heart pounded, and he perspired.

A secure elevator accessed the parking area, but Ahiga wasn't sure whether he should use it in case people were waiting for him on the floor below. He could hear shouting and footfalls as the militia breached the apartment and stormed in, searching each of the rooms. Things suddenly went quiet. They must have realized the apartment was empty.

He needed a plan. Ahiga assumed they knew he had been in the apartment so they would either start searching the building or searching the apartment for a hidden refuge. The room had reinforced walls, but they could break anything with enough force. He paced the floor, desperate for a plan and wishing he had the maser pistol from the safe deposit box. He suddenly remembered his father had another safe in the panic room, inside a display cabinet. It had a biometric lock similar to the one at the house. Ahiga hoped his father had given him access. The safe clicked open and Ahiga's spirits lifted as he sighted a maser pistol. He adjusted the settings as trained long ago. He placed it behind the belt line of his pants in the small of his back. *Just like in the holo-movies,* he thought with dry amusement.

He heard banging on the safety room door. They had found the opening. He had no option now but to take the elevator. He descended to the basement parking garage. Waiting inside the compartment as the elevator doors opened, Ahiga hugged the wall, frantic, listening for any sound. Keeping his hand on the maser, he lunged forward, hoping to surprise anyone outside. He realized that he'd look foolish if anyone was watching and the coast was clear, but he wanted to give himself a chance of getting away. His heart was pounding a thousand beats a minute as the adrenalin coursed through his blood.

Ahiga lunged, rolling over on his back as he rotated to face the elevator. No one was there. He exhaled deeply, grateful for the reprieve, as he stood up and scanned the parking station for intruders. He couldn't see anyone. He went to his father's AGrav and programmed it for a two-hour return flight at maximum speed by manipulating some settings and adding a five-minute time delay. He slinked out of the AGrav and waited in a secluded spot of the park for the program to kick in. He hoped the accelerated launch would attract the attention of his pursuers so he could return to the apartment and retrieve his things.

The AGrav sped out of the park. Seconds later Ahiga heard shouts from the entrance as the sentries at the doorway watched it disappear, thinking they had failed to prevent his departure. There were further shouts and relayed messages from the members in the apartment. Five minutes later three of the paratroopers emerged from his father's building and jumped into their AGrav, pushing the throttle full forward in pursuit of an empty capsule.

Ahiga waited to make sure it was safe. He crept towards the elevator and, once inside, he removed his maser from his belt and pointed it towards the doors.

When they opened, a menacing intruder was turning at the noise as fast as his reactions would allow with practiced military ease. Their eyes met momentarily, the intruder's glowing black with malice. With fear in his eyes, Ahiga adjusted the maser and fired before the attacker could bring his weapon into position. Surprise registered on the intruder's face as he collapsed on the floor, jerking from the effects of the stun gun. Ahiga had adjusted the controls to a powerful setting.

Ahiga stood where he was, stunned as much by his audacity as his luck. He couldn't move, couldn't decide what to do next. He finally came out of his trance as he realized he had to get moving before the others returned. He went to the bedroom drawers and took three belts out of the third drawer. Returning to his victim, he strapped the man's ankles together with one belt, rolled the man onto his stomach and strapped his wrists behind him with the second belt and looped the third belt through the other two and tightened it so the man's feet and hands were almost touching.

His assailant secured, Ahiga went into the bedroom and packed his bag. He called a taxi and went downstairs to the front of the building where the taxi was waiting. He directed it to the Ceti Interspacial Hotel, the most luxurious in the system, where he checked into the penthouse.

Ahiga got a beer from the bar and looked out at the surrounding mountains cradling the capital in their lap, like a mother cradling her precious child. *How had those men, kidnappers probably, known where he was?* Ahiga concluded they must have known he was on the arriving flight and followed him back to the apartment. He had to be more careful. He was fairly certain nobody had followed him to the hotel. Taking his comm from his pocket, he called the police to report the break-in at the apartment, pretending to be a neighbor without identifying himself. He sipped on his beer, thinking about what to do next, realizing he needed somewhere no one could reach and the hotel wasn't a viable long-term option.

Ahiga was certain that Malo was the key to his father's murder. He also knew the chip Feng had given him held some vital information that pieced together the whole puzzle he had swirling around in his mind. Reviewing his options, he decided to go to Procyon to meet Malo. If he chartered a private yacht, he would have the privacy to view the chip. *I should make a copy and put the original back in the safe deposit box at the bank.*

His father regularly used a charter company for his travels. Ahiga rummaged through some old message files his father had sent him to find the company's contact details. After some discussion and negotiation on price, Ahiga booked the yacht to leave at 8:00 in the morning. The captain, Ferris, would meet him in the immigration hall at the spaceport.

Ahiga put the copy of the chip in his room safe and deposited the original in his pocket. It was now 4:00 in the afternoon. He could get to the bank before it closed, if he hurried. He dashed the couple of blocks from the hotel and made it in time to secure the valuable package in the vault. It was almost 6:00 by the time he returned to the hotel.

Ahiga considered the hotel's dining options and decided to try the rooftop bar and restaurant where he could stay off the streets for the evening. As he changed into one his new trendy suit, he realized he still had the maser tucked in his pants! How had the bank not detected that?

He entered the bar just after seven that evening. There were few people there. *It's probably early.* He sat on a stool at the bar and grabbed the barman's attention.

"What can I get you, sir?" the barman asked.

"A beer thanks and drop the sir please," Ahiga said.

The barman warmed to the informal tone and introduced himself as he topped off the beer. "There you go. I'm Klah."

Ahiga smiled. "Pleased to meet you, Klah, I'm Ahiga."

Klah's eyes opened wide. "I thought I recognized you. You're the son of the murdered Ambassador, aren't you?"

Ahiga nodded. "Yes, I am."

"Sorry about your father."

"Thanks."

"What brings you here? Do you have a house here or are you just dining tonight?"

"Yes, I have residences, especially now but, to be brief, I prefer not to be in any of them tonight. I would also prefer it if you didn't advertise to anyone that I'm here. I'm trying to keep a low profile at the moment."

"No problem. You're the customer."

Someone at the other end of the bar was trying to attract Klah's attention. "You have a customer over there," Ahiga said, pointing with his chin.

"Oh. OK," Klah said. "Hope you have a pleasant evening."

"Thanks."

Ahiga felt hungry but didn't fancy the look of the nearby restaurant. He grabbed Klah's attention, "Do you serve meals in the bar?"

"I'll grab a menu for you." Klah walked away to the other end where the stacked menus lay, took one and came back. "There you go."

"Thanks." Ahiga read through the menu, made his selection and ordered. He also ordered a bottle of wine. Klah delivered the wine and glass and served the wine professionally. The meal came promptly, and he ate it, intermittently sipping at his wine. A waiter took the empty plate away.

Ahiga looked around. Lounges were scattered throughout. He grabbed the bottle of wine and his glass and moved over to one that looked comfortable and had a view of the surrounding panorama. A holo screen was showing the evening's entertainment line-up.

It approached nine, and the bar started filling up with people. Ahiga relaxed, enjoying the flavor of the wine. He noticed two women about 10 metres away in animated discussion and they occasionally looked his way. One was nudging the other with her elbow, trying to encourage her in Ahiga's direction. The other was unwilling. She seemed embarrassed and shy. Ahiga smiled in bemusement at the comedy playing out before him. He could see that she was nervous by the greenish red color of her aureola. He was fairly sure they wanted to come over, but one was reluctant, avoiding the other's coaxing. Eventually the harassed one shoved the other's elbows away, took a deep breath of determined resolve, and started walking towards him. The other followed. They were both dressed well, in Ahiga's opinion, the harassed one with a seductive touch while the other was much more conservative in her taste.

They finally arrived in front of him.

"H... H... Hi," the harassed one finally got out. Ahiga could sense the embarrassment in her, as her aureola flushed a slight green, and felt sorry for her.

"Oh. Don't be silly," the other one said, fed up with the other's inability to converse normally. She turned to Ahiga, "Hi. I'm Chooli and this is Mai. Do you mind if we keep you company for the show tonight?"

Ahiga laughed. "You two are hilarious. I was watching you over there. A very entertaining interchange, but I embarrass you. I'm sorry. I'm Ahiga. Good to meet you, Chooli and Mai. It would be a pleasure to have some company. Is there a show here tonight?"

Chooli gestured for Mai to reply. "It's all right for you," Mai grumbled to Chooli. "You've already got someone wherever he is at the moment." She turned to Ahiga, "Y... yes there is. The Cretan Novas are playing tonight."

"Really? I like them," Ahiga said. A sly expression came on his face. "I take it you are the one being encouraged to get better acquainted with me?" he asked.

Mai turned bright red and her aureola deep green. "Yes," she mumbled.

"Not to worry. Grab a seat and we can talk while we wait. You like champagne?"

They both nodded. Ahiga's seat had room for two so he moved over a little and Mai sat next to him stiffly, unnerved by the closeness. Chooli found a single lounge chair and moved it into position so she could chat and still watch the show.

Ahiga ordered an expensive bottle of champagne and toasted his new companions as they raised their glasses: "To becoming friends."

"Friends," Chooli said, raising her glass and sipping.

"Friends," Mai whispered, a sparkle in her eyes.

Ahiga gasped in astonishment at Mai's eyes. He'd never seen ones so beautiful. He was nervous with embarrassment himself now, but said what was on his mind anyway. "To beautiful women." He returned Mai's gaze.

Mai looked down, delighted with the compliment.

Chooli watched Mai with a cheerful expression, but also a little bemusement as she witnessed the interplay before her. "Shall I leave?" she asked.

"No," Mai almost shouted, tearing her eyes away from Ahiga and giving Chooli a chastising look.

"Please don't," Ahiga agreed. "Looks like she needs you."

Mai gave him a nudge. "No, I don't."

Ahiga laughed, Chooli laughed, and eventually Mai laughed too.

Ahiga and Chooli took a sip of their drinks. Mai took a large gulp to calm her nerves.

Mai asked Ahiga, "What do you do?"

Ahiga replied, "I used to be a maintenance engineer on the ship maintenance platforms orbiting the planet but now I'm an idle trillionaire." Ahiga sobered as he finished the sentence, deep sorrow lining his face.

Both Chooli and Mai's eyes opened wide at the mention of his wealth.

"You look sad," Mai said as she saw his pain.

"My father died recently."

"Oh. I'm sorry."

"Thanks. What did you mean before when you said to Chooli that it was all right for her, she had someone?"

"She met someone recently. In this bar actually, but he's away somewhere solving a case."

"Is he a police officer?"

"He's from the GIA."

Ahiga sat silent for a moment, processing the information. "He wouldn't be Chief Inspector Detective Alex Warner by any chance?"

Chooli's eyes widened in amazement, "Yes he is. How do you know him?"

Ahiga laughed out loud at the irony of the situation. "He interviewed me as part of his investigations into my father's murder."

"You're Ambassador Tse's son?" Both of them blurted out a little too loudly.

"Yes, I am and could you please keep your voices down. I don't want it getting around that I'm here," Ahiga rebuked.

"Sorry," Mai replied.

"So where is he now?" Ahiga asked Chooli.

Chooli was not sure if she should say, but decided it would not hurt the investigation Alex was conducting. "He went to Eta Cassiopei to look at a similar murder. He said he wouldn't be long and would be back soon," she said doubtfully.

"Oh."

"So why are you here?" Mai asked, trying to regain Ahiga's attention.

"Long story. I don't really want to talk about it at the moment."

"Sorry," Mai said, disappointed that she seemed to say the wrong things all the time.

"Don't be. What brings you here then?"

"We go to the university. We room together and come here every so often to see if we can get someone to buy us a drink," Mai admitted, a little abashed.

"I'm sure you're very successful," Ahiga acknowledged.

"Mostly," Mai giggled. "We haven't been coming so often since Alex left. Chooli doesn't want to get into any compromising situations. We came to watch the band tonight, really. When we saw you, I couldn't keep my eyes off you," Mai confessed. "Chooli had to push me to come over, though."

"I noticed."

They all laughed.

Ahiga was relaxing, and he saw that Mai was, too. She seemed fun and didn't behave any differently knowing who he was and how rich he was. Ahiga said, "Well, if it's any consolation, I wouldn't have had the nerve to do what you did."

"You're kidding!" Mai exclaimed.

"No. I'm very shy."

Mai giggled and looked at Chooli, who gave a barely perceptible nod of approval.

The band came on and Mai slid slightly closer to Ahiga, which he noticed. He moved towards her in approval. He saw how contented and happy she looked as she leaned against him and felt her comforting warmth. He didn't know what it was, but there was something different about her he hadn't experienced with any other woman. They both sat back in the lounge, relaxing against each other.

Chooli watched the band, enjoying the music. Ahiga saw a man walk up to her, whispering in her ear. Her eyes turned to fiery darts at him, her aureola black with rage, and she slapped him hard. He staggered back and retreated. She looked around at Ahiga and Mai, pretending to poke her finger down her throat and then settled down to watch the band again.

They all enjoyed the rest of the night together. Ahiga knew he should have gone to bed long ago, but he couldn't bear to leave Mai.

The band finished playing, and people started packing up and leaving. Mai had snuggled up close to Ahiga, not wanting the night to end.

"We need to go," Chooli said.

"I need to go to bed too," Ahiga said.

Mai looked into Ahiga's eyes but saw no invitation for the rest of the night. "Will I see you again?"

"I'll be away for a while. I'm leaving tomorrow morning." Ahiga was conflicted but realized there was something special about Mai and he wanted to see her again. "Give me your contact details and I'll call you when I get back."

"Really?" Mai said, a beaming smile appearing. She quickly got out her comm and relayed her details across to him.

Ahiga smiled in return. He shook Chooli's hand but gave Mai a long hug.

He watched the two leave, talking animatedly as they went, and went to bed.

AHIGA WOKE EARLY, packed his bags and went to the spaceport. He found Ferris. They boarded his yacht and set off for Procyon.

Ahiga sat for some time thinking about Mai. He wondered what chance of fate had brought her into his life when he was having such a terrible time everywhere else at present. He smiled to himself. She was so shy at first but was full of bubbles, bursting with enthusiasm and excitement once she became comfortable with him. He supposed she wanted to make a good first impression. What surprised him was that it didn't seem to make a difference that he was one of the wealthiest people in the system. Money was of secondary importance to this person. He liked that. He would definitely contact her.

Ahiga roused himself from his daydreams and started to examine Feng's files. Ferris had assured him he could remain completely isolated from the hyper-hive aboard the yacht. He opened the file called Malo's Plan.

Ahiga read slowly and carefully. From his understanding, the protest and civil unrest on the planet was being instigated by Malo's agents. *That's why there are so many protests,* Ahiga thought. He wondered if these agents were also after him. Malo's next step was to have the CDF stationed on standby in each Cetusian system. At his signal, the agents would initiate demonstrations and riots on the system planets, which would trigger the need for CDF intervention and martial law, control of all the Cetusian worlds being transferred to human political governance. Ahiga's jaws clenched at the thought of Malo's treachery. *Why would he want that?* Ahiga wondered. *Why is his hatred so intense?* He wondered why Feng himself had not used the information to stop Malo. Maybe the reason was on the other files on the chip. He opened the one titled Tse's Plan. He started reading.

There were two lists of names in the file. One list contained confederates who his father had been working with. Feng was one name on that list. Ahiga was shocked to realise that all the other people on the list were now dead. That would mean Feng was in mortal danger. *Feng must know that,* Ahiga thought. The other list contained names of people on each Cetusian world.

As he read on, he felt proud of his father as he came to understand his plan. Ahiga also felt sorry for his father as he had to participate in some distasteful activities. His father would tell each world, in secret, of Malo's plans. The second list contained his father's agents in each of the systems as the interface between Tse and the security forces. The local security was to reinforce the system security stations to defend them from the CDF. Once his father knew that the takeover was imminent, he would signal the agents to arrest Malo's agents, preventing any possible riots. His father would then send evidence of the treachery to the Confederation Security Council President, with the positions of the CDF naval fleets.

Ahiga was teary as he now understood what his father had been trying to do. His father knew what Malo's plan was, or at least the basics. What was to happen now that his father was not there to implement his strategy? Ahiga wiped his eyes and decided he had to finish what his father had started. He had to confront Malo and stop him. He now had the evidence he needed and hoped that it was not too late.

Ahiga opened the third file on Feng's chip. It was about a husband and wife couple, Shallum and Cajsa Tsadoq. Cajsa was Malo's PA and Shallum, his political attaché. Cajsa died six months ago. The cause was listed as suicide, but Shallum didn't believe it. He demanded an autopsy, but the authorities refused, which devastated Shallum. According to the information in the file, Malo had the death quickly dealt with.

The file continued with evidence that Cajsa had stumbled onto Malo's plan and confronted him. She apparently never told Shallum, maybe to keep him out of danger. It was highly likely that Malo had Cajsa killed to prevent her divulging the secret. Malo had convinced Shallum that there was a conspiracy group that his wife had uncovered and Malo was on its tail. He trickled information about the group's activities to Shallum periodically. The conspirators were coincidently all members of the Confederation who opposed Malo's legislation and who were being murdered one by one.

Ahiga was even more astounded. There was no hard evidence in the file, but the reason for the murders now made sense. It even made sense that Shallum may be the murderer, seeking revenge for his wife's murder. Malo had a lot to answer for.

27

AFFECTION

Alex and Nascha made themselves comfortable on the yacht as they sped towards Procyon. Alex shut himself in a private room and connected the hyperlink. He set up to call Chooli. He didn't know why, but he missed her. Her abrupt, direct way of speaking brought a smile to his face. The radiant light she exuded was contagious. Her intelligence amazed him.

"Hello." Chooli answered on audio only.

"Hello," Alex repeated, smiling to himself.

"Who's this?"

"I'm insulted."

"Alex!" Video suddenly flickered on with Chooli's beaming face emanating from the screen, her eyes sparkling like blazing white stars. Her aureola glowed with a golden radiance.

Alex laughed. Chooli laughed too, realizing her exuberance was on display.

"It's so good to see you, Alex. Where are you? What've you been doing? When are you coming back?" Chooli was out of breath.

"Whoa. Let me answer one question at a time," Alex said, still beaming with joy. He couldn't believe how happy Chooli made him feel. "First question, I'm on a yacht traveling to Procyon."

Chooli looked puzzled. "What are you doing going there? I thought you were going to Eta Cassiopei."

"We've been to Eta Cassiopei. Then another murder happened on Xi Boötis, which we inspected. Now we're going to Procyon to interview some people of interest."

"Oh. You get around. I didn't think commercial vessels traveled that fast."

"I don't think they do. I had to charter a private yacht, and this one is very fast."

"Well, look who's the hyper-ship setter then. I'm jealous."

Alex chuckled. "Yeah, it's all right. I wish you were here to share the experience."

"I wish I was there too."

"Enough about me. What have you been doing?"

"Why?"

Alex rolled his eyes, "Because I'm interested in you."

"Oh. Sorry. Old habit. Nothing much. Went to the Ceti Interspacial bar to see the Cretan Novas again with Mai. You'll never guess who we bumped into. Someone you know."

A tinge of jealous wariness came over Alex. "Who?"

Chooli laughed, "Look at you. No, I didn't go after anyone else."

Alex blushed with guilty embarrassment for not trusting her more. "Well, who then?"

"Ambassador Tse's son, Ahiga."

"Oh. Hope you got more out of him than we have so far."

Chooli laughed. "He's charming and down to earth. Mai thought he was very diablo. The feeling was mutual, I think. You should have seen Mai. I virtually had to drag her over to introduce herself."

"Really? I didn't pick Mai as the shy type."

"Me neither. I think she really liked him and didn't want to ruin her chance. He said he would contact her again when he got back."

"Where was he going?"

"He didn't say. He just said it wouldn't be long. Oh. Another thing. I just read on the news feeds that someone broke into Tse's apartment in the capital last night. They arrested someone all tied up when they got there. The feed said there was an anonymous tipoff. Bit of a coincidence, don't you think?"

"Yes, it is. It's too much of a coincidence. I wonder why Ahiga wasn't staying there. Maybe he doesn't have access. Another question to ask him when I catch up with him. He is very elusive when he wants to be."

"Hmm. When are you coming back?"

"Not sure yet but two or three days, I hope."

"I miss you," Chooli said, her eyes misting with barely concealed tears.

Alex looked down. Too much emotion poured through him to answer immediately. He gained his composure. "I miss you too. In all my relationships, I have never wanted to be with someone as much as you. I don't know what's happening."

Chooli's aureola turned a mottled orange and emerald blue.

"What's happening with your aureola?"

The coloring went green and her face slightly red, "I'm embarrassed to tell you."

"Come on."

"That was the sweetest thing anyone has said to me and the coloring was me radiating back love. I couldn't help it. It's hard for us to hide our emotions."

"Interesting." Alex was humbled. He wondered if he had the same feelings. "I'm sorry I embarrassed you."

"Don't be silly. I just wish I could hold you just now."

"Me too."

The moments passed as a silence and peace of shared tranquility reverberated between them. They looked into each other's eyes, their souls. The juncture passed.

"I had better go," Alex said.

"Please!"

"I know. I wish we could have more time. I have some things to do before we reach Procyon."

Chooli looked sad, "OK then." Tenderness radiated from her, "I love you."

She caught Alex off guard. He was suddenly flustered and didn't really know what to say. He reached into his emotions to work out what he truly felt, "I love you, too."

Chooli's face instantly blossomed into the largest smile, like a budding flower bursting open in the glory of its bloom. "Diablo."

Alex was all smiles too, "Yeah, diablo. See you soon."

"See you."

Alex cut the link. He sat back in his chair. This all seemed to be too fast and yet not fast enough. His feelings confused him and he took a deep breath to calm himself. He hoped he would get back to Caerus soon to see her again. He was glad he had called. The information about Ahiga was interesting. Alex wondered where Ahiga was going and why. He changed his focus and thought about what they would do when they arrived on Procyon.

He found Nascha watching a holo-movie in the general area of the cabin.

She looked up, "Finished our secret comm then?"

The comment irritated Alex, but he kept his composure, "Yes, I'm finished."

ALEX AND NASCHA arrived on Procyon at 9:30 in the morning. They went to a hotel and checked into separate rooms to freshen up. Alex found out that Malo had just returned to Procyon, so he placed a call through to him.

"Hello, Malo Metam's office," Malo's PA said over the comm link.

"Hello, I am Chief Inspector Detective Alex Warner of the GIA. Would I be able to speak to Malo Metam please?"

"I will see if he can speak with you. Just a moment, please."

There was silence while the PA contacted Malo. Malo came on the comm after about 30 seconds, "Hello Chief Inspector, How may I help you?"

"Hello Mr Metam. I was wondering if my associate and I could come over and talk to you sometime today."

"Humph. I am a busy man, Chief Inspector. What is this about?"

"I am sure that you have kept up with the news about Ambassador Tse's death. I understand that you were acquainted with him and I would like to ask you a few questions. It's a routine matter and won't take up much of your time, I'm sure."

"Well, yes, I knew him. I suppose you are doing your duty. Very well. Let's see. Will 5:00 this afternoon be all right with you?"

"That will be fine. Thank you. There is just one more matter. Do you know how we can reach a Shallum Tsadoq? I believe he works for you." Alex noted a slight delay before Malo answered.

"Well, yes. He is my attaché. He is away on business at present. I think he is returning tonight some time. Why do you want to talk to him?"

"Just routine questions. We will just have to wait until he returns then. We will see you at five and thank you for your time." Alex disconnected the comm link.

Alex thought the change in composure when he mentioned Shallum Tsadoq was interesting. There was a knock on the door. It was Nascha. She had changed and freshened up, something Alex had not done yet.

"What's happening?"

"I just got off the comm with Malo. We have a five o'clock appointment. Apparently Shallum is away and returning tonight sometime. So, not much at the moment, I'm afraid."

"So, what do we do till then?"

"We can look over everything we've got so far."

28

CONFRONTATIONS

Ahiga arrived on Procyon just after 3:00 in the afternoon. He called the home contact number for Malo from the spaceport.

"Hello, the Metam Residence. Whom may I say is calling?" a butler asked.

"Hello. My name is Ahiga. I was wondering if I could talk to Malo Metam."

"I am sorry he is not here at present. You can contact him at his office."

"OK. I have his office contact. I will do that." Ahiga broke the connection. Malo was at the office and not off world, as Ahiga had hoped. He had called Malo's residence to make sure. Ahiga intended paying Malo a visit in his office instead of calling him.

He hired an AGrav from one of the hire companies at the spaceport and keyed in Malo's office location. The vehicle sped away. It estimated the trip would take 30 minutes. Ahiga sat back, thinking. He had to stop Malo somehow. He had to get him to see reason. He had to tell him he knew about the conspiracy to take over the Cetusian worlds. He knew that Malo was indirectly behind his father's murder through Shallum. He had to make Malo believe he would fail because his father had put a counter-plan in place to stop him and these worlds were ready for him and his CDF traitors. Ahiga took a deep breath. He hoped he was ready.

The AGrav arrived at Malo's office building. He parked it and went to the elevators to Malo's office. He used the elevator and arrived at Malo's floor, exited the elevator and looked around. It seemed empty, but he could see Malo's office area up ahead and to the left. He walked the distance, determined, and turned to the entrance of the office. A reception area confronted him, elegant and neat. A Personal Assistant sat behind a reception desk. She looked up.

"May I help you?" she asked.

"Yes, my name is Ahiga. I would like to speak to Malo Metam please. I am the son of Ambassador Tse from Caerus. I believe Malo knew him well."

The PA looked at Ahiga skeptically. "Please have a seat. I will see if he can see you." She knocked on a door and entered, closing the door behind her.

Ahiga assumed the door was the entrance to Malo's office. He waited some time before the PA reappeared.

"Mr Metam will see you shortly," she said, an air of distrust exuding from her.

"Thank you." Ahiga waited.

Malo came out of his office after about five minutes and walked up to Ahiga. "I wish I could say it's a pleasure to meet you but, under the circumstances, please accept my deepest condolences on your loss. Tse was a wonderful friend to me and he always talked about you."

Ahiga stood. "Yes, I wish I could say the same," he said with a wary dry tone.

Malo caught the nuance of the reply and Ahiga saw him inspect his face for any signs of where the conversation might go. Ahiga also saw a hint of disgust in Malo's expression.

"Well, let's retire to my office where we can talk in private."

Ahiga politely nodded and started walking to the door of the office. He walked through. Malo entered behind him, closing the door after him.

"Please sit," Malo said, pointing to a chair facing the office desk.

Ahiga sat and waited.

Malo walked around the desk and sat in his office chair. He studied Ahiga for a moment. "How may I help you?" he asked.

Ahiga steeled himself. He gulped and then said, "I would like to know why you had my father killed."

Malo's eyes shot open in astonishment and then a wary guise set on his features as if he were facing a challenging political opponent in the parliament. "That's a bold accusation."

"So you do not deny it?"

"Of course I'm denying it. It's preposterous. Tse was my friend. I had nothing to do with his murder. Why would I have done such a thing?"

"Oh. You didn't do it yourself. You had someone else do it for you."

"You are obviously distraught and wanting to find answers, which is understandable, but what evidence do you have to substantiate such a monstrous claim?"

Ahiga stood up and started pacing the room as he considered his line of questioning. "You are aware of an organization called Scorpius?"

Ahiga caught a brief look of surprise on Malo's face. "I have never heard of it."

"Cut the pretense, Malo. I know you have heard of it. You are the head of it. You see, my father left me some files detailing much about the organization and many other things. Come to think of it, maybe that's why I've had people following me on Caerus. Maybe they were trying to tidy up any loose ends."

Malo replied cautiously, "Well, yes. I am the head of an organization called Scorpius, but it is just a philanthropic group."

"I think it is much more than that. I think it is an organization prepared to kill people to extract information from them. My father left a holo-recording."

"You must be mistaken. I would never have sanctioned that. What your father did is no responsibility of mine."

Ahiga slammed his fist on the desk and shouted, "You sanctioned it. The other person on the recording said so."

Malo jumped in his chair and gulped. "Circumstantial. You can't prove that."

Ahiga studied Malo with bitter disgust. He didn't realize how degenerate Malo was. "Just like I can't prove you had Cajsa Tsadoq liquidated?"

Malo jumped again at the name. He reddened with rage. "I did no such thing. Now if you intend continuing with these preposterous allegations, I insist that you leave."

"I will leave when I get some answers," Ahiga shouted. He calmed again and said in a softer voice, "I have seen the police records. It was you who had the investigation shut down and a determination of suicide as the cause of death. It was you who made sure they didn't perform an autopsy. It is all there in the report."

"I didn't want Shallum to be more distressed than he already was."

"But it was Shallum who wanted the autopsy. He didn't believe that she committed suicide, did he?"

Malo started showing worry lines on his brow from the stress. *He's holding up to the pressure very well. He's not sweating yet,* Ahiga thought.

"He was in denial."

"He wanted the truth, and you denied him that."

"He was becoming demented, obsessed."

"That brings me to the next topic. The unfortunate deaths of some diplomats."

"What about it?"

"They were all members of your Scorpius organization, were they not?"

"I don't think so."

"Don't lie. You know very well that they were and each one who died was the next in the alphabet in the reverse order. It wouldn't surprise me if Feng is dead by now. He is Beta, which you already know, so I would get very nervous if I were you, you being Alpha, unless you are the instigator of these incidents."

Malo squirmed in his chair at the connection and accusation. Ahiga noticed small beads of sweat appearing on his forehead.

"Why would someone murder Feng? He is number two in the organization."

"Maybe for the same reason someone murdered my father. They know what you intend doing and they are not in concurrence with your intentions. In fact, everyone who has died so far seems to have disapproved of what you intend doing."

"You cannot know that."

"I can and I do."

"Even if I was behind the deaths, which I'm not, how could I have done it, anyway?"

"You have the perfect instrument - a deranged husband. Shallum works for you. All you need do is convince him that a splinter group was hatching a political conspiracy which Cajsa found out about and led to her death. You just need to feed the names to Shallum one at a time for him to do the rest."

"Ha! You really have a vivid imagination. Why would I do such a thing?"

"To cover up the real conspiracy. That's why."

To Ahiga, Malo seemed to feel like he had the upper hand again. He had a slight smirk on his face.

"And what would this conspiracy be?"

"To use the CDF to overthrow the Cetusian members of the Confederation. Am I close to the mark?"

Malo sat shocked. He was speechless. He was like a cornered wild animal looking for a means of escape, his mouth half open as if about to say, 'How did you find out?'

The door of Malo's office opened, and Shallum walked in. He paused when he saw Ahiga. He closed the door again slowly. Malo looked at Shallum. Ahiga turned and looked at him too. Ahiga saw a man with crazed eyes, as if hypnotized into performing a pre-programmed routine only to have a bug in the software stop him.

Ahiga turned back to Malo. He saw Malo's face turn into malevolence. Ahiga saw the wheels turning in Malo's mind as he contrived a new scheme, a means of escape from his predicament.

Shallum spoke. "I was not aware you had company, Malo. The PA was not at her desk. This makes the situation awkward."

"I'm glad you came, Shallum," Malo said. "I would like you to meet Ahiga, Ambassador Tse's son. He was just telling me how he helped his father in the murder of your wife."

Ahiga looked at Malo in utter disbelief. The audacity of the lie dumbfounded him. He looked at Shallum, who was looking at him in a confused and yet maniacal way.

Shallum said in a mechanical and emotionless voice, "What letter is he? I don't recall him being a member of Scorpius. I thought I only had one more to complete the job. I only have to exterminate Alpha and my retribution will be complete."

Malo started to panic. "Alpha had nothing to do with your wife's death, Shallum. I told you I would advise who the culprits were."

"Yes, you did. I took care of Beta. Pity about his receptionist, though. I don't enjoy wasting life."

Ahiga didn't like the direction the conversation was taking but stayed silent, watching the interplay between Malo and Shallum.

Malo rose from his chair and slowly walked around the desk. Shallum walked forward a few steps.

"You just have this loose end to deal with," Malo said.

"But he is not Alpha. He is out of order. He cannot be one of them. He is out of order."

"I was unaware of his involvement until now."

Ahiga decide he had to jump in before he was in serious trouble. He was right about Feng being on the list. He felt sad. He had liked Feng. Ahiga could see why he got along with his father. "Shallum. Listen to me. Malo is lying. I had nothing to do with your wife's death and neither did any of the people you have killed. It is Malo who had your wife murdered."

Shallum turned from Malo and looked at Ahiga. "Why would Malo lie? He has always looked after me like a son."

"Malo is the head of a conspiracy to overthrow all the Cetusian systems and replace them with human governments. Your wife found out and threatened to expose Malo."

Shallum turned to Malo again. "Is this true?"

"Of course not. Ahiga is as slippery as an eel with his words. He is trying to get out of being exposed."

Shallum stood motionless, like a robot stalled in its ability to react. A crazed smile appeared on his face. He said to Ahiga, "Did you like the final touch with your father's death, the removal of his aureola? I did that before he died. It was very agonizing by the contortions on his face. Then I broke his neck."

Ahiga's face went pale at the confession. His stomach clenched knowing that he faced his father's murderer. He did not like his options. Surely Shallum would not want him to escape with the knowledge.

"Your father said the same thing that you are saying. Malo had my beautiful wife murdered, but why would he? He loves me. He would not do something like that... or would he? I'm so confused."

"Why else would he object to an autopsy, Shallum?"

"Why else? I'm getting a headache. There are too many things to think about." Shallum put his left hand inside his suit pocket and pulled out a maser pistol. He did the same for his right suit pocket and pulled out a kinetic pistol.

Ahiga and Malo stepped back two paces.

"Which one shall I use?" Shallum asked himself. "If I kill him straight away, I might not get the answers I'm looking for." He put the maser on stun and shot Ahiga.

Ahiga screamed.

ALEX AND NASCHA walked into the reception area of Malo's office just before 5:00. Alex was just about to announce their presence when he heard a scream from behind the office door. He saw that both Nascha and the receptionist heard it too, and he became instantly alert. "Who's in the office?" he asked the receptionist.

"Malo and a person called Ahiga."

Alex and Nascha looked at each other.

"Surprise," Alex said. He started walking to the door.

"You can't go in there," the receptionist said. "Malo's in a meeting."

"Meetings rarely include screams," Alex replied.

Alex continued to the door. Nascha followed. He placed his finger above the door-opening button and looked at Nascha, gesturing with his other hand that he would move left when they went through and that she should go right. Nascha nodded. He pressed the button. Alex rushed through to the left and Nascha to the right.

Two men standing and one lying on the floor confronted them. He saw that the one on the floor was Ahiga. He was in pain but still conscious. Malo was facing them, and another man had his back to them but was turning. Alex saw the man was armed and prepared to use his weapons. He tensed his muscles, ready to spring into action like a stalking cat about to jump its prey.

"Let's calm down," Alex said, trying to get some kind of control of the situation. He could see a crazed look in the man's eyes even from a side angle.

"It is too late for calm," Shallum said. "People killed my wife and they have to pay. I almost have my retribution, but I have one left. You should not have come."

Alex saw Shallum lock his eyes on Nascha. Shallum reset the maser to maximum and moved to aim both pistols at her. Alex jumped towards Nascha just before Shallum fired, knocking her away from the path of the shots as they discharged their means of death. The maser shot hit Alex in the upper arm, disintegrating some flesh and muscle. Shots of pain flashed from that area to his brain. The bullet from the kinetic pistol penetrated his ribcage, smashing one rib as it pushed through and lodged in the lung, narrowly missing Alex's heart. He could hardly breathe. His chest felt tight, and he bled profusely. Events seemed to turn to slow motion. He saw Nascha on the floor next to him. She looked winded. He was glad she was safe for the moment. One of his prime rules was to protect the people under him. He had not failed yet, and he did not intend to fail now. He turned his head to the rest of the office.

Alex saw Shallum look at the place he was aiming at, turn his head and look at him, then Nascha. He started altering his aim.

At the same time Ahiga, agony etched on his face, took a huge lunge at Shallum's legs. He smashed into Shallum behind the knees, buckling them and unbalancing him. Ahiga wrapped his good arm - the other one hung numb and useless from the maser stun - around the falling torso, ensuring an ever increasing and heavy drop to the floor for Shallum. Shallum's calves were under Ahiga and the rest of him was on top. His head gave a loud crack as the back of it hit the floor. The kinetic weapon fired into the ceiling as Shallum fell and both pistols flew out of his hands.

Nascha recovered and flew into action as her training kicked in. She rolled over to the maser and grabbed it while raising herself up from the floor and jumping to the kinetic pistol, grabbing that too. She put the kinetic pistol in her pocket and aimed the maser at Shallum. She held her chest in pain where it had met the floor. Backing away, she took a quick look at Alex. "That was a stupid thing to do," she said.

Alex coughed, a trickle of blood coming from his mouth. "I know."

Nascha looked back to Shallum and Ahiga on the floor.

"Looks like you came just in time," Malo said as he walked forward.

"Stay where you are," Nascha demanded, "or you will know what being stunned with one of these feels like."

Malo stopped instantly. "You can't believe I have anything to do with this?"

"I don't know what to believe at the moment. What I know is he shot at me, my boss is injured, and we have the culprit on the floor with someone we can't quite keep track of. Sit on that chair." Nascha pointed to a chair in the corner. It was where she could keep an eye on him and the others.

Nascha pointed the maser at Shallum.

Shallum was recovering from his dazed state and trying to get off Ahiga, but was being hindered by him, Ahiga's arm keeping him in position.

"Let him go, Ahiga. You," Nascha said, gesturing with the pistol to Shallum. "Get up slowly to your knees and place your hands on your head or I will stun you."

Shallum slowly obeyed, tears filling his eyes. "I must complete my retribution for Cajsa's death."

"You will get your retribution. Ahiga, roll away from him."

Ahiga obeyed and stood, using his good side to lift himself. He hobbled back.

"What is your name," Nascha demanded.

Shallum turned his face to look at Nascha, "Shallum Tsadoq."

Surprise appeared on Nascha's face.

Alex coughed again. "All our eggs in the same basket for a change," he quipped. Flashes appeared before his eyes. His breathing labored. His arm was in excruciating pain and oozing blood where the maser shot had destroyed and cauterized the flesh. He coughed again.

"Save yourself," Nascha said, not taking her eyes off Shallum. "I've got this. Shallum. I want you to lay face down on the floor and put your arms behind your back."

Shallum obeyed.

Nascha moved to him, taking hand arrestors from her pocket. She placed one arrestor over one wrist and the other over the other wrist, immobilizing his hands behind his back. She moved away and relaxed slightly. She looked over to Alex again, concern on her face. She turned to Malo. "Call the police and medical help."

The receptionist poked her head around the door, pale as a sun-bleached shell. "I have already called the police," she said. "I'll call for a medic too, Malo."

"Do that," Malo said, his body slumped in exhaustion.

Nascha moved over to Alex. She looked at him, examined his wounds.

"How bad is it?" Alex asked.

"I've seen worse. Why did you do that?"

"One of my rules. Never lose one of your people," Alex wheezed, the viscous consistency of the blood affecting his vocal cords.

Nascha looked at him harder, respect for the man in front of her appearing on top of the worry.

"Take me back to Caerus," Alex said.

Nascha sniggered, "We'll have you back to Chooli in no time."

"How did you know?"

"I'm a detective, aren't I?"

Alex chuckled but quickly stopped as pain speared across his side and chest.

He heard voices from the reception area and then one at the doorway. "Drop your weapon," a police officer said to Nascha.

"I'm GIA," she said and showed the officer her identity chip.

He saw the chip and lowered his weapon. "What's the situation?"

Alex slowly sank into unconsciousness as he saw Shallum disappear into a trance.

∼

"Shallum, Shallum."

"Cajsa?"

Shallum stood in a space that was all white. He did not know how he got there. Cajsa appeared before him, as beautiful as ever. Her radiance reflected in her smile.

"It is over now, Shallum."

"Where did you come from? Have your come to take me with you?"

"Not yet, my love. Not yet." Sadness appeared on her face.

"Is what that person said true? Did Malo have you killed? Were all those other people innocent? Am I a monster?"

"Yes, it is true. Malo had me killed for knowing too much. I should have told you, I am sorry. But you are not a monster, my love."

"But all those innocent people. I have caused so much anguish for their families. What have I done?"

"Shh, my love. He tricked you. I forgive you. They will reveal the actual murderer in due time."

A calm smile came over Shallum's face and he started laughing like a maniac, a laugh that did not stop.

29

THE INTERROGATION OF SHALLUM

Once they bundled Alex off to the hospital, Malo had left and the police had removed Shallum to their prison cells, Nascha looked at Ahiga with suspicion. "What were you doing here?"

Ahiga looked contrite, "I was trying to get some answers."

"Answers about what?"

"About my father's murder."

"From Malo. Why were you talking to Malo? Did you suspect that Shallum was the murderer?"

"Not until now, not positively anyway. He confessed in front of Malo, although I don't think Malo will admit it."

"Why not? What has he got to hide?"

"I believe that he encouraged Shallum to murder my father and the others."

"What for? Why would he do that?"

"I'm not sure," Ahiga lied.

Nascha looked at Ahiga closely but decided not to pursue the matter further at present. Instead she said, "You're coming with me to the station so we can have a longer discussion after I've had a chat to

Shallum. I hope he hasn't totally gone around the bend yet. His lunacy as he left worries me."

Ahiga looked annoyed and put out but conceded, "OK. I suppose it's the least I can do."

"Why are you so maddeningly secretive? We are trying to help you, you know," Nascha said as she led Ahiga out of the office and to the AGrav that she had hired.

"I know. It's just how I am, I suppose."

They arrived in the parking area. Ahiga went to his AGrav.

"Where are you going?" Nascha asked.

"I have my own AGrav."

"Oh no, you don't. I'm not letting you out of my sight for now. You're coming with me. Tell the AGrav to return to its hire site."

Ahiga looked the picture of innocence, "I would have followed you."

"Sure," Nascha said cynically.

Ahiga did as he was told and got into Nascha's AGrav. They drove to the police station where Shallum was being held and went to the Detention Officer's desk. She looked at the holo screen of the cells, Shallum's in particular. Nascha studied his behavior. He was looking unblinkingly straight ahead like a statue as he sat on the only seat in the cell. Now and then he released a maniacal cackle and then returned to complete silence. She looked at the Officer on duty.

"He's been like that since he came in. He's unresponsive to our directions, although he's given no trouble either."

Nascha nodded. "Can you get him to an interrogation room for me?"

"Sure," the Officer said and picked up his comm to relay the request.

It was 9:00pm. Nascha was exhausted from the excitement of the day. Her excesses of the night before didn't help either, she reflected with regret. She was pleased that Alex hadn't gone off the deep end with her for it and that he didn't torment her about it either. She wondered how he was. She found out where they had taken him and asked about his condition. The nurse on duty said that he was in surgery and that was all she knew at the moment. Nascha thanked her and hung up. She hoped that Alex would be all right. She had only realized on the way to Procyon how deep the relationship was between him and Chooli. She had been very jealous when she met her but realized that Alex and her would never work, anyway. They were both too temperamental. It would have been a stormy relationship that ended in tears. Reflecting on what little she knew about Chooli, she thought she would suit Alex's personality although Nascha was not sure what had affected him so much in his previous relationship. It must have been very traumatic for him from the little that Alex had disclosed.

She came out of her reverie as an officer came up to her.

"We have him in Interrogation Room C, if you will follow me."

"Lead the way. Ahiga, come with us."

They went to another part of the station. Nascha and Ahiga went into the observation room for Room C. "Stay here," Nascha ordered Ahiga.

"I'm not sure it would be worth my while not to," Ahiga said sarcastically.

Nascha sniggered under her breath and said, "I'll restrain you to something otherwise," as she left and went into the adjoining interrogation room.

Nascha studied Shallum as he sat in his seat. He didn't acknowledge her presence but stared directly ahead with no expression or emotion. Nascha noted the steady rise and fall of his chest as evidence he was alive. She sat opposite him and looked into soulless black eyes. It was like looking into black holes. There seemed to be nothing there.

"Can you hear me, Shallum? It is 2106 and Nascha of the GIA is interviewing Shallum Tsadoq."

He blinked as he heard his name and looked at her.

"I have failed. My love told me Malo tricked me. Those people were innocent."

"Which people?"

"Pi, Mu, Lambda, Eta, Delta and Beta. And that poor PA."

Nascha looked at Shallum, a little confused by what he was saying. Alex had not shared enough information with her. She knew that Tse was Eta, Samir was Delta and Feng was Beta but who were the others. They must be the other deaths Alex had mentioned. She continued, "When you say Eta, do you mean Ambassador Tse from Caerus?"

"Of course. He is Eta of Scorpius. I was told that he killed my love."

"And Samir Kumar is Delta?"

"Yes."

"Xiang Feng is Beta?"

"Yes."

"Who are Pi, Mu and Lambda?"

"Nguyen, Owen Renshaw and Koanang."

"Who told you?"

"Malo, Malo told me. He said they were planning something secret, something terrible, and that my love had found out. They disposed of her before she could tell anyone. He was so kind and understanding. He told me who they were. I had to extract my retribution." Anger appeared on Shallum's face. "But he tricked me." He moved to get up and rush out. Nascha jerked back in fright at the sudden violent move but the restraint to the table solidly secured him, the table being bolted to the floor. He strained for a few moments. Nascha composed herself again. "Please sit down, Shallum."

All energy left him, and he resigned himself to sit again.

"Who tricked you Shallum?"

Anger reappeared. "Malo, Malo tricked me," he shouted. Furious eyes bored into hers like laser blasts. She felt fear like she had not felt for a long time. She suddenly realized that the person in front of her had no feeling, no remorse and no sanity. He had broken down into obsession and become a complete psychopath from the grief of his wife's murder. "I know now. Malo had her killed. It was his plans that Cajsa had discovered and threatened to reveal."

The interview went on for several hours and it was past one in the morning before she finished. She thought she knew the facts of Tse's murder now. She went to the police on duty and asked them to bring in Malo, but they couldn't locate him. His family was deeply distressed, as they didn't know where he was either. She went back into the observation room. Ahiga was sitting in a chair asleep. She wished she could do the same, but she still had things to do. She woke him up. "I should put you in there now but I don't have the energy."

He yawned. "Why? I'll tell you what I know."

Nascha looked at him suspiciously but let it go. She was undecided what to do next. She called the hospital again. They told her that Alex was out of surgery and in a stable condition but still in a coma. She was glad that he seemed to be out of danger. She looked again at Ahiga, "Have you booked a hotel?"

"Yes."

"You can go there then. I'm off to the hospital. But don't skip the planet or your life won't be worth living."

Ahiga realised the seriousness of Nascha's order. "Sure... Since it doesn't look like I can go anywhere without you, I may as well get rid of my yacht and hitch a ride with you. I'll pay any expenses."

Nascha thought that was one way to keep an eye on him. "Sure, do that. I'll see you later today. And you are not to mention anything to Alex until he has recuperated a bit or I'll have your balls."

30

RETURN TO CAERUS

Alex woke up in a hospital on Procyon. His arm was in a rejuvenation bandage and his chest felt normal again, if slightly sore. He could breathe properly, which was a relief. He tried to sit up but quickly changed his mind as pain radiated from his broken rib.

"Good of you to join the world of the living again," said a nurse as she busied herself reviewing Alex's statistics.

"Where am I?"

"You're in Procyon Space Centre Hospital, the best in the system. The people who brought you here knew what they were doing."

"How long have I been unconscious?"

"Oh, about 12 hours. It's just after seven in the morning. You're lucky to be awake from what I've been told. It was touch and go there for a while."

"Oh," Alex said as he thought about the fragility of life. *Life is for living, he thought.* "How long will I have to stay in here?"

"Not long. Apparently they want to take you back to Caerus. 'As soon as possible' they said. You can leave when the doctor confirms that you are stable enough to travel."

Alex's spirits brightened. He sensed Nascha's involvement in the arrangements. "Can't I sit up or something? I'm bored already."

The nurse laughed. "You men. You're all the same. I know - I married one."

Alex grinned. "Would you rather we were getting up to mischief?"

"Not on your life. Anyway, I can raise the bed now that you're conscious." She adjusted the controls so that Alex was in a semi-sitting position. "That will do for now. We don't want too much pressure on that rib for a few days."

When she left, Alex looked around his room. He was grateful to have it to himself and grateful to have a window overlooking a garden that was being slowly lit by the rising sun. Two birds in a tree greeted it with song.

Alex wondered what had happened in Malo's office after he had lost consciousness. The last thing he remembered was Nascha explaining things to the local police and Shallum laughing like a lunatic. He guessed he would be told, eventually.

There was a knock on the door and a face popped around. "Mind if I come in?" asked Nascha

Alex was pleased to see her. "Of course!"

Nascha carried a chair closer to the bed. "The nurse said I could have a few minutes with you now that you're awake. How are you feeling?"

"Sore. Let's have an update."

Nascha laughed. "No way. The nurse will have my aureola for her dog's breakfast. You're supposed to rest. Now that we know most of what's happened, thanks to Ahiga, I can wrap up the case. There's a surprise too, but I'll save that for another day."

Alex grunted with annoyance. He folded his arms gently across his chest, careful not to aggravate his smashed rib. "That Ahiga will have a lot to answer for when I get hold of him."

Nascha laughed again. "Don't worry, I've given him a hard time overnight. He still knows more than he is letting on. I have him in detention in his hotel at the moment, but enough of that. Have you been told when we can move you?"

"I thought you looked tired. Have you been up all night?"

"Pretty much. I dozed off in the chair in the waiting area when I got here. The nurse woke me when you came to. Well?"

"Well, what?"

Nascha threw her hands up in exasperation. "When can we get you on a ship home?"

"Oh, that. Soon, I think. The doctor has to see me. I can go if he thinks I'm stable enough."

Nascha's mood sobered. "Thanks for what you did. I think I would probably be dead if you hadn't."

Alex looked at Nascha approvingly. "It's one of my rules, but you're welcome. Thanks for the tidy up work after. I was a little immobilized," he said with a wry grin.

Nascha smiled back. "We'd have all been in trouble if Ahiga didn't do what he did."

"Humph! Yeah, I suppose."

A doctor interrupted their reflections.

"How are you this morning?" he asked.

"Had better days but I feel good, considering."

"Yes, you look better than I expected."

"I think I will go," Nascha said to Alex. "I can use some sleep. The hospital will contact me when we can move you."

"I wouldn't go too far. It might be sooner than you think," the doctor said.

Nascha sighed. "OK. No rest for the wicked. I'll wait outside while you do your examination."

The doctor conducted a few tests. He ran a scanner over the damaged arm and chest and examined the results. There were a few mm-mms while he did his work. He finally said, "You are a remarkable man, Mr Warner. You have recovered very well so far. We will get some breakfast into you, organize some medications and have a nurse take care of you along the way."

"That's great," Alex said. "I don't like hospitals."

"I didn't say you were out of hospital for good. Just for the trip back to Caerus. You need to be admitted to a hospital there for a few days."

Alex's enthusiasm faltered with the news, but he was still glad to be going back to Caerus and seeing Chooli again.

"I'll let your partner know. I'll sign your transfer chip and organize a nurse to get you to your ship."

A few moments later, Nascha returned. "So, good news I hear. Jacques will be pleased. He wasn't too happy when I told him we might delay our departure."

"It shouldn't worry him. I'm paying by the day."

"You know how they are. That type usually can't stay in one place for one-second longer than they have to, unless there's some action. We'll have an extra passenger. We couldn't see the point of Ahiga going back on a separate ship, so he's tagging along. That way I can keep an eye on him."

"That'll cost us extra," Alex protested.

"No, it won't. Ahiga has promised to pay for the whole voyage back. 'His treat,' he said. It seems he has more than enough money now."

"Oh."

A different nurse joined them and announced she would be accompanying Alex on the yacht back to Caerus. "Make sure you don't get into any trouble."

She was a beefy matronly woman in her early 50s. "No chance of that," he said.

Nascha held back a snicker. "I'll let the hospital know where to take you at the spaceport and I'll get Jacques and Ahiga organized at the other end."

"OK. See you there," Alex replied.

About four hours later, Alex was on the ship and Jacques came out of the cockpit to greet him. "Hear you had some action," he deadpanned.

"Some I didn't need," Alex replied.

Jacques chuckled. "Well, we'll be leaving in a moment and I'll try not to hit too many bumps along the way."

"Appreciated."

Alex lay on a transportation trolley and could only get up to walk to the toilet, as he still felt very weak. He had lost a lot of blood. The bandage on his arm had to stay there for a few weeks while the tissue regenerated and he had a healing patch on his chest over his broken rib. The doctors had taken a long time extracting the projectile from his chest cavity. The bullet had lodged close to his heart and one of the major arteries. A miss-cut would have had dire consequences. He was content to do what he was told for the time being.

Ahiga came over to talk to him once they had taken off and were on their way. "How are you going?" he asked.

"Could be better, but I'm not complaining. That was a brave thing you did."

"I was fairly sure that I would've been dead if I did nothing so I took the opportunity when it came along. You had good timing in coming when you did. That was an impressive move on your part."

"One of my maxims is to protect my team. If I can't do that, I don't deserve to be their leader." Alex looked at Ahiga for a moment, sizing him up. "You could have told us you had more information, you know. You're lucky I don't arrest you for obstruction of justice."

"I had nothing that I could prove. I needed more evidence first. Anyway, I've been told not to discuss anything about the case with you until you've recuperated more."

"Who told you that?"

"Nascha."

Alex groaned with irritation. "They going to lock me away or something?"

Ahiga changed tack. "I believe we both know a certain couple of women back on Caerus."

Alex brightened at the thought of Chooli. "So I've been told. How did you meet them?"

"I stayed at the Ceti Interspacial Hotel for one night before I left. I went up to the rooftop bar to relax and have some dinner. I was minding my business, and they were standing some distance away looking at me and in a heated discussion." Ahiga chuckled, "Chooli was trying to persuade Mai to approach me. Mai looked scared stiff at the prospect!"

Alex also chuckled, bearing the pain in his chest. "That's right, I forgot. Chooli told me, but I thought Mai was the outgoing one."

"No way. It was quite a comedy act at the start, but she was sweet once she relaxed."

"Will you see her again?"

"I think so. There was something about her."

"I know what you mean. I feel the same about Chooli."

"What impressed me the most was that, when she found out who I was and how wealthy I was, she didn't change her attitude one bit."

"Well, if you want it, I hope things work out."

"I hope that when you're well enough and if Mai and I are seeing each other, that we might go out for dinner. The four of us."

"I don't see why not. It's a deal so long as you tell me what it is I'm not supposed to know."

Ahiga looked around and then down, thinking. "I'll tell you everything when you've recovered."

Alex grunted in frustration. "You're not making me like you very much."

Ahiga laughed. "I suppose not, but I don't want to get on the wrong side of Nascha."

"Oh! Well, I think I can forgive you there. She can be a handful."

31

AMBUSH

The yacht finally docked at Caerus spaceport. The nurse reviewed Alex's condition and allowed him to get out of bed and walk. A wheelchair was available if he tired. They cleared immigration and customs and arrived in the general concourse area.

"Alex!"

Chooli ran towards them, fear and anxiety on her face. Alex burst with love and was surprised by his emotions but then realized his physical safety was more important at that point.

"Whoa, whoa, whoa," Alex said, gesturing with his good arm for her to slow down.

Chooli slowed to a walk as she approached. She looked him in the eyes, relief on her face. "Idiot."

Alex laughed. "Good to see you, too."

"Well, who else would go off without me and get shot?"

The others watched on with amusement, especially Ahiga.

"There was more to it than that."

Chooli stood in front of Alex, hands on hips, for a moment longer, then wrapped her arms around him and hugged him tightly, loosening her grip when he complained.

Alex cherished the affection, although he felt a little embarrassed in front of the others. He wrapped his good arm around Chooli. "Who told you what happened and when I was returning?" he asked as he looked around at the others, feigned accusation in his voice.

Nascha looked away, pretending something had caught her eye at the other end of the concourse.

"Thanks Nascha."

"Who? Me? I had nothing to do with it," Nascha said with a smirk.

Chooli let go of Alex and looked at him again. "I'm glad you're back."

"So am I."

"This reunion is very touching, but how about we go to the limousine I've hired?" Ahiga said with a little impatience.

"Excellent idea. I need to sit down and rest," Alex agreed.

The nurse came forward and offered the wheelchair. "Well, you had better use this then."

"I'll make it to the AGrav."

The nurse gave a huff of disapproval.

"That's an order," Chooli commanded.

Alex looked at her in surprise. He realized that she meant it and she wasn't taking 'No' for an answer. "OK. OK. I get the hint. Getting bossed around already," he complained.

The others laughed.

Chooli went behind the wheelchair and volunteered to push him along, although Alex could have controlled it himself with the motorized system. He decided not to get himself into any more trouble with Chooli. The troupe resumed walking to the spaceport exit where a chauffeur escorted them to the limousine.

Just as they reached the vehicle, loud cracks rang out as they came under attack. Someone was shooting at them with a Maser pistol, missing them and striking various objects. Everyone ducked for cover except Alex, who sat stranded in the wheelchair. Chooli realized his predicament and rushed out to bring him under cover behind an AGrav as, another volley of firepower sprayed their way.

"Got a pistol?" Chooli asked.

"In my bag," Alex replied.

"See how many there are and where they're hiding."

"I counted four. They're not very good shots."

"Thank the gods for that. This one?" Chooli asked as she grabbed a bag.

"No. That one," Alex said, looking around for the others. "Where's the nurse?" Then he saw her, on the ground with half her head missing. Alex gritted his teeth. "Bastards. They'll pay for that." She had volunteered to look after him and had sacrificed her life.

Chooli found the pistol and activated it, ready to fire on maximum stun. "Those snipers won't stop until they've killed who they came for."

Alex saw Nascha had her pistol out, seeking a target. He noticed with surprise that Ahiga also had one ready. He turned to Chooli. "You can't use my pistol."

"Shut up. You are in no condition to use it."

Alex realized Chooli was right and he might place them in more danger if he persisted. "You know how to use that?"

"Of course. Now help me find these pricks."

Alex sought out the bullet holes around the spaceport exit and mentally traced the shots back to points of origin. The shots were all coming from one general direction. "Over there. These people are amateurs. This isn't a professional ambush."

Chooli aimed his pistol where Alex was pointing. The others did the same.

Alex had an idea. "Let's see how jumpy these clowns are" he said as he threw the emptied bag into the air and towards the dead nurse.

The shooters took the bait and instantly fired at the bag, one disintegrating it to shreds, as Chooli, Nascha and Ahiga took aim at their position.

"I didn't like that bag, anyway," Alex said.

"Give me some cover while I circle around," Nascha told the others.

Chooli and Ahiga nodded.

"On three," Nascha said. "One... two... three."

Chooli and Ahiga fired off several rounds of maser shots while Nascha rushed over to the side, crouching to give herself as much cover as possible. Alex was nervous at having Nascha go on her own, but realized he was no help and they needed to get out quick. He trusted her training. She had shown good precision before. Chooli and Ahiga stopped when Nascha reached protection, circling the snipers' position. The attackers fired off another volley and Chooli fired off occasional shots in return to distract them from Nascha, taking turns with Ahiga.

A gun battle suddenly erupted from the snipers' lair. *Nascha*, Alex thought, dreading the outcome, as his heart pounded in his chest and his rib started aching with the tension. The firing stopped. Alex closed his eyes, anticipating the worst.

Chooli was standing before him, worried. "She'll be OK."

"I hope so. I wasn't there to take the heat this time."

Chooli looked at Alex strangely, not understanding.

Just then Nascha walked out of the building with two men in front of her, hands above their heads, a pistol aimed at each of them.

Alex and the others sighed in relief. Chooli and Ahiga relaxed their grip on the pistols they held. Nascha marched the attackers to where the others were and told them to stop.

"Keep your pistols trained on these two," she ordered, as she tied their arms behind their backs with the restraints she had retrieved from her bag.

Alex rose and walked over to the nurse, feeling sad. *She didn't know I would be her last patient*, he thought with regret. He heard sirens approaching and looked up. Police AGravs rushed towards them, coming to rapid rest around them, encircling their position to prevent escape. Alex and Nascha both got their GIA identity chips out and raised them above their heads. "GIA," Alex shouted once the sirens silenced. Chooli and Ahiga placed their pistols on the ground and put their hands up in surrender.

The police got out of the vehicles and the sergeant in charge came over, looked at the chips to confirm the identities and told the others to relax their guard. "What happened?" he asked.

Alex explained the events of the previous half hour and told them to take the culprits in and charge them. He wanted to question them later. Other police secured the scene and the site where the snipers had fired from, and where two more dead bodies lay.

The chauffeur came out of hiding. Alex had completely forgotten about him and wondered where he had been. The chauffeur looked at his AGrav and shook his head. It had suffered some damage from the exchange of fire. "How am I going to explain this?"

"Send me the bill," Ahiga told him.

Two men walked up to Ahiga just as they went to get into the AGrav. "Sorry we didn't get here in time," one of them said.

"And you are?" Ahiga asked.

"Your father recruited us for a certain purpose."

Ahiga raised his eyebrows. "Yes, you may have been useful."

"Who are these men?" Alex asked. "Don't tell me you can't say or I'll stun you."

Ahiga decided to share what he knew with the GIA. "My father recruited them to counteract a coup being planned by Malo Metam that is to occur sometime soon. I believe our brief altercation just now was Malo's attempt to silence us, silence me, before I could reveal his secrets."

"What? Are you sure of that?"

"Yes, I am sure. Isn't that right, men?"

"We don't know the big picture but Tse recruited us just as Ahiga said," one of the men said. "He was to give us a signal to round up the ringleaders of the uprising just before it occurred. He was talking to the government to boost personnel on our defense stations in the system, to counter an attack the CDF planned to overthrow the government. Ahiga got in contact with us yesterday and told us he was taking over where Tse left off."

Alex shook his head in amazement. "This just gets better. Did you get a look at the two we arrested? Do you know them?"

"Not a close look, but I think I recognize one of them at least."

"Can you two meet me at the Central Police Headquarters,

please? We need to continue this conversation, you too Ahiga. You're as slippery as an eel when it comes to sharing what you know."

"What did I do now?" Ahiga complained.

"It's what you haven't done," Alex castigated. Alex was feeling tired from his injuries and the excitement. His arm was troubling him too, but he tried not to show any pain, especially in front of Chooli.

Alex and the others got into the limousine, Chooli next to Alex facing the front. Ahiga and Nascha sat opposite them. Alex sighed in relief.

"I'm watching you two," Nascha jokingly said.

The atmosphere in the AGrav lightened, relieving the tension of the previous events. Chooli said, "You can watch all you want. That won't stop me."

Ahiga grinned. "Stop that you two, please, I just want to rest."

They all laughed.

Alex closed his eyes. Chooli snuggled up next to him. He could feel her warmth and it felt good. It felt normal, peaceful, contented bliss. He could sit next to her and forget the rest of the world forever. He opened his eyes again after a while and looked at Ahiga. "Have we walked in on a conspiracy, then?"

"Yes," Ahiga replied.

"Well?"

Ahiga thought for a moment. "See what you can get out of the ones that shot at us first. I will fill in the blanks."

Alex rolled his eyes. He was too tired and in too much pain to argue at the moment.

"Are you going to give Mai a call?" Chooli asked Ahiga in a furtive tone. "She keeps asking if I've heard if you're back."

Ahiga blushed. "None of your business," he said. His expression became shy. "Probably."

Chooli squealed with glee.

"Ouch!" Alex complained, as she bumped his rib.

"Sorry," she said, chastened but still smiling.

They arrived at the Ceti Interspacial Hotel.

"What do you want to do, Nascha?" Alex asked. "Do you want to go to your place first?"

"Yes, I will. I'll meet you at the station. Can the driver take me home, Ahiga?"

"Yes," Ahiga said. He gave the instructions to the driver and got out.

Alex and Chooli followed him. The porters removed the luggage from the vehicle. "Where is your wheelchair?" Chooli asked.

"Must have left it at the spaceport," Alex replied. "Didn't like it, anyway. When are you going?"

"You've got to be joking. I'm not letting you out of my sight after what happened last time."

Alex rolled his eyes, knowing there was no point arguing.

32

COUNTER ATTACK

Alex arrived at the Police Headquarters just before 4:00 in the afternoon. He had a terrible time convincing Chooli she couldn't come. "It's police business," he repeatedly told her. She had finally relented and sat in the hotel room moping. He prepared himself for the interrogation, even with his injuries. He determined that the time for playing games was over. He sensed that the stakes were getting too high, if what Ahiga and the other mysterious agents had said was true.

Nascha walked in 10 minutes after him. The two agents hadn't arrived yet. That was OK with Alex. He needed to interrogate the assassins first.

"Have you got a pistol handy?" Alex asked Nascha.

Nascha raised an eyebrow in surprise, "Yes, I do."

"Can I borrow it?"

"Shooting them won't get them to talk."

"Don't worry, I won't kill them. I just want to scare the shit out of them if I need to. We need to get them to talk and quickly."

"OK then. You're the boss."

Nascha pulled out her pistol and gave it to Alex. Alex secured it in the small of his back, the barrel under his trouser belt, and hid it from view.

"Let's go do this," Alex said and walked to the interrogation room.

Nascha went to the observation room to watch.

Alex walked into the room. He saw the prisoner seated in a chair, forearms resting on the table, a smug look on his face. *I'll wipe that look off you*, Alex thought.

"This conversation is being recorded. It is sixteen fifteen. Let's start with your name."

"I want a lawyer," the prisoner said, looking at the wall.

"You will get a lawyer when I say you get a lawyer," Alex said, starting to get angry.

"You will get some answers when I get a lawyer." The prisoner slowly turned his head and looked at Alex, a smug grin plastered firmly on his face. "I know my rights."

Alex paced his frustration. He stopped and faced the prisoner. "I don't think you understand. Conversation ended at sixteen seventeen." He walked over to the recording device and turned it off. "I'm not the local police. I'm from the GIA."

The prisoner jerked towards Alex at the mention of where he was from, the smile fading to concern as he watched Alex warily.

"The GIA don't have to play by the rules and I really don't want to after being shot at this afternoon, so I suggest that you talk and tell me your name and why you were shooting at me."

"I'm not saying anything," the prisoner said flatly.

Alex stared at him malevolently for several seconds. He sashayed the length of the room, letting the atmosphere intensify. He walked to the side of the table, next to the prisoner, and put his hand behind his back, slowly pulling out the pistol, watching the detainee as it came into his view. His eyes opened wide in alarm. Alex casually caressed the weapon in his hands. He quickly lowered it and fired at one of the chair legs. The leg disappeared, the chair sagged, the arrested man yelping in surprise.

"Excellent shot, don't you think," Alex said with a malicious smile. "Better than I thought, actually. I thought part of your leg might have disintegrated too. Must be your lucky day."

The prisoner was unnerved. "I'm Sigmund Johnston."

"Ah! See what a little persuasion can do." Alex lowered the pistol.

Sigmund squirmed in his seat, trying to find a position where he wasn't in danger of falling off the unbalanced chair.

"Now Sigmund," Alex emphasized 'Sigmund.' "Why were you shooting at us?"

"We weren't shooting at you. We were told to eliminate Tse's son. You just happened to be with him."

"Really, and who told you to 'eliminate' Tse's son."

"Orders from above."

"Do you often go around shooting people because someone asks you to?"

"Of course not."

"So why did you this time?"

"Orders. You obey orders or you might be the one in the sights."

"Orders from who?"

Sigmund sat silently.

Alex's pistol shot up and vaporized the back of Sigmund's chair.

Sigmund almost fell as the back of the chair move backwards on one side. He changed position in the chair, so he was only half on the chair on the good side. "From the organization hierarchy. I believe the order came from Malo Metam."

Alex smiled with satisfaction. "Why do you believe that the order came from him?"

"Because he is the head of Scorpius."

Alex looked puzzled. "Scorpius? What is Scorpius?"

"It's the code name for our organization."

"What does Scorpius do?"

"I don't know what happens in the other parts of the organization, but we are to generate unrest in the Tau Ceti system to give the impression that the government can't control its people. We are to generate massive riots soon, when we get the coded signal. The CDF will then come and restore order, which we help with by dispersing the rioting crowds. I think Malo believed that Tse's son knew too much about the plan and wanted him out of the way."

Alex looked at Sigmund in disbelief. He paced the room, thinking.

"You said this would happen soon?"

"Yes, when the CDF fleet is in place. I believe similar events are planned for the other Cetusian systems so we are probably waiting for the entire fleet to be in position in all the systems."

"Do you know where this fleet was to assemble in this system?"

"Not exactly. Just outside the monitored limit of the system but in quick reach of the defense stations."

Alex realized that, if what Sigmund said was true, they might not have much time to avert this catastrophe. He had to act fast. He joined Nascha in the observation room. "What do you think?"

"He's telling the truth, at least the truth as he knows it."

"I agree."

"A bit heavy in there. Hope you never interrogate me," Nascha said approvingly.

"I wasn't going to get answers tonight any other way. We need to interrogate the other one, but first, let's get some fake blood and splatter it around the room. Make him think his partner didn't get off too well."

"You are evil."

"Yeah."

They arranged for some blood and brought the other prisoner into the room. He started talking immediately and confirmed what Sigmund had said.

"What now?" Nascha asked after they finished the questioning.

"We need to go talk to your security forces and see if we can confirm that the CDF is in your system, ready to attack."

Ahiga walked into the room. "The people up front said you would be here. Find out what you needed to know?"

"Do you know about the plot to take over the system?"

"I found out a few days ago when I read the chip that Feng gave me and Malo confirmed it when I confronted him."

Alex threw his arms up in exasperation. "Why didn't you tell us and where is this chip?"

"Initially, I wasn't sure and then things moved too fast." He reached into his pocket and pulled out a chip. He gave it to Alex. "That's a copy."

"Does this say where the CDF fleet will be positioned for the attack?"

"Not specifically but there's only a few logical locations."

"OK. Let's get to the Security Forces Headquarters," Alex told Nascha. "You're coming with us too, you slippery little eel."

ALEX, Nascha and Ahiga sat in the primary meeting room of the Tau Ceti Security Forces Headquarters. The First General was there with his chief aides. Alex had just explained what they knew about the plot to overthrow the Cetusian government. The First General cleared his throat. "This would normally be a little hard to believe," he said looking at each of them with drill-like eyes, piercing into their souls. "Fortunately, Tse had discussions with me on this specific topic, so I am inclined to believe you. Tse was not one to divulge things at this level on hearsay and gossip. The stakes involved require at least an investigation to confirm the story."

"Do you know the likely location where the CDF might gather until they get the signal to attack?" Alex asked.

An aide brought up a hologram of their system and the First General pointed to a position.

"We believe we do. It should be here," he said pointing to a position in the out system. "It is closest to our primary defense stations and within fast approachable distance to Caerus."

"Good. We need to get there with a large enough force to get them to surrender."

"I presume they were counting on the element of surprise, so hopefully they won't have too large a fleet. Otherwise we may be in trouble even if we catch them off guard. OK, let's assemble our sixth and seventh squadrons to leave in three hours. They are at the ready. We will bring squadrons one, two and three up to 'Command to Engage' status."

"We need to be on the command ship," Alex said, including Nascha and Ahiga as well. "There might be one other."

Nascha and Ahiga looked at him, puzzled.

"OK then," the First General said. "Be ready at the disembarkation lounge in our Caerus Space Base at O-one hundred hours."

"Will do," Alex said. He sat back and closed his eyes, feeling tiredness and his injuries catching up with him and the day wasn't over yet. He grabbed his chest as a spear of pain lanced his cracked rib.

"Are you OK?" Nascha asked, concerned.

"Just a war injury. It's been a long day." He stood after a few moments. "Let's go." He walked out of the meeting room with Nascha and Ahiga in tow.

"Who's the fourth person?" Nascha asked Alex in the AGrav back to the hotel.

"Chooli," Alex said. "She would murder me with her eyes if I left her again at such a time, she's already tried calling me half a dozen times, and she has some skills that may be useful."

"If you say so."

"Do you need to get anything from your home?"

"No, I'll be fine."

They arrived at the hotel and alighted from the AGrav. Alex went to his room, as did Ahiga. Nascha waited in the lobby.

"Where have you been? I've been worried sick something else happened to you. Why didn't you call back?" Chooli exploded when she saw him.

Alex couldn't help but smile. "Calm down, Chooli. I'll explain."

Chooli rushed up to him, held him tight and kissed him passionately. He winced. She continued to hug him, a little gentler. "You scared me. I thought something happened as you can't look after yourself."

"I'm sorry. We just had to do a few things. We had to talk to the security forces once the assassins told us the details of what's happening. Apparently there's a CDF fleet positioned just outside detection range, ready to force Confederation military rule on the system."

Chooli let go. "What? That's ridiculous. They can't do that. It's against the constitution of the Confederation."

"Malo Metam, one of the Confederation Parliament members, has apparently organized it. He's set this up through an organization he put together called Scorpius. He seems to have a particular hatred for Cetusians. When did you get to be such an expert on the Confederation constitution, anyway?"

Chooli blushed. "I have an interest in Intersystem politics."

"Oh. Good to know. Anyway, pack some things. We're going on a trip to find this fleet, if it's out there. I thought you might be useful and you wouldn't have let me go otherwise."

Chooli looked surprised. "You're right about not letting you out of my sight. Lucky I got a few things while you were out."

They both packed a bag and were ready to leave in 10 minutes. They went down to the lobby where Nascha was waiting. Ahiga was there too, with a small bag.

"We all ready?" Alex asked.

The others nodded.

"Let's go find a fleet then."

Alex led the gang out of the hotel and to the waiting AGrav, which took them to the Caerus Space Base an hour's flight away. A military contingent met them and led them to a shuttle that took them to the Lead Cruiser in the Sixth Squadron, the command ship.

The counter force sped away to the suspected location of the CDF fleet 20 minutes after Alex and the others came on board. A person led them to individual accommodation rooms, which Chooli initially complained about but Alex placated her with the reasoning why, and then escorted them to the command deck soon after.

Admiral Klah, the commander of the Sixth Squadron and leader of the offensive, met them. "Hello Chief Inspector Detective Warner. I'm Admiral Klah," he said.

"Hello Admiral Klah. Please call me Alex. This is my fellow GIA Agent Nascha, and I have brought along Ahiga, the late Ambassador Tse's son, and Chooli, both for information they may have or special analytical skills."

"We should approach the rendezvous point in three and a half hours," the Admiral said. We have discussed our plan of attack if we find our target there and they put up a fight. The Seventh Squadron will circle them and come in from their rear in a triangular split formation. They will enter normal space in that formation in the assigned position at the designated time. Rest in the meantime. I'm told you've had a busy day."

"Yes, we might just do that," Alex said. "Is there anyone who needs us?"

"No, not till the action is about to start."

Alex and the others soaked in the panoramic view from the forward window of the command before retiring to their rooms. Chooli snuck in with Alex as soon as she could.

"I know I shouldn't be here but I haven't seen you for so long."

"It's OK."

Alex lay on his back with his head on her lap. She stroked his hair as she gazed at him. He looked back at her, not believing how lucky he was.

"How's your arm and ribs?" Chooli inquired with maternal concern.

"OK. My arm feels good, but I wish I could get it out of this sling and move it again. My ribs ache, though. My breathing is fine. The lung healed quickly."

"Anything I can do to make you more comfortable for a while?"

"Apart from things we can't do here, you're doing it."

Chooli punched his good arm. Alex snuggled his head in her lap and closed his eyes. He was asleep in 10 seconds. They woke to knocking on his door.

"Rendezvous in 10 minutes, sir," a sailor announced.

"Oh. OK! Let me wake up and I'll go with you." Alex turned to Chooli. "That was embarrassing."

"We weren't doing anything."

"I suppose not. Let's prepare for what's coming."

The Admiral looked up as they arrived, "Five minutes."

Alex felt the tension mount as the minutes passed. The squadron personnel seemed calm with practiced efficiency.

The time came and the CDF fleet appeared exactly where they predicted. Admiral Klah directed his communications officer to jam all outgoing communication systems and hail the intruders.

Five minutes passed, and an admiral in CDF uniform came on the screen. He sneered as he said, "This is Admiral Boyd of the CDF. What is the meaning of this intrusion?"

"This is Admiral Klah of the Tau Ceti Security Force. I would like to ask you the same thing. Why have you intruded into our system?"

"We are not in your system."

"What are you doing here?"

"That is CDF business."

Admiral Klah was getting frustrated with the lack of cooperation. Alex gestured that he wanted to talk to the recalcitrant Admiral. Klah agreed.

"Admiral, I am Chief Inspector Detective Alex Warner of the GIA. I would appreciate it if you confirmed a few things for me."

"If I am able."

"What is the nature of your mission here?"

"That is classified."

"Are you here to take control of the Tau Ceti defense stations on a command signal?"

The sneer disappeared from Admiral Boyd's face. "We are on a simulated exercise, yes."

"Are you to take control of the Tau Ceti defense stations?"

The Admiral was becoming visibly nervous. "We are of the understanding that the Tau Ceti authorities are aware of the exercise."

"We have no such knowledge," Admiral Klah interjected.

"Is that the full extent of the exercise?" Alex continued.

"We... are to hold positions and await further orders."

"Are you not meant to proceed to Caerus and take control of the planet?"

Admiral Boyd tensed at the accusation. Perspiration appeared on his forehead. He looked from side to side, avoiding eye contact, a sign to Alex that he was spot on the mark. "I am not authorized to answer that question," he said finally.

"Authorized by whom?"

"General Langdon. He has personal control of the complete exercises."

"Exercises? What other exercises?"

Admiral Boyd realized, too late, that he had said too much. "I cannot answer that."

Chooli whispered something into Alex's ear. Alex nodded. "Do you know of an organization called Scorpius?"

Admiral Boyd was taken by surprise. He then became defensive, "I may have heard of it."

"Is Malo Metam the head of that organization?"

"I do not know."

Admiral Klah took control of the conversation again. "I insist that you stand down your fleet immediately."

"What, because of what I see in front of me? I don't think so."

Admiral Klah looked at the chronometer and confirmed that it was time for the Seventh Squadron to appear. "Not just what you see in front of you but what's behind you."

"There is noth..."

The Seventh Squadron appeared.

Admiral Boyd turned away from the screen and reviewed his changed circumstances. His face set with determination. "No."

"Then I will have no alternative but to open fire on you and take you by force. Three more squadrons will soon be here."

Resistance left Admiral Boyd when he heard of the imminent arrival of the additional squadrons. He was visibly deflated. "Very well. I will stand down."

"A sensible move, Admiral. Prepare for us to board your ship."

Admiral Klah cut communications. "It looks like we thwarted that invasion," he said, looking around at Alex and the others.

"Yes, but not the whole conspiracy. I need to get to Earth immediately to inform the President of the Security Council about what's planned and stop the CDF. I need to get to Procyon to stop Malo too," Alex said wearily.

"There is nothing quicker than one of our super destroyers. I can authorize one for the journey."

33

RECALL THE FLEET

During the voyage, Alex thought about how his attitudes and opinions of the Cetusians had changed. He originally had no empathy for them. People could accuse him of being species prejudiced. Cetusians had deserved all the ridicule and abuse they got, in his opinion. They kept complaining about being victimized and abused. The 'halo thingy' was a calling card for being ostracized. The interesting thing was that he hadn't really known any of them then. He based his judgments purely on his prejudice. He also felt that his betrayal had been a factor in how his bigotry had developed over the years.

Alex found it incredible how Chooli had changed his attitudes. He realized he saw the woman instead of the Cetusian, and she was one amazing woman. He could honestly say that he had known no one like her before. At that moment he knew he would do anything to protect her, even sacrifice his life for hers, if it meant saving her. That was a turnaround he struggled to accept.

Why was humanity like that? What made them think one way at one time and another way at a different time? Alex could never fully understand the depth and flexibility of the human psyche. He had the revelation that all the prejudice and discrimination came to nothing if the survival of humanity was at stake, including any cospecies.

He thought about all this as he sat next to Chooli, who fussed over him and his injuries. The attention would have normally annoyed him, but now it felt natural and deserved.

"Will you stop fussing over me?" Alex finally said to Chooli, annoyance softened by tenderness.

"Well, you won't look after yourself!" Chooli retorted.

The others looked on, amused.

"I survived before."

"You had to. You didn't have me before."

"You're right," Alex said contritely. "I didn't, and I was the worst for it."

Chooli stood back with wonder. "Thank you."

"Whatever happened to that cool, detached personality I saw when I first met you, anyway?"

"It's still there and will fully return if you don't behave yourself."

Alex sighed.

"Will you two stop please," Ahiga said shaking his head. "You'll be at each other's throats next if you're not careful."

Chooli and Alex looked at each other. They laughed as Alex realized what they were doing, and he was sure Chooli realized the same. They didn't display open affection in front of the others. It wasn't appropriate.

They arrived on Earth the following morning. Admiral Klah wasn't joking when he said the destroyer was fast. Alex quickly organized a meeting with the President of the Security Council, thanks to some persuasion from his boss Commissioner Harris.

Alex and the others arrived at the President's office and his PA escorted them in.

"Welcome. I am President Chandra," the President said as he rose and navigated around the desk to greet them.

"Hello President. I am Chief Inspector Detective Alex Warner and this is Agent Nascha from Caerus, Chooli and Ahiga, the late Ambassador Tse's son," Alex said as he pointed to each of them as he introduced them.

"Commissioner Harris has spoken highly of you, Alex," Chandra said. He turned to Ahiga. "I am sorry about the loss of your father. He was truly an exceptional man."

"Thank you," Ahiga said.

"I hope you catch the offender soon," Chandra said, turning back to Alex.

"I believe we have and that he is responsible for a string of other murders, but there are other matters afoot, which is why we are here," Alex said.

"I am glad of the news. So what is it you wish to discuss?"

"We believe your CDF ships are positioning themselves to attack all the Cetusian Confederation systems on orders from Malo Metam."

Chandra frowned as he absorbed the information. "I find that hard to believe. I know Malo has his differences with the Cetusians, but that is extreme. What evidence do you have of this and who in the military would listen to him?"

"Well, for one, we have just come from Caerus where the Tau Ceti system security forces have caught the CDF congregating for just that purpose. We got a confession from the commander in charge. Ahiga here has chips with information from his father and the late Representative Feng the plans. And I believe General Langdon is part of this conspiracy."

Chandra looked at Alex in disbelief. "You can't be serious! I've known General Langdon for years. He is a distinguished officer."

"I wish I was joking President, but I'm not."

Chandra was silent, deep in thought. "I'll get to the bottom of this. I'll see if First Admiral Reagan knows anything." He went behind his desk and retrieved his secure comm from a drawer.

"First Admiral Reagan," the Admiral greeted.

"Reagan. Chandra here."

"Oh. Hello Chandra. What brings you on this channel?"

"I have a Chief Inspector Detective Alex Warner of the GIA and others here who have just given me some disturbing intelligence. Can you tell me the current location of your fleets?"

"Well, as far as I know, most of them are here or on routine patrols but let me check." Reagan brought up information on the whereabouts of his forces on his data plate. A puzzled expression came on his face, which Alex caught. "That's odd. What are all those doing there?"

"What do you see, Reagan," Chandra probed.

"There seem to have been recent fleet movement to position squadrons around the Cetusian systems."

Chandra looked at Alex and back to Reagan. "Do you know why they're there?"

"Not the slightest. I didn't order it."

"I believe your General Langdon may have information, according to Chief Inspector Warner."

"Why would he be moving ships without my knowledge?"

"May I?" Alex asked Chandra, signaling for the comm.

"Admiral, I believe this is a covert operation that aims to overthrow the Cetusian governments. You need to recall those ships immediately," Alex ordered.

The Admiral paused. "Wait!" he yelled. He picked up another comm and spoke to someone for a while until he exploded. "What do you mean they're on practice maneuvers and we can't contact them? I want them recalled immediately and I want you in my office now!"

Flushed with anger, the Admiral spent several seconds regaining his composure. "I will send an immediate recall message to the ships involved. I will also send a security alert to the affected systems advising them to place their Security Forces on full battle status."

"Thank you, Admiral. You may have saved many lives," Alex said.

"That may be, but it should not have come to this at all. Langdon has some explaining to do, as will I probably before all this pans out."

34

STOPPING MALO

Alex and his entourage arrived on Procyon in record time thanks to the super destroyer. Alex called ahead to the local authorities with orders to arrest Malo but he had disappeared. His family was distraught with worry. They were certain he was still on the planet, though.

"Where would he be?" Alex asked, as much to himself as to the others.

"Let's go to his office," Ahiga said. "I have a hunch."

"Like what?" Alex asked.

"I don't really want to say but can you think of a better place to start?"

"S'pose not."

Chooli seemed lost in thought.

"What's on your mind, Chooli?" he asked.

"I was just thinking, if I was orchestrating this operation, I would need a communications room to coordinate operations and monitor progress. He must have a secret room somewhere and Ahiga's suggestion that we start at Malo's office is a good first step."

"Hmm. She has a point," Nascha said.

Alex saw the logic. "Let's go then," he said. "I'll get the police to meet us there."

They hailed a taxi and piled in. Alex contacted the police. They sat quietly while they went to Malo's office. Ahiga seemed to do something with his comm unit, sending a message or something from what Alex could tell, but Alex didn't bother finding out. He thought Ahiga probably wouldn't tell him, anyway. They arrived at Malo's office and got out. The police were already there.

"Let's go up," he said to the police sergeant in charge.

"We already know he's not there, sir," the sergeant advised.

"Do you have a device to tell if the wall is solid or whether there is a sizeable space behind it?" Ahiga asked the sergeant.

"Yes, we do."

"Please bring that with you."

The sergeant looked at Alex, and he nodded. The sergeant asked one of his constables to get it from their patrol AGrav. The constable returned, and they all went up to Malo's office. They walked past the protests of the PA sitting in reception and into Malo's inner office area.

Alex and Ahiga looked around. The others watched. Ahiga went out to the reception area and back into the office again several times.

"What are you looking for exactly?" Alex asked.

"I am not sure but... can you test to see if this wall is solid?" Ahiga asked the constable, pointing to a wall in Malo's office.

The constable turned on the device and scanned the wall several times. "There is a considerable cavity behind here," he said pointing to the area. "The rest of the wall seems solid for a reasonable distance to suggest that there is just wall there and nothing else." He changed the setting on the device and conducted another scan of the suspect area. He chose a fresh setting and scanned the entire wall again. He changed the setting a third time and did the same until he stopped at a particular location. He turned to the others to explain, "This area I first mentioned appears to be some kind of doorway and the rest of the wall seems to be solid under normal scrutiny. However, with closer interrogation with the device, I have found that the wall is just thicker to give the impression there is no space behind it." He paused.

"Go on," Alex coaxed with mounting tension.

"There is a considerable space there and also, there is an infrared signature showing there is a human in the room."

"Yes!" Ahiga exclaimed.

"So, how do we get in there? There must be a secret door with a hidden latch," Alex said as he scrutinized the wall. There was a holograph hanging on the wall and Alex moved the frame. Nothing happened. He removed it from the wall and found a button mounted flush into it. He looked at the others, "Shall I?"

"I presume it's not going to blow the place up," Nascha said. "You may as well."

Alex pressed the button; a part of the wall dissolved, and a rectangular doorway appeared.

The police officers withdrew their maser pistols from their holsters as did Alex and Nascha, although Alex's injuries meant he wasn't as agile.

A hallway 10 feet long led to another doorway. Pale lighting illuminated the hallway.

"I suggest you leave this to me," Nascha whispered to Alex. "You only have one arm at the moment."

Alex nodded. "I'll cover you from here."

Nascha and a constable gingerly crept down the hallway until they reached the door where the constable braced himself against the wall and aimed his pistol through the door ready to fire.

"Malo!" Nascha said, raising her voice.

"Who's there?" Malo's said in surprise.

"Alex Warner and Nascha from the GIA and the police."

"Ah! Come in. I am not armed."

Nascha looked at the constable. She signaled she would have a quick look from a low position. She lowered herself to her knees, pistol poised, pointing to the ceiling. She pivoted her head past the doorframe and back in one rapid motion. Nothing happened. She looked through the door again. "Clear," she said. "Cover him constable."

The constable stepped into the doorway with his pistol trained on Malo.

Alex put away his pistol. He and the others walked down the hallway, and they all piled into the room. Malo sat in front of a bank of holovision screens. He turned his chair to face them, seemingly unperturbed by the intrusion.

Alex scanned the screens and saw that each was showing large public demonstrations on all Cetusian planets. Reporters were giving updates on the mass of protestors congregating in the streets and riot police closing around them. "What's this?" he asked, wincing as he moved his injured arm.

Malo had a smug smile. "This is a day to go down in the annals of history. This is when I will finally put Cetusians in their place as servants of humanity and not as some upstart alternative life form, thinking they can push humans around with no consequence. You are witnesses to the overthrow of the Cetusian governments today. All will know that you do not bully a Metam and get away with it. I have spent years getting even with you Cetusians," he said looking at Ahiga. "I have spent my entire life planning this moment and now it has arrived."

Nascha and Chooli stood in shock as they watched the screens. Alex couldn't believe what he was hearing. "Are you crazy?"

"No. I am not crazy. This is revenge."

Only Ahiga seemed unfazed by the dramatic events. Alex wondered why.

Malo noticed Ahiga's calmness as well. "I am sorry about your father. He was an excellent ambassador but he got in the way. He knew too much. He was influencing too many members of my organization, but I do not understand your attitude. Are you not shocked as well?"

Ahiga regarded Malo evenly. "Yes, I am shocked. I have pity for you. You have done all this because of something that happened in your childhood? You held a grudge for that long? What did those

Cetusian children do to you? Tease you a little? Does that constitute a reason for murder? For the suffering and pain that you would have inflicted on millions, maybe billions, of people."

Malo's triumph and confidence wavered a little. "What do you mean 'would have'?"

"Do you think my father joined your organization because he believed in your cause? He had a concern that developed into a fear of your intentions. He joined it to stop you, first to gain your trust, then to know your plans. All that time he was making plans of his own..."

From the bank of screens, one of the commentators from the Lalande system started speaking. "We have news just at hand that a CDF squadron is moving in to provide support to subdue the uprising." Confusion appeared on the commentator's face. "The squadron is moving towards the Lalande defense stations. The reason for this is unclear at present. We will keep you posted as events continue to unfold..."

"You see. You cannot stop this," Malo said.

Alex cursed under his breath. We are too late, he thought. He noticed that Ahiga still seemed untroubled by the unfolding situation.

"Oh! That is where you are wrong. As I was saying, my father was making plans of his own. He had identified all the ringleaders in your network who were fermenting the rioting in each of the systems. He created his own network of agents and had secret meetings with the relevant government officials."

Doubt appeared on Malo's face for the first time. "But Tse is dead."

"His plans are not. He left them with me."

A reporter on the planet Chiron in the Alpha Centauri system spoke through the holovision. "We understand the authorities have arrested the ringleaders of the protest movement. Police are dispersing the crowds here and the city is returning to calm..." He stopped to listen to his earpiece where someone was talking to him. "... We also understand that a CDF squadron, stationed just outside the Chiron system boundary, has been recalled to base. There is no comment on why the squadron is positioned in that vicinity. Our reporters are trying to verify the circumstances behind this as we speak."

Malo turned red with rage. "What have you done, you little flea?"

Ahiga's disposition remained unchanged. "I contacted the agents my father recruited and put in place a plan to detain your trouble-makers as soon as the protests started, so the crowd no longer had a focal point to keep them hyped up and rioting. We also had the CDF in the Tau Ceti system impounded and informed the President of the Security Council of the CDF presence in the Cetusian systems. He had the First Admiral order an immediate recall of all ships to base."

Malo lunged at Ahiga in uncontrolled fury, trying to grab his neck to strangle him. Ahiga sidestepped the attempt. The police immediately intervened and manhandled Malo into submission as he continued to wriggle and struggle to resume his attack on Ahiga. Malo eventually stopped his exertion. "I will get you for this," Malo said with hatred in his eyes.

Ahiga's face showed sorrow and pity as he walked out of the room.

The police cuffed Malo and led him away.

Chooli approached Alex. "You did well. You and Nascha both." She turned to Nascha and nodded.

"Me? One-armed bandit? We should thank Ahiga," Alex said, "even though I should arrest him for concealing information, the rat." His voice had no conviction.

"I'm sure people will thank him when all this settles down and things return to normal again."

"I just can't understand what would motivate a person to do such a thing," Nascha said.

"Sometimes an experience can burn such a deep wound it becomes your entire focus and motivates you for good ... or evil," Alex replied. He thought of his own behavior as he spoke.

They returned their attention to the holo screens. Crowds were slowly dispersing. Not much damage had been done, thanks to Ahiga and his father's planning.

"Shall we go home?" Alex said finally, his face drawn with exhaustion. He could feel the last few days had taken a toll on him.

"Yes," Nascha and Chooli said in unison. They collected Ahiga who was waiting in Malo's office and went back to the destroyer and Caerus.

35

ALEX AND CHOOLI DINE WITH AHIGA AND MAI

Once they returned to Caerus, Alex told Commissioner Harris that he was having some time off. This surprised the Commissioner, as Alex rarely took time off. He granted the leave and said that Alex needed time to recover from his injuries, anyway. Alex spent the time getting to know Chooli more, although he made sure she continued her studies. The more he found out about her, the more he realized how special she was and how much she meant to him.

Ahiga made good his promise of a dinner with Mai, Chooli and Alex. They went to the most exclusive restaurant on Caerus. Alex wore his most formal clothes. Chooli dressed in an exquisite gown that he had helped select for the evening. She was a bundle of nerves, being so overwhelmed at the thought of going to such a fancy place.

"Calm down," Alex said, trying to get Chooli to relax.

"But what if I make a fool of myself," Chooli replied.

"That didn't seem to be a problem when you met me."

"You idiot. That was different. We weren't going to an exclusive restaurant."

"Well, I'm insulted," Alex said teasing. "You get all uptight about going to some restaurant but I'm just another person who came along."

Chooli became flustered. "I didn't mean that and you know it."

Alex smiled and held Chooli still for a moment, looking into her eyes. "I know this is a big thing for you. You have never been to a restaurant like this. Nor have I, but just pretend that it is just another restaurant. I've taught you some etiquette. That will get you through and if you do something untoward, I'm sure no one will even notice. Believe me. I'll protect you from embarrassing yourself too much. That might be a full-time job, though. My reputation is at stake, you know."

Chooli hit Alex hard on his uninjured arm.

"Ouch!"

"You deserved that."

"Well, did I," Alex said as he came closer to her and restrained her for more amorous activity.

"Don't please. I don't want to ruin my outfit and makeup," Chooli said, not convincingly but enough for Alex to relent and give her a loving peck on the mouth.

"The things I have to suffer for you."

"Let's just go before I do something you might regret."

"Promise?"

"Men!" Chooli said in frustration, but also with a note of satisfaction, as she stomped to the door.

Alex had booked an AGrav to take them to the restaurant, not wanting to take any chances of being late. There had been many celebrations over the days since the thwarting of the conspiracy to subjugate Cetusians to Human rule, making movement in the cities difficult sometimes, and the availability of taxis even more difficult. They went down to the lobby of the hotel and waited.

The restaurant was lit up with scenes from prominent landmarks on Caerus. Chooli stood agog in amazement at the spectacle.

"I'd close my mouth before an insect goes in it if I were you," Alex commented cheekily.

"But, it's just so diablo, don't you think?"

"Yes, it is. What I find so amazing is that a person like Ahiga can go from his old life to this one and adjust so quickly without going crazy."

"Yeah. I suppose, but he was born into it. He was only doing the engineering job to prove that he could forge his own life without relying on his father for his entire existence."

Alex took Chooli's arm in his good arm and led her to the restaurant entrance. His injured arm was still in a sling, mending. Holographic cameras flashed around them as they crossed the threshold and a reporter wanted a few words from two of the people who saved the system from tyranny. "No comment," Alex said and pulled Chooli forward to the dining area.

"I am sorry about that Madame, Monsieur. We unfortunately could not keep them out once they found out that Monsieur Ahiga and yourselves were patronizing our humble establishment," the Maître De said apologetically. "And may I take this heartfelt opportunity to thank you sincerely for what you did to save our system from disaster."

The appreciation humbled Alex. The only words that came out were, "You're welcome. I was only doing my job."

The Maître De smiled knowingly and offered to escort them to their table. Ahiga and Mai rose from their seats to greet Alex and Chooli and the women immediately fell into an animated conversation, as they had plenty of catching up to do.

"How's the injuries?" Ahiga asked.

"Mending well. I should get out of the sling soon and my chest doesn't ache like it did. I'll be ready for fighting again before I know it. The boss will probably want to give me the next case straight away when he finds out."

"We must make sure that doesn't happen," Ahiga said with a sense of conspiratorial connivance in his tone.

They both laughed jovially.

"What about you? What are you going to do now that your

father's murder and his business with Scorpius is out of the way?"
Alex asked.

"I won't be going back to my old job, if that's what you meant. I
need to get my head around my father's business interests and start
running them myself. It will be hard not having him around to teach
me the ropes," Ahiga said sadly.

"You'll have to find a coach."

"I may have found one. I don't know her very well yet, but Mai is
good with money."

"Is that right," Alex said with dismay. "Maybe the gods brought
you two together."

"Yeah. Maybe. What about you two? I can't imagine two cops
living together. Won't you both be trying to find out what the other is
doing?"

Alex laughed. "Maybe. I can't imagine finding out too much about
Chooli if she doesn't want me to know. That's what frustrates me
sometimes. It's like getting a gram of Astatine from Earth."

"Yeah. Look at them. Like two schoolgirls talking about the latest
trend," Ahiga gestured in Chooli and Mai's direction.

Alex looked at them. Chooli and Mai sensed being watched and
stopped talking and turned. "What?" they both said.

"Nothing," Alex replied. "We were just enjoying the view."

Both Chooli and Mai blushed with pleasure at the compliment.

Alex continued with Ahiga, "You know I should haul you over the
coals for being so difficult with us."

"Maybe. I know you won't though."

"Really? What makes you say that?"

"This business would have been a lot messier without me doing
what I did and a lot more people would have been hurt."

Alex conceded Ahiga's point. "Yeah. It would have."

"Anyway. Are we going to eat or are we going to chat all night?"

They had their entrees and main course before Ahiga became
serious again.

"Alex. I've been thinking ... I hope you don't mind but I've been
doing a little digging into your background."

"My files are supposed to be sealed by the GIA," Alex said, surprised and a little put out that his history was being investigated.

"Forgive me. Everything has a price, but I had to know more about you. I have a proposition for you."

Chooli and Mai stopped talking to listen into Alex and Ahiga's conversation.

"Really?" Alex said, curious. "Continue."

"Well, one thing I found out is that you are a very honest man, although you have been wild sometimes. We all have our moments, but you always seem to have an intuition when something doesn't seem right. Even in this case, I have seen this talent displayed. What I am trying to say is I could use someone of your skills on my team, both in security matters and business transactions. I am offering you a job, if you're interested. We can discuss remuneration and other matters later."

Chooli's eyes opened wide in amazement. She looked at Alex, waiting to hear what he would say.

Alex did not reply straight away. He pondered what Ahiga had said and what he was proposing. *It would allow me to be close to Chooli,* he thought. He couldn't imagine going back to Earth and continuing the relationship from afar. He hesitated. Everyone was looking at him, wondering what he would say. He had to say something. Finally he said, "I won't say no yet. What you have proposed is a big change for me. I've always been in the police force and I love the job, so to leave would be a big decision. I'm not sure if I really want to stop what I'm doing. It gives me a buzz when I solve a case. I feel I'm doing something for the good of Humankind, all of it, not just Humans themselves. I'm making the confederation a better place. There again you have offered an enormous opportunity. We would have to sit down and discuss exactly what it is you want from me. Let's have a proper business discussion about it sometime soon."

Ahiga smiled. "That's the answer I was expecting. Anything else wouldn't have been the genuine Alex. I was hoping there might be something, or more to the point, someone tempting you to stay." He looked at Chooli.

Chooli grabbed Alex by the forearm. Alex looked at her, love in his eyes. He turned back to Ahiga, "Now you're not being fair but you're right, I like Caerus a lot." They all laughed.

"What about me?" Chooli protested.

"What about you?" Alex questioned, pretending indifference.

"Humph! Men," Chooli said, hitting Alex on the upper arm.

"You two look like a bickering couple already," Mai said.

"Are not." Chooli replied.

"Aren't bickering or aren't a couple?"

"Ugh, you're worse."

Alex sat bemused. He loved Chooli even more when she had her little fits of outrage. "A particular person is especially interesting to me," he finally said.

His comment brought an instant sparkle to Chooli's eyes. He adored her sparkling eyes.

"Anyway, what about you two?" Alex asked.

Ahiga looked at Mai and back to Alex. "At the moment we are exploring possibilities."

"Good for you."

"I was very nervous at the start," Mai said modestly.

Alex chuckled, "So I heard, but that's a good trait to have sometimes. It can keep you out of trouble."

They had dessert then and continued talking until late and finally time to go. "Thank you very much for the dinner tonight, Ahiga," Alex said.

"You're welcome. A small repayment for the frustration I caused you and Nascha. Remember. Think about my offer. You won't be disappointed if you accept."

"I will think about it and get back to you soon to arrange a meeting."

Ahiga and Mai left in his limousine. The restaurant was near to Alex's hotel so he and Chooli walked back since the night was balmy. Chooli threaded her arm around Alex's waist and Alex rested his on her shoulders as they strolled, enjoying the scented air emanating from the blossoming trees lining the boulevard.

"You should take that job," Chooli said. "It would be a great opportunity for you."

"Maybe... do I sense a bias from an interested party though?"

Chooli giggled at the mild accusation. "Probably."

They walked on for a while.

"Do you like me?" Chooli asked.

Alex paused before he replied, thinking about what he truly felt for her. "No," he said and stopped walking, pulling her around so she faced him. She looked worried. "I love you." The fear exploded into shear joy. Her aureola radiated a golden yellow. She immediately wrapped her arms around him, her head against his chest. He felt the dampness of tears seep through his shirt. She looked into his eyes. "I love you, too," she said hardly able to control her emotions, and her tears, her aureola turning a mottled orange and emerald blue.

Alex felt a sense of completeness with the confession of his feelings. He had bottled himself up from close personal relationships since the betrayal of his previous partner. He had vowed never to open up to anyone again. Chooli had changed all that. His resolve had melted as soon as he first saw her, he realized. It had completely thawed when she had almost demanded he take her to his bed. She was so fresh, so honest, so innocent in her own way and he knew she could never betray him but where to from here? If he went back to Earth, how would their relationship develop? Did his existing career mean more to him than she did? These were questions he needed to answer before he could give Ahiga his answer. He came back from his reverie, placed his arm on her shoulders and started walking again. Chooli followed his lead, resting her head against the side of his chest. Her hip against his swayed in synchronous rhythm as they walked.

"How would we see each other if you went back to Earth to your job?" Chooli asked.

Alex could sense worry in her tone. "I don't know. I would find a way, but let's not think about that tonight. Let's just think about how delightful tonight has been and is."

"... And could be."

Alex looked at Chooli. She looked back with ravenous desire. "Diablo," he said.

"Diablo," she whispered.

36

PAPA'S BLESSING

Alex woke late. Chooli was already up and sitting by the window in one of his shirts to cover her nakedness. She had her feet on the front edge of the chair with her chin resting on her knees as she chewed on something. He saw by the reflection in the window she was thinking. She had a frown of concentration. He watched for a time, fascinated by her demeanor, her sharpness of perception.

"About time you woke up."

Alex laughed. Her words reflected what he was thinking. "You would keep me up all night."

"I didn't hear any complaints" Chooli turned with an enormous smile of affection.

"What were you thinking about?"

Chooli hesitated but finally seemed to decide. "I want you to meet my parents."

Alex sat up, surprised at the request, almost demand. "I'm not sure it's time yet."

"It will never be the time. Don't worry. They won't eat you."

"I didn't mean that," Alex said, confused about his reaction and emotions. Things were going fast, maybe too fast for him. What was holding him back? He thought it only natural to be nervous about meeting her parents. Maybe he feared rejection, which surprised him. Finally he realized he would have to meet Chooli's parents eventually if he wanted to continue the relationship, which he did, so he may as well get it over with. He was sure they would be very nice people. They couldn't be too bad if they produced a person like Chooli. "OK."

Chooli stood and came over to him, giving him a passionate kiss. "I'm as shit scared as you."

Alex laughed. "I doubt I will ever get used to your bluntness."

Chooli smiled. "Well, no point delaying the inevitable."

"I s'pose not."

"Are you going to get up and make me some breakfast or am I going to gnaw your arm?"

"I'm very much attached to my arm. I want to shower first, though."

"Thought you would never ask," Chooli said as she dragged Alex to the bathroom, removing her shirt as they went.

"It's late for breakfast. We'll have brunch," Alex said, once they were both dressed.

"Whatever. I'm starved."

They went downstairs to a cafe around the corner from the hotel. It was pleasantly warm, so they sat outside. They enjoyed a meal together, chatting small talk mostly until Alex started thinking about Chooli's parents.

"Tell me a bit about your parents."

"Not much to say. They're my parents."

Alex looked at Chooli, a frown of fake annoyance on his face.

"OK. OK. Let me think. Well, I already told you Papa pushed me to follow my talents, which is why I'm here, and I told you we are comfortable financially but not well off. Papa has worked very hard all his life for his family and expects his family to do the same." Chooli frowned.

"Go on," Alex encouraged.

"They are very traditional. They like things being the same. They realize the galaxy is changing, but the traditional values of our people are important to them. They can be very stubborn, especially Papa. Family honor is very important. It comes from our cultural background."

"Have you told them about me?"

"Probably don't need to with all the media attention but yes I have, sort of."

"What do you mean, sort of?"

Chooli was feeling uncomfortable. "Well, I told Mama that I met someone special, and she started interrogating me about you."

"Ha! I would love to see someone interrogate you."

"Stop it. Anyway, she sort of suggested I introduce you to them. She said I needed Papa's blessing."

"Blessing for what?" Alex felt trepidation rising as the meaning escaped him and he was not sure he liked the terminology.

Chooli tried to calm him. "They just want to know you're treating me right, that's all. Anyway, they'll love you."

"If you say so. When are we going?"

"Tomorrow. For dinner."

"But..."

"You're recuperating and on vacation. You have something else to do?"

Alex looked sheepish. "I s'pose not."

Chooli smiled sympathetically. "You'll be fine."

"Yeah right."

They finished brunch and Chooli took Alex to the zoo to show him the native animals of Caerus. Alex enjoyed himself but was a little embarrassed by the looks some people kept giving him. "Why are people looking at me, us, strangely now and then?"

"We have been all over the news and I suppose it's unusual to see a Cetusian and a Human together on Caerus. That's all. I'm not worried about it. I want to show you something. We will have to get a taxi but it's not very far away."

"What is it?"

"I'll tell you when we get there."

They ordered a taxi, and Chooli directed it to a location on the outskirts of the city. They alighted from the taxi at the entrance of a garden. It intrigued Alex why Chooli had brought him there. They entered the garden and walked down a path for about 300 yards, eventually coming to a smooth obsidian rock.

"What is this?" Alex asked.

"I think I told you we haven't been on Caerus long enough to have legends, but I forgot about this. It is said that this is some kind of portal to another dimension or something. The story goes that when this world was first explored, they found this. The people suspected that it was something special but didn't know what that was initially. As the planet was not completely suitable for human habitation, because of the low oxygen level, they didn't investigate it further for a time and they went to our sister planet that had a suitable oxygen concentration in the atmosphere. They colonized that. After a time two original settlers remembered this rock and came back to investigate it further. It is said that a portal opened somehow, and they walked through, never to be heard of again. I suspect they have changed the story to add a bit of mystery."

Alex looked at the rock, fascinated. "Who were they?"

"Look at the plaque," Chooli said, pointing to the polished metal plate embedded on one side of the rock.

Alex moved closer and read: 'Where Jade and Ethan Richards left this Universe. We await their return.'

Alex was taken aback. He had a memory of reading something similar in his childhood, but he thought it was a fairytale. "Well, I'll be. But your name is Richards. Are you related?"

"I don't know."

THE NEXT DAY they prepared for their trip to Chooli's home village. The trip was to take four hours in a hired AGrav. They left straight after lunch. The changing scenery along the way fascinated Alex. They left the city's coastal plain and slowly rose into the surrounding foothills where farming intermingled with tropical forest enclaves. As they rose in altitude, the vegetation changed to cooler climatic species and farming became rare. There were maybe better, easier terrains for farming, Alex thought. They stayed in a mostly Mediterranean climatic zone in their travels, but Alex could see snow-peaked mountains in the distance, barricading them against intrusion of the other side of the range. They eventually came to an elevated plateau that was a lush carpet of green with patches of brown where farming land lay fallow, ready for the next crop.

"That's my village," Chooli said, pointing with one hand as she had her other arm around his.

"It looks small."

"Yes, just a few thousand live there."

They approached the outskirts of the village and entered. People stopped what they were doing to look at the strange AGrav as it passed. Alex saw many were sweaty and dirty from a day's hard work. Some seemed to walk back to where they lived. They passed through the center of the village where many shops and businesses stood, turning down two traffic ways and finally stopping in front of a house.

"This is my home," Chooli said.

Alex saw a white, double-storey building, set back a few feet from the street front. An entrance on the side allowed an AGrav to park there and provided entry to the rear backyard area, which seemed large. The front of the house had several windows and an entrance door, exquisitely colored with a frame displaying various images. Alex noted other houses had the same door display, but they were all different in detail.

"What does the artwork around the door mean?" Alex asked, curious.

"It tells us who lives there and their tribal background. I'll explain it later."

"Interesting. I'd like that."

Alex saw that Chooli was nervous. He was nervous too. He did not know what to expect, but it was too late to back out now. Chooli knocked on the door. She turned to Alex with a tight smile as they waited.

Her mother answered the door. "Oh, Chooli, why didn't you just come straight in?" she said as she looked at her and then at Alex with interest.

"Mama," Chooli stepped forward and gave her mother a hug. "I didn't want to intrude. I've been away for so long."

Her mother paused, looked at Chooli, momentarily intrigued about something. She decided not to say what was on her mind. "Well, are you going to introduce your friend?" she said instead. She looked expectantly at Alex.

"Of course, Mama. Mama, this is Alex. Alex, Mama."

"Hello Alex. Call me Haseya," Chooli's mother said as she held out her hand.

"Hello Haseya. Pleasure to meet you." Alex shook her hand. He could see some resemblance to Chooli in Haseya's face, a family connection obvious. She was the same height but had filled out slightly as middle age crept in, still quite a slender figure though. She wore a fresh dress and makeup to look her best for the meeting. She had an apron on. Alex assumed she had been cooking.

"How rude of me. Come in, please."

Haseya ushered both in and closed the door.

"Who's at the door?" they heard from somewhere in the depths of the house.

"It's Chooli and her friend," Haseya responded.

A cautious "Oh," returned to them.

Alex looked at Chooli, anxious.

Haseya walked down the hallway. Alex and Chooli followed. They rounded a corner and through a doorway into the living room. Chooli's father sat in his easy chair, reading the local news plate, which he put down when they entered and stood up. He was tall, taller than Chooli by a head and still had his muscular, trim figure. He was obviously Chooli's father. He wore a judgmental expression.

"Papa," Chooli said as she walked up to him and hugged him.

"Chooli. It is good to see you. Hope you have been studying hard."

"Oh Papa! Of course I have." She looked at her father with the loving eyes of a child toward her parent.

Her father's expression softened a little as he frisked Chooli's hair in play.

"Stop that. You'll mess my hair," Chooli complained in fake annoyance.

Her father smiled with tenderness. "They grow up so fast." His stern expression returned as he looked at Alex. "Introduce me to this friend of yours then."

"Papa, this is Alex. Alex, this is Papa, Naalnish."

Naalnish gave a quick surprised look at Chooli before returning his attention to Alex. Alex extended his hand. "A pleasure to meet you, Naalnish."

"It is good to finally meet this friend of Chooli's I've been hearing so much about, both from her and on the news. If nothing else, you seem to have improved Chooli's diction."

"Oh! Papa."

Alex smiled. "She has made an effort."

"Let's go out on the porch while the women prepare dinner. You want a drink?"

Chooli frowned in annoyance at her father's chauvinistic assumptions.

"Chooli and I have things to talk about anyway," Haseya commented and led Chooli to the kitchen.

"Yes, I'd like a drink. What do you have?"

"I'm having a beer. Good enough for you?"

"Perfect."

Naalnish went into the kitchen and came out a few moments later with two small bottles of beer. He handed one to Alex, "Follow me." Alex followed his lead as he walked out of the back of the house and onto a porch area in the backyard. There was a table, and six chairs there. Alex presumed they sat there for meals sometimes. Alex waited for Naalnish to select his chair, the head of the table, and chose one adjacent on the side.

Taking a sip of his beer, Naalnish looked towards the native vegetation behind the house where a small creek flowed past the property. The sparse tree and bush populated grassland extended out toward a more densely treed forest area about two hundred yards distant. He could imagine Chooli and her siblings exploring the forest when they were children.

"You high in the GIA then?" Naalnish asked, starting his interrogation.

"Not really."

"What? Chief Inspector? Isn't that high?"

"I suppose. It's too high, if you ask me. I enjoyed my job much more when I was just a detective."

"Why did they pick you?"

"Pick me for what?"

"This murder investigation."

Alex smiled slightly. "Please don't be offended, but I can see where Chooli gets her bluntness from."

Naalnish chuckled. "That's why I was so pleasantly shocked before. Well?"

"Well, W... Oh. They thought I was the best for the job, I suppose. I usually get results quickly and they wanted the case solved immediately, for political reasons more than anything, I think."

Alex could see Chooli peer out from the kitchen window now and then, looking worried. It must be harrowing for her.

"Well, you seemed to have pleased the politicians here for a change. They're a complaining bunch if I ever saw one."

"I think they were happy we thwarted this conspiracy to overthrow the Cetusian confederation systems more than solving the murder. They were related."

"Nasty business, that. What's your views then?"

"Views on what?"

"Cetusians and Humans."

Alex thought seriously about how to answer. "I admit I had some prejudiced views of Cetusians due to ignorance. I believe you are as equal in this confederation as us. Chooli has educated me a lot on the Cetusian cultures and psyche. We are all the same."

"Humph! Where are you from?"

"I come from Sydney, Australia, on Earth. I was the middle child of five. My father worked hard as an AGrav mechanic to get us through school. I went on to university to study criminology, entered the police force and they eventually invited me to transfer to the GIA where I've stayed for eight years."

"How come you're not married?"

Pain crossed Alex's face at the memory of his betrayal. "I was in a serious relationship a long time ago. She betrayed me. It has taken me a long time to heal. I have also been traveling with my work too much to form a serious relationship - until now."

"Shit happens!"

"Yes, it does."

Alex saw Naalnish looking at him judgementally again. He wasn't sure why.

"You travel a lot, then?"

"I have been, yes. Because I'm single, I get the out-of-system cases."

"You have a girl at every spaceport then."

Alex didn't like what Naalnish was implying. "No, I don't," he said defiantly. "Chooli is the first woman I've been in a relationship with since my last one fell apart. She is different, special."

"Don't get all upset. She is someone special and I intend to make sure she stays that way."

Alex couldn't understand where the questioning was heading, or why, but remained amicable for Chooli's sake.

Chooli appeared at the back door. "Dinner's ready." Alex saw she still had a worried look.

Alex and Naalnish stood and Alex followed him into the house and the dining room where he sat patiently, looking for a lead on what to do next. Chooli and the others folded their hands, so he did likewise.

Naalnish said, "May we be truly grateful for the sacrifices of the animals and plants we eat tonight."

Haseya and Chooli said, "Indeed." They all started eating.

After a while Naalnish asked Alex, "So, do you think she will make a good detective?"

"Papa!"

Alex chuckled. "I've noticed that she is very intelligent and remarkably perceptive, two qualities essential for detective work. I think she will make a fine detective."

Chooli looked at her lap, embarrassed by the compliment.

"Good. She didn't want to go. I wanted her to make some use of that brain of hers."

Chooli helped her mother clear the plates and brought out a large bowl of fruit from which Alex selected two native fruits he had previously eaten at the hotel and liked.

As they were finishing, Naalnish cleared his throat. "Alex, I have given this much thought. I will be blunt with you. You will go off somewhere to another case on another planet soon. Chooli will just become a memory to you. This will bring dishonor to her, and to us through her. I cannot allow this to happen. I cannot let this relationship continue."

Alex was lost for words. Chooli, distressed to the point of shaking and her aureola turning an ashen gray, gave a loud wail of grief and rushed from the table. Haseya looked alarmed too, but said nothing. She rose and left to console Chooli.

Alex felt a flood of anguish. He could feel his heart being torn apart. Finally he said, "I'm sorry to hear that you think I would do such a thing to Chooli. I don't think you understand how much she means to me."

"I'm not saying that you would intentionally but, being away would eventually allow temptation and, with temptation, dishonor."

Alex felt frustrated. He didn't know what he could do to convince Naalnish that he was worthy of his daughter.

As if Naalnish could read Alex's thoughts he said, "I have made up my mind. You are welcome in our house, but you must stop this relationship. It cannot continue any longer."

Alex was deeply distressed. He was fearful for Chooli, as he had seen how emotional she was when she left the room. He rose, excused himself and left the room to seek Chooli. She was upstairs in her old bedroom. Her mother stood at the door, pleading with her daughter to let her in so they could talk. She was very unhappy. "I am sorry. I can do nothing. I want to console Chooli but she's locked the door."

"Let me try." Alex gave a gentle tap on the door. "Chooli. It's Alex. Can I come in, please?" After a while. he heard footsteps and the door unlocking. Chooli tried to give him a brave smile. It was holding, but wouldn't last long. Alex looked at Haseya to see if it was OK for him to go in. She nodded. Chooli instantly grabbed Alex in a hug, her head on his chest. She sobbed uncontrollably. Tears came to Alex's eyes, and he didn't know what to do. He didn't want to see Chooli in this state. He stroked her hair, trying to calm her.

Eventually Chooli calmed down. "I should never have brought you here. Should never have sought Papa's blessing."

"You know you couldn't have done that. You have too much respect for him to do that."

"But I can't live without you." Her sobbing flooded her again like a cloudburst of rain. Alex's shirt ended up wet.

"Shh. Shh. It's OK. I'll think of something."

"There is nothing you can do. Once Papa has decided, it's final."

Alex ran Naalnish's words through his head again. Maybe there was a possibility. "Chooli, I'll go now. I will stay the night, but I want to go out on my own tomorrow to think things through. I might go for a walk in the forest. I'll come back for dinner tomorrow night. OK?"

Chooli stopped crying. She looked at Alex and eventually nodded her head.

"I'll think of something. I promise. Now, your mother is worried about you. Will you let her in to talk to you? For me... please?"

Chooli nodded again. Alex kissed her gently on the lips and they hugged, feeling each other's warmth, knowing it might be the last time. They released their embrace, and Alex opened the door for Haseya to come in. Before she went in, he asked, "Where will I sleep tonight?"

Haseya became flustered. "Where are my manners? This room here, I'll show you."

Alex stopped her. "Chooli needs you more than me now."

Haseya stopped what she was about to do. "Yes, of course. You are a good man, Alex."

Alex went downstairs and out to the AGrav to get his bag. He grabbed it and went to his room. It was all laid out immaculately. Alex smiled. Haseya had truly wanted to impress him. Things were as they were. He couldn't change that now. He had to think. He prepared for bed and turned out the light but couldn't sleep.

ALEX SAW the light outside brighten with sunrise, sure that he had not slept all night, but he may have nodded off without realizing it. He got dressed and left his room, looking momentarily towards Chooli's room, wondering how she had slept. He silently sneaked out of the house through the back door and into the natural environment beyond. He wasn't hungry and walked into the forest and kept walking, making sure he didn't get lost.

Chooli's honor, and the family honor, was paramount to Naalnish. Alex worked through the conversation and pronouncement of the previous day. With everything said, there seemed to be one thread that dominated the decision. That Alex would leave and go back to Earth, continuing his job, darting about the Confederation investigating crimes and leaving Chooli stranded, futilely waiting for him to return. He could see now the fear Naalnish had for Chooli and how that related to her, and their honor. If he went away and did not return, it would make her look foolish. Alex didn't want that to happen either. He loved and respected her too much to hurt her. In a sense, he would be doing to her what had been done to him all those years ago.

So, what was he to do? He started thinking again about Ahiga's offer. He wouldn't have the exhilaration of hunting down some of the worst criminals in the Confederation, but he wouldn't get shot at either. It seemed his role in Ahiga's business empire might be whatever he wanted to make it. He would still travel, maybe even extensively sometimes, but he would always return to Caerus. Caerus would be his new home. Chooli may even come with him on occasions. It would also mean that there would only be one partner in law enforcement, assuming Chooli graduated. The more he thought about it, the more he liked the idea, but would it be enough to persuade Naalnish to change his mind? That was their only hope as far as he could see. He felt better within himself now.

Alex wandered the forest for the rest of the day. It was very peaceful and reassuring, giving him a sense of permanence. Leaves covered the ground where they fell, carpeting the floor of the forest. The sunlight mottled the covering where it broke through the foliage above. He hoped there weren't any predatory animals around. Presumably they didn't come this close to civilization. He heard birds singing now and then and small creatures scurrying through the underbrush.

Alex eventually returned to Chooli's parent's house as daylight faded and dusk began. He was starving too.

"There you are," Naalnish said. "We were getting worried you had become lost."

"Sorry to put you through the worry. I've always been an excellent walker." Alex looked at Chooli. She looked distraught still and in need of sleep. Her face was like a statue, no emotion emanating from it. It was as if all life had drained from her. "Hello Chooli."

Chooli gave him a brave smile. "Hi."

"Hello Haseya."

"Hello to you too, Alex." He saw the strain on her face.

"I might just freshen up before dinner, if that's OK?"

"That's fine," Haseya said. "It will be another 20 minutes yet."

Chooli looked at Alex strangely. He thought she may wonder why he didn't look as distressed and lifeless as she felt. He hoped he could surprise her tonight. He went upstairs.

Dinner was being served when he came back down, so he sat down straight away. Naalnish was already there. Haseya and Chooli sat after they had placed all the meals on the table. They ate in virtual silence after they expressed the ritual blessing.

After they had eaten, Alex braced himself with the courage to present his proposal to Naalnish. "Naalnish, may I talk to you."

"Certainly."

Chooli looked at Alex, startled and terrified, not wanting to go through the same trauma as the previous evening.

"I have been doing a lot of thinking today as I walked the forest behind your house. Did you know that the late Ambassador Tse was a wealthy man?"

"There have been reports of his wealth in the news now and then, yes."

"His only son has now inherited his wealth and all the businesses generating it. He has to come to terms with running this extensive business empire on his own. Chooli and I had dinner with him a few nights ago and he offered me a position. I haven't given him my decision yet. If I accepted, that would mean that I'd make Caerus my home. If I accepted this offer, would you reconsider your decision regarding Chooli and me?"

Naalnish looked at Alex with hardened eyes. "You would do this for Chooli?"

Alex saw a reflection of Chooli in a mirrored cabinet behind Naalnish. She sat wooden faced, not wanting any more emotional heartbreak and disappointment, but there was also a glistening of hope in her moistened eyes. She sat still like a rock, as if not wanting to move in case she cracked. "Yes I would," Alex said, looking Naalnish directly in the eyes.

Naalnish sat in silence for some time, looking intensely at Alex and, in turn, Chooli. Alex saw that Chooli wasn't game to look at her father. She looked straight ahead instead. Haseya sat holding her breath, showing as little emotion as possible. "If you would do this Alex," Naalnish finally said, "you and Chooli have my blessing." A smile appeared on Naalnish's face.

Chooli yelped in delight and glee. She jumped from her chair and ran around the table, wrapping her arms around her father's neck.

"Papa, Papa. Thank you, Papa," she said as she kissed him on the cheek with tears rolling down her face.

"Thank you, Naalnish," Alex replied.

"Now, if Chooli will stop choking me, I think this is cause for celebration."

"Oh, Papa," Chooli said as she released her hold and wiped the tears from her face with the backs of her hands. She looked at Alex with love and pride.

Haseya beamed with joy. Chooli went to her and gave her a hug. "You make sure he doesn't think he just made an enormous mistake now," she instructed Chooli.

"Never Mama, never." Chooli beamed at Alex. She released her mother and walked around to Alex, who rose from his chair. They hugged each other tight. Chooli looked into Alex's eyes. "Thank you," she whispered.

While this was going on, Naalnish had left the room. He returned with a bottle of Caerus sparkling wine. "Glasses Haseya." He opened the bottle, which popped when he removed the cork.

Haseya got four glasses from the display cabinet, and Naalnish poured the wine. Alex and Chooli had their arms wrapped around each other's waist.

"To Chooli and Alex," Naalnish toasted.

"To Chooli and Alex," Haseya repeated.

They all clinked their glasses and took a sip of wine, Alex and Chooli gazing into each other's eyes as they did so. Alex could see the life returning to her. They all sat down again.

"Fruit?" Haseya asked.

"Yes, please," they all responded.

Haseya went to the kitchen and Chooli reluctantly took her eyes off Alex to help her mother.

They ate and talked until late.

The long day and previous sleepless night eventually started getting the better of Alex, so he said his good nights and departed for bed. Chooli followed him into the bedroom and they kissed passionately, Chooli wrapping her arms around Alex tightly.

"Thank you so much," she said. "You will never regret this."

"I know I won't." They kissed again. Chooli kept hugging him as if he would disappear if she let go. Alex allowed her, enjoying her warmth against him. Eventually he said, "I had better go to bed. I'm exhausted. We can do something tomorrow. Maybe go for another walk in the forest."

Chooli released him reluctantly. "OK. I can show you all my old hiding spots." They kissed again one last time, and she left, leaving Alex alone to his bed and sleep.

ALEX SLEPT SOUNDLY AND LONG. He woke mid-morning to a knock on his door. Chooli opened the door wearing a radiant smile and impeccably dressed in navy blue colored slacks and a red shirt. She styled her hair in the fashionable front and rear ponytail look of the time. It brought instant joy to him to see her so happy again. "Hi."

"Hi sleepy. You ever going to get out of bed or do I have to come in and drag you out."

"You can try."

Chooli tried to grab Alex's hand to haul him out but he pulled her onto the bed instead. She let out a squeal of surprise but allowed herself to tumble on top of him. They kissed.

"You look gorgeous," Alex said.

"You don't look too bad yourself."

"Are you going to make me breakfast?"

"I wish we were alone so we could have some other delights first."

Alex chuckled. "Let me get up and I'll get ready so we can spend the day together."

Chooli pouted. "Can't we spend it here?"

"You're incorrigible," Alex said as he slapped her on the rear.

Chooli squealed again but got off the bed and went out of the room.

Alex used the bathroom, showered and dressed. He then came downstairs to the kitchen where Chooli was with her mother.

"Hello Alex. Did you sleep well?" Haseya said with a smile.

"Hello Haseya. Yes, like a baby."

"Good. You have a seat in the dining room and we will bring you your breakfast in a moment."

"Oh, that isn't necessary."

Haseya gave Alex a look that said, 'Obey if you don't want to upset your girlfriend's mother.'

"OK. I might just do that," Alex said, amending his comment. He went into the dining room. He heard Chooli giggle behind him.

It seemed to Alex then that traditional Cetusians ran a very patriarchal family system where the male was the breadwinner and the female looked after the home and fed the family. He didn't think Chooli would continue that tradition with him if they went that far, although she had already proved her persistent determination in getting her way in looking after him. He sat down opposite the window which overlooked the front of the house. It was quiet outside with neither AGrav nor pedestrian traffic in sight, although he saw a person gardening.

Chooli came through holding a plate that had the Caerus equivalent of bacon and eggs and a glass of a citrus fruit juice. She went back into the kitchen and came out with two cups of steaming hot coffee. "Eat up, you'll need your strength today," she said with a little smirk of amusement as she sipped her coffee.

Alex obeyed and welcomed the unique taste of the home-cooked breakfast. He finished eating and drank his juice. He then drank his coffee, which was still hot. Chooli just sat looking at him the whole time. It seemed like she was idolizing him. Alex finally said something, "What's up?"

Chooli hesitated. "You were a very brave man last night. Few people would have had the nerve to say what you said to Papa. He is a very demanding man and people can rarely persuade him to change his mind once it's made up."

Alex felt a little embarrassed by the compliment. "The prize was worth it," he said.

"I'm just something to win then, am I?" Chooli responded with fake indignation.

"Well, that's how it goes when us men have to get into serious negotiations," Alex replied, playing along.

"Humph! You wait."

"Promise?"

They both laughed.

"Anyway. I've packed a picnic basket for us. I'll take you to a spot I love by a river near to here. We can have a picnic lunch there."

"Sounds wonderful. I'll just go upstairs for a moment and get some things out of the way and be back soon."

Alex contacted Ahiga to make an appointment. He also sent a message to Commissioner Harris announcing his intention to resign, if things worked out as he was expecting.

He came back down and joined Chooli. She sat reading in the dining room while she waited. "All ready. I've arranged to see Ahiga tomorrow mid afternoon so I'll have to leave in the morning. Will you come with me?"

Chooli gave Alex a strange look. "Of course I'm coming. I'm not letting you get away now."

They grabbed the items they needed for the picnic and went out into the forest. It was a warm sunny day. The atmosphere was perfect for a romantic liaison. Chooli led Alex down a path, rarely used judging by the overgrowth. They walked for about 45 minutes until they passed through a gap between two hedges and arrived at a grassed area next to a gently flowing river .

"This is delightful," Alex said, impressed.

"Yes, I used to come here often when I needed to get away to somewhere peaceful to think."

Alex shook out the picnic rug close to the riverbank and they sat admiring the view. Alex saw some flowers not far away. He got up, picked some and gave them to Chooli. She smelled the sweet scent wafting from them as she placed her head in his lap. They enjoyed the time in solitude together, sharing the food and drink they had brought with them.

They finally returned to the house. Alex announced that they would leave in the morning to complete arrangements for his new job.

ALEX STARTED WORKING with Ahiga a few weeks later once he had fully recuperated. He went back to Earth for a week to wrap up things and move his belongings. Commissioner Harris was disappointed to lose him. Alex suggested he consider Ruth for his position, as she showed great potential in Alex's opinion.

Alex returned to Caerus and began his new life with Chooli.

The End

The Zodiac Series continues with book 2 - Libra (Continue to check out the first chapter or purchase.)

Thanks for reading this book. If you loved the book and have a moment to spare, I would appreciate a quick review on the site where you purchased the book, as this helps new readers find my books.

The exciting intrigues Alex and Chooli encounter continue in Libra, the second book of the Zodiac Series. Type https://books2read-.com/libra-jw in your browser to find out more.

Subscribe to my Newsletters and receive three free episodes of The Chronicles of Gatacus Todd.

Type http://subscribepage.io/g4r4f8 in your browser.

ALSO BY JOHN WEGENER

Books

Reach For The Stars Trilogy

FTL

Centauri

Ceti

Reach For The Stars Box Set (Books 1-3)

Loki's Fall

Zodiac Series

Scorpius

Libra

Halwende's Legacy Series

Halwende's Redemption

Halwende's Resurrection

Halwende's Reincarnation

Halwende's Legacy Box Set (Books 1-3)

Solar Dawn Series

Lunar Rift

Other Stories

The Dark Ages

SAGI

Short Stories

The Love Particle

ABOUT THE AUTHOR

John Wegener grew up in the Adelaide Hills of South Australia. He now expresses his imaginative dreams by engaging in writing after a 34-year career as a Chemical Engineer in the steel industry, which has taken him to many countries and allowed him to experience many cultures. John currently lives in Wollongong, Australia with his wife and children.

Click on johnwegener.com to find more of my books or read his blogs. Type subscribepage.io/g4r4f8 to subscribe to my emails for more stories and information.

f